Her Druid Desire

BOOK ONE OF THE
AMBER DRUID SERIES

TRISH F. LEGER

CAJUNFLAIR
PUBLISHING

Praise for Trish F. Leger's writing…

"It is dangerously sensual and the story simply mesmerized me. Author Trish F. Leger could not have written a better teaser for her AMBER DRUID series than HER DRUID TEMPTATION."

Pamela @ Romance Junkies (4 ribbons)

~

Amber Druids, dangerous men, an investigation, hostility, and sexy, steamy love scenes are all rolled up in Trish F. Legers "Her Druid Temptation".

InD'Tale Magazine (4 ½ Gold stars and a Crowned Heart)

~

"I really enjoyed reading Liana and Trevan's story...the characters are likeable and their sexual chemistry is smoking hot!"

Amazon Reviewers

Also by Trish F. Leger

Scorching and Sensual Romances…

HER DRUID TEMPTATION-*prequel* to the Amber
Druid Series (e-book only)

HER DRUID DESIRE-Book One of the Amber
Druid Series

HER DRUID FANTASY-coming Summer 2013

Sweet Romances…

SEASONS OF LOVE: Hearts, Hearths & Holidays
(Anthology)

THREE WEEKS BEFORE CHRISTMAS

Connect with Trish:

wackycajun@hotmail.com

Facebook: Trish F. Leger-author

www.trishfleger.webs.com

ISBN 13: 978-0-9857192-6-5
ISBN 10: 0985719265

CAJUNFLAIR
PUBLISHING

P.O. Box 641

Kinder, LA. 70648

www.CajunflairPublishing.com

http://www.facebook.com/CajunflairPublishing

Dedication…

To those out there who have the courage to hold out hope
for the things they want most of all.

Acknowledgments…

I would like to thank my husband, for putting up with me sitting in front of my computer, ALL THE TIME. See babe, me being on the computer does have an end result!

For family and friends, always.

For the most awesome book club ever!

To Kim @ The Killion Group, for the great cover, thanks!

And thanks to everyone for being so patient with me while preparing this book for publication.

Chapter 1

Anger, rage, pettiness-those were things she could deal with. This…this pain-that by all rights she shouldn't even feel, was something so very new to her.

Nadia Morales gripped the steering wheel tightly between her fingers. The weather matched her mood, wild and unmanageable. Wind buffeted the Land Rover, causing the powerful vehicle to lurch, which of course caused Nadia to focus on staying on the road instead of swimming in the ditch.

Hated tears burned in her eyes, causing her focus to haze. She longed to hang her head against the steering wheel and give into the absurd female emotions that were pulling her under, but she couldn't. She needed to get home. She needed the cozy, inviting retreat of her cottage to soothe her shock, and bring her peace of mind back. Nadia needed to calm down, but saying that was easier than doing it.

Another bright flash of lightning was instantly followed by a sharp, threatening clap of thunder. Nadia jumped as the sound receded to a mere rumble. Trying valiantly to steer the large vehicle in the blinding rain was becoming increasingly hard.

"Breath, just breathe, and keep calm," she said out loud, hoping to quiet herself with the sound of her voice.

Bad weather had always been her Achilles heel. Ever since she was a young girl, storms had pricked her curiosity and her fear. Hiding in her bed with pillows and blankets over her head was the norm. Living in southern Texas hadn't helped one bit. The weather was always unpredictable and ferocious.

The rainstorm, the emotions of the moment, and the fear that slid through her veins like slick black oil, all coalesced together. It took everything inside Nadia to bully through the moment as if nothing bothered her, when that was a lie.

There was only about a mile to go and then she could let go in the privacy of her own home. Then a black blur ran out in front of the truck.

"NO!"

She jerked the wheel to the right, but it didn't help. She felt, more than heard, the sickening thud of the blur hitting the left front of her bumper. Ever so slowly she pumped the brakes, not wanting to risk slamming them and sliding off the road.

Hands trembling, she glided the large vehicle to the curb and put on her flashers. A glance in the rearview mirror showed a distinct black mound lying against the rain drenched blacktop. Through the rivulets of rain, she determined the shape to be that of a small dog.

"Why?" she whispered to herself.

As if the past hour hadn't been hard enough on her, and now she might even be the murderer of some innocent dog. Nadia peered through the rain-distorted glass on the back of the Rover, but she couldn't make out movement. She adamantly refused to leave an animal out there in the elements, especially if it wasn't dead.

She grabbed a bat that was under the back seat of the Rover, then opened the door and cautiously went to check on the injured animal. It might be injured, but living in the country had prepared her for animals infected with rabies, and wild, half-crazed, hungry dogs that roamed freely when she was young. She felt remorse, but she wouldn't be a chew toy for a vicious dog, half-crazed or not.

Cool raindrops slid under the collar of her shirt as she cautiously moved her way towards the black mound. Steam rose up from the hot pavement as the cool rain hit the blacktop. Dark woods on each side of the road teemed with wildlife that chattered amid the noise of the now-dying storm.

Wind whipped her long black hair into her face, but she heedlessly shoved it away, and noticed the rise and fall of the animal's torso as she approached. In some macabre, weird way she could thank this small animal for running out in front of her because the spotlight was off of her pain for one second.

She stopped about three feet from it when it lifted its head in her direction. Even though the wind blew rain and hair into her face, she could clearly see large brown eyes peering at her wearily. Her heart all but melted, and then she heard a soft whine, followed by a slow wag of the dog's tail.

"Oh, poor baby, I'm so sorry."

The black and white fur of the Border Collie was matted with rain and blood, and the more she looked, the more she knew what needed to be done. Another soft whine cemented her decision.

"Baby, you are going to be fine. I'm going to get you some help."

She spoke softly to the dog and moved closer. It seemed to understand her, which Nadia sensed was odd. Tentatively, she reached out to stroke its fur, gripping the bat tightly in the other hand in case she might need it. To her astonishment, the dog didn't seem to mind being touched. She then placed the dog in the back seat of the Rover, feeling the warmth curling through her system at having been able to do something right tonight.

For one moment something else needed her attention, and it wasn't her problems; for that, Nadia was grateful. She pulled out her I-phone and scrolled through listings for twenty-four hour vet services. When the list came up with Safe Haven Animal Shelter and Clinic among the names, her heart stopped. She glared at it for a few seconds, long enough to still her beating heart and then realized she was closer to the clinic than she first thought.

Thirty minutes later she was pulling into the parking area. As a large, state of the art facility on the outskirts of Beaumont, Safe Haven came about more than twelve years ago. Local man Drake Thompson, business owner, investment guru, and the guy with an all-around lucky touch with everything in life, started this place to do exactly what it is called. The haven also included a vet's clinic. At the moment, the whole place was dark, except for security lights on all sides, and around back where the large pens were. A heart-wrenching whine echoed from the backseat.

"I know baby, I'm trying to get you some help."

She opened the door and dodged fat raindrops to bang on the door. That was when she noticed the hand written sign taped to the door. When lightning flashed, Nadia jumped, but she held her phone up to the door to read the sign.

Emergency on ranch outside of town. Call 555-3927 if in need of assistance.

Why in the world would the vet leave a contact number belonging to the owner of the shelter? Nadia itched to know, but kept her questions to herself. "Damn it," she muttered, thumbing through the list of numbers on her phone, because she already had his number stored. Then she ran back towards the Rover, wondering what in the world she had done to piss God off this time. This run of bad luck was turning legendary already.

On the third ring, she realized God's twisted sense of humor, as a deeply accented, Texas drawl slid over the line. Out of the frying pan and into the fire. Nadia calmed her rapid breathing and tried to remember what she was calling for, instead of her reaction whenever she heard this man's voice.

"Drake, this is Nadia. I have a dog here and I believe it needs medical attention. I found your number taped to the Safe Haven clinic door for use in an emergency. What should I do now?" She hoped she sounded calm, cool and collected, but she highly doubted it. After having the worst surprise of the year, hitting an adorable dog, and now having to hear *his* voice, she had come to the conclusion that her night couldn't get worse.

"Nadia, do you know how badly the dog is hurt?"

"I'm no vet, but I think that she has a broken back leg. She appears to be breathing normal, if a little fast, and there is a small bit of blood. I didn't mean to hit her," Nadia added in a low tone.

Sounding completely businesslike, he said, "Do you know where Ridgeland Lane is?"

Her heart sped up in her chest. Of course she knew where it was, half the town of Beaumont knew where he lived. A couple of years ago he'd built a massive, sprawling log cabin out along the quiet banks of Ridge Lake, and from then on it had been like a mad house of crazy females to see who would be the woman to tie down the infamous Drake Thompson. The property was gorgeous, the house was amazing, and the man was Croesus rich. So far no woman had been successful.

"Yes, I can be there in ten minutes."

After telling her he would have the gates open and waiting, she hung up and glanced to the backseat of the Rover. Large, hypnotically beautiful brown eyes stared back at her. A piteous whine came from the depths of the female Border Collie. She turned back around and reservedly put the vehicle in drive. She would get this dog some help, no matter where she needed to bring her for that to happen.

***

A little over ten minutes later the lights of her Rover were bathing the trunks of his trees with a lazy circle of bright blue halogen. The blue picked up everything, including a large handsome sign that proclaimed this to be 118 Ridgeland. The beat of Nadia's heart told her she was close. She didn't even need to see the damned sign.

Large indigenous trees, oak, sugar maple, silver maple, pine and dogwood, all vied for attention as the wind whipped their healthy foliage around. The rain finally stopped, and just like he told her, a large wrought iron gate was left open.

Nadia drove for what seemed like another ten minutes, until she found a clearing and got her first full glimpse of Drake's house in the moonlight as she cleared the opening. A huge, sprawling log and natural stone affair took up a large amount of space. The place was at least four thousand square feet, with rough timbered logs and natural paving stones that led to the front doors. Lights spilled out from the massive windows, illuminating people milling around inside.

She parked her Rover right next to a silver Tesla, a big black Hummer, a low slung Audi and a new model Chevy pickup then stepped out, murmuring to the dog the whole while. Seconds later, she stepped out and gently grasped the dog in her arms.

Please be okay, she muttered to herself, as she made her way along the meandering flagstones towards the front door. The last thing she wanted to do was walk up to Drake's front door like a guest, when she resembled nothing more than a drowned rat, but she didn't have time to waste on looking for another entrance.

Looking down into the dog's sorrowful brown eyes caused her throat to close up. But at least she was here getting her some help instead of leaving her to die in the road.

Nadia made it up to the large double oak doors whenever the Border Collie started shaking in her arms. "Shit, shit, shit..." Tightening her arms around the shaking dog, she began kicking the door, praying for someone, anyone, to open up and help her. Just when she was about to start shouting, one of the large doors opened.

Drake Thompson stood in the opening, as imposing as Nadia remembered him being in person. Before she had the chance to drool over him, he immediately leaned over to scoop up the shaking dog into his arms. She didn't hesitate to hand over the poor animal. It was a well known fact that even as the owner, Drake spent just as much time at his business as his vet's did. Nor did she have the chance to soak in his voice when he told at her to follow him. When she cleared his foyer and got a good look at the people in his living area, she remembered exactly what she must look like at the moment. The past two hours of her life had been more than emotionally draining, especially with her running around in the weather. Well, needless to say, it hadn't helped her appearance one bit.

There were four men and three women standing around a counter between the living area and the monstrous kitchen. It was clear to Nadia that these people were the crème de la crème of society. Wealth dripped from huge diamonds that adorned the women and the clearly tailored lines of the men's clothes. After giving Nadia a dismissive glance, they turned back to their conversation, clearly telling her without words that she didn't belong here, even if she could buy her way into their clique with her new money. To them, it didn't matter if she'd inherited the Rockefeller's assets, she was still a newcomer into their elusive and highly critical world.

She shook off the feeling that she truly didn't belong, and got a brief glance at the imposing ruggedness and masculinity of the house before having to run and catch up with Drake as his long-legged strides led her through his house and then into a mudroom of sorts.

The dog stopped seizing and was now lying still on top of a long counter covered in various garden tools and lawn care spray bottles. Her liquid brown eyes were closed now, but Nadia could see the rise and fall of her labored breathing. She took a deep breath and thanked God that the seizure hadn't harmed the dog any more than necessary.

Drake's body was huge beside hers, which was nothing new for Nadia. When you are 5'2" it is almost a foregone conclusion that you will meet an adult in the eye. Not only was he tall, he was just all around big.

She sensed something, some kind of powerful ripple in the air around her, as his hands ran over the dog's body. The instant connection between this massive man and a small, wounded dog was clear to Nadia. No wonder he had started the shelter and clinic; it was obvious to anyone with eyes that he was an animal person. He was gentle, thorough, and within minutes he was finished checking the dog. He immediately grabbed his cell from his pocket and dialed a number.

Nadia just stood there, still wondering if the dog was okay or not. Instead of blurting out questions, she let Drake do what he needed to do. He knew more about this than she did anyhow.

"Chase, how's the mare?" Drake questioned, while one large hand stayed firmly on the dog in case she decided to bolt. To Nadia's untrained eye it seemed as if the female was more than happy to stay right where she was, regardless of her injuries or pain, and with her eyes closed she seemed extremely relaxed.

"Good, look, I have an injured dog here," he stopped for a minute, his light brown eyes leaving the dog, and spearing her where she stood, "Possible broken back leg, multiple cuts, but she is alert and comfortable right now." Drake looked back to the dog, and Nadia was immediately relieved to have those intelligent, all seeing eyes off of her. "Ten minutes? Alright, we'll be here."

Keeping his hand on the dog, he ended his call and looked back at Nadia.

"Chase Williams, he's the vet on night duty this week, just finished up with a mare out on the Circle T Ranch. He should be here in ten minutes."

"Good, I was so worried and I needed to make sure that she would be okay. Do you think that any of her injuries are life threatening?" Nadia asked, trying to ignore how intimidating and wholly masculine he was. The harsh, fluorescent lights threw him into stark relief.

With his broad forehead, low slashing brows and beautiful bone structure, it was like staring at a sculpture, all except for his penetrating brown eyes which bored holes into Nadia.

Thick, dark russet colored hair was cropped somewhat close to his head, but it still managed to look unruly and wild. His body was muscled, without being overblown, and his overwhelming height made him seem much larger. He moved with a grace, a slow as molasses saunter, that had given Nadia warm flutters more than once.

"She's lucky you are such a compassionate person. Most people would have left her there to die."

The deeply accented Texas drawl shook Nadia out of her secret appraisal of his body. She mentally slapped herself out of the trance she had sunk into.

"I couldn't leave her there," Nadia murmured, more to herself than to him. Her fingers sank into the dog's fur and immediately Nadia remembered what had happened earlier. With all the drama of the thunderstorm, and injuring the dog, she'd almost forgotten the emotions from before. Now it came back, sizzling through her like a firestorm.

Tears hit the backs of her eyes, while humiliation slammed into her body like a wave. She should get used to this. Certainly shame and humiliation would be her constant companion once the truth hit, and she knew it would. For all of its charm and small town flair, Beaumont was a bustling city. Its citizens were good, honest, hardworking people but, like always, and mostly in the wealthier groups, there were those that would gossip. She would have to learn to live with it.

She remembered the people milling around Drake's living area. That was his crowd. The super-rich. The elite of society. He'd been born to this. The ins and outs of this world ran through his blood by right. She, on the other hand, was an upstart here. The denizens of this crowd regarded her with something akin to horror and smug defiance. If it were up to them, she would never make it in their world.

The only person who had thought differently, and helped her maneuver the vagaries of her new social calendar, was now enemy number one. Thank God she was a quick learner; otherwise, she would be left out, floundering, and lost to the cruelty of society. Well, she'd learned her lesson and she doubted she would trust so openly again.

Dear God, how would she ever face anyone after this?

Was she strong enough to do this?

She stepped back from Drake's overwhelming presence. Out of the corner of her eye she saw him regarding her intensely. Of course he was. She was practically having a nervous breakdown in his house.

"I have to leave, but please send word, or call me whenever you find out something. You remember where to find me, right?"

He nodded, and without stopping her, let her leave. The look in his eyes when she turned around showed her that he knew something. Somehow Drake Thompson realized something wasn't right, and Nadia knew that if she allowed it, he might make everything worse than what it was already. That was the last thing she needed.

***

Camera's flashed and snapped. Every paparazzo was out for a surprise shot. Drake Thompson knew better than to let one hint of unsettling emotion cross his face. That would only invite their specific brand of torture.

He pressed his arm tighter around Laura's waist, slipped a lazy, one sided grin on his face and pretended that this was exactly where he wanted to be at the moment. Which was a lie. What he really wanted was his back porch, a cold beer, and his comfortable deck chair to lounge around in. With the sounds of wildlife that was so abundant in south Texas, Drake could unwind and listen to nature calm him like always.

As for right now, he stood there obediently and mentally chanted a small spell which would turn every picture on every frame into a blurry haze for him, a light Amber Druid trick that he incorporated to keep people from getting a clear view of him on camera.

Ten minutes later he was inside the large ballroom that was set up for a certain animal charity tonight. The plate fees were set at two thousand a piece, but with all the proceeds and donations going to shelters and clinics around Texas, Drake hadn't minded forking out the money. The place was packed, filled to the brim with politicians, ranchers, and business folk who knew just how important this funding could be. Drake refused to get on his soapbox. He would rather work hard and talk less, but he knew his appearance tonight would be remarked upon and might draw generous donations not only for his clinic, but also for others.

Society was like a mistress. You needed to charm her every once in a while, well, a bit more often than that, and if you were nice you might get lucky every time you stood in her presence. Drake kept that phrase in his mind when he thought of all of the invites he received in the mail. There was no need to attend every single one, but every so often it was needed to keep the peace, so to speak. Drake was a business man first and foremost, so coming out and playing polite every once in a while helped.

"She is an upstart bitch."

The phrase was scalding and came from across the room. With his Druid ability, the statement cut through the room like a knife with deadly accuracy. Drake could feel the tension rise. Even with every other conversation going on at the moment, the drone of whispers from across the room was amazingly accurate, and Drake didn't have to look to see where the women were sitting.

"I heard from Tammy the other day that she walked in on Donavan with Suzanne Harrows. They were going at it like rabbits on his office desk in his house. When she noticed, she ran, and no one has seen her since."

"Do you blame her? I wouldn't show my face either. Everyone knows he was only with her for the money, and she couldn't keep him happy one bit." This was whispered by another woman in the group. Drake could taste their excitement over the juicy gossip that was being shared.

"Ever since Linda Browning died a little over a year ago, Donavan had been sniffing around the new protégé's tail hoping against hope that she might give in and let him inside. Well, he was let in, and was just getting his hands all up in that particular cookie jar, when little Ms. Upstart caught onto what he was doing."

Drake continued to glance around the ballroom, make small talk with Laura and a few other guests, but the conversation across the room was giving him more answers than anyone else had over the past week. He usually wouldn't take anything they said at face value, but for some reason this particular gossip fest felt true, especially when he knew Donavan to be an ass already.

The appearance of Nadia on his doorstep late last Friday night had jarred him a bit. After examining the animal and gleaning a bit more from being in her presence, he could now see what should have been more than apparent to him when he first opened the door. She'd been extremely upset, and not just because of what happened to the animal. Something else caused the anger, hurt, and betrayal to seep from her pores, shimmering above her in luminescent waves.

The new, young protégé of the deceased Linda Browning was a twenty five year old newcomer into the world of horrendously wealthy, diabolically smug socialites. In Texas, wealth was only frowned on when you were newly minted by its clutches. But along those same lines, it was forgivable if you were thrown headlong into the fray. In Nadia's position, Drake knew that it was pure jealousy and back biting arrogance that was giving her nothing but, hell, ever since she had taken over the reins of Linda's business.

Apparently Linda had seen something-some bright, focused light inside the young woman that cemented the decision in her mind to move her up in the world. At twenty-four, Nadia became president…Numero Uno… over the brain center of The Browning Corporation. She worked her way up since the age of eighteen, and now, in turn, ran a huge corporation that managed three magazines; two boutiques, one in Beaumont, the other in Houston; and numerous charity organizations. Not to mention, it kept her in a state of luxury that continued to amaze the young woman that came from a lower class working family.

The will hadn't been that shocking, at least not in Drake's estimation, and he knew that the job was more than a handful. But the ever resourceful and determined Nadia could make anything run smoothly.

When they first moved to Texas, back when Nadia was twelve, her father, Matt Morales, worked for him until the day of his and his wife's death when Nadia was a green sixteen year old. Matt had been one of the best accountants that Drake ever employed, and upon his death, Drake had kept an eye on the young and impressionable girl that was left all alone then shipped off to a foster home, but he never forced himself in her life.

At the age of eighteen, right out of high school, Drake pulled a few strings with Linda, promising her that he would find someone perfect to be the assistant to Linda's personal secretary. He'd gotten Nadia the interview, without her knowledge, and from then on anything that caught Linda's eye had been all Nadia.

Now sitting here, suffering through this fanfare event, Drake listened to the gossipy hens on the far side of the ballroom, and was sick to his stomach at what had surely caused that hurt, painful stamp around Nadia's aura the other night. She was a lovely young woman, brimming with drive and fire, and he only hoped she could come back from that pain and move beyond it.

Now he would just have to contain the urge to rip Donavan Hamilton's limbs from his body the next time he saw the bastard.

Chapter 2

The hot Texas sun beat down on Nadia's uncovered head as she sat beside a clearly upset Franco Magana in the outside corner of a trendy downtown restaurant. The establishment's high walls halfway protected the wealthy clientele from the press, but just twenty minutes ago their waiter had to call the police to pull a photographer from the tree beside Nadia's table.

The madness was already beginning.

The man was raving about trying to get a picture of the elusive "ice princess," as Nadia was being called now.

She sunk her fingers into the muscles around her neck, trying to ease the tension away. The model she used for high profile shoots like these hadn't shown up this morning, which was the last thing she wanted to happen since she was trying to make Mr. Magana happy.

"Darling, I need models that show up on time. With no models, we have no picture taking. I know you realize this, no?" Franco's head tipped slightly sideways, as his accented voice poured over Nadia's stretched out nerve endings.

"Mr. Magana, I'm so sorry. I will call in two other models for tomorrow. How is that?" Nadia questioned, hoping to soothe the irate Italian photographer. She needed him for the new spread. *The Trend* was on pace to join the ranks of exalted magazines everywhere, and when you were being compared with the likes of *Vogue*, *Cosmopolitan*, and *Vanity Fair*, every department needed to be running like a ship in top notch performance. This was the first time since she'd come on board as the new president that they were this close to matching those fine journals. She was determined to do everything to make that happen, without losing her vision or her mind along the way.

"Call me Franco, love, and of course that will work. I love you and what you are doing with this company. I know Linda would have loved it too. That is why I work with you, no?" Franco said with surprising honesty.

The middle-aged photographer to the stars was on everyone's list. For Nadia, she pulled the coup of the decade getting him to shoot a spread for her magazine. So far he was acting totally out of character. She'd heard very bad things about this man, how he was vainer than ten supermodels, an extreme perfectionist and numerous other things, but looking at him now Nadia was just damn glad she could placate him enough to have him come back and try this all over again.

"Darling," his voice deep with an Italian accent, "you need to let these worries you have pass you by. It is not good for you or for your business."

Nadia shook her head "I know." God, did she ever.

She looked up over the table to the handsome Franco and sent him a gracious smile. "Please, let me apologize once more, and like I said, we will be back where we need to be tomorrow with more models than you can shake a finger at."

A smile full of Italian charm slipped over his features. "Good, I cannot wait to capture the beauty and fire of this great city for your magazine."

Two hours later, Nadia was beginning to cool off in her downtown office in Beaumont, when Renee opened the door.

"Here are the messages from yesterday that I forgot to hand you, sorry, and also you have an enormously sexy man waiting for you," Renee told her with a wide smile. The woman was the same age as Nadia, but a little more outspoken with her sexuality than Nadia would ever be. With her dark red-gold curls and an hourglass figure, it was hard for men to have a decent conversation with her, but for Nadia it was Renee's sharp mind that kept her in this office. She was a shark-ruthless when she wanted information and downright mean when crossed. Nadia was more sedate, but loved Renee's outlandish moments. The office place was never boring with her around.

"I just got here," Nadia whined, sitting back in her swivel chair and rubbing those muscles again. She swore she could feel the tension ebbing back into them. The day was never going to end.

"Please tell me that you aren't going to make me turn him away." Renee's blue eyes practically begged Nadia, "If not for the sake of him needing to see you, at least let me tell him that you are busy so that I can keep him occupied in the front."

He must really be something for Renee to get all worked up. Usually her eccentric secretary knew her worth, but kept the men to a distance, not caring one way or the other if they found her attractive or not. It seemed to Nadia that she really wanted to get her hands on this one.

"I couldn't care less what you tell him, but allow me to grab something for my head before you send him in," Nadia murmured, as she went through her top drawer searching for the bottle of aspirin she usually kept there.

"I'll give you a few moments to unwind before sending him in, kay?" Renee gave Nadia a wink then turned and walked out, closing the door behind her.

After taking the aspirin, Nadia leaned her head back on the headrest and tried, unsuccessfully, to relax. The past week had been hellish and like she assumed, the ugly rumors spread, fueling gossip and more gossip. She wanted nothing more than to crawl under a rock and sleep the next year away. Hopefully, by that time the gossip mongers would find something else to sink their teeth into.

Without giving a thought to what she looked like, she pulled the clip from her hair in the back. The tension eased ever so slowly. Usually she didn't have to travel to Houston all that much. Her company headquarters were here, in Beaumont, and with Derek running her large office in Houston, she was lucky to stay close to home. Today's visit was specifically to placate Franco, and she managed to do so.

The afternoon sunlight slipped through her office windows highlighting the beautiful green walls and numerous bookshelves that lined them. Nadia got up and took off her light business jacket, hanging it on the coat rack beside the door. She pulled on her shirt, making sure the edges were still tucked in to her trousers, and then went and sat back down, determined to see what her mysterious "sexy guest" wanted. Then she could send him on his way and finally relax.

Right before Renee buzzed him in to allow him entrance into her office, there was a slight charge in the air, almost as if a jolt snagged through the air and into her body. With some alarm she watched the door open, and not surprisingly, Drake Thompson walked in.

The tingles gave him away. It was always like this for her, even when she had been a young twelve year old girl, new to Beaumont. Back then the tingles had scared the bejesus out of her. Now, she knew deep down inside her body, where she let no emotion reach, that this strong, deeply masculine man touched something far inside of her that had never been visible to anyone else.

His body, massive and honed to hard perfection, paused inside her office doorway. Testosterone oozed from him, stifling the air around him and letting her know that he was a bit more dominant than any other man would ever be. Nadia realized that no matter how persuasive he could be, how tactile and convincing, he was still the suave Texas gentleman, not entering her office until she deemed him able.

"Drake," Nadia greeted him with a slight nodding of her head, telling him without words that he was welcome. She moved back to her chair and sat behind her desk, hoping the monstrous piece of wood would help her feel a bit more balanced and in command with him nearby. So far it wasn't working.

"Nadia," he murmured her name with all the rich vagaries of an exotic slur. To her it seemed to take him forever before he finished. His voice rippled like slow molasses warming in the hot sun. Tipping his head, he moved farther into the office and then lowered his body into one of the two chairs across from her desk.

She admired the ease in which he crossed one booted ankle over the opposite knee, sprawling in her chair as if it were a recliner, his body deceptively lazy looking in a half slouch. An older, snap front western shirt covered the broad expanse of his chest, while tattered denim hugged his long legs. Large, worn leather boots covered his feet. The dark warm chocolate of his hair was a bit long around his ears, but what really drew Nadia's attention were his eyes. A decadent, sinful caramel color, warmed to a rich golden brown. Dark, heavy lashes fanned out around those scorching eyes and Nadia felt her body rise ten degrees hotter.

The buzzing of her phone slapped her back into reality.

"Excuse me," she murmured to Drake and picked up the phone. "Yes?"

Renee's eloquent voice came over the line, "Isn't he just delicious?"

Nadia couldn't even think of a decent reply, except for the furious blush that was working up her throat at the moment. She mumbled, "I'll buzz you when I'm done," then hung up the phone, praying the blush wasn't as furious as she thought.

Clearing her throat, she looked back at Drake. "What can I do for you?"

"I tried to come by on Tuesday but you weren't available." The piercing eyes looking over at her from across her desk were intelligent and deadly accurate. Nadia didn't even blink wrong, knowing instinctively that he might take something from that and glean the truth. She knew he might already know, but him knowing, and her telling him, were two different things. Her heart couldn't handle any more excitement at this moment.

"I was out of the office on business." Changing the subject seemed like a great idea. "How is the Border Collie? Were you able to patch her back together?"

"She is doing wonderful. Her spirits are up and her vitals are good. The back leg was merely fractured, but she is in a cast. Although she is so lively, I doubt it would have stopped her if she had lost her leg at all."

He spoke warmly of the animal, and Nadia knew that he cared for the small dog. She wished that she could have bounced back so easily from her own problem.

"She is under care at the Haven, as I'm sure you figured, but I have not placed her on the list for adoption just yet, and I won't, if you want first dibs at her." Cunning brown eyes zeroed in on her and Nadia knew that he had seen through her thin shell the other night, and today as well. He'd sensed something was wrong, and he knew that the small dog would take her mind off of that. She understood she needed the distraction of the dog, but how did he know that?

His hand stroked the arm of the chair, and Nadia was mesmerized by the slow touch of his finger against the grain of leather. Silently shaking her head, she thought about bringing home a dog. Her back yard was large and fenced in, there was ample room in her cottage just in case she wanted the dog inside, and it wasn't like she didn't have the means to take care of the animal.

Drake spoke, as if sensing her hesitation. "She will be fixed, if you are wondering what you would do with an unexpected litter of puppies. And she will be up to date on all of her shots when you pick her up."

"You are a born salesman, you know that?" Nadia told him.

He shrugged his massive shoulders with a grin on his face, "Some things just come naturally."

There were too many things that came naturally for Drake Thompson. Nadia took it as a fact of life that he was magnetic, driven, and extremely lucky when it came to women and business.

"Look," he told her as he leaned forward in the chair, "we both know that you felt something for her, enough so that you made sure she would be okay, even while you were having your own problems." He didn't go into detail and when Nadia leveled a hard look at him, he just continued. "Don't make me give her to someone else that I know won't show her the love or affection that you will. She deserves a good life too."

Nadia let his words pour over her. She heard and understood the hint. Her life was better than it ever had been. She was president of a large company, was more than covered on any money situation that might arise, but yet her personal life was a mess. Nadia knew he was trying to take her mind off what happened; she understood that, but she doubted any of it would work.

The truth was she needed that dog. If anything could help her through this rough patch, it would be that sweet bundle of fur. She had the time, didn't she? Besides, didn't she owe it to the dog?

"Okay. I'll do it."

When she caught the knowing gleam in his brown eyes, she didn't feel as if he was playing upon her weakness for hurt animals. She felt that she was doing something good, something that *she* wanted to do for a change. And knowing that the adorable Border Collie would be hers to care for made her maternal instinct kick in. Now she would have something to help take her mind off of all the gossip and pain.

"Good. She needs you too, Nadia."

She looked up, surprised at his words. Why she was surprised, she couldn't say. Drake had always been a very astute man. For him to see beyond her tough front was nothing new. Ever since she was sixteen it had been a battle to keep her feelings hidden. Her adolescent crush turned into a burning, all-consuming love for this man. She never deluded herself into thinking he would be hers. It was almost a rule of nature that he would never be tied down by any woman, much less her. The pain of seeing him with other women would never fade, especially when she knew that he didn't think of her as someone desirable.

Heat drenched the backs of her eyes. She looked away, blinking furiously to clear the tears forming there. Clearing her throat she said, "Thank you for giving me the option to have her before anyone else."

"Her name is Belle."

Nadia resolutely kept her gaze on the papers she was trying to straighten on her desk. "Belle. It suits her."

Quiet descended on the office, and for a moment a feeling of relief overcame her. Then he spoke.

"Nadia…"

As he said her name he placed emphasis on each syllable, making it sound foreign and mysterious. Her heart fluttered, while hidden, forgotten parts of her anatomy stood up to take notice.

"Look at me."

Please don't make me.

She knew what he'd see in her eyes if she did. The feelings she fought so hard to hide the past week were at full brim. His presence always screwed with her inner balance somehow. She felt off kilter, lost, and floundering.

"Nadia," he murmured, his drawl drawing out the word.

She focused her gaze on the intriguing opening of his shirt. There were two buttons open, exposing the dark, luscious tone of his skin. It was roped with tendons. His Adam's apple bobbed. Her stomach fell to the floor as she finally brought her eyes to his.

Warm, rich colors swirled under dark lashes. His eyes weren't merely brown. They were alive, bursting with life and some other fiery sentiment. It was the most unusual thing Nadia had ever seen. But she refused to look away. He held her there, suspended by her emotions and the raw, primal power she sensed in him. His eyes were beautiful, deep and mysterious. Barely hinting at the inner man she never thought she would see.

"Everything will be fine."

His deep voice resonated in the room. The sound, the genuine amount of sincerity in that hypnotic drawl, caused her eyes to flood with tears. She could see that he understood, even if he hadn't heard the full story. By some weird cosmic act he understood her broken trust, the horrifying rawness of her feelings. Amazingly enough, he never once said, 'I told you so.'

Nadia sat there, floored by his level of understanding and shook her head in affirmation. She couldn't speak. It seemed as if all sound was torn from her vocal cords, but looking into Drake's soulful eyes, she realized it didn't matter. He understood more than mere words, and that made the pain of not having him hit even deeper than before.

She watched, in a trance, as he stood up, tipped his head courteously in her direction then quietly left her office.

***

She broadcasted her emotions far too easily. And since they were out in the open, Drake had soaked up every bit of sensation she had let slip.

His Druid senses picked up on them easily in her office, but sometimes it was harder. There was no way for him to ignore them. Her nerves were all over the place today, and it made her emotions harder to hold back.

There were determining factors to reading someone. If you were close to that person, emotions and feelings got in the way. The process was easier if you didn't know the person you were trying to decipher.

Drake closed the door to his work truck and started it up. A rock station blared to life, but he ignored it, focusing instead on the light green eyes that he had seen minutes ago. Within seconds, the emotions he knew she was so good at hiding, were apparent to him. Nadia had always been intensely personal and private, but even with that she still couldn't block the way she felt. Drake knew that even if he wasn't a Druid, he would have still been able to see the abject pain in her eyes.

Drake felt more than a little protective of her. With her small stature and delicate build, he always felt territorial, as if she were too young and naïve to get along without him. The past few years had proved him wrong. He watched her move up from assistant, to president of the Browning Corporation. And she handled it with grace and aplomb. But even through all that, especially after taking the head job little more than a year ago, Drake could still sense the underlying emotions she was trying to conceal.

This afternoon's episode was proof that she needed something, something relaxing, something to make her slow down a bit. Drake couldn't even remember the last time he'd seen her laugh, since seeing her out in Texas society was about as close as he'd been to her recently.

As both his personal and business life were chock full of charity work and invites to exclusive gala's and events, it was a given that he would see her often. Drake knew that it was all business to Nadia. Every event, every society function, was overtime for her. She never enjoyed the functions, and Drake knew part of that reason was Donavan.

Donavan Hamilton became a slug the minute Linda passed, as if sensing that maybe the new protégé would be a bit more willing to slough off some of her money to a suave businessman with loads of charm. Drake admitted to himself, Donavan knew business. As the manager for a firm of accountants, he had a pristine business reputation. But it was his personal financial situation that caused him to scent out the richest woman in the area and try to freeload. His gambling addiction was only *one* vice that needed to be reined in.

Nadia allowed herself to become embroiled in a fantasy world of Donavan's making. She had allowed him to help her, and if there were any business problems, she went to Donavan.

That was a bitter pill for Drake to swallow. But he knew it was because of him that she allowed herself to be pulled in Donavan's direction, because she didn't want him to think she was leaning on him too heavily, as she'd done so in the past. That knowledge hurt him; it still did. But he knew then, and still did now, that it was better this way. Although, Drake was damn happy to know that she now realized exactly what kind of man Donavan was. Drake knew for certain Donavan would be nothing but history, if he wasn't already.

At that thought, a pleased smile crossed his face.

***

After dropping off menu suggestions and decoration ideas at her organizer's house, Nadia was finally on her way home. She had a fairly large charity event at the end of the month that was draining what was left of her creative energy. When she pulled up in her driveway, she almost drooled at the sight of her front door.

She needed a damn vacation.

It wasn't like her staff couldn't handle everything if she decided to take one. They were more than capable of doing what needed to be done. It was her, Nadia reasoned, that was hesitating. She couldn't get past the thought that if she stayed home she might just lose her mind.

Glimpses of Donavan and Suzanne kept flashing through her mind. She had known better than to let herself fall for him. But he was charming, handsome, and so knowledgeable with business. And with Nadia desperately trying to show Drake that she was okay in this new job, Donavan had been the answer to her prayers. Seems like her plan to make Drake realize a few things was coming back to bite her on the ass.

She should have known better than to think things would ever run smoothly again.

After checking her emails one last time, she sent a reminder to Amy to be ready to shoot tomorrow morning with Franco at eight sharp. After a quick shower, Nadia sat down in her recliner and waited for the loneliness to set in. Nighttime was always the worst.

Even though Donavan had been the answer to her prayers, he was sometimes a smug bastard. In comparison sharing a few intimate moments with him hadn't made half a spark light up inside of her like it did when she just *looked* at Drake.

It went against everything she wanted. Inviting someone that she knew she didn't fully trust into her life and into her heart. But it was easier to handle that, than it was to get her heart stomped on every time she turned around. Nadia kept up the pretense of being around Donavan simply out of necessity. Even with all of his faults, he was a charming, funny man who for a brief time kept her mind from wandering to Drake.

She thought back to her parents. Neither having any family, they had both been lonely and alone when they met. That changed after moving to Texas from Louisiana. Within weeks her father, Matt, found a good paying accounting job, and her mother, Anna, found one working for a local department store. Friends soon followed. Nadia, an only child, had been raised with strict morals and values. She knew from watching both of her parents hold down jobs that she would never be a spoiled little rich girl like the ones she met at school. She had been a young, shy and very mature girl for her age. There had only been one person that made her feel gauche, naïve, and so ungainly that she wanted to hide beneath something whenever she met him, and that was Drake Thompson.

A smile caught at the edges of her mouth as she thought back to those early days. Her parents had been alive and happy, and she was too young to notice anything about men. There were many company picnics, days to visit the animals, and even more days when she would show up after school to meet with her father. Of course for Nadia, the big deal was watching for Drake. By the time she reached her sixteenth year, she could manage to say more than a few words to the large Texan without blushing and tripping over sentences. She knew, by then, what those sidelong glances and crooked grins did to female hearts and bodies. It was a dream of hers that when she got old enough, she would make Drake realize she was a woman, and after that, everything would fall into place.

The death of her parents changed all of her dreams. The funeral was taken care of with a small amount of insurance money that her parents managed to keep up with, but every other necessity was covered by Drake. The tall, sometimes brooding, and eerily perceptive Texan had stepped in whenever Nadia felt her world falling apart. Sitting beside him in the funeral home and the large church service had been a soothing balm to her young, bruised heart.

The days after the funeral, Drake had been her everything. When the state of Texas had sent her to stay with an older couple in a foster home, Drake brought her there. When she called him every week to say how she was doing, per his instructions, he listened with avid interest. When Drake called her for her seventeenth birthday and invited her out to eat, Nadia felt her young heart start to beat with renewed fervor-until Drake picked her up and Nadia noticed he wasn't alone.

That day she realized something. Though she was seventeen, and a budding woman, Drake would never see her as what she dreamed. He would never see her long, flowing black hair, her light green eyes, and small, slightly curved, short frame as anything sexy and beautiful. She would never be able to compete with model tall and waspishly thin women that he paraded around with, especially after he told her that she would never add up. Why would Nadia want to anyway? They giggled like school girls and grasped at his body as if he were a precious temptation that they couldn't help but want. The one that he'd brought that night was a new one, but Nadia knew that she would join the long list of women that Drake discarded with amazing speed.

After that night, Nadia no longer called Drake. She no longer waited upon his arrival of a visit as if it was the highlight of her week. She did her damndest to ensure that when she did see him, she didn't stare like some lovesick teenager. Instead, she coolly held a conversation with him and did not respond to his teasing ways.

She became driven, and after getting a job as assistant to secretary of the president of a large company at eighteen, Nadia almost forgot Drake.

That hadn't stopped her from dreaming, wishing, that one day his feelings toward her might change. Of course, the reality was, Drake would never stoop to dating her or even see her as someone desirable. By the time Linda had passed on, and Nadia inherited everything, she gave up her secret desires. She would never have Drake. Her body would always want him, her mind would fall asleep with thoughts of him, but the real her would never have the experience of being his woman.

At the first society function, where Nadia was acknowledged as the new president of Browning Inc., Drake was in attendance. When Donavan Hamilton asked for a dance, Nadia felt the slow tingle, and body warming charge of Drake's presence close by, but she ignored it and accepted that dance from Donavan, even admitting to herself that the small part inside of her that lusted after Drake wanted him to be jealous by that snub. Now, little more than a year later, Nadia was starting to believe God didn't want her to be happy.

Sitting in her quiet home it was easy to think that, especially with that snub from a year ago still haunting her. She had known that further enticing Donavan into some semblance of a relationship would cause the hordes of society members to think that was exactly what she wanted.

That couldn't be farther from the truth. She was cold, and abnormally indifferent to men. The only man that caused any kind of reaction in her was the one that she had been trying to get away from for the past ten years. Of course, no one in Texas society knew that, nor would they.

She'd latched onto Donavan for her sanity. She knew that with her new title, money and prestige, she would have many questions, and need some direction. The board had helped, but Nadia had known early on that she would need a confidante, someone she could pester when she needed help. It had been easier to let

Donavan latch onto her, rather than call upon the one man who caused her insides to light up like a fourth of July firework display.

Now her confidante was gone, but thankfully, she had a year's worth of experiences under her belt. She was pretty sure she could handle anything now, especially with the horror of last week still fresh on her mind. No way in hell would that happen to her again.

Now comfortably snug under her comforter, with small slices of moonlight creasing through her blinds, Nadia allowed herself to finally relax. Thoughts of Donavan, and of how she put herself into this mess, didn't stick, neither did thoughts of Drake, and of how downright sexy he had been this afternoon in her office. Her breathing deepened, her body molded to the soft, pillow top mattress, and soon the blessed peace of sleep had pulled her under.

Chapter 3

"Ms. Morales, it is so nice to see you tonight."

Nadia gave Mrs. Penelope Harris a sugary sweet smile, ignored the hidden meaning behind that statement, and replied, "You too, Mrs. Harris. I hope you find the evening to be extremely entertaining." Then she deftly maneuvered herself away from the Harris's and the other barracuda's that were filing in around her. The only thing she wanted now was to hide in the ladies room until this whole farce was over. Of course that wasn't an option, but Nadia couldn't squelch the 'want to' that formed in her stomach.

The Drossier family was one of the chief benefactors of the Browning Corporation. Nadia had been putting together this event for over six months, and now it was finally here. The wealthy family gave generously to the arts and humanities. And for over ten years, they held a yearly ball/charity function that drew numerous faces. The crowd ranged from business sharks to Wall Street types, and as Nadia looked around she even saw a few Hollywood icons in the mix. It was a lavish affair and a large feather in the hat of Nadia's company to be able to pull it off without a hitch. This was one of the many 'large' projects that her company handled during the year. Nadia usually loved every single moment of it, but now she wasn't so sure she could keep it together for the rest of the night.

Donavan was here, with Suzanne. It was as if he was flaunting what society had guessed at for the past three weeks. He hadn't made it around to her yet, but Nadia knew before the night was over, he would find her. They would have to meet face to face, in front of everyone in the ballroom.

The hurt that she managed to live with for the past weeks slithered through her veins, reminding her of what happened. She still felt bruised, battered, and left out in harsh elements, after what she had seen.

That's what you get for allowing yourself to care about a man that you never wanted to begin with.

She had known what kind of person he was. She'd just refused to let her mind dwell on that. And what had started out as a business relationship, turned into a small bit of contented placement on Nadia's part. She allowed herself to feel at ease and comfortable in thinking that even though she didn't love Donavan, he would never leave her side and go to another. The whole pseudo-relationship had been a front. They'd been more friends than anything else. That was all that Nadia had been able to give.

So why had finding him with another woman hurt so much? Why did she feel like the wounded party in this scene out of a horrible play?

Hell, she cried over a man that she wasn't even sure she cared deeply for. Sure, she had trusted him, to some degree, and there were many evenings where she knew if she had been able to give more, things could have turned into something totally different. But she hadn't, and things stayed the same. When she'd seen him pounding into Suzanne as if he couldn't get enough of her, Nadia felt the world shift, and her balance had been screwed ever since.

As she walked amid the throngs of people, she allowed the music from the band to try and calm those stretched out nerves. Nadia had to admit that the place was decorated specifically by her directions. Sheer, dark blue silk hung from a center point on the ceiling, while beneath the silk twinkling white lights blinked, creating a hazy, outside feel deep inside the ballroom. Blinding white tablecloths covered every table, and long, tapered silver candelabras held candles which emitted soft, wavy light in the large ballroom. The large chandeliers were dimmed, and the atmosphere was soft, comfortable, romantic, and hopefully inductive to writing large checks.

She made her way to the ladies room, then stopped at the sitting area and checked her appearance out in the long, tall mirrors that took up one wall.

Her dress mode was never flashy, more understated and elegant. She didn't care for the flesh revealing designs that most of Texas society women bought; instead, she leaned more towards clean lines and classic looks. The only boldness she allowed in her clothes was the color. The deep, midnight blue of her gown tonight was what drew Nadia in the first place. The dress was formal, floor length, and was stunning in its simplicity. So far, her appearances in public hadn't put her on the worst dressed list, which surprised her because of all the cattiness that surrounded this culture. She still got a feminine thrill whenever she opened the paper and saw her own image looking back at her from the best dressed section.

An hour later, after eating a small bit of food, and holding a few conversations with some donators, a small charge lifted the hairs on Nadia's arm and neck. Warmth flowed deep into her body, and she grew hot even as a chill skated upon her skin. Looking up from the table where she sat with Renee, and a few other office workers, Nadia searched the area knowing that Drake was nearby.

Seconds later, she spotted his tall, dangerously sexy body across the way. His dark, rumpled hair gleamed mahogany in the candlelight, while the wavering shadows highlighted his rugged, sharp bladed nose, and beautiful, all seeing eyes. Firm, sensual lips smiled at something his date said. Nadia felt her thighs tighten in anticipation.

His body was draped in a black tux, and instead of a bowtie, he wore a white dress shirt with silver vest on under his tux jacket. The stark colors made him look dangerous, and jealousy twisted deep in her gut. He was every dream, every wish, of a man that she had ever wanted. After years of hoping, it was still a forgone conclusion that she would never have a chance with him. But damn, a woman could dream, couldn't she?

The darkness suited him. With his sinister good looks, scorching sensuality and seductive Texas drawl,

Nadia understood how every woman felt when she was introduced to him. He was a devastating man.

"Ah, I see your lovely ex-boyfriend made it to the festivities," Renee drawled as she looked at Donavan over the rim of her wineglass. "And of course he brought a date. What a surprise to see it is Suzanne."

Nadia didn't even look in their direction. "It was bound to happen, Renee. We both knew that." The words felt like dust in her throat.

"Yeah, honey, I know you are right, but there is something called subtlety and Donavan doesn't know the meaning of it." The other woman licked her lips, and Nadia could clearly see the bloodthirsty gleam in her eyes. "Or, he just didn't care one way or another."

"It doesn't matter anymore. It was all a mistake to begin with."

Blue eyes leveled on Nadia with speed and accuracy. "Don't you dare put all the blame on you. He's a man and if he wanted out, for any reason what so ever, he should have ended things before deciding that he was going to screw some other woman while you were still considered to be *his*. Doesn't matter how the relationship was going," Renee said with a cutting motion of her hand.

Nadia listened to what Renee was saying, knowing that her secretary cared for her like a friend, but still she felt alone in this full ballroom even with her friend at her side. Her eyes unerringly searched out the area across the ballroom, once again landing where Drake was sitting with his date, and a full table. The woman was Natalie Ramos, a well-known author, and society darling. Tall, blonde, and stunningly beautiful, she sat beside Drake as if she belonged there. In Nadia's estimation, she did.

Drake's arm was around the back of Natalie's chair, and every once in a while he would send the woman a crooked grin, one that made Nadia's heart beat faster and her palms sweat. Nadia could see the flow of conversation at the table, mostly between Drake and Natalie, and felt the old familiar need pulse low in her body. She'd wanted that man before she'd even known what wanting meant. Now that she was older, and you would think wiser, the need hadn't changed. The pain was the same.

He smiled that one sided grin again. Nadia shivered. The backs of her eyes felt like they were on fire, and ever so slightly, she felt the threat of tears. Damn. *Why*? Why did she have this burning, all-consuming feeling for a man she would never be able to touch, much less have for herself?

No one else had ever made her feel like this. And now, after a year of her emotions being dulled by the presence of Donavan, he was out of the picture, and her old wants were making her remember exactly why she had allowed Donavan so close. She needed someone, a man, to be a buffer between her and Drake. She would never have a chance, and probably end up making an ass of herself over him, if she didn't have some damage control. Donavan had been her damage control. Now he was gone.

Nadia blinked out of her thoughts and instantly felt speared by heat. From across the ballroom Drake was staring at her. Stilling instantly, she blinked, thoroughly caught in the snare of warm brown eyes, and an instinctual maleness that made her tremble. Her fingers caught the soft fabric of her dress and clenched.

This wasn't the same look that he had given her when she had allowed him entrance to her office weeks ago. It certainly wasn't the look that he threw her when she'd shown up on his doorstep with the injured dog. It was scorching. Hot. Raw. And it made Nadia's mouth go dry. While a sharp, painful blush climbed up and over her cheeks.

She tore her eyes from his and took a deep, calming breath, just as Renee cursed softly.

Nadia looked up from the table, and met the green gaze of Donavan standing by the table.

As if her night couldn't get any worse.

"Nadia," he nodded in her direction, not even saying hello to Renee. Thank God he had come alone, leaving Suzanne somewhere in the ballroom. "I was wondering if I could speak to you alone."

Renee scoffed at him under her breath, while sending out signals that said she would be more the willing to peel his skin from his body. Nadia held her calm composure. The other members of the table were now dancing, leaving only Renee and Nadia to greet Donavan. "You can say whatever you need to say right here. Renee is a close friend of mine, as you already know."

And besides, Nadia knew if she left the table with him, the raw hurt she felt every time she saw Drake nowadays might lead her to accept his apology-and whatever else he wanted the minute they were alone.

He chided her with his eyes and tried again. "Dia, honey, we don't need to talk with her around. This needs to be said in private." His tone was slightly pleading, and it grated on Nadia's nerves.

"Hmph, I see no reason to say what you need to say in private. You sure as hell weren't thinking about Dia's welfare whenever you were doing Suzanne, were you?" Renee spoke out, much to Nadia's dismay.

"Renee, hush now," she told her friend, hoping to calm down her bulldog attitude before Renee decided to do harm to Donavan.

"You know he doesn't deserve any breaks, hon. He is only trying to 'pretty up' what he did wrong," Renee told her, sending killing glances towards the man in question.

"You need to stay out of this, Renee. This is none of your business," Donavan glared right back at Renee.

Well, that certainly wasn't the right thing to say.

Renee jumped from her seat, pointing her finger in his face. "It became my business whenever I had to console her after she found you humping Suzanne on your desk, asshole."

"Renee! Sit down!" Nadia furiously whispered, hoping to calm her friend into some kind of order. They were starting to draw curious stares. Thank God the music was loud enough to drown out their argument.

Blue eyes flashed to her, and Nadia could feel her friend's anger. "I will handle this, okay?"

Renee snorted, but kept her gaze trained on Donavan as Nadia grabbed his arm and pulled him away from her table and around the ballroom. She found one of many French doors and pulled it open, leading Donavan out into the warm, balmy Texas evening.

"Say what you need to say to make yourself feel better and then leave," she told him, as she whirled around and stood before him.

"Dia, honey, you know I'm sorry. You know I never meant to hurt you." He brought his hands up to her shoulders, and for one insane moment Nadia wanted to lean into him, to allow him to console her, to make the emptiness go away, even though she knew he wouldn't be able to. That depressed her, knowing that she was so starved for human emotion, for another person's touch, that she would allow it from the man that caused some of the pain in the first place.

"I don't know anything anymore." Was that her? That woman that sounded wounded, hurt, and confused?

"Ah, my Dia, you are too sweet, too gentle to be in this cutthroat world of society. Suzanne is just sex to me darling. She could never take your place in my world."

Nadia could hear him talking, but curiously enough she didn't feel anything but emptiness. She felt dead, to him, and every other emotion. He was still going on, rattling about how he had needed sex and Suzanne was an easy lay, nothing more. Nadia just continued to stare at his bowtie, feeling as if the world had ceased to exist. She had somewhat trusted this man and he had taken that and cleaved it in two. But the pain, the hurt from weeks ago numbed, and now she just felt disgusted with men in general. This is what she got from trying to do the right thing. She should have known it wouldn't work.

New sounds came from behind Donavan and he, thankfully, halted his voice in midsentence. Nadia looked beyond his shoulder, disinterestedly, and could barely make out the tall shadow of a man standing there. The minute he spoke, she knew immediately who it was.

"I see you are still trying to worm your way under Nadia's radar, Donavan. Don't you think that by now she has realized what a bastard you really are?"

And that easily she felt awake, every nerve ending alive and thrumming. Donavan exhaled an indignant scoff, and tried to peer through the darkness at who would dare insult him, but once Nadia had heard his voice, she didn't need to see who it was. What really surprised her was that Drake would take it upon himself to come out here and confront Donavan. By his words, he wanted him gone. That pissed Nadia off. As if she couldn't handle Donavan herself.

"Thompson, you go too far," Donavan told him. Nadia could clearly sense his anger.

Drake slid out from under the shadows and Nadia suppressed a shudder at how eerie he looked standing there. Never before had she noticed how attuned this man was to the darkness.

"Clearly Donavan, I don't go far enough. For the past year you have made her the laughingstock of Texas society. Seems like you keep doing a bang up job month after month."

Donavan bristled again, but Nadia calmed him a bit by placing her hand on his arm. She turned him to her. "Ignore him, and let me tell you this, whatever happened, happened. Don't think that I will welcome your attentions now. Please, go back inside and go to Suzanne." She hoped he would take the hint and leave. She was through with him, and didn't want him around her again.

Instead of saying anything, he sent Drake a disgusted look, and turned to go back in the ballroom. Even as he left, Nadia realized this wouldn't be the last time that she would have to lay down some rules between them.

The minute he was gone, Nadia whirled on Drake, furious.

"What in the hell were you thinking coming out here and baiting him like that? This is none of your business, Drake. None! I could have easily handled him." She tried not to yell, but it was hard. She took deep breaths and focused on his dark silhouette against the stone of the building. The words he just said rolled around inside of her brain. He'd called her a laughing stock.

"Handle him? The man needs more than just words spoken to him. He needs a good boot up his ass." There was enough venom in those words to make Nadia's skin crawl. Drake sounded furious, which was a first for her.

He shifted away from the building, causing more shadows to fall upon his tall frame. Darkness slithered around him like a living thing, wrapping his body in swatches of moonlight and obscurity. Nadia noticed he looked more menacing in the dark too. Shivering slightly, she tried to hide her anger and find a nice way to leave him and go back to the security of the ballroom. It wasn't as if she was frightened of him. She was more wary than anything else.

"I still don't understand why you came out here." She sounded as if she cared that he came to her rescue. Damn. Clearing her throat, she looked anywhere but at him. Not that it helped. She could be blind and still know he was around. His smell, his presence, just him breathing was enough to make her body stand up and take notice.

Instead of answering her statement, he sauntered closer to the edge of the small portico where they were standing. The play of muscles in his shoulders was highlighted by moonlight. Nadia clenched her fingers against the material of her dress.

"I knew what I was getting when I allowed Donavan close to me." Now why in the hell had she admitted that? That was none of Drake's concern.

Shut up, Nadia!

"Did you really, little Dia?" The endearment sounded condescending when he said it. Donavan had been the one to start calling her that. Many other society members picked up on it also. "The man gambles most of everything he has away. He barely has money for his own business to stay afloat. He loves rich women, I'm sure I don't need to tell you why, and among other things, his taste runs towards rough sex."

Those words went through Nadia like a shockwave. She knew some of it, and a few other things that he hadn't mentioned, but it was still wicked to hear him talk so base to her like that. She looked towards him in the dark, and could barely make out his facial features. Strong emotion wafted off of him.

"He is scum, Nadia. Filth. So far beneath the purity of you that I'm surprised you didn't turn brown when you touched him." He turned to look in her direction, and Nadia swore she saw a flash of golden light where his eyes were. She shivered and wrapped her arms around her upper body, not able to deal with this new side of Drake so easily. Exactly what had she just seen?

"I'm glad that you caught on to the truth before he was able to strip your wealth away or hurt you indefinitely." He left the edge of the portico and slowly walked towards her. Her heart kick-started into a dangerous tempo. Something was different tonight. Something was causing Drake to act even more territorial towards her. Nadia wasn't sure how to feel about that.

She could barely breathe whenever he stopped in front of her. His tall, massive frame made her feel ultra-feminine. Her forehead came to his breastbone, and that was only because she was wearing high heels. The breeze turned, and Nadia could smell the tinges of some spicy, woodsy cologne that he wore. She inhaled, taking in the smell, recording it to her memory for the months to come. He was so warm. And it took every ounce of her conscience not to give into the notion to walk up to him and beg him to hold her. Just to feel those arms cradling her, protecting her, caressing her…

The air stirred near her head, and instinctively she knew he had brushed his fingers there. She almost moaned low in her throat, but killed the noise instantly. There was the slight tug on her loose hair, and then she felt his finger trace her jaw line. Nadia almost dropped to the ground at his feet. Her breath crystallized in her lungs, and she knew in the back of her mind that this was affecting her more than him.

"I don't think you realize the kind of hurt he could have given you, Nadia."

She tried to swallow, but her mouth was too dry. The moment was so acute that she was able to feel the calloused skin on his fingers when he brushed her jaw again.

"You are too small, too delicate, and so much more than that, to allow him to mess with your life like he was doing."

The words touched something deep inside of her, and Nadia clenched her teeth from screaming out, *but you don't understand! This was all to keep me away from you. To keep the temptation of reaching out to touch you away from my hands, away from me!*

The threat of tears returned. Oh dear God, what was she going to do? This was too dangerous. She knew better than to dwell on anything he was doing or saying. But it was so hard when he was saying all the right things, and touching her in all the right ways.

You can't have him Nadia. You knew that years ago, and you still know it now.

Listening to her conscience warring inside her head, she pulled her chin from his hold then locked the memory of his fingers on her skin in the vault of her mind. Slowly stepping away from him, she put space between them, even as her insides screamed at her not to do so.

"Whatever danger I was in with him around is no longer apparent," the words came out low, and deep. Nadia cleared her throat and continued, without looking directly at Drake. "He will never be welcome in my life again."

Without giving him a chance to say anything, she turned and left him standing out in the moonlight, with only the sounds of night as company.

***

What in the hell just happened?

Drake clinched his fists, ground his molars together, and literally stopped himself from breaking the top of the stone portico ledge in half. After a few seconds the need to change had passed, but as a defensive mechanism, his fangs were scraping his bottom lip.

"Fuck."

The word was murmured low. Even humans couldn't hear it, but just saying it eased the tension coiling tight inside his body.

Movement jostled the small bush next to him on the outer perimeter of the portico. His enhanced vision could see clearly in the night, and as he peered into the bushes a small nighthawk gazed back at him coolly, her yellow eyes warm and friendly. The bird let out a soft trill, a short hoot that fell on Drake's ears warmly. To any other human it would only be the sound of a bird squawking. To Drake, he understood the emotion behind it. The hawk felt sorry for him. Apparently the bird sensed his tension.

"Believe me, I don't even understand it, friend."

The hawk tipped her head curiously to the side, peering fiercely at Drake, then flew off to find more interesting company.

The barrage of emotions from Nadia left Drake feeling as if the floor had been scraped out from under him. It wasn't often he was left standing around with his thumb up his ass and nothing to say. Actually it was a very rare occurrence. Usually he was able to cut through the bullshit and get to the point. With Nadia, he couldn't do so. He had the horrible feeling that he would hurt her feelings if he did, so he never pushed her too far.

Brushing his hands through his hair he let out a growl, shook whatever tension from his body that he could, and pushed the confusing thoughts away. He only came out here to make sure Donavan, the ass, didn't try something stupid. Something that might warrant Drake kicking him into the next century. Of course that hadn't happened, much to Drake's dismay. But damn, it would have been fun to take out his frustration for the dumb bastard on the very man that caused Nadia's pain in the first place. Just thinking of that particular form of exercise got him all worked up again.

Remembering the pain, hesitation, and confusion that warred around and mixed in her aura minutes ago was what had made him so confused. He hadn't known whether to console her, hug her, or leave her the hell alone. The blood inside her body had also been at full alert, zinging around, rushing through her veins and calling out to Drake, which told him that there was something happening here that he wasn't quite too sure of.

At first he sensed her depressed emotions, then tinges of wanting, of needing something badly had come to the fore. When she walked away, the total adjustment back to the real Nadia, the one that held her cards close to her and never allowed anyone to see, was final. He knew better than to try and dissect what he felt all at once. It would take a while for the essence of her true feelings to be signaled out.

After a few minutes of settling down, he managed to go back inside. Within minutes he had zeroed in on his date and was about to leave, when Nadia's small frame plucked at the edge of his radar.

He couldn't remember ever seeing her look so damn enticing. The wicked blue gown suited her far better than those other, oversized frocks that she wore in society. Well, the dresses weren't that bad, but they sure as hell were nothing compared to what she was wearing right now.

Dark blue clung to every curve of her body. Drake had never seen *that* much of her before. Now that he was, he was admitting that she was curved in all the right places. The bare patch of shoulder led to her long, elegant neck, and as he looked back down his eyes caught on the silver arm cuff that she was wearing. For some reason that little extra jewelry made all the difference. She looked pagan, dangerous, and fey-something not entirely of this world, and that added to the mix of chameleon like fronts that had him so confused tonight.

He was just about to tear his eyes away when they lit and stayed on the long length of one leg extended from the daring little split in that delicious dress. Long, shapely and so damn beautiful. Before Drake could blink to take it all in again, it was gone, back under the folds of the long gown. His gums burned, so did his eyes. How in the world did such a short woman have such long legs? How was it possible?

Why in the world does it matter to you? It took you this long to notice she is a nicely put together woman. Leave it at that and don't worry about how the rest of her looks under that dress.

Nadia was almost like a daughter to him, not a woman that deserved to be drooled over. Shaking those thoughts from his mind, he found Natalie and made for the exit as if flames were licking behind his heels.

***

Nadia fingered the delicate silver chain of the necklace that her parents had given her for their last Christmas together. The tears she hadn't shed yet, even after tonight's emotional battlefield, still didn't fall. They merely rimmed along the lower lids of her eyes, causing everything to blur and basically drive Nadia crazy.

The soft, but still fragile edges of the silver covered feather pricked her finger. The feather came from a small hawk that Nadia had taken a liking to after she'd noticed it at the Haven. The victim of a random vehicle accident, the hawk had been picked up and taken to the

Haven. The beautiful, regal looking bird touched something deep inside her, causing her heart to stutter every time she saw it. After doing what they could for the bird, it still passed after dying from internal injuries.

Unbeknownst to Nadia, her father mentioned to Drake her feelings for the bird, and Drake in turn had acquired one of the small feathers from the animal, gotten it plated in silver, attached it to a delicate necklace, and Nadia's parents gave it to her as a Christmas present.

Now with the light from a few candles burning in her living area, Nadia let her fingers trail over the frail edges of the feather. She always felt that even though the gift came from her parents, Drake instead gifted her with something from his world of animals, something full of healing and mystery. He held that inexplicable air of understanding and knowledge about animals that she would never comprehend. Watching him work with them was something unexplainable and beautiful, and if a person watched too long, the connection between animal and man took on a respectable and strong alliance.

One afternoon while waiting for her father to get off, she saw Drake and a few men out in the paddocks working with an abused horse. Just the simple act of trust, of allowing one small touch between human and animal, was something that was instantly met with hostility from the sadly abused equine. That first afternoon Nadia saw Drake enter the paddock and simply stand there, about twenty-five feet away, as he watched the animal while humming something low beneath his breath. He never really approached the animal. It was more along the lines of a gentle seduction of the horse's emotions. His long, tall body would walk side to side, while his hands worked with a small lead rope, and his eyes tracked the animal at all times. To Nadia it was like poetry. Something incomprehensible with mere words, but she knew that Drake would sooner or later overcome the issue of trust and the horse would accept him. Within weeks the animal had.

She shook her head and looked at the tiny flame of the candle nearest to her. The way she felt for him was similar to that flickering flame. She knew better, but would her feelings for him ever be extinguished?

For the sake of her sanity she hoped it would happen soon.

Chapter 4

"I'm getting a dog."

Renee's blue eyes peered over the lenses of her chic glasses, straight at Nadia. "A dog? Since when have you started feeling maternal and wanting to nest?"

Nadia shook her head as she answered, "I'm not nesting, or feeling maternal, but the dog needs a home and I'm open for a change of scenery." She slung a questioning look over at Renee, "Why would getting a dog mean that I'm nesting?" Did she project her loneliness that much?

Renee rolled her eyes and ignored the question, "Ahh…this must be the dog you mentioned injuring the night you found out about Donavan. I remember you saying something about the dog being at the Haven," she told Nadia, as her fingers slipped over the edges of a ton of papers on Nadia's desk.

Nadia joined in the search for the one paper that they couldn't find. "Yeah, Drake offered her to me before he put her up for adoption. After thinking about it, I have decided to go ahead and accept his offer."

Renee's blue eyes slid over to her again. "Drake? Is that the same Drake from a couple of weeks ago that came into the office looking all delicious and much too *Texan* for me to handle?"

Nadia couldn't help but smile at Renee as her fingers continued flipping through papers. "That's him, although I'm not too sure he would like to hear you talking about him like he was the new flavor of the month."

Renee huffed. "Flavor of the month? Honey, try flavor of the year. That man oozes so much sex appeal that my beloved great grandmother, Esther, would claw her way out of the grave to just look at him."

"Well, I have decided to go ahead and adopt the dog. Hopefully I won't live to regret it," Nadia told Renee, even as she was still smiling over Renee's statement about her great grandmother.

Renee's hand covered hers over the huge mound of papers between them. "Honey, you know as well as I do that you love animals. That dog will love being there with you." Then she pulled her hand away and continued looking.

"You are right. I have no reason to worry about anything," Nadia agreed. "And anyway, it will be a few more weeks because she has a pretty weighty cast on her leg, and she is receiving the best care at the Haven right now. There is no need to move her."

There was also no need to throw herself into Drake's presence right now either. Their last little meeting had taken place the weekend before, and Nadia was just now starting to feel as if her life was returning back to normal. A dose of Drake didn't fit into the picture.

"Found it!" Renee's vastly relieved statement woke Nadia up from her silent musings. "I'm going to input this into the computer for you, and then we can both go home," Renee told her as she waltzed out of Nadia's office.

After Renee's departure the abrupt silence that ensued made Nadia's ears ring. The last thing she needed to be was alone. She couldn't trust herself when she was depressed, and she still was, even though it had been almost a month since she walked in on Donavan.

Moving around papers on her desk, she finally found her datebook knowing that she would see Cole Walker's invitation written down. Cole Walker held an annual barbeque at his home in Houston, but the unique thing about this get together was that half the proceeds went to various charities and organizations. With the plate prices varying from $200.00 to $500.00, and with a large number of guests attending the lavish event, the charities were always happy when they received the check. Nadia's part in the event was distributor of funds. The part she didn't like was that more than half the people she couldn't stand would be there. Thank God the gossip about Donavan messing around with Suzanne was starting to die down.

Why not go? Enjoy good food, maybe take in the beautiful environment that Cole Walker lived in, and let go, just for a little while? But would she be able to? Not giving herself the chance to back out, she grabbed her phone.

Seconds later Cole's secretary answered. Even though it was close to four-thirty in the afternoon, Nadia knew he was still there, and after she asked the secretary to speak to him, he was on the phone.

"Nadia, how are you honey?" Cole was the consummate Texas gentleman, suave, debonair, undeniably handsome, rich, and loaded with southern charm. He was more than just a great catch. He was turning out to be a good friend.

"I'm fine, Cole. I hope the invitation to your barbeque is still open, even if I had already cancelled once before?"

"Darlin', you could deny every invitation that is sent to you, but you should know better than to think that I would refuse you anything." Silky incitement fluttered in his voice, and Nadia knew, like she had for almost three years now, that if there was the least bit of a nod from her, he would do his damnedest to mark his territory around her. He was nothing but a harmless flirt, but she had known from the first moment she met him that he would make some woman happy someday. But that woman was not her. Thank God he never pushed the issue.

"Well, I'm planning to attend tonight."

"My guests and I will be waiting patiently, honey. Just make sure you bring your dancing boots. I'm sure I won't be the only one waiting in line for a dance with you."

"Shameless flirt, but thank you. I will see you tonight."

After hanging up the phone to Cole's laughter in her ear, she smiled and thought to herself that she might just have a good night after all.

***

"I see the earlier rain shower didn't stop your guests from showing up on time," Drake told Cole Walker when he finally managed to snag a moment of his host's attention.

Cole shrugged his shoulder and returned Drake's smile. "You know us Texans. If you promise us food, beer and dancing, we show up in drastic numbers."

Drake knew Cole was right.

The early evening was more than a little warm, but with that earlier rain shower, a breeze now kicked up from the south. Everything smelled fresh, damp, and Drake had a feeling that his night was about to get better. Where that thought came from, he had no idea.

"How are the animals managing with all that fancy new fencing and high tech gear you have over there?" Cole asked him before he took a sip from his beer and nodded at another guest that walked past him on the large outdoor patio.

"I'm sure it takes some getting used to, but the new fencing and other gadgets my people put up around the area are equipped with some pretty damn good sensors. If the animals in our northern pasture piss wrong, we will all know about it."

Cole grinned at that. "Well, at least you know the animals will be safe while they recuperate from whatever injuries they sustained before."

Drake nodded then took a deep draw from his own beer while letting his gaze take in the huge event. He and Cole kept up a light conversation about the current stock market woes while Drake took in his surroundings.

Cole's large, rambling ranch home was behind them, while around two hundred people milled in Cole's large yard. The ranch was just east of Houston, so the drive wasn't too horrible from Beaumont. With the large number of guests, Drake was sure that Cole would meet his quota of donations before the night was over with.

Cole Walker was in his mid-thirties, a good ole Texas boy with loads of charm, loads of money, and a fair amount of brains in his head. Drake liked to maintain good company, and Cole was one of the best. He was one of the top dogs in a firm of lawyers in Houston, and even though he made good money putting the bad guys away, he didn't need a dime of it. Cole's family was tremendously wealthy in oil, banks, and many other endeavors that Texas had generated over the past hundred or so years. Drake had known his ancestors on a friendly basis for almost two hundred years now.

"Damn, she did show up," Cole's statement and following whistle caught Drake's attention. "And she brought company. Would you look at that pair of lovely women? The night couldn't get any better."

Drake followed Cole's nod, and when he caught sight of the women, he became stock still.

He should have known with this being a charity event that Nadia might show up. But when he first got that thought in his mind, he had chased it off. Never before had he looked for reasons to go out of his way to ignore, or get away from her company. Lately, for some reason, he was finding it odd he was having those thoughts in the first place.

Her curvy, flame haired secretary was with her. But for all Drake knew, Renee could have been Cindy Crawford and he still wouldn't have looked twice at her. Now *that* was a thought that he *didn't* need to dissect. Damn, he just needed to stop thinking all together.

"Who is that beauty beside her?" Cole questioned, and Drake watched his eyes follow the tall Amazon beside Nadia.

"I'm surprised you don't already know. That's her secretary, Renee Allemande."

"Renee, hmm…I believe Nadia mentioned her before, but I don't remember ever seeing her until now. Besides, how could you forget a woman like that?"

"Now that you mention it, it's been only lately that Nadia has brought Renee with her to many other charity events," Drake mumbled, clearly getting a new direction of thoughts on why Nadia would do that.

"She is drawing confidence from a lady that clearly has plenty to draw from. I'll bet anything that she is doing that because of what Donavan did to her."

Drake turned and looked at Cole. It wasn't too often that a human picked up on something so hidden, that only a Druid or witch would have seen. Apparently Cole listened to his gut about as much as Drake did. It wasn't often that a human impressed him. Now was one of those times.

"I believe you are right. Renee is obviously very confident in everything she does; it fairly oozes from her. Nadia must have been more hurt by Donavan than she lets on."

Just thinking about that ass caused Drake's hand to itch. The urge to beat him to a bloody pulp, castrate him, *then* show him what kind of harm that he could really do, surged through Drake. This wasn't the first time he wanted to kill a human. He was sure it wouldn't be the last.

With a blink he changed his thoughts. It wouldn't be wise to allow his anger to override his judgment. What a show that would be.

***

She felt his eyes on her from across the yard.

Now it was a forgone thing to ignore him. There was no way she would be able to get away from him if he wanted to readdress their discussion from the other night, bullshit about mundane things, or just tell her hello. She was well and truly stuck. And here she had thought her night would be amazing. How was it possible for it to turn crappy so fast?

Her eyes slid over him quickly. She didn't want to be caught staring, and from what she saw, he was still making all the women drool. Didn't matter if it was an outdoor party or black tie, the man was simply dangerous.

A plain black tee shirt that had the Safe Haven seal on the left side covered his upper torso. Dark washed blue jeans fit him tightly, and a trusty pair of boots was on his feet. He looked relaxed, at ease, in the early twilight that filtered through the many trees, the last rays of sun touching him, bringing every detail of his finely molded body into high relief. Even while she noticed him looking at her, she felt his relaxed stance. She couldn't fight off the knowledge that he was more comfortable at night, in the darkness, where for some reason she sensed the subtle layer of privacy cloaking him really came down, baring the real man, the man that she itched to know.

Those light, caramel colored eyes tracked her movement until she was standing before both him and Cole. Nadia had about half a millisecond before Cole grabbed her in a huge hug and squeezed her.

"It's good to see you again, Nadia. I'm glad you changed your mind," he told her as he let her go and sent a wicked look towards Renee. Nadia was more than happy to introduce her secretary and let Cole's interest be pushed onto someone else.

"This is Renee Allemande. She has been my secretary since I became president, but I have known her for almost three years," Nadia told Cole.

"Miss Allemande, it is my pleasure," Cole said, as he held out his hand.

"It is lovely to meet you, Mr. Walker. I have heard nothing but good things about you." Renee sent him a sly glance, long enough to take him in, then gave his hand a hearty shake.

Cole grinned, "Call me Cole, and with Nadia doing the talking you never know. But I'm glad to hear they were good things."

Nadia rewarded him with a slap on the arm. "Keep it up and I might tell her more than you want her to know." She sent a wink in his direction, softening the threat, then turned to Drake who had been silent through the introduction but had a small grin on his face.

"I'm sure you remember Renee, right?" Nadia asked Drake.

Drake smiled his crooked grin, leaning in as he shook Renee's hand. He was so tall that he had to bend a bit to look her tall friend in the eye. "Renee, I hope you enjoy yourself tonight. Cole makes some of the best barbeque in the state."

Renee shook his hand and gave Nadia a quick look, "I'm sure I will enjoy myself. I just have to make sure that the boss lady here does the same." Renee leaned in towards both men, as if she were about to impart a juicy secret, "We all need to do our part to make sure that happens, don't we, boys?"

Only Renee could get away with calling two virile, mature men, "boys", Nadia thought, while she silently fumed at her secretary's underhanded attempt to make sure she had a good time.

Minutes later, Cole managed to steal Renee away, which left Nadia alone with the one person that she shouldn't be alone with.

She looked everywhere, except at him.

Huge oak, sugar maple, and pine trees dotted Cole's overly large yard, but they were spaced at certain intervals, which led Nadia to assume that all of this had been designed by human hands, not by Mother Nature. Even so, it was still extremely lovely and breathtaking.

Flower beds were also trailing along at different angles, some at the base of the trees, some with their own beds closer to the large patio. People mingled, music blared from the side of the house, and Nadia could feel Drake's presence like a drug in her system.

The warmth from his body singed her right side, but no matter how much it bothered her, Nadia knew she wouldn't move away. She took any moment with him as one that should be savored.

"I might as well get it out in the open and tell you that I won't apologize for sending Donavan off the other night." The words were low, about as softly spoken as Drake would ever get, and even still his voice was deep, rich and melodic with his drawl.

"I knew better than to assume that you would," replied Nadia.

"Well, since we have come to that conclusion, do you want something to eat?"

Nadia finally allowed her eyes to glance at him and nodded. Seconds later, they made their way to the patio where huge tents were set up covering the dance floor, the pits cooking the meat, and more than a few guests that were sitting at large round tables.

Nadia grabbed a plate and Drake did the same. They both stood in line and served themselves, buffet style. After piling their plates high, each of them went to the open bar and grabbed something to drink. Nadia ordered a soda while Drake got a beer.

Nadia walked out of the tented area, back towards the quieter atmosphere of the patio. She selected a table that was only large enough for three and so far in the corner that it was relatively dark and even a bit lonely. Thank God Renee was still with Cole so she wouldn't fuss. Before Nadia could take her first bite, a shadow fell over her. She glanced up, surprised to see him standing there. Didn't he have a date to sit with?

"Is this seat taken?" Drake gestured to the seat across from her, and Nadia's heart sputtered. She so didn't need this.

"Uh…no, go ahead," she nodded, almost in a daze, to the empty chair.

With his heavily laden plate and beer in hand, he accepted the seat and gave her a weird look.

"What?" She questioned, not knowing what could have caused him to glance at her like that.

"I have the horrible feeling that every time you see me, you expect a woman to be hanging on my arm." He shook his head slightly and grabbed a drumstick, which he promptly bit into. Nadia almost forgot the words in her throat. Hell, even watching him eat was intriguing.

"It's kind of hard to imagine it any other way, when you know that is the truth." Had she actually said that? She looked up and caught the look he threw her and Nadia realized she *had* said it aloud. *Way to go Nadia. Are you trying to antagonize him?* Ignoring her thoughts, she grabbed a forkful of beans and stuffed it into her mouth. Hopefully, no other words would emerge to embarrass her.

"At least I realize how you see me now."

Nadia didn't look up from her loaded plate. That would be an accident waiting to happen. "Sorry, but you know it's true."

Instead of him answering, seconds turned to minutes and before long they were both finished with their food. The table, which had once been roomy enough for Nadia to be alone, had shrunk in size since Drake had decided to accompany her. The lantern shades that had been hung around the perimeter of the house outside were now fully lit. Beyond the patio, in the wooded area of Cole's yard, Nadia could barely make out anything of significance. It was a beautiful night for a charity benefit and Cole always did a bang up job. Now that twilight was deepening into night, the band was picking up tempo.

"Apparently Cole's feelings for you didn't go that deep."

Drake's deep voice slid over her ears, and Nadia turned to him when he spoke. He gestured to the dance floor where Cole and Renee were dancing with about ten other couples. Renee had herself glued to every square inch of Cole's tall body, and he didn't appear to mind in the least.

"It was never anything more than a harmless flirtation," Nadia told Drake as she watched the dancing couple.

"Hmm,…if you say so." His words had her turning to look at him again.

"Just what does that mean?" She asked him, begging him to keep going, to bring up something, anything that they would be able to argue about. When they argued, she didn't have to hide her true feelings.

His eyes narrowed to suspicious slits. Leaning back in the chair with his long, big body reclined, he looked at ease, supine, and so very lazy. But Nadia knew better than to think that he had ever had a lazy bone in his body. It was all a front. He raised his beer bottle and took a swig, drawing Nadia's eyes down to his Adam's apple as it moved. She turned her head away sharply, trying to ignore the pulse of pure want deep inside her body.

"Why does it get you so angry when I say that a man was interested in you? Why does that bother you so much?" She rolled her eyes, knowing he could see the action, and licked her lips while she thought of an answer. Drake spoke before she could.

"I know for a fact that Cole Walker is an open book. He has no gambling tendencies, doesn't hook up with rich women so that he can take their money, and as far as I know, he doesn't like to rough house with women during sex." He stopped talking long enough to take a swig of beer, and just when Nadia's mind was starting to finally wrap around what he said, he kept going, shocking her into even more silence. "Although, I will admit, some rough housing can be quite fun."

Nadia made the mistake of turning to look at him, and had to stop herself from dissolving into a puddle of need right there beside his boots. *Rough housing can be fun?* Dear Lord, just the statement caused all kinds of images to run rampant through her mind. She turned her head away from his thorough gaze and swallowed deeply.

"I have never wanted Cole in that way, although I have known for years now that with the slightest invitation on my part, he would have taken over and gotten past our friendship stage." Just why was she explaining herself to him?

"I knew that. I just wanted to see you get riled up over something without me having to bring up the Donavan incident. I wanted a more relaxing conversation, not something so damn serious that we can't even speak to one another."

His words caused her to look back at him. The night was a bit darker now, and with the way he was sitting only one half of his face was caressed by the lantern light. The side that wasn't was the picture of being devilishly handsome.

Nadia forced herself to think of nothing but lighter thoughts. She understood what he was saying. Every time they managed to end up sharing the same airspace, they had nothing but severe conversations. Drake was letting her know he was sick of it, and if she was being honest with herself, so was Nadia. She might as well enjoy his company since she was in it, although it would be hell on her heart to spend quality time with a man that never had and never would want her.

"I'll bet you can't wait until football season starts, huh?" She sent him a sideways look and caught the slightly crooked grin that stole over his sculpted mouth before he stopped it and donned a serious expression, and then ruined it all when he busted out laughing.

Nadia was floored. "What? You wanted a lighter conversation. That's exactly what I was doing, starting a lighter conversation!" She huffed and turned away, silently laughing along with him, but acting mulish on purpose.

"Ah Nadia," he told her when he finally regained his breath. "I distinctly remember you saying how much you hated football. I also remember a few guys asking you to football games when you were in high school, and you adamantly turned them down."

She looked at him in shock, "I was a teenager for crying out loud. Hell, I never knew what I wanted then." She huffed, "And anyway, I asked *you* the question."

You are lying, lying through your teeth. You wanted the man sitting beside you. Even though you didn't know at the time what wanting meant. But you do now.

Drake's words caused her mind-rambling to stop.

"I clearly remember you when you were a teenager." She caught his eyes whenever he glanced at her. The comfortable feel in the air put her at ease, so did the deep, hypnotic quality of his voice. "So slight, so delicate, and you always wore your hair in long braids."

Nadia rolled her eyes again, "I hated those darn braids." They couldn't really be talking about her hair, could they? "Mom said if I didn't take care of it, it would fall out." A light laugh escaped her, "Mom always knew how to make losing my hair sound like the end of the world as I knew it." Nadia stopped as another thought popped up in her memory. "Although I remember Carl Browning commenting on how pretty my hair was in braids. I think that is why I wore them for so long."

"How old were you when that happened?" His deep, silky voice slid out of the darkness next to her.

"I would say around thirteen. At the time, I thought he was the hottest guy for giving me a compliment."

Drake chuckled. Nadia gave him a glance and asked her own question, "Okay Mr. I'm Untouchable, I'm sure there was someone in your past that caught your eye. Everyone had somebody when they were younger that they were crushing on."

"Crushing on?"

"Yeah, you know, you liked this person, even though you knew you would more than likely never have the chance to ever date them." Damn, this was starting to sound like her life story.

"Hmm…I'm sure there was someone, but that was a long time ago."

Nadia peered at him through the slight shadows and barely caught the smile on his face. The smartass was fooling her. He probably remembered the girl's name, knew her age, and where she lived. Damn lucky girl. "You can't tell me that you don't remember."

He shrugged his massive shoulders and took another swig of his beer. Nadia narrowed her eyes good-naturedly, trying to show him her mean face. Instead, he busted out laughing again. He was seriously too happy tonight…must be all that beer he was drinking.

"What's wrong, you getting too far up there in age that your memory is taking a few hits?"

"Oh, that's a low blow, Nadia," he said it seriously, but she caught the smile he sent her way.

"Okay, back when you were a teenager, you know around the Inquisition, there had to have been someone that caught your eye."

He smirked at her and said, "I really don't remember."

Nadia smiled at him. "Damn, that's horrible. A whole lifetime lost to the ravages of dementia." He laughed out loud, and Nadia couldn't stop the smile that appeared. She loved the sound of his laughter, deep and melodious. "Does it run in your family? Because if it does, you might want to go get it treated right away. You wouldn't want to waste the memories that you still have."

He moved, sitting straight up in the chair, and Nadia's easy going nature left as she remembered just exactly who he was and what he did to her insides. For an instant there she had forgotten all of the years she had ached for him. It had been a different moment all together, something she had never had with him. Now she was missing it already.

"I never knew this side of you existed. But I know for damn sure that I like it." Then he grabbed his empty plate and got up from the table, leaving a very confused and very mystified Nadia behind.

Chapter 5

What the hell had he been thinking, voicing the thoughts in his head? He knew better than to dangle a comment like that in front of Nadia. Ever since he had first laid eyes on her when she was twelve, something damn close to hero worship had been in those green depths. Over the years she had apparently learned to hide her thoughts and emotions.

Not that it mattered worth a damn.

Ever since that double glance when she was younger, he had felt her regard for him with every look, hesitation, and wide-eyed peek. Back then, he had thought it funny and kind of cute.

Now, it caused reactions in him that shouldn't even be considered. For thirteen years he had thought of her like a daughter, looking after her whenever her parents passed had cemented that territorial feeling inside of him. But ever since he found out what Donavan had done, and her odd reaction on the terrace last weekend, all he could think about was how grown up she looked, and how he was starting to read her body and mannerisms like any other human he came into contact with.

Being an Amber Druid was like being on link with every person's emotions within a fifty yard distance. Sometimes, if you were strong enough and dedicated to ignoring it, it was very possible to simply act as if the other person wasn't there. Drake was able, and had been for a while now, to do just that. He had learned early on to train his abilities and not let them rule him or his life. But with those abilities came drawbacks, or chinks in the armor. Sometimes there were certain people that he simply couldn't ignore, and others that were too complicated to read.

Nadia was a mixture. At times, she was as easily read as a book. Her emotions were painted upon her face and she expressed them completely. Her body responded with blood pooling happily in certain areas, causing her pearl colored skin to blush in the most interesting ways. That was happiness so extreme and pure that she couldn't hide it. As far as he could remember, he'd never seen this side of her before. Other times, her expression was closed off. Her eyes were shuttered and her breathing was choppy, as if she had just run around the block. The translucent color of her skin was ruddy, caused by rushing of the blood so close to the top of the skin. It was during those times, when she was angry or upset, that Drake had a hard time figuring out exactly what had caused her to become like that.

On the terrace last weekend she'd shown him so many varying emotions that even with his specialized abilities, he still couldn't put an exact finger on what had gone on. The only thing that stood out to him then was that she felt many degrees of pain, heartache, and such blazing want, that Drake's body immediately zoned into change mode.

When such a level headed woman like Nadia sent out such screwed up messages, a man like Drake couldn't help but wonder what had caused it. But the deeper he got into this puzzle, the more intriguing his object became.

Looking at her now, still sitting at the same table they had occupied about thirty minutes before, it seemed as if the placement of the table and the darkness of her corner did nothing but pull her in and enfold its dark arms around her. She was so slight, so much smaller than him. That was another reason why he was so protective of her, even though he did know she had a buried steel backbone under that delicate exterior.

Her long black hair was pulled up in a clip on the back of her neck. A tee shirt that had TEXAS emblazoned on the front covered her from the waist up, while a low slung pair of boot cut jeans clasped her legs and ended in a pair of pointy-toed cowgirl boots. Even though he knew her to be twenty-five, she still managed to look all of eighteen years old. Too damn young for him, no matter what age.

But even as he thought that, he started walking back in her direction. For some reason, unknown to him, everything inside of her called out to him.

It's only because you can't read her clearly.

Drake knew better than to read anything into his interest in her for tonight. It was lack of company that had him returning to that seat. Another excuse was he hadn't really, *really* talked to her in years. He missed little Nadia. That was the only *plausible* reason for him to go back and meet her at the table.

***

Drake sauntered back towards her with all the grace of a panther on the prowl. His long legged stride ate up the distance between them with unerring speed. His beer from earlier was gone, and she hadn't seen him grab another since. As he walked, the shadows from strategically placed lanterns gleamed off of him. Chocolate colored hair turned russet in the lowlights, and the lines of his body were starkly delineated. People seemed to glide out of his way, as if anticipating when he was coming near and simply moving away from his purposeful stride.

*Take a breath. Don't let him see how much he affects you. This should all be routine by now....*until she remembered his comment about rough housing during sex. For some reason, that sent her blood pressure up and away. Thoughts of him and sex, period, were enough to fulfill fantasies for a very, very long time. But when she added images of him being just a little rough, hell, Nadia felt her ears burn.

Women had always melted around him. Even the most frigid ones Nadia had ever seen were no match for Drake and his slow but dangerous approach to seduction. He took his time with everything, so Nadia assumed that same quality would be applied to his sexual appetite.

Stop this! Your imagination always gets you in trouble.

She distinctly remembered one of those times when she had been sixteen, and the bus had dropped her off at the Haven to meet her father that afternoon. Since her mother worked later hours, instead of going home by herself, Nadia would meet her dad at the Haven most afternoons. That afternoon proved to be one of the best of her teenage life.

One of the large barns on the grounds of the shelter was being renovated and enlarged to house more animals. About fifteen men were working on the barn when Nadia got there that afternoon. She barely gave any of them a glance. Instead, she went inside to let her father know she was there, then she came back out through the back part of the shelter to read in quiet. Minutes passed in silence while Nadia got comfortable beside the large, wild bird cages. Sitting under a huge oak tree with her back to the base, she squinted in the sunlight as she heard a man walking by. Drake came into view, with his slow saunter, and torso bare to the harsh Texas sun.

Nadia's breath evaporated in her lungs.

She had seen younger guys without their shirts on, but never before had she felt the rush of warmth through her system as she was now. Licking her dried lips, she watched with hot eyes as her father's boss passed not but twenty feet away from her, walking towards the barn with a large hammer in his hand. Drake always made her feel inconsequential, but he was never mean or rude to her, like other guys that she knew. But Lord, he was some kind of handsome, even more so than she had ever seen in her young life.

Dark, luxurious hair, wet with the humid air, clung
to his head. Rivulets of sweat moved in streams from his
dark head, down onto his neck then it dripped onto
large, muscled shoulders, making his skin slick from the
stuff. Like a well-oiled up statue, he moved in the barn's
direction slowly. His long, slow, sure stride causing
Nadia's heart to beat so fast that she feared she might
pass out. Her eyes followed his stride, and she couldn't
help but feast on the sight of his butt covered in blue
jeans.

She was about to look away when he stopped
abruptly and turned in her direction. His eyes zeroed in
on her sitting there beneath the tree, and Nadia froze in
fear. It was one thing to openly stare at a man without
him knowing; it was another thing for him to find out
about it while it was happening. Instead of some kind of
recrimination towards her, he gave her a slow nod, then
turned and continued on his way towards the barn.
Nadia's heart continued beating.

Her friends at school would die when she told them
just how beautiful her dad's boss was without his shirt,
and sticky from sweat. As it was, her palms were itching
and she wished she was old enough and pretty enough to
even be considered his.

For weeks and months after, the images of Drake in
those tight jeans and sweat coursing from his body had
made an indelible mark on Nadia's brain. When she
became older, she had dreamed of the situation, but it
had been a bit different. For one thing, she was older, so
in her mind she could think of things to do that wickedly
sexy body of his. Another thing was no one else was

there except them. When he turned and caught her staring, well, the grown up version of her gave him a sly wink, and stood up from the base of the tree to walk over to him seductively. Drake had stood there, slick with sweat and waited for her to come to him.

The dream always ended when she made it close enough to touch him. For some reason the closer she got, the more her dream Drake changed. His dark, good looks turned harsher, more devilishly sexy, and his eyes changed to a glowing gold color. Nadia would stare in shock and then zap out of the dream breathing deeply, trying to get her mind back in order, while the sheets beneath and around her were twisted against her body.

The dream was always the same, sexy in the beginning, and then turning odd whenever he looked at her with that gold gaze, singeing her where she stood. Nadia had no explanation for it and probably never would. But it hadn't stopped her from wanting to get her hands on him, even when she knew that would never happen.

Coming back to reality, she took a deep breath when she realized how close he was getting to her. And God help her, but after their conversation earlier, she couldn't help but feel a bit more curious about him and his life before she had even met him. Sudden questions pushed at her mind.

What was his favorite color? Was he a boxers or briefs kind of guy? What was his favorite food? Just how old was he?

The last question was the gnawing one. After all these years she still didn't know his true age. He seemed to be somewhere in his mid-thirties. Nadia had always guessed that he was just as private about his age as he was everything else.

"You're still here," his deep voice slid against her ears as he pulled out the same chair he had been sitting on earlier.

Nadia shook off her thoughts. "Yeah," she looked in the direction of the dance floor where Renee and Cole were still dancing. "I keep thinking she might get tired and then be ready to leave. So far it hasn't happened," she turned to Drake with a slight smile.

He looked at the couples dancing then back at her, "Why aren't you dancing? I know it's not for lack of partners asking."

Shock held her mouth quiet as he spoke. So apparently he had seen the two guys earlier that had asked her to dance. He hadn't danced with anyone either. More or less it seemed he was here just to donate and network, which he had done when he had left her table. That was Drake to a tee. There was always a reason to drum up sponsors, donations, or even interest in helping animals.

"I just didn't feel like putting on a false front for some man I didn't know," she answered, and it was an honest answer.

"I don't see why you should have to have a false front for anyone. If they don't like what they see, they wouldn't have asked you to dance."

"That is some eloquent thinking and the truth, but I just don't feel like putting up with anyone right now."

Her eyes caught and held his for one moment. Hot molten caramel turned her insides to liquid. It was always like this, this burn from the inside, even when they were having a normal conversation.

"Would you like me to leave?"

Ah, he was such a gentleman to even offer. "No, I'd rather you than someone else."

A crooked grin covered his mouth. "How surprising that I have moved up in your estimation. No wonder we had rain earlier today." Apparently her comment had sounded a bit insulting.

She rolled her eyes, "Sorry."

He laughed at that. "You have to admit, Nadia, that you haven't always been such a warm person to me lately," he told her, his grin gone, nothing but a serious expression on his handsome face.

Nadia felt her insides flare up. She could not tell him the reason for that. Never would she explain why she had to act a certain way around him. Instead, she shrugged her shoulders and kept staring at the dance area where people turned and swayed to the music, never guessing that she was about to lose her mind with a serious case of the nerves if Drake didn't stop asking questions that she couldn't answer. And if she kept trying to turn the subject, he would wonder.

"Take it from me, that it isn't you making me like this, but more like recent circumstances that have hardened my so called shell," she told him, still not looking at him. The torn edges of his dark washed jeans, and shined tips of his boots, were in her line of vision. She could feel his heat and warmth beside her arm on the top of the small table. Her gut clenched. Would she ever be able to touch him? The only time he had voluntarily touched her was when her parents had passed. The memory of his arms closing around her shoulders was something that Nadia had never forgotten.

"I'm sorry that you had to learn the hard way about Donavan and Suzanne," He told her. Nadia couldn't help herself; she had to look in his direction. But now he was looking at the dance floor. "There had been rumors for weeks that they had something going on, but of course a rumor is a rumor. And it wasn't as if we had the kind of relationship that gave me permission to walk into your office so that I could warn you about the man you were seeing."

He stopped speaking, and the muscles in his jaw tensed and rippled. He seemed oddly upset about something that really was her fault. After all these weeks she had had time to think, and it seemed to her that even though she was the wronged party, she had caused all of this herself. She was to blame for her own shame and humiliation.

First of all, she had basically allowed Donavan to date her simply so she could keep her mind off of Drake. And even though she knew that she couldn't have the kind of relationship that he wanted them to have, it would have to be enough to keep her mind and thoughts away from the dangerous man at her side.

"I knew what I was getting into when I started dating him," she told Drake, as he turned, giving her his full attention. His eyes were light in the dark shadows on his side of the table. A warm rush filled Nadia. God, he was a beautiful man. All hard ruggedness but with a soft, sensual mouth, that at the moment, was firm and businesslike.

"Why would you do that to yourself? Isn't that like aiding the enemy?" Those eyes narrowed seriously before he spoke again, "And you can't lie to me and tell me that you actually wanted the man. Every time y'all were together it seemed as if there was an icicle wedged between you two."

Nadia gasped lightly but managed to still keep it quiet. The amazing insight that Drake had was scary to her. How was he able to read her so easily? How would she ever get away from the way he made her feel? Maybe she should make plans to move away.

"Let's just say it was something that was easily worked out between us." She licked her lips and didn't go any further.

He scoffed from his side of the table. "I hate to see you wasting your time and energy on someone like Donavan. You could have the pick of Texas society, yet you settle on that trash."

I could have you.

Nadia silently scolded herself, and tried to think of a way to change the subject. The present one was upsetting her, causing her to think of things that she shouldn't.

Drake's sudden movement out of his chair startled her. He walked directly in front of her chair and held out his hand. "C'mon, come dance. You don't need to be sitting here and moping around about some dick that couldn't do anything right." His tall body was a huge shadow in front of her and she couldn't see anything except his outline from where she was sitting.

"Excuse me?" she questioned. He wanted them to dance. Them, both of their bodies swaying closely while music played. Wouldn't that be dangerous?

Yes, it's very dangerous. Don't do it Nadia!

"Yeah, you know, dance. We will move to the music and forget about this ugly conversation we were having about your recent ex-bastard of a boyfriend."

His words sent a warm thrill shooting through her body, but Nadia was still up in the air about it. Apparently he could sense her hesitation.

"Nadia…come." He gestured with his hand.

"Oh hell," Nadia whispered, but didn't question anything in her mind. She shut off all cognitive function and stood up beside him, shaking in her boots the entire time.

"That sounded extremely convincing," he muttered to her, but when she glanced up at him, he was smiling that crooked grin of his, and Nadia's heart almost exploded from pure excitement. How had he heard her whisper?

They neared the dance area where a huge parquet wood floor had been laid and more than a few couples were dancing. The band was local and the song they were playing was just ending when Nadia and Drake walked up. Immediately they started a slow song. The strains of a recent Brad Paisley tune hit the air with a sweet melody as Nadia stopped by Drake's side.

She was eye-height with his breastbone when he turned. Almost instantly, he grabbed one hand with his larger one, and the other settled at her hip, burning her through the denim. Her mouth dried and her stomach caved. This was one thing she had dreamed about since she'd been old enough to enjoy dancing. The hard musculature of his body was inches, mere inches from her own, as he began to move in time to the music.

Excitement was too dull a word; not even "enthusiasm" could cover how she felt at this moment. Sheer pleasure bloomed deep inside her body. Every fingertip tingled with anticipation while her booted steps kept in time with his. He wasn't holding her too close, but she was closer than most of the other women were to their partners. The soft, sensual, woodsy smell of his cologne tickled her nose whenever his big body moved. Her eyes caught on the neck of his tee shirt. Even his neck was roped with muscle and tendons. She was sure if she looked close enough, she would be able to see his pulse beating there too.

Shivering slightly at the thought of just how close she was to him, Nadia immediately stopped as she realized her nipples were hard.

Shit.

"You okay?" His voice was deep, gravelly, and so damn sexy that she almost fainted right there at his feet when he leaned down to whisper in her ear.

Oh, kill me now. "I'm fine," she said and continued to move, hoping like hell he wouldn't realize that her nipples were hard enough to cut glass, and they were probably poking holes in his shirt right at this moment. Damn.

When seconds passed and he hadn't made any jokes, Nadia relaxed a bit, until his fingers tightened, bringing her even closer to that hard, hot body of his. Now Nadia's hips were moving daringly close to the front of his jeans. Hell, she could practically feel the denim rubbing against her own. He maneuvered her slightly, until their legs were opposite of each other, and every time she moved her feet, her thigh rubbed the inside of his.

Her body erupted in heat. Never before had she felt this hot, this keyed up. With every sway of his hips, and movement of their legs, her body was pulsing in time to the music and their actions. Nadia couldn't get enough of it, and it was becoming harder to control her breathing when her body was zinging in all the right places. Even the denim of her jeans was causing her sensitized skin to quiver.

Oh, he feels so good. I knew he would. I have known it all along. All those gorgeous muscles, moving like liquid fire against me, sliding those long fingers over and around my hip with every sway. Dear God, let them play another slow song. However, Nadia doubted she would survive if that happened.

When the song ended, Nadia immediately stepped back. She was full of nervous energy, and she knew better than to even glance at Drake. Thank goodness Renee chose that moment to come charging in.

"Girl, my feet are about to fall off. Are you almost ready?" Renee gave her a wrung out expression and looked towards Drake. "You don't mind if I steal her away do you?"

Nadia heard him say, "Not at all," in his deep drawl, but she didn't look back towards him. Instead, she kept her gaze firmly on Renee as she started to propel her towards the house. She saw Cole standing with some businessmen on the patio, engaged in deep conversation, so she didn't stop, but kept right on walking until she stopped at her Land Rover. She could call him in the morning and tell him her 'Thank you' then. Right now all she felt like doing was getting home where she would be able to dissect every moment of that dance with Drake.

Renee was a wonderful friend and Nadia was glad she had brought her along, even if they hadn't spent any time together at the party. Nadia learned that Cole had asked Renee on a date and it was unusual to see Renee so exuberant over a man, but Nadia was happy that Cole was focusing his attentions on someone beside her.

The drive was not that long, and Nadia pulled into her driveway around midnight. She had almost made it to her back entrance, when a rustle in the bushes beside her house made her jump. Looking towards those bushes with wide eyes, she grasped the small light on her keychain and shown it in that direction. Small, yellow eyes stared back at her. The leaves rustled once more and the small hawk flexed its wings and twitched its head directly at her. Nadia had the distinct feeling that it would understand if she spoke to it.

Okay, those long hours are catching up with you honey. You need to get inside and go to bed.

But she continued to stand there, transfixed with the small, regal looking little hawk. Moments later it chirped out a little sound then took flight, causing Nadia to jump and shake her head as she went inside, muttering to herself about talking to animals when she knew they couldn't talk back.

***

Drake hung up the phone after confirming with his pilot that he would indeed fly out at 8:00 a.m. tomorrow morning. The trip to New York couldn't be put off. And since his mind and body were still in shock, he figured the event he was flying out for would take his mind off of what he had just learned. But he still had his doubts about that.

Sliding open his French doors that led out to his deck behind the large home, he inhaled the early morning air, and let the soothing qualities sink into his bones. The back of his home faced nothing but woods and Ridge Lake, something that he was immensely fond of. This was the one spot where he could do or say anything and no one would know about it. Since he was constantly catalogued in the real world, by his every movement, it was nice to know that no one could scale the large fence he had erected around his property and get in his private domain.

The night air was humid, but still comforting as Drake stood there in his jeans, barefoot, and let the sounds of wildlife cascade over him.

A small sound hit his ears. He turned towards the west and saw the little nighthawk make her way into a graceful landing on the railing that surrounded his deck. She preened for him, lifting her wings, spreading her feathers and Drake smiled at her show. Her intelligent, yellow eyes looked directly at him and she set her head into something that resembled a nod.

Ah, so Nadia *had* made it home okay.

"Thank you, honey. I appreciate the fine job you did."

She gave a little trill of sound and then fluffed her wings before taking off into the night sky. Drake watched her go until she disappeared from sight. Even after all this time, it was still amazing to him that he could converse with animals almost as easily as if they were human and holding a conversation with each other.

Ever since his change at twenty-five, he had been gifted with a particular specialty. That was one of his main abilities, among a few others that every Amber Druid had. Each Druid had their own special skill, their calling card of charms, so to speak.

Ramsey McMurray was a master of touch and could charm, sooth, and even kill with that power alone. Brenan McKinnon was telekinetic, able to move objects with his mind. Traven Campbell could spark electricity from his fingertips. Little Liana, who was like a sister to Drake, could walk through walls. Kale Morgan was one of the most powerful Druids that Drake had ever met. His abilities were almost endless, mind reading, stopping blood flow, and his skill at healing was absolute. The list of Druids and their powers went on and on.

Thinking of his powers caused him to rehash the scene from the barbeque earlier.

The conversation that had popped up between him and Nadia had been interesting, but what really caught his attention was what happened when they had started dancing. He never would have guessed that touching her would have answered all of his questions. He was used to assessing the situation without having to touch anyone or anything. To say he had been surprised was an understatement. Now he remembered the fire that arced from her and sent heat flaring inside his body.

Pure sexual desire had smashed into him the instant he had pulled her body within inches of his. He hadn't been expecting it and it had caught him off guard, but just as immediately he stopped any reaction of his. The last thing he had wanted was to send her running away from him, even when he knew that is what he should have done at that moment. The hot trail of lust slipped under his radar and slapped him into reality.

At first his mind couldn't contain all the information she was sending him. *This* is what she felt every time he came into view. This burning, all-consuming want that radiated off of her in waves had left him pole axed, and he barely continued dancing, knowing that at every moment, every time he was in her sight, this is how she felt.

How could she stand it?

The pulse of sexual yearning in her body was a number of things he had sensed, another one was the need she had to touch him. The slight huffs of breath against his shirt, her fingers clenching against the back of his neck and his hand, the rushing of blood to her core, were other clues. He knew without having to use his powers, that she was slick with want. He had practically felt the heat rising from her body. He could almost taste the spiciness of her on his tongue at that moment.

To know that this young woman, the same young woman he had thought of as nothing more than a family friend for the past thirteen years, now wanted him as she might want a lover, sent a shiver down his spine and his fangs threatening to expand, along with other parts of his anatomy. It had been hellish to hold in all of those things on that dance floor. He still had no idea how he'd done it. Thing was, she didn't even comprehend that he'd had this realization. If she did, her embarrassment might be too much for her to handle. Drake could sense the importance she placed on her emotions.

Night sounds interrupted his thoughts. Just what in the hell was he going to do now? He knew that he could never have some random relationship with Nadia. And never would he have more than that. Casual sex was his thing, his code, and the women he did it with were more than understanding, which is of course why he picked them. They knew the game and how to play it. Keeping his Amber Druid status secret was the first thing he worried about with women. No one knew what he was. He wanted to keep it that way.

Nadia would never be casual sex, never.

Her parents had raised her with morals and values that Drake knew she used in everyday life. She had an invisible sign above her that screamed "marriage material." Drake knew better than to get caught up in that. Plus, they shared a past, something tangible and real that he could never sweep under the rug. And even if he wanted to ignore her, he couldn't. Her life and his were intertwined by their business acumen. They both were leading members of Texas society, and they both were firmly cemented in that grasp.

The only thing to do was to act like nothing had ever happened, like he had never felt that electricity shooting from her emotions, or the sweet zap of energy that she had charged him with when she touched him. Those things would be locked away, hopefully forgotten along with almost two hundred years of other sacrifices that he had made because of his honor.

He would keep thoughts of her when she was a teenager with braids in her hair, along with images of her and her family coming to Christmas parties at the Haven together. He would remember her father and just how down to earth he had been. He wouldn't confuse what happened on the dance floor with what she was to him. There was no reason to ruin his image of her with thoughts of her small body pressing close to his, her small hands reaching out to touch him, and those pink tinted, lush lips, opening on a soundless scream as he brought pleasure to her body.

No. None of that would happen. Nadia would forever remain nothing but a casual acquaintance to him. He would do his best to keep it that way. His honor demanded it.

Chapter 6

Drake Thompson, one of Texas's leading wealthy bachelors lights up the red carpet with Lorelei Winfield on his arm. The dashing southern devil is wearing Armani, and the lovely Lorelei is draped by none other than a vintage Valentino masterpiece. They were among many celebrities, and newsworthy people attending the gala World Wildlife Federation fundraiser in New York, Tuesday night.

The headline screamed out, silently grabbing Nadia's attention from the shelves at the Wal-Mart in Beaumont. She couldn't stop her hands from picking up the latest weekly copy of the social magazine, *Social News Weekly*. It was a conglomeration of the many social happenings in all the major cities across the U.S.

The picture under the heading was of good size, and Nadia knew if she ever had the opportunity to shoot pictures of Drake and put them in her magazines, she would make them of decent size so that the consumer could see every luscious detail of the large, attractive man in full color. Sometimes when she looked at pictures that had been taken of him they were hazy and unfocused, but this one was alarmingly clear.

"Miss, the total is $78.05."

The voice of the woman working the register was annoyed, but it snapped Nadia out of her reverie of

Drake and the luscious redhead that he was with in the picture.

"Sorry," she told the woman, and then paid for her purchases and left, leaving the tempting picture behind on the shelves at the checkout. She sure as hell didn't need to bring it home with her and drool over it depressingly.

The past week had been harsh. She had fallen behind in the magazine ratings. Three of the models from the firm she used had become infected with a virus, and all Nadia heard at work from Renee was how amazing Cole was. Maybe she *should* have dated the man. Hell, the way Renee went on about him, he sounded absolutely fantastic. Renee had informed her that Cole was taking her on a weekend date to the Cayman Islands, and no matter how hard Nadia tried not to be jealous, it was tough to be around someone who was actually having a great life right now.

A while later she was unloading her groceries when her phone rang. After maneuvering around all of her packages she finally managed to grip the handheld.

"Hello?"

"Ms. Morales?"

"Yes, this is Nadia."

"I'm Chase, from Safe Haven Animal Shelter. We have a border collie here that has your name and other personal information on her call sheet. I understand that you were to adopt her soon. Am I right?"

Nadia's heart tripped to a stop in her chest. "Yes, I'm waiting for her to heal properly before bringing her home." Dread bled thickly through her limbs and veins. "Is something wrong?"

When he took a deep breath, Nadia steeled herself for bad news. "An infection set in probably two days ago. We are doing our best, but she is fading fast, Nadia. I called you out of courtesy before any drastic measures are taken to give her peace."

Give her peace? No, oh no! This wasn't supposed to happen!

Nadia gripped the phone harder, squeezed her eyes shut against an acute pain for an animal she barely knew, but cared for. She spoke into the phone, "I can be there in about thirty minutes."

"I'm deeply sorry for such bad news," he told her, then hung up the phone.

Seconds passed, the dead line started beeping, and Nadia shut it off without conscious thought. Little black spots danced before her eyes as she stared at her fenced in backyard that she could make out through her back window. Belle would have come and lived with her in probably three more weeks. The large fenced yard and quiet, low traffic country living would have suited her fine, and after visiting her numerous times, Nadia knew that firmly.

A fine mist covered her eyes, but Nadia refused to cry. Her life was crappy; this just certified it for her. Everything she touched fell apart.

Even though she knew she was acting irrational, she couldn't stop one thought from forming in her mind. If Drake would have known about this, he would have done everything in his power to save that animal.

But you know he has the best people working for him.

Still, she centered that pain, and the motherly instinct that she hadn't been able to show the injured animal, onto his shoulders. He was the one that had saved that dog for her. He was the one that told her Belle needed her as much as she needed Belle. He was also the one that was gallivanting around New York with Ms. Vintage Valentino right now as her world was slowly disintegrating. Her world that had become the way it was because of him and the way she felt about him-her world that she didn't even know how to live in anymore.

He had known weeks ago that she needed a distraction, some form of distance from her job and Donavan. He had offered Belle, and she had taken that offer. But now his option was being torn from her before she had the chance to care for it and love it like it deserved. And even though it wasn't precisely Drake's fault, Nadia was projecting her pain and anger onto the one man that she needed to keep her defenses around.

As she finished with her groceries, tried to control her tears, and finally made her way out the door, Nadia silently fed the antagonism and hurt, pushing it to the back of her mind where all of her thoughts and feelings for Drake were cemented. She had prayed for a way to make him not so enthralling to her. She would use anything to make that happen, anything.

***

"Mmm…you taste amazing."

Lorelei's wine-scented breath brushed across his jaw, and Drake clenched every muscle in his body as her tongue crept out and licked another path from his ear to his collarbone.

This had started when they walked in her door. Usually sexual dalliances were no problem for him, neither was keeping the woman happy, sated, and delightfully numb when he finally left her bed. But for some reason, the sugary sweet smell of Lorelei's perfume, her artfully coiffed red hair along with the tight, extremely short black dress, was throwing any thoughts of having sex out the door, just as it had Tuesday night after the gala.

Now, even with all of that, Drake could still admire a fine body when it was pressed up in his face. With all of the plastic surgery around these days, Drake had to admit that Lorelei's breasts were her own, and they were delightfully bouncy and perfectly round as they dangled in front of his face, her pert nipples flushed a raspberry red with arousal. She had pushed the top of her clingy dress down so that he could feast on her skin like she was doing to him. He just hadn't bit the bullet, so to speak.

Her fingers were making short work of his shirt buttons as he sat there and basically let her undress him. Still, he felt not a damn thing when she pulled open the offending material, and then slid down between his legs, her hot eyes fixed on the prize, the prize that was at the moment only half-hard, and still needed some attention before he could reach any state that would satisfy the witch in front of him.

"So submissive, but I like being in control, makes me all the more ready to work you until you scream my name."

Drake rolled his eyes as she opened his trousers. He didn't stop her from pulling the two pieces of material open, and she saw how uninspired he was, but for some reason he got a smile from that.

"I see I will need to do a little more for you before we move on to the main course, but that's okay. I'll make it so hard for you baby that you won't ever want me to stop."

He chuckled at that, but she ignored him. That was when the truth hit him. This shouldn't be happening. He was an Amber Druid. Members of that class had certain more primal urges than most humans. There was no reason why he shouldn't be sporting a hard on so amazingly rigid that even Lorelei would seem anxious about it. No justification for sitting submissively before her—her nipples stiff and alert, enticing him for closer inspection, for a taste—In the low light of the room.

Drake considered himself a connoisseur of women. He loved a sweet, slow seduction, but rarely had the time for it. He loved all women, no matter their sizes, shapes, colors or personalities. He adored the way he could make them smile shyly at him when he turned on his Texas, good ole boy charm. Every inch of their skin held numerous erogenous zones. When tasted, caressed, or licked, he could turn even the frostiest of women into nothing more than a blubbering mass of want. He prided himself on doing that to every woman he had the chance to sleep with.

For some reason he was losing his patience with this woman, who was at the moment, on her knees about to take his half flaccid cock into her wet mouth. The damnedest thing was, he should be as hard as a rock, and he wasn't. Even when her fingers brushed the sensitive area underneath the head, still not one whisper of a zing moved through him.

Drake peered across the room, towards the wall and began to feel a spiking of rage flow through his system. He knew why this was happening, and he didn't like it one fucking bit. The rage built and built, rising to a level that was deadly, and not what he needed. When his emotions reached the limit, or when he picked up anger from a human, his change started. Right now he could feel the heat of his eyes shifting from brown to amber, and one move of his tongue caught the edge of a fang slipping into a point. Damn.

Lorelei's mouth was an inch away from his cock, her breath staining his skin, and he still didn't feel any spark of lust for her. Instead he shoved her away, watching from under lowered lids, her breasts bouncing, as she landed on her ass on the floor. He got up and started buttoning and zipping his clothing back into a decent state.

She was whining in the background, saying how she could make it all better, but Drake ignored her and called his driver back to come get him. He knew she would probably spread rumors of how he couldn't get it up, but right now if he so much as got into any sparring match with her, his full change would take place, and there was no way to explain that. As it were, his eyes were on full Druid mode, so were his fangs, and he could feel that his face was changing also. He had to get the hell out of there.

Thank God she never stopped him.

***

When Drake got back, a week to the day since he left, he came back to heartbreaking news.

"I noticed she was acting funny around Tuesday." Chase explained while Drake stood there in the surgery prep room of the Haven and stared dumbly at his Vet. "You know some of the symptoms, vomiting and diarrhea, very uncommunicative. She didn't want to come out of her area, and since she was such a lovable little thing I knew something was wrong." Chase shook his head sadly, "We, Trent and I, did everything we could, even did a deep clean around her wounded leg, but we knew after some tests that the infection was internal."

Drake stood there in shock, running his hands through his hair and basically feeling lost. That little dog had been special. She was two years old and had been in prime health until the accident where Nadia had hit her. When Nadia had brought her to his house, Drake could sense the instant imprinting between Belle and her. He knew then that Nadia needed to feel that small dog's presence in her own life. Nadia needed to heal from her disastrous mistake of seeing Donavan with Suzanne. Sometimes animals were better than humans in dealing with pain and anger. Drake sensed the absolute unwavering love that Belle could have given Nadia, and it pained him that the small dog hadn't pulled through her infection.

"Shit."

Chase's eyes came to his face. "I know man, I know. It isn't a good day when you lose one like that. But we have plenty of other animals here that are healing nicely if Ms. Morales wants one of those instead. She was pretty upset when she came in yesterday afternoon."

Drake's eyes zeroed in on him immediately, "Nadia was here? You called her?"

Chase looked directly contrite. "But that is routine, by the book. You know that. Why *wouldn't* I call her?"

Drake turned and tried to imagine just how upset Nadia had been yesterday. He could see her in tears, sobbing for the life of the small Border Collie. Damn, this wasn't supposed to happen. She had always been deeply emotional; that incident of Donavan cheating had hurt her far more than anyone imagined. Drake feared this just added to the hurt.

"She declined adoption of another animal right now," Chase told him.

Of course she did, Drake thought to himself as he watched Chase glance at his watch.

"It's almost five. I'm heading out. Max is on night duty this weekend since Trent needed the weekend off." Chase glanced back at him and Drake could sense that the other man thought he had done something out of code in dealing with Belle's death.

"Ms. Morales, was she very upset?" Drake asked, although he sensed the correct answer.

"Yeah, it was hard to break the news to her that we would have to put Belle down. I knew once we started talking to her that she cared for Belle."

Drake drew his fist over his mouth, imagining what Chase was saying, "Alright, I guess I will see you Monday then. Try to have a good weekend."

"You too, boss."

After watching the young man leave, Drake left the prep room and made his way to the office he had at the back of the compound. The large, masculine space instantly soothed him, calming him in a way that being around nature did. He stared out the window, glancing at all of the large areas that were fenced in, where animals were mending or being cared for in a way they never would away from here.

Thoughts of the little dog, Belle, infused his mind. She had been a pretentious thing-a little spitfire of a dog, the perfect foil for Nadia's cool, calm, and collected personality. Belle had also been hurt in the past. Her huge brown eyes had told stories of pain and a mean-spirited owner before she had run away and ran into Nadia's path.

Drake could see some of his crew leaving for the night and he knew, in the back of his mind, that he needed to check on Nadia.

Don't do this man. You are getting too worried about her. She needs to be far, far away from you right now.

He ignored the voice in his head, grabbed his keys from his pocket, and strode from the building, heading for the one woman that he shouldn't seek out.

Thirty minutes later, his big rig was pulling up in front of her small, cottage-style home on the outskirts of Beaumont. He had known for years where she lived, but actually driving up in her driveway gave him a funny feeling in his chest.

Going to her door, he glanced around, noting the small touches she had given the old cottage. Azaleas and Iris's were blooming in landscaped portions of the front and back yard, and tall, mature oak and maple trees gave the place a homey feel. He glanced back to the door and liked that the front door was painted bright red, which offset the rest of the neutral home. Apparently Nadia had a flash interest in color. For some reason that made him smile.

He could sense her on the other side of the door. And for a few seconds, he felt her curiosity until she got closer to the door, and when she looked through the peephole, he felt that curiosity turn to raw anger.

Staring bemusedly at the door while she opened it, Drake wiped his expression and kept his thoughts to himself.

"Hey," he told her, when she opened it fully and glared at him from her diminutive height. It was almost laughable, really, that she could stare him down when he was more than a foot taller than her.

She nodded in his direction but didn't smile. Peering around his body she pointedly glanced at her front drive. "Are you lost?" Then she pulled those green eyes back to his.

Man. The animosity in her stance, permeating the air around her, almost choked him. Was she blaming him for Belle's death? Surely not, surely she understood that he had been out of town, and he hired only the best to work in his clinic. His eyes catalogued everything about her, and he sensed the blood flow in her body as he watched a ruddy blush climb over her neck. She was pissed, highly so.

"Why would I be lost?"

Her lush mouth firmed in anger, "You never came to visit before, so how was I to assume that you knew my address?"

He ignored that angry statement. "Can I come in?" If it was possible her eyes turned greener than they were before. But he knew that was emotion trying to spill over from the inside. She scoffed. A soft noise that told him a lot about what she was feeling. Then she gave him a tight smile, "Whatever you need, you can surely tell me right here."

He was shocked. Never before had Nadia turned her anger on him. Belle's death must be hitting her harder than she wanted to admit.

A breeze fluttered the old tee shirt she had on that was loose around her body. All the while, the purple color brought out the paleness of her skin and the black length of her hair. Her old cutoff shorts showed him long, sexy legs, and he tore his gaze away, coming back to her face.

He cleared his throat, "I know about Belle."

There it was. That brief flash of pain that she held so deep inside. He knew it wasn't good for her to do that, but she was stubborn, and always had been. Morales's daughter had grown up with spunk; he knew that, but it was surprising to see it, when all he saw from her was the polite façade that she showed to society.

"I know. They did everything possible to save her." Her throaty deep voice was raspy. In that instant he realized she had cried all night over Belle. He watched her look back to the inside of her house, and he knew she was hedging about leaving him standing on her front step.

"If you know that, why am I still standing on your front step instead of in your house?"

Her manners were bred into her, and even though she was vibrating in her anger, she slowly opened the door fully and moved to the side. Drake walked in and immediately felt as if he were drowning in sorrow. Her acute pain was so deeply imbued in the house that he could feel it in the air around him.

"I would ask you if you want something to drink, but I don't feel all that hospitable at the moment." Her eyes surveyed him closely as he stood in her living area, and he began feeding off all of that negative sensation she was sending him. He could sense her pain underneath the anger, and had the insane urge that he should hug her, make her understand that everything would be okay.

"It is hard to lose something that you were looking forward to having around."

She scoffed again. He was coming to hate that sound.

"Look, maybe you should get out, go out tonight, find some friends and have fun, Nadia. You don't need to be home alone right now."

Apparently that was the wrong thing to say. She turned the full force of her green eyes on him and the heat of her emotions stung his skin. He had never, ever beheld such pain before, and he had been around for a long time. Even when her parents had passed, she had been wracked by hurt, but this was pure anger.

"You have no say over me Drake. And don't pretend worry when we both know that you only think of me as baggage from your past."

Whoa. Yes, there was some definite fury here. He needed to tread lightly. If he got caught up in her emotions too much, she might learn more about him then he wanted her to know.

"Whatever you're saying is based on pain. I am concerned for you, Nadia. You are like family to me."

She stood behind the sofa and sent green daggers in his direction.

"That's funny. I'm like family to you? What the hell ever Drake. Don't try to pull your head games over on me." She threw her hands up, as if she were done talking.

"This is no game, and I have no idea why you are so pissed at me. I employ the finest vets in three states. Belle was in the best care possible. I had no id--."

"No idea!" She screamed it, finishing his sentence for him, and then continued her rant.

"Of course you didn't." Her finger pointed in his direction, and Drake could see her chest rising with harsh breathing. "You were up in New York, with Ms. Vintage Valentino, probably fucking her brains out! Of course you were too busy to see about one little dog that you promised to me!" Green eyes slammed like lasers against his brown ones. The tension in the air went up about ten notches.

"You don't know what I was doing in New York, and even if I was 'fucking Ms. Vintage Valentino', like you say, it is none of your damn business." Seething anger pushed through, tingeing his voice with a gravelly drawl, trying to come to the surface. Drake held tight to his control. His skin was tightening, the blood rushing through his system, and his gums burning, but he kept it under wraps.

"That was a promise, Drake." Tears swam in her eyes, but she didn't stop. "You were supposed to let me have her. I needed her, don't you see? You were right, I needed Belle." She touched her upper chest. The tears that threatened now spilled over her cheeks, but instead of giving into harsh sobs, she held her ground. Those eyes of hers seemed to be huge green orbs in her small, slight face.

His anger dissipated. He felt glued to the floor in the middle of her living area. Emotion swam in the space between them as she held onto some vestige of her tattered pride. Her small delicate chin wobbled, and Drake felt his hands twitch. The need, the compunction to hold her, to console her, rose to unbelievable heights inside of him. Never had he thought he would see this strong woman break.

"You were away, gone, and she was there." Nadia pointed in the distance, while her green, pain filled eyes rose to his, and Drake felt as if someone had hit him with a Mack truck. 'I'm sorry' seemed so minute, so puny, and wide off the mark in the face of such sorrow. He had known that she needed Belle. He hadn't known how much. Now it was clear that she was going to fall apart if something didn't happen soon.

"Nadia, I—"

"Please, just leave. I can't do this right now." Her voice that had ripened with anger was now whispery thin. He felt her falling slowly apart, even as he saw it with his own eyes.

Standing there he knew, without a doubt, that she would not welcome any reassuring gestures from him right now. And even though he hated to do it, he turned and went back to her front door. Stopping at the door, he turned and took in her hunched shoulders, head facing the floor while tears brimmed over her eyes. The power coursing through his body at that moment told him that he could ease her pain and anger, if only she would allow him to touch her. The shield she had surrounding her chased that idea from his mind. She would sooner touch a snake than his hand right now.

Clearing his voice he told her, "Don't hesitate to call me if you need something, Nadia."

A burst of condescending laughter edged from her throat, but she didn't reply. Drake opened the door, and walked out of her house, dreading each step that took him away from her while she was in this state. He knew he could help her, but she didn't want that. He had to acknowledge what she wanted and not push her, even if that might make her hate him even more.

***

There had been many instances in her life where Nadia had felt such horrible emotion. This surely wasn't the worst, but now she would remember it as the day that she had driven a stake between her and Drake.

But that was what you wanted, wasn't it? You needed something to drive you away from him, something to keep your mind from conjuring up images of him at every turn, just so you could live a normal, healthy life.

Well, now she was stuck in the one scenario she had hoped for. She just hadn't thought she would lose Belle over this. But she had. There was no way around it and after realizing that, things had been a bit better. But her irrational anger at Drake had burned red hot and out of control when he had come to her home.

All the time he talked to her, the only thing she could see was Lorelei's body wrapped tight around his. She wanted to smash the pretty woman's head in. When she had accused him of fucking the woman's brains out, that had been anger talking-until Nadia realized that he had probably done just that.

That sent a wave of remorse flooding through her, but she knew that was only jealousy making her think that way.

With tear-filled eyes, she sipped her tea, and stared out onto her back porch. Moonlight gilded every edge of furniture, patio equipment, and her overgrown grass yard. Fireflies buzzed around, their small bodies lighting up the denseness of the dark. Nadia took another sip and tried to stop her emotions from overreacting.

Just the idea that Drake had been with Lorelei was like a killing blow to her middle. Nadia wasn't sure of how many more images she could conjure up with Drake and that woman, but if her brain flashed one more shockingly descriptive picture, Nadia just might consider becoming an alcoholic. Being drunk made her sleepy, and sleeping was the only way to stop seeing them doing the deed over and over in her mind.

God, she had been rude, terribly rude, but what she told him hadn't been prettied up at all. Every vehement word had spilled out, and she felt a slight bit better.

The tears gathering in her eyes once again mocked her. She knew that she was crying because of what she had done, rather than what she had lost with Belle. Furious with her emotions, she wiped her wet cheeks and remembered the shock in those warm caramel eyes of his when she had basically yelled out his actions with Lorelei. Apparently he had never assumed his little Nadia would rant and rave about him having sex before. Now he knew just how hot her temper ran when stoked. She wanted to crawl under the floorboards.

Other than admitting just how attracted she was to him, she had just planted a huge sign on her forehead that screamed *Jealous*. With Drake being the astute man he was, she was damn sure he would figure it out real soon.

Then what will you do?
Nadia had no idea.

Chapter 7

Bright and early Monday morning, the first bouquet arrived.

The beautiful arrangement instantly made Nadia suspicious, and her suspicions were confirmed when she opened the card and read Drake's elegant scrawl:

No words can express how sorry I am. Enjoy the flowers.

Drake

Nadia brought her eyes back up to the spray of Orchids, Tulips, and other fragrant flowers and met Renee's wide eyes over the bouquet.

"Damn," she muttered, giving Nadia a look that stated just how surprised she was. Nadia could agree. She had never received flowers from Drake before. She ignored the warm glow and looked around Renee to the delivery guy still standing in the office doorway.

"Please return these and you can tell him that it was a lovely gesture."

Renee gasped and the guy shrugged, reaching out to grab the large bouquet and then he left the office, leaving Renee standing behind him, her mouth working like a gasping fish.

"What the hell?" Renee's eyes instantly went to Nadia's face. "Are you sick? That yummy man sends you flowers, *flowers*, Nadia, and you send them back?"

Nadia told herself that she had bared enough to Renee when she had called her Sunday, she shouldn't need to say more. "I just want to go on about my life without thinking of anything that happened Saturday." And that was the truth. She wanted to forget her humiliating actions in front of Drake.

She had just sat back at her desk when Renee said from the hallway, "Girl, I don't know what you have planned in that head of yours but I have a feeling you had better line up your next shot. This Drake fellow doesn't seem like he would give up that easily."

That was what worried Nadia.

An hour and a half later her worry grew.

The same delivery guy was back in her office with the same bouquet. "He isn't happy and he said to make sure you read the card."

Nadia's insides trembled, but she brushed it off and gallantly took the card from between the fronds of baby's breath and greenery. Apparently this delivery guy was working directly from Drake's office for his bold scrawl was once again on the card.

I knew you were stubborn, but this is ridiculous. Just accept the flowers.

Drake

A slow smirk grew on her face, but she stopped it from forming fully. She thrust back into her mind all of the reasons that she shouldn't accept this gift from him. Imagining herself thinking depressing thoughts of him while she held the flowers to her chest was what cemented her actions. She would not pine for him anymore.

She placed the card back and gave the delivery boy an apologizing glance.

"Don't worry, I don't mind at all. Every time I leave his office he tips me," the young guy told her, and Nadia couldn't help but laugh as he left the building once more with the bouquet firmly in his grasp.

***

Across town Drake was not exactly good company right now.

His attempts at apologizing to the most stubborn, hardheaded little lady this side of the Mississippi was not working, and he wasn't pleased about it. The delivery guy had come and gone three times already. When he came back with the bouquet in his hands again, Drake gestured for him to leave it with his secretary and then he could go.

She *would* accept something from him as an apology, even if he had to be underhanded to get her to take it.

He pushed papers around on his desk until his phonebook appeared and as he flipped through, he tried to understand this burning *need* to give her something in the first place. Could it have been because she had looked like a wounded black haired angel when she cried Saturday? Maybe it was because even after his changing over 200 years ago he still couldn't handle tears from a woman. Whatever the reason, all Drake knew was that he had a burning aspiration in his gut to see her happy again, and he wouldn't rest until he carried forth on his plan.

An hour later Drake was wearing a shit eating grin and feeling about ten feet taller as he left his office for field work. There was no way in hell Nadia could return his gift now and just knowing that caused his blood to heat.

He adamantly refused to dissect any reason why his body grew hotter when he had thoughts of her.

***

The card arrived the next day in the mail.

Nadia slid her fingernail under it and pulled out the heavy vellum paper. The Saunders Spa was located in one of the ritziest neighborhoods in Houston. Nadia had done a few write ups on the large business for one of her magazines and she had loved the neutral elegance of the place. They catered to wealthy patrons, but every year at a couple of Nadia's events they would send out gift baskets that included spa days and other goodies. Her eyes went over the small note and Nadia remembered meeting Gwen, the manager, at one of her events a few months ago. Gwen had basically said that she wanted to thank Nadia because since they had been sending out those goody baskets, their business had skyrocketed and she had included a day pass for her in the envelope.

Dang, she could use this, and it was the thing she needed so that her mind could be at ease while her body got pampered. Before she allowed her mind to change, she called the number and accepted the generous gift.

The week passed relatively fast, and with no more flowers from Drake. In the back of her mind, Nadia had hoped she would have seen more, but she knew once she refused him three times she would not be seeing the lovely bouquet again.

You had your reasons to do that.

She had, but thinking about it a week later she was seeing just how impolite she had been to turn down his gift. What really surprised her was how easily he had given up. Like any other Texas gentleman she knew, Drake was a surefire charmer and could easily smile or drawl his way past any woman's defenses. Since it hadn't been him delivering those flowers, it was easier for her to stay immune from his charismatic ways.

Anyway, she thought to herself, if he had wanted to charm her he could have done so Saturday at her house.

Just remembering what she had told him that day sent a fiery blush traveling over her skin. It had to have been more than clear to him just what those yelled words meant. She only hoped that he didn't care about her jealousy.

Yeah right.

If she knew Drake, and she did, not only had he noticed the green monster in the room with them that afternoon, he was also waiting for the perfect time to get to the bottom of things.

She sure as heck didn't need that. Hell, she was barely hanging on by a thread as things were now. Drake was an intense man. If he wanted to, he would have her emotions laid bare in mere moments. Saturday, they had been all over the place, and he had only been there ten minutes. Nadia knew if there was something he wanted to know, he wouldn't waste time. The ruthless businessman and hardnosed animal activist in him would rise to the surface and leave her in shambles.

Pushing thoughts of him away, she focused on the relaxing day she would have at the spa instead. She would not waste the spa's generosity on emotions she could do nothing about. There was no way to change her feelings for Drake. She had loved him for years and would continue to do so, no matter how much it hurt her to know that he would never care for her that way.

She knew now, after the Donavan incident, that trying to push those feelings onto another man, or even using another man to hide behind, would never work. All that had done was waste her time and screwed up a friendship and developing trust between her and Donavan.

There was no way to escape Drake and what he made her feel. She had accepted it, but she knew her life would be miserable because of it.

***

The weeks flew by and surprisingly enough Nadia was so busy that she rarely had time to focus on Drake. In between meetings concerning photo shoots, headlines, and hot topic events, Nadia also had her hands full with numerous charity functions, and trying to stay on pace with other national magazines, all without losing her sanity.

Three weeks had passed before Nadia caught the feeling that Drake might be nearby. Her internal radar had never failed her before. With her interest held on a conversation with Amy Morehead and Leslie Tierney, Nadia noticed Drake from the corner of her eye. While

Amy talked about her first year of marriage, Nadia's nape prickled in awareness. The slow thrum of heated responsiveness slipped past her defenses and tickled her belly. Her attention was drawn to his tall frame as he stood with his back to her a good distance away.

The dim lights in the Galleria hotel slipped over his dark chocolate hair and massive shoulders. The knowledge that he was here, at this event, spilled through her body like warmed honey. It was almost as if their argument had never happened. Her body still reacted to him in that same dangerous way. But in Nadia's mind she knew things weren't the same.

Those easy conversations they had shared when she was younger, along with the ones at Cole's barbeque just weeks ago, seemed like memories now. Like always, Nadia would be able to hide what she felt under a cold and indifferent nod or look. What scared her was if Drake would come out and ask her about her jealousy problem. Would she be able to play it off? She wasn't sure.

When he turned, Nadia noticed the tux was absent tonight. He still managed to look seductively handsome in his black trousers, dark midnight blue button up shirt and patterned tie. Even though the dress code wasn't black tie, he outshone every other man there in his understated elegance.

Those beautiful eyes of his scanned the area while he still managed to keep his attention on the conversation with the men around him. When his bold gaze came too close to her, Nadia snapped her eyes back towards her friends, but she had the feeling that he had caught her staring.

After getting drawn back into the conversation, she surprisingly forgot about Drake's presence.

Another thirty minutes passed as Nadia laughed and gossiped with the girls. These two women were the only true society women that she trusted. With their easy going manners and open, friendly attitudes, it was easy to get along with both of them.

"I see whatever it is you are doing is working perfectly."

Drake's deep drawl snapped her to instant attention. Nadia noticed he barely hefted his voice above a whisper, so the other ladies hadn't heard him. With her back ramrod straight and her eyes still on her friends, Nadia let her emotions and senses open to his nearness.

His tall, hard, hot body was standing very close behind her. She could feel the heat radiating from him in waves. Since the gathering was massive with people milling around closely everywhere, Nadia knew the other women hadn't given Drake's closeness extra attention. The small hairs on her body lifted minutely, as if rising to meet him. Her fingers tightened on her wineglass whenever he spoke again, as his warm breath teased her bare neck.

"You are relaxed, smiling, and you look happy."

A warm thrill shot through her. He noticed her, or rather, something about her and that was something she hadn't expected.

The thread of conversation was still heavy around her. Nadia listened to the girls talking, but for the life of her she couldn't understand what they were saying.

"I guess that trip to the spa did its job?"

Those few words thrummed through Nadia's brain. It took her a moment before she realized exactly what he was saying. Her eyes widened and her body stiffened even more. That sneaky, sneaky man!

Turning, she whispered, "You underhanded, devious, conniving…" She was so furious that she ran out of words to spit at him.

"Ah darlin', sometimes that is the only way to make a woman see reason. You have to do things a little dishonestly." His words were deep with his delicious drawl, and Nadia hoped Amy and Leslie couldn't hear their furious whispering.

She fumed silently while Drake's eyes sparkled at her with hidden humor. The bastard was enjoying this! He liked seeing her flustered. Those eyes of his were warm on her face as he looked down at her, and Nadia watched as a sexy, wicked grin kicked up one corner of his mouth. Her insides quivered as he nodded to the other ladies vaguely and said, "Ladies."

His eyes slammed once more into hers and Nadia felt rooted to the floor.

"I'll be seeing you around."

He worded it like a promise, putting emphasis on the 'you' part. In reality those softly spoken words made her want to find a hiding place right this second.

Whispers from behind her drew her attention but she couldn't help but watch Drake as he walked away from her, his large, powerful body moving fluidly, muscle by muscle.

***

The stinging of his gums acknowledged the fact that the sight of Nadia after three weeks of not seeing her proved more than his vaulted control could take.

Drake continued walking until he had maneuvered around throngs of people to the refreshment table where a beer was waiting with his name on it. After that first bracing cold drink, his body cooled somewhat. He nodded to a few people he knew around the table but maintained his distance from them for the time being. He had all he could handle right now with Nadia crowding his thoughts.

She still stood about thirty feet from him, but even with that distance between them, Drake could feel the pulse of awareness that had thrummed through her body, and still did, when he had walked up behind her. The responsiveness of her body had called out to him at that moment. Drake had stopped himself from giving the delectable, exposed nape of her neck a long hot lick, but even now his mouth still watered from the action that he had halted.

With all of her glorious dark hair piled on her head, her shoulders, nape and back was bared to everyone's gaze. The black, strapless gown was stunning in its simplicity. With Nadia wearing it, it became a walking temptation. Drake's hands tightened into fists at his side. He almost crushed the frozen beer bottle in his hand, stopping himself mere moments before he knew he would have heard a crack in the glass.

Shit. This was ridiculous.

But his body didn't think it was. At that moment Nadia laughed, and the sound caused something inside Drake's chest to tighten almost to the point of pain. Dreading the action and telling himself he shouldn't, he brought his gaze back to where she was standing and soaked up the sight of her with a blinding smile on her face. Her eyes were lit up from within while she spoke to one of the women on her left. The front of her dress was just as simply made as the rear, but with it wrapped around her body, to Drake it became something that showcased all of the curves that he had overlooked for years now.

Well, he was catching up real fast with reality.

The young girl with the coltish legs and stick body was nowhere in sight. Now he was faced with a dark-haired beauty. Smoldering green eyes showed him almost every emotion she felt and her adolescent skinniness had disappeared, giving her a more feminine, rounded appearance. Ripe, womanly curves were splendidly on view for his approval, and boy did he approve.

Surprising long legs, for such a small woman, took up half of her height. The only other thing on her that competed with her long legs was her long black hair. When it was down, the very tip brushed her lower back.

Drake felt his fists clench again as an image scorched his brain with heat. He could imagine her long, delicate neck thrown back, her body magnificently flushed with arousal as she tilted her hips to receive him, her long hair tracing fire along his thighs with every backward dip, as she screamed his name.

He growled and moved away from the table. Fuck this. She was Nadia Morales-daughter of an old friend that he had trusted and cared deeply for, not only for him, but for his young family too. This rabid want that had him fired up and wanting to do things to her that he shouldn't even dream of, was ludicrous.

With his thoughts in the gutter, damn good thoughts, but still inappropriate, Drake downed his beer, tossed it in the nearest trash can and headed for the woman that had been giving him delicious looks all night.

Her name was Josette, and that was all Drake needed to know. The only thought in his mind was to get Nadia's image out of there, and if he had to do his best to fill his mind with someone else, then he would. Josette was more than happy to dance and while they did Drake tried not to see the glance that Nadia gave him. It was almost as if she knew what he was doing, as if she knew how he felt in that moment.

She knew nothing about the overwhelming need pounding through him right now. Nothing about how he was burning up for a woman he shouldn't even feel this way for. Nothing about those fragile, wounded eyes knew anything about the intensity of his lust at this moment, and if Drake had any say in it, she would never know. No matter how gentle he could be, the beast that lived in him, that breathed the same air as he, but managed to only come out at times of high stress or emotional moments, would tear her apart. His Druid abilities were strong and sometimes Drake felt the primal edge of that hidden danger pulse inside of him. The last thing he needed to do was unleash that upon the one woman that he wanted only to protect.

You know damn well you want more than that from her.

He clenched his jaw and tried to ignore the burning of his gums. Josette's left leg slipped into the small opening between his. Her hip brushed his groin and he felt the excitement rushing through her veins. The tall brunette was more than experienced with the way he handled things than Nadia could ever be. Even the aura around her hinted at a wealth of hidden sexual vices that he could easily imagine would keep them busy all night long. But when he glanced down at her brown eyes that all but promised him heaven, Drake felt anxiousness crawl into his chest.

Even with her obvious interest, her tall, svelte form, Drake still couldn't manage a hint of interest in Josette. And that pissed him the hell off. All he wanted to do was bury himself deep in another woman and forget about Nadia.

When the dance ended, he politely, but firmly, brought Josette back to her table with the rest of her guests. The look of shock and hunger in her eyes made him even angrier, but he didn't know what to tell her.

Sorry darlin', but you aren't what I want. For some reason, that little dark haired woman-child in the corner over there makes my blood run hot, but a purely delicious carnal woman like you can't get me hard.

Drake scoffed at his subconscious and left the ballroom. He would stop this madness. He just wasn't sure of how long it would take him.

***

Nadia looked in the mirror once more. She wiped gently at the tear marks on her cheek, sniffed and then threw the tissue in the trash. She reached out to grab her small clutch and noticed the fine shaking skittering along her fingers. And that was all it took to make her chin wobble again.

She slammed the clutch down on the counter in her anger.

Why should she continue to do this to herself? What was the point? She was only making herself depressed when she allowed her eyes to follow him around. When he had taken Josette Perkin's hand and led her to the dance floor, Nadia could have sworn that her heart had sunk to her ankles. The pain that had invaded her system at that moment had been intense. She had almost run to the restroom for privacy.

She wanted him so much that she felt sick with it.

Letting out a puff of air she stood straight up. She stiffened her shoulders and placed an iron hold over her emotions. He would not get to her this easily. He could dance with whomever he wanted, he could flirt with whomever he wanted, and he could sleep with whomever he wanted. Nadia would remain immune. She told herself these things, but for some reason she didn't believe one word.

Surprisingly enough, when she walked back out to the ballroom Josette was still there with a sullen look on her face while Drake was nowhere to be found.

***

Nadia had just settled into bed, tugged the covers up to her chin and rolled onto her side, determined to not dream at all, not even about Drake, when her phone rang. Huffing out a breath in irritation, she grabbed her iphone that was emitting the annoying sound and answered.

"Hello?"

"Hey, I just wanted to make sure that you made it home okay." Drake's thick-as-molasses tone slid into her ear. Every single inch of her body come to immediate, throbbing life.

"Yeah, had no problem at all," she said, still wondering why he would call in the first place. All the jealous thoughts she had had of him earlier in the evening unfurled once again in her mind. She tried to shore up her I-couldn't-care-less-what-you-think-or-feel-at-this-moment emotion, but it wasn't happening. Hearing his breath on the other end of the line was having the opposite effect on her sensibilities.

"I'm not bothering you, am I?"

Even when he asked something like that, the sensual note in his voice rang out, appealing to her every nerve ending, almost as if he had one finger over the phone strumming her pulse in tune to his every whim.

Nadia cleared her throat, "Of course not."

Damn girl, you could have played it up a bit more. Made it seem you might actually be doing something naughty for a change. Don't want to sound like too much of a middle-aged spinster, do you?

Shucking those thoughts she asked, "Is there something you needed?" even as she prayed he wouldn't let her off the line yet. This was a different connection than what they usually had. And the more she thought about it, the more she realized that there were many things that could make this conversation enriching-like the fact that she could hide from him, in plain sight, or hearing, rather.

The sound of him shifting rang out, and Nadia almost, *almost*, groaned as she imagined him lounging around. Her fingers clenched around the slim body of the I-phone and she heard the otter box protecting the device click in obvious strain.

"No, I didn't need anything." Another deep breath, then, "Just wanted to rub it in some more that I know you enjoyed the spa treatment."

Nadia could practically hear his smile over the phone. The devil. He knew she was still fuming over his deception on getting the upper hand. And Nadia could be the better person in this situation.

"Okay, I will admit that I enjoyed the spa very much. And I'll even thank you for the gift." She cleared her throat, "Thank you, Drake."

He chuckled, the resonance of that sound sifting into Nadia's bloodstream, heating it to boiling. "I'm glad you liked it, darlin'. Since you wouldn't accept anything else, I convinced myself that I'd found something you would never be able to turn down."

"Well, I would have turned it down if I had known it had been from you."

"I'm glad you didn't. I only wanted to make you feel good, honey, that's all."

If only you knew…….Nadia thought to herself.

She stretched in the bed, and then said with all honesty, "It worked." And almost as if a little demon sat on her shoulder she decided to take things further. "It worked very well, almost too well. I think I floated on cloud nine for about a week. My muscles felt less tight, my emotions were less tangled, and I can't remember being more relaxed. Overall, it was a very good gift."

"I'm glad, because you deserved it."

He didn't voice what they were both thinking. That the death of Belle had hurt her more than he had thought it would at first. Nadia was glad for him leaving that out of the conversation. At first she hadn't really known what kind of direction to take this phone call in. Now it seemed that she was willing to do anything to keep him on the line.

"Have you ever been to a spa before? I mean, I'm sure it's not something that busy men like you, or men in particular, actually admit to doing, am I right?"

Another sigh floated on the line, and when he spoke, his voice sounded deeper and even more intimate, if that were possible. "I've never been, but I have had massages before."

Nadia could imagine the lucky woman that had the supremely ultimate chance to touch, massage, and basically run her hands up and down Drake Thompson. Lucky witch. "Did you enjoy them? I know it took some getting used to for me. I can't handle a masseuse with heavy hands."

"I enjoy them alright, I guess. It was more of a conditioning thing after working out for long hours."

"Oh."

Seconds passed with the sound of their breathing echoing on the line. Nadia didn't feel the need to clutter up the quiet with conversation. She just sat there and listened to Drake breathe and shift on his bed, obviously, and considered herself a very happy woman.

And then he spoke again.

"You looked gorgeous tonight."

Warmth burst through her body at that intimate compliment. Her breath quickened, her heart tripped and her blood sped up and out to every single inch of her nervous system that hadn't been awakened by his voice yet. Her nipples pebbled against her night shirt, causing little pricks of awareness to bloom in her belly.

"Thank you."

"God, you're more than welcome, baby. More than welcome."

Nadia wanted to moan at the simple thrust of desire that had taken her unawares in mere moments. But she held it back, barely.

"I guess I should let you go so that you can get some rest."

Nadia bit her lip, silently begging him not to hang up with her, but knowing that if she wanted to keep him on the line, she would have to share more than just social niceties with him. Could she do that?

"Drake, don't go yet."

Oh my God. There, she'd said it. She actually went out on a limb and let him know with a few words that she wanted his conversation, attention, basically whatever he would throw at her. Nadia could hear the hesitation on the other end. Please God; he hadn't hung up on her, had he?

"It's just…this is nice, that's all, and I don't want it to end yet."

God, can you sound any more pathetic, Nadia?

"You're right. This is nice." A few seconds of silence and then, "And for the record, I didn't really want to get off the phone either."

Nadia smiled at that. "I'm glad I wasn't the only one."

"But, unfortunately, I have to leave in four hours for a business trip."

Despair crashed in on Nadia's little party. And she had just found the courage to speak to him without cursing herself afterwards. "Oh, well, I understand of course."

"But it would have been an interesting night, I'm sure, if I wouldn't have to attend that damned meeting."

Nadia felt her pulse flutter at his words. "I guess so."

"Darlin', I know so."

Wow, had things just gotten hotter in here? *No, it's only your imagination firing up, honey, that's all.*

Nadia stuffed that thought. "Well, I guess I'll see you when I see you."

"I'll hold you to that. Good night."

"Goodnight," she whispered back, and slowly ended the call.

Lying back in her bed, Nadia let her mind calm down from the exciting call. Too bad it would take her body another two hours to do so.

Chapter 8

Humid summer air wrapped around Nadia's ankles. She stepped around rain puddles on the sidewalk, and hummed *Back in Black* by AC/DC under her breath as she made her way to the long, meandering front entryway to the Hollis's house.

The large get-together was more of a summer party, and with the recent rain the party had been moved inside the large two and a half story monstrosity that Darlene Hollis called home. With its stately southern façade, Hollis House reminded Nadia of plantations one would see in Louisiana, not in Texas. The massive white house had a large gallery that wrapped around the frame of the structure. Tall mature trees added to the southern charm aspect, while night sounds echoed in the air around the home, giving it a touch of mystery.

She finally made her way to the front door where Darlene was standing amid a group of people while she greeted newcomers. Darlene's eyes landed on Nadia the minute she cleared the massive double doors.

"Ah, little Nadia, welcome honey. I'm so glad you could make it." Darlene, ever the southern lady, kissed both her cheeks and pointed in the direction of what Nadia knew was a coatroom off of the foyer. "You can put your belongings in there sweetie. And you are here as a guest, not as coordinator tonight, so you will have a good time!"

"Thank you, Darlene. How are the grandchildren?" Nadia asked with a smile. She loved the older southern lady because she was bluntly honest and never missed an opportunity to push business in Nadia's direction, which not only helped out Nadia but it helped out charities that Nadia dealt with.

"Tommy is here with his new fiancée. You will have to meet her, such a nice girl. Now Randy, on the other hand, is stuck in Rome this weekend." Darlene rolled her eyes. "He said he had business to attend to and couldn't cancel."

Nadia wouldn't have minded being stuck in Rome, but she kept that to herself. "I'm sure he knows he is missing out." She gave Darlene a hug and then left her side to mingle with the rest of the guests.

The large home was lit up like a Christmas tree for the dinner and in Nadia's estimation there had to be at least over fifty people in attendance. Huge buffet tables were set up against the left wall and Nadia made her way over to them, her stomach growling its appreciation.

She had just filled her plate and was turning to find somewhere to sit whenever a chill skittered over her skin. With the small hairs on her neck alive with tension, Nadia turned and caught the large frame of Drake Thompson moving in her direction.

Her plate wobbled precariously, but she managed to avoid dropping it on the floor. Stilling herself, she pulled up her indifferent look and took in his appearance. A button-up dark maroon shirt, clearly tailored, covered up his magnificent chest. He wore dark grey trousers with boots, and for some reason that made Nadia smile slightly. Two weeks had passed since she had seen him in Houston for the fundraiser. She had spent two weeks of trying desperately to avoid thinking of him at all, but she knew that probably would never happen, especially since that phone call the same night.

"Hey," the softly spoken word was drawled near her. Nadia came to the present and noticed he was standing directly in front of her. Caramel eyes were hooded by dark brown lashes and his mouth had a slight smirk to it.

"Hey," she said back, hoping that she could garner more of a vocabulary where he was concerned. Shuffling the plate she tried to grab a wineglass from the table, but only proceeded to almost drop her plate on the floor. Cheeks burning, she tried again.

Drake's hand came out and he asked, "Which one do you want?" He asked as her progress towards a glass stopped.

"The white wine please."

His hands grabbed the glass delicately and he held onto it while looking at her. Seconds passed and Nadia felt at a loss for words. What was he waiting on?

"Is there a problem?" She asked finally, watching as his smirk turned into a full crooked grin. Her stomach dipped to her feet. The man was too sexy for his own good. And too tall, she had to lean her head back to see him, even in heels.

White teeth flashed as he spoke, "Where would you like to sit?"

God, she was a dumbass. She looked around, trying to hide her heated blush, and noticed some chairs off to the side in the hallway. "Over there is fine," she told him as she gestured towards the hallway.

Without giving her a reply, he moved in that direction. Nadia walked behind him and took in the sights, which were damn good from where she was looking. Minutes later she sat in a chair and instead of walking off, he also sat. She tried to dredge up the charming conversationalist she had been on the phone that night, but her muse must have picked that moment to become shy.

Instead, she picked at her plate and tried to study him covertly. Warm eyes looked back and the slow tingling started in her blood, heating up her whole body. She stuffed something into her mouth, she didn't know what. She just needed something to keep from stating how damn good he looked. Flavor exploded on her tongue seconds later. Eyes tearing up, she immediately reached for her wineglass, in his hands, and gulped the chilled liquid.

"Are you okay?" He asked her. Nadia sensed his worry, but she also sensed his laughter.

Fire burned in her throat but she managed to croak out a wobbly, "Sure." That's what she got for trying to not state the obvious.

Minutes passed, and Nadia realized she didn't have the need to utter one word. She studied his dark hair and the way it drooped over his ear. Dark beard stubble was hidden right under the skin and Nadia wanted more than anything to feel it against her hands. That brought back images of the last time she touched him. Her skin burned in reaction. That dance was still making her want things she shouldn't.

Her attention was snagged by a man passing close to her. He walked in the opposite direction and she noted that it was Donavan. He went towards the buffet and grabbed a plate, but never once turned and acknowledged Nadia or Drake. It wasn't as if Nadia hated his guts, but she would rather not be drawn into his company. She knew he was a sly one. It was much easier on her well-being if she stayed away from him.

"I see you noticed him." Drake drawled in a low tone from beside her.

"I'm sure I would have sooner or later. The party isn't that huge," she told him, taking another sip of wine and catching the hard look on Drake's face.

"He is one of those people you just can't trust as far as you can throw him."

Nadia silently agreed as she continued watching him. "But he is such a great liar that you would believe anything that came out of his mouth." Seems that she should have caught onto that part of his personality earlier and saved herself a load of trouble, but at least she learned somehow.

"I'm glad you aren't tied with him anymore."

Her shocked gaze flew to his. Warm honey colored eyes glinted at her from beneath a fringe of dark lashes. The wine she was drinking lodged between her throat and stomach.

"He basically seduced Suzanne and left her dazed at how fast he swindled some of her money."

"The bastard. I never really knew him at all, did I?" Nadia mumbled, feeling supremely sorry for Suzanne. The urge to slap Donavan rushed through her.

"Just be relieved it wasn't you, darlin'," Drake told her. She turned back to where he was sitting and noted the relaxed look he was giving off. She didn't buy it one bit. He always had animal fast reflexes.

"I see Jacob Ritter is here. There is something I need to speak with him about. I'll see you later."

Nadia nodded and watched him walk towards the large living area. He moved slowly, surely, as if he had all the time in the world to get where he was going. She wasn't sure why he was actually hanging around with her, when she had expected him to ignore her after their confrontation.

Slight movement rustled near her side and Nadia looked up into Donavan's face. Damn, the last thing she needed was arguing over how he had been so very sorry about his screw up with Suzanne. But Nadia pasted a bright, fake smile on her face anyway. *Keep up social niceties, Nadia...*

"Nadia, you look beautiful tonight. It is so nice to see you."

She wanted to cringe but answered politely instead. "Thank you, Donavan."

"I still never got a chance to apologize to you without being interrupted." He looked perfectly embarrassed and his eyes were like a puppy dog that had gotten kicked to the curb. Nadia didn't want to feel sorry for him, but she had known him for a good while and during that time he had never taken her money, treated her badly or done anything to make her think he would eventually cheat on her. Maybe what Drake had heard about Suzanne was a lie. Maybe he was just trying to make Donavan look horrible to her.

"You apologized already Donavan, and I forgave you."

An earnest look crossed his face. "Please, let's walk a little. I've missed your company."

Nadia quelled the urge to tell him no, besides what could he possibly do with so many people wandering around? Not only that, she could also feel a few stares in their direction. She stood up and placed her half eaten plate and wineglass on the table beside her. "We can walk for a minute, but only to the porch."

He gave a charming smile and grasped her elbow as they walked towards the large French doors behind the buffet tables. "Are you doing okay?"

"I'm fine, just extremely busy with the magazines and other charity works." She started to slide into a familiar camaraderie by the time they made it to the veranda that wound all the way around the house. Nadia noticed a few people were on the north side of the porch, she could hear them talking but couldn't see them, but she still felt safe.

They talked lightly for a few minutes. He told her of hearing about her rankings in the polls with other prestigious magazines and he also said that his accounting firm was on the up and up about to open up another branch in Dallas. Before Nadia realized it, ten minutes had passed. The darkness was full now, but with the soft gas lamps attached to the porch she didn't feel any fear, nor did she notice that the other people had left the porch.

When Nadia finally noticed that Donavan was too close, it was too late. Staring at his hard face in the shadow of the gas lamp the first true touch of fear slid into her body.

"I think I should go back in now."

A slight smirk crossed his lips. He leaned even closer. Nadia moved back, but felt the hardness of the house wall at her back. There was nowhere left for her to go. "Why would you do that when we are just starting to get reacquainted?" His hand came up to grasp her right arm as he leaned his much larger body into hers. She tried to work her legs between his so that she could knee him, but as he leaned, he pushed her open legs outward, removing that particular threat.

Nadia wasn't about to be taken advantage of right outside Darlene Hollis's house with a party going on. She shoved with all she was worth. When he stopped stumbling only two feet from her, his eyes swung in her direction and Nadia was shocked at the depth of anger she saw there. Battling down a sick feeling in her stomach, she told him coldly, "Don't you ever, ever put your hands on me again."

The angry look in his eyes calmed instantly and Nadia started backing away from the wall of the house and him, not trusting him one bit.

"Now honey, all I wanted to do was talk. I deserve to have some of your time, don't I?"

The thick underbrush surrounding the house scraped against her ankles, but Nadia continued her slightly backward walk. She had the awful feeling that if she gave him the opportunity he might just tackle her in the yard. But no, Donavan wouldn't draw attention to this little mix up, would he?

"You don't deserve shit from me. I gave you more than what you deserve."

Feeling just a bit stronger since there was more space between their bodies, Nadia turned her back but kept glancing over her shoulder every few feet while her legs swallowed up the distance back to the front of the house. When she noticed he wasn't really following her, just standing off of the corner of the house, she turned fully and went back into the party, breathing a sigh of relief as she did so.

Trying to ignore the painful beating of her heart, she took in a lungful of cool, air conditioned air and grabbed a wineglass from the tray in the foyer. For about ten minutes no one really bothered her, and her eyes never caught sight of Donavan coming in the door, thank God. After twenty minutes, she started to get her bearings back when she caught sight of Darlene waving at her through the crowd.

She was introduced to the grandchildren, who were men her age, and as they all conversed in the large library, Nadia's eyes took in Drake's form over by the large wall of books. His dark chocolate hair was mussed, as if his hands had burrowed there repeatedly, and his hands moved slightly when he spoke to the three other men standing around him. Their conversation was deep and more than likely businesslike, Nadia assumed. But as she turned back to the sound of Darlene's laughter, Nadia realized she felt extremely safe in his presence.

An hour later she said her goodbyes and almost walked back in the library where Drake was still talking to the men, but she decided against it. He didn't need to know when she left the party. And he probably didn't care either way. Shaking her head, Nadia grabbed her belongings from the coatroom and slipped out into the humid summer night. There were a few other people leaving, so she didn't feel alone, until they all left through the front entrance and made it to the sidewalk. When the woman and man she followed out turned the opposite way from Nadia, the fear came back. But she shoved it away as nothing more than paranoia. There was no reason to fear walking to her car, which was parked around the block from the grand house. This was Beaumont, not Houston.

The huge oak trees from Darlene's yard hung over the sidewalk as Nadia walked, lending the mysterious night air something a bit more sinister and forbidding. She grabbed her purse tighter against her, fished out her keys so that she would be ready to start her Rover right up and started walking fast.

When she turned on the sidewalk, the extremely dark, narrow lane where she parked screamed at her to go in the other direction. Ignoring the warning and wrapping her keys around her fingers, like a pair of brass knuckles, she forged on. Darlene lived in the historic district of Beaumont where the streets were narrow and there wasn't that much traffic at night. *Don't remind yourself of that right now,* Nadia admonished herself.

When she got within twenty feet of her Rover, beeped the doors and saw the light come on inside the huge vehicle, pure relief swamped her.

With her heels clacking on the pavement, she raced around the side of the vehicle to get in, and out of nowhere a huge hand clasped over her lower jaw, silencing her efficiently, while another hand threw her keys to the ground before she could set off the panic button. She started kicking immediately which apparently pissed off her attacker, because he hauled back and slapped her, hard.

Nadia slumped, dazed, against her vehicle as her vision blurred before her eyes. Even sounds were going in and out, whooshing through her head with alacrity.

"Now that I have your attention you will do nothing to screw this up, do you hear me?"

He didn't say his name but Nadia knew the voice. With her legs trembling beneath her, her body shaking heavily and tears brimming in her eyes, she needed to get somebody's attention. She tried to suck in enough air for a scream when his hand covered her mouth again.

His breath ruffled the hair close to her cheek and Nadia cringed away. His palm tightened against her arm and Nadia knew she would have a bruise there tomorrow. "Don't move away from me. You know I have been nothing but patient with you."

Oh please make him stop.

The whispered litany was repeated in her head when his mouth slithered onto her neck. "We don't want any one to intrude on our reunion, do we honey?"

Tears fell from her eyes when he let go of her arm and used the hand that had covered her mouth to push away her dress strap. "You little tease. You tied me in knots for a year, and now I see you making eyes at Thompson? There's no way I'm letting you give him what I've been very patiently waiting for."

With her mind foggy from pain, she took another deep breath and screamed for all she was worth. The sound reverberated down the small street and deep into the night, shocking in the silence.

He hauled back and slapped her again, sending her into another slight daze. "You little bitch." With vision murky from his abuse, Nadia stood there confused while he murmured words she didn't recognize.

That's okay, someone heard me. Someone will come soon.

Her fear along with his abuse was causing her to float about in this odd state where what was happening to her seemed like a dream. That was, until he leaned back slightly and then suddenly, he wasn't there anymore.

Slumping against the hard body of the truck, she huddled with her eyes closed, tears streaming down her cheeks, shaking like a leaf in a hurricane while a fierce growl reverberated in the air around her. She didn't open her eyes to look, terrified as she was by the sound, but just stayed hunched over, rocking herself on the small road, and wanting so badly to wake up from this horrible nightmare.

There was a rough curse, then shuffled footsteps, and Nadia felt tingles shoot up and down her arms right before a shadow fell across her body. She scooted away on the pavement as fast as she could and would have gotten past the corner of the vehicle when the shadow spoke.

"Baby, don't do that. Come, it's me, Drake. Let me help you, okay?"

The timber and tone of the deep voice carried to her ears, and Nadia knew it was him but everything inside of her was telling her, screaming at her to run. Instead she sat there, in her ruined sundress with no telling what kind of bruises and dirt stuck to her. She was a huge ball of fear. Trembling, she looked from the corner of her eye and noticed the tips of Drake's cowboy boots, right there in front of her. She could tell he was squatting down beside her, and all at once she realized she should cover herself, cover up the damage that Donavan had done.

His hand reached out to grasp hers gently, and Nadia flinched. She heard a low, vile curse, but allowed him to grab her hand in his own. He gently, ever so slowly, helped her up. When she stood fully, her legs gave out, and instantly she found herself being picked up in his strong arms. She felt a moment's hesitation, a cringe against him out of fear, but then at the same time a sob tore from her chest, and with a small cry she curled into his chest and shuddered, while harsh sobs tore from her throat.

***

Drake clenched his fingers so hard against the steering wheel that he heard a small ripping sound. With one look he realized he had popped the elegant stitching on his wheel. Damn. This was his favorite pickup truck. The frayed ends of the leather cover showed up blue against the immaculate glowing backdrop of the dashboard.

Thank God Nadia was asleep in the passenger seat. He would have no excuse to cover up his display of rage. He needed this to be a lesson for him.

Control yourself man.

He did have one good thing to say for himself. Donavan was still alive, although he probably wished he was dead instead. Drake had maintained some form of control, enough to realize that he should live so that he could spend the rest of his sorry life in jail. Donavan was in a Beaumont hospital at the moment. The broken jaw and fractured arm Drake had given him were nothing compared to the areas of internal bleeding that were being monitored. He should be damn lucky that was all he had wrong with him.

Drake looked in Nadia's direction. Pale, watery moonlight illuminated her profile. Long dark lashes crested the gentle rise of her cheeks, while her gently upturned nose and bruised mouth quivered with slow, deep breaths. She was safe now. Safe from Donavan, that was. Drake refused to think about his certain weakness where this young lady was concerned.

He couldn't even begin to describe the sheer rage, the gut wrenching reaction that had come over him whenever he heard that high pitched scream and he had known, deep down, that she was in trouble. With his abilities, he was able to be at her side in seconds and when he had seen Donavan leaning over her prone body, up against her Rover, Drake had known then that the bastard had sealed his fate. Drake had gone into killing mode, not caring who was around, just knowing that a low, vile, piece-of-shit human, was violating something that belonged to him.

Drake knew he could have easily been found out. Hell, there might be someone out there tonight that could have seen him change, but knowing that Nadia was alive and conscious beside him made everything else pale in comparison.

Somehow, some way, he had calmed the second he touched Donavan. Rather than killing, he had inflicted small damage only. To him, that was his good deed for the day. But it could have so easily turned into a murder scene, especially when he saw the damage done to Nadia up close. Instead of going back to the asshole and ending his life, Drake had picked up Nadia and made sure she was covered, before walking back into Darlene's house and informing her of what had just happened right outside her gated yard, while he made sure one of the guests called the police.

The guests had been shocked, outraged, but that was exactly what Drake wanted after he told them where to find Donavan, out cold on the road beside Nadia's vehicle. Now there were no excuses or ugly rumors that could be started that the fifty or so people from the party couldn't stop in its tracks. Donavan would be forever branded an attacker of women while everyone already knew of Nadia's gentle, caring nature. Donavan would go down, in more ways than one.

That was the only thing about this night that caused him to smile.

After contacting the Beaumont Police, Drake had only given them enough time to ask pertinent questions before bringing Nadia to the hospital where he wanted her thoroughly checked over. Yes, he had admitted to the police that he'd seen a woman being abused, and that's why the attacker was in such bad shape. Needless to say, Donavan wouldn't be pressing charges against him. Drake had taken care of that with a little threat of his own.

After an hour spent there and a full exam, Drake found out from the E.R. doctor that she had suffered two blows to the face which had caused a split lip and more than a few bruises and small cuts from the ring that Donavan had worn. She had numerous bruises on her upper arms and a few on her knees, but that was all.

Drake knew it could have been much, much worse. Just the thought sent a deep burn into his eyes and his gums. He clenched his jaw, forcing his fangs down and carefully clenched his hands on the wheel.

Seconds later he covered her hand with his and sent a calming, soothing sleep spell deep into her body. Since she needed the rest, Drake didn't feel quite so bad about his underhanded approach to making her relax. She would sleep the rest of the night and long into the day, and if it were up to him, he would be there if nightmares threatened.

Chapter 9

A slight tingle, much like the one that she felt whenever Drake entered her personal space, slithered through her body while the dark, starless night closed in around her, Nadia shivered but kept very still.

Tall, mature trees stood like massive sentinels in the dense wooded area surrounding her. The moon was a small slash of cream against the black backdrop where no stars shone. Night sounds permeated the still, foggy air around her. Whippoorwills called and every few minutes a lonely, chill inducing whine came from the darkness.

Wrapping her arms around her shoulders, Nadia peered into the darkness that hovered around the trunks of every tree in her line of vision. She couldn't pinpoint exactly where she was but the only place this wooded that she knew of was Ridge Lake. The smell of sweet gardenias was thick in the air, and Nadia knew that there were many of those bushes that lined the wild areas of the lake.

A sound caught her attention. Nadia swiftly turned her head in the direction and waited. Seconds later she didn't see anything, but the hair rising on her arms and that persistent tingle kept her eyes on that particular area. She didn't feel apprehensive or afraid. The emotions inside of her at the moment were more engrossed with the strange surroundings than anything else.

Her eyes picked up on a large shadow lingering near the edge of one massive pine-about fifteen feet from her. She was just allowing herself to move her vision from the ground up when she realized that it was a man. Even though it was particularly foggy and highly dark where they were standing she was able to make out his large frame and the width of his shoulders. As her eyes traveled up towards where she assumed his face would be, a startled gasp escaped her mouth.

A beautiful glowing gold, something that resembled the deep brilliant color of a 24 karat nugget, gleamed in the darkness where his eyes would have been. Nadia was intrigued and fascinated. She knew she probably should feel a deep, resonating fear, but she didn't. She wasn't terrified at all.

The large man with the odd eyes moved closer and immediately Nadia felt faint. Seconds later, she blacked out.

***

The house was dark when Nadia woke. The odd dream lingered in her mind, not frightening or scary, just different and unusual.

Sunlight filtered in from her window, just barely illuminating part of the hardwood floor with its soft yellow radiance. She turned in the bed, opened her mouth to yawn when severe pain caused her eyes to fly open and her hand to come up to her cheek and lip. Images from last night flashed through her mind like an old movie still, showing her again and again just what had taken place.

Shuddering, Nadia's fingers came up to touch the bruised skin on her cheekbone, and the small gash on her lip. The bastard had done a good job on her face. Thank God Drake had shown up when he had.

As if thinking of him heralded hearing his voice, a slightly raspy, deep Texas drawl sliced through the quiet of her bedroom. "Don't fool with that too much darlin.' You'll start it to bleeding again."

Nadia let her eyes, swollen from crying the night before, fixate on the corner of her bedroom, where the voice had come from. Her fingers stopped fiddling with the swollen flesh instantly. It wasn't necessarily stark panic that had her frozen at the sound of that deep baritone. It was more like awareness, an overwhelming *knowing* that the substantial man sitting in her small, very feminine bedroom was a devastatingly masculine one. He all but sucked the very oxygen from the room just because he was in it.

His face was in one of the many shadows around the room but Nadia was able to make out certain things, like the broad, straight blade of his nose, the mussed ends of his hair and the harsh, uncompromising jut of his jaw. An old, worn blue tee shirt covered his huge chest while worn, frayed jeans clasped muscular, hard legs. White socks were on his feet and to Nadia that was almost as intimate as him being here in the first place.

She could barely make out the light, rich color of his eyes from where she was sitting, but she knew he was looking at her. The knowledge that he had stayed the night here slid through her veins like warm molasses.

Don't read anything into that.

"Does it pain you?" He asked, pulling her back to the present as he moved from the soft wicker chair in the corner to the side of the bed. When he drew near Nadia had the automatic reaction to move away from him. It wasn't as if she were afraid of him, it was more or less that her conscious made her move before she even realized she had done it. When he saw her reaction he stopped all together.

Nadia sat there feeling humiliated. Drake had never before done anything to warrant this behavior from her. She knew the attack last night was what caused this wary feeling but it made her feel sick to know that he was probably thinking that she was more affected by this incident than she let on.

"Sorry," she whispered, not even knowing if she had said it loud enough for him to hear. She didn't look up at him standing there so close, rather she kept her hands busy threading the soft fringe of her chenille throw through her fingers. Apparently he hadn't pulled the covers back when he had laid her here. Instead he had covered her with the soft blanket. He couldn't even bring himself to change her clothes to make her comfortable.

You have known for years how he feels about you. And sexual desire isn't it.

"That's fine," he spoke right above her and Nadia had to stop her heart from jumping out of her chest. "It's understandable with what happened last night." His huge body sat beside her on the bed, but not too close. "You never told me if it pains you or not," he told her, gesturing to her face with his right hand.

"It throbs a bit, especially my lip." She dared a glance while he was sitting beside her. Long, brown eyelashes with tangled ends hovered over caramel eyes. His cheeks were rough with bristled whiskers, but the look in his eyes kept her spellbound.

Nadia's heart picked up tempo, and after a few seconds she felt as if one word from him would send her into some deep, dark oblivion where he was the one calling the shots. Those light brown eyes of his were full of knowledge, secrets and things that Nadia would never know the answer to, no matter how much she wanted to.

"You know the doctor gave you a prescription for pain that I got filled this morning while you slept. If you want, I can go grab you some." The look in his eyes was unreadable.

Nadia nodded her answer and seconds later her bedroom felt like hers again. When she was sure he had made it away from her door she plopped down on the bed. "Damn." She didn't need the object of her desire in her home, waiting on her hand and foot while she pined away in some pool of lust for him.

Even though she had known for years how he felt only familial affection for her, her body and mind still gravitated towards him as if she could change his mind somehow, even when she knew she couldn't.

Damn, she knew better than to let her mind lead down this type of road. Ever since her teenage crush on him she knew he had been inaccessible. Hell, she had never been accused of being stupid, but she knew an unreachable dream when she saw one.

The ceiling above her was not going to give her the answers she needed, but she stared at it anyway. Seconds later Drake walked in carrying a prescription bottle and some water. Nadia sat up in the bed and pushed away every salacious thought she had of him. It wouldn't change anything and she couldn't do anything about it, so she might as well live with it.

***

After dosing up Nadia and watching her make her way into the bathroom for a shower, Drake went into her kitchen. The day had turned slightly overcast, with clouds gliding over the blinding sun every few minutes. As the spotted light crept through the window, Drake made a pot of coffee but skipped the breakfast. It was almost lunchtime anyway.

The bright, cheerful sound of a mockingbird slipped into his ears. Drake braced his hands on Nadia's countertop and controlled the urge to rip it in half.

He had felt rage before. Christ, he had been alive for over 200 years. Every emotion known to man had flooded through his body at one point or another. Sorrow, heartbreak, fear and all-consuming wrath when his family had been taken from him. Yes, he thought to himself as the mockingbird flitted over to window and trilled especially for Drake, he had known many feelings throughout his long life. It was only now that he was considering hunting down Donavan and actually plunging headlong into the fray of anger that had hold of him, that he *wanted* that sick human's blood on his hands.

He was considering murder-killing another human being! Drake shook his head and dropped it between his shoulders. He had been raised by loving, strict parents, and had been taught moral codes and values that were sometimes lacking in today's generations. If his parents, heck, his family could see what he was thinking now, he would be swallowing a couple of his teeth from his mother's slap, while his father would be asking him if he needed help hunting down the bastard. It didn't matter that his immediate family had been dead for a long, long time. He could sense them turning in their graves.

It wasn't as if he had never taken a human life before. He had, but that had been during war and times of major upheaval in Texas. Things had been different then for the new state and its warring people. But this, this was something that Drake knew was wrong. Premeditated murder was not something that was forgivable. The bad thing was his Druid nature sometimes overruled his human nature. Things that seemed so cut and dry as a human were slightly more fuzzy and unrecognizable when his powers were on full force. The push of his energy was telling him that he needed to right this wrong. What had been done to Nadia last night was a punishable offense. He knew better than to think that Donavan would go to jail. The asshole had too many connections and probably had favors to turn in. Fucking bastard, he would walk around, more than able to taunt Nadia at his pleasure.

Drake had to make sure that she put a restraining order against him. Last night she had been in pain and too upset to finish everything at the police station, but if Drake had his way, he would drag her back there kicking and screaming the moment she left the shower.

"You're still here?"

Nadia's voice kicked thoughts of murder and bloodshed to the curb. Drake turned as she walked stiltedly into the kitchen. Long black hair was damp and curling at the ends. Her face was devoid of makeup and she was wearing jean shorts and a tee shirt that claimed, *I read minds…and you should be ashamed of yourself.*

Drake couldn't help the smile that tilted the corners of his mouth. He was still awed that she had managed to slip past his radar and sneak up behind him, but the shirt made up for it. It wasn't often that he saw her relaxed enough to wear something like that around him or anyone else.

He ignored her question. "Nice shirt," he told her as he leaned back on the counter behind him.

The blush started at her collarbone then traveled up, tinting the tops of her cheeks. He could feel the surprise and astonishment that she felt, not to mention the slightest bit of sexual desire drifting from her, now that he knew to look for it. His heart sputtered then resumed with such force that Drake cleared his throat and automatically turned his feelers off. No way would he be able to get through a single conversation with her if he kept imagining his hands on her body.

"Thanks," she murmured, brushing past him on her way to the coffee machine. "Thanks for making the coffee too."

"No problem."

Minutes later she sat at the table with a huge mug of steaming coffee while Drake stayed by the counter with his own cup, knowing better than to get too close to someone that intrigued him that much.

She cleared her throat, "About last night…" Huge green eyes peered up at him from where she was sitting and a fist squeezed his heart. He had saved her from Lord knew what last night. Just the words brought reality smashing down on him. Donavan could have raped her, murdered her, or violated her and left her broken, lying there on the pavement. Drake counted his blessings again for attending the party last night. He didn't want to think about what would have happened if he hadn't been there.

His eyes slid back to her because he knew she wanted to thank him properly. That was the way she had been raised, almost with the same morals and values as he. His breath sputtered when he noticed the sheen of tears in her eyes and the trembling of her small chin. It was enough to make a grown man feel inconsequential.

"I can't thank you enough for what you did." She fiddled with the handle of the huge mug she had in front of her as she spoke, "I never…never would have thought that Donavan would do something so horrible…and to me of all people." Those large haunted eyes of hers swam in tears as she looked up at him. Her fingers left the mug and went to her mouth, then to the back of her neck. He imagined she was feeling more than stressed. Hopefully the pills would help with that.

"I never expected to see you out there. I thought my every option to get away was gone."

Drake shook his head negatively, trying to pump up her self esteem, "With the way you screamed, I knew in that instant something wasn't right." He put his cup down on the counter beside him, then turned his eyes back to hers, trying to will some of his strength into her small frame. "Don't think that you weren't doing enough to protect yourself…you were. I'm sure if I wouldn't have come along you would have maimed him in your own way." He smiled slightly, trying to inject some humor to lighten the situation. He would rather see her smile than cry.

She did smile, but it wasn't near what he wanted to see. She looked all around then came back to him leaning there. Her eyes sparkled with unshed tears and in that second Drake realized that Nadia had grown up right before his eyes. She had a confidence, although bruised and battered, that radiated her self worth to those around her. Even with the incident last night, she still sat straight and solid at her table. She was only teary eyed because of her gratitude, not because of what had happened. To be on the receiving end of that honest, pure emotion made Drake feel about two inches tall.

She was no longer the small, gangly, uncertain daughter of his accountant. She was no longer the teenager that followed him around with huge, innocent green eyes. She was a woman. She was capable, strong, and beautiful, but most of all, the innocence, the purity, and that unknown sparkle in her eyes were still there. Her progression from young lady to full blown woman hadn't changed her. Drake admired that.

He was still extremely glad that he had arrived when he did last night, but that didn't mean that he didn't think she couldn't have gotten her way out of that situation. When Nadia wanted something, she was damn determined. He would never put anything past her.

"Thank you, again. I will never be able to repay you." Her voice was slightly scratchy and hoarse but Drake latched onto the word 'repay' and turned it over and over in his mind.

"You're welcome," he told her, but in his mind he thought of ways he could get her to repay him. And he knew all of them would shock her silly. Immediately, he blocked those thoughts. Nadia should never feel as if she had to repay him for anything, especially with something like this.

Drake shook those thoughts from his mind. This was still Nadia, the same Nadia that he had watched over from a distance for years. And even though he knew she found him attractive and desirable, that didn't mean that he was going to give in and start seducing her with the intent of sex.

You just keep reminding yourself of what and who you are, your past with women that get too close, and what Nadia would think if she knew the real you. That should stall any thoughts of lust at once.

Turning, Drake went back to the counter and stared out the window.

Listen to that voice in your head. You know its right.

Yeah, but the bad thing was that Drake knew that if he allowed it, Nadia would turn out to be much more than just sex. And there was no way that he could allow her to twist herself into his life and heart.

***

By Tuesday of the next week Nadia had finished up with the police reports and restraining orders, much to Drake's enjoyment. If she had to hear from him one more time about the pros of a restraining order, she would lose her mind. She knew it had to be done, so she'd done it. Of course the nightmarish scene from the street had played out in her mind since then, so that had also given her some incentive to get the order immediately.

"Girl, have some more dessert," Renee's voice slipped in under Nadia's radar and snapped her back to the present. She was having dinner at Renee's house, and Renee was doing everything she could to fish out details from the night of the incident.

"I honestly don't think I could eat anything else," she told Renee as she placed her empty plate in the sink and turned to catch the frown on the redhead's face.

"I can't ever remember you turning down another serving of my 'better than sex cake.' Now I *know* you are still feeling ill effects from last weekend." Renee gave her a small smile and poured her another glass of wine. "C'mon, come sit back down and tell me how Mr. Drake Thompson made everything all better." She gave Nadia a salacious wink as she said that and moved towards her living room, pulling Nadia along with her.

Plopping down in a deep, soft loveseat Nadia tried to evade Renee and her questions, but she knew it was a foregone thing. "He did what he had to do to secure the situation and then he made sure I felt okay before leaving me alone." Nadia listened to herself explain the rescue in some clinical way, but all she really remembered was the smooth, almost unhurried way that Drake had disposed of Donavan.

Her mind had remembered other things hours and days later, like the strong current that had slipped in and around her body when Drake had interfered. Another odd thing was the growling noise she heard. It had sounded like an animal, something wild and thoroughly upset. Her dream image of the man with the bright eyes popped up in her mind immediately.

"He stayed with you overnight?" Renee gushed. "You are one lucky, lucky woman."

Nadia rolled her eyes. "He was only making sure I was okay. It wasn't as if he had ulterior motives for coming to my house, Renee."

"Honey, when a man like him comes to your house, you make him find ulterior motives." Blue eyes full of friendship peered at Nadia. "If you care for him as much as you say you do why don't you make a move? I honestly don't think he will toss you away if he knows how you feel."

Nadia had told Renee about Drake and how she felt for him just two days ago, right after the incident with Donavan. Since she had been on medication for anxiety, she chocked that up as an excuse for letting her secretary know her personal business. If she was being honest with herself though, it was like a load off of her chest to be able to share the news with another woman, one that she considered a friend.

She shook her head and took another cold sip of wine. "I wouldn't waste my time on him."

Renee reared back in shock. "Waste your time? Honey, have you really taken a good look at the man? Dear God, he's beyond delicious, and he is settled. He has his own business; he has money. I could go on and on."

Nadia nodded, "I know."

"Then why are you so broken up about it? I have never known you to be so determined to ignore something that I know you want. I can name numerous times in the past where you have been like a bulldog with something that you wanted badly for your magazines or your charity work."

Nadia sat there listening to Renee, knowing what she said was true, but also knowing Renee would never understand her viewpoint. Renee was a go getter with men, like Nadia was with business. With her upfront, in your face sexuality, Renee was someone that Nadia wished she could be like when it came to a masculine God like Drake. Unfortunately, she knew that would never happen. She was wired differently.

"Let's get something straight right now. I will never be a forceful, sexual go getter. And even if I were, I'm not attracted to anyone like I am to Drake." Nadia brought up a finger to make a point. "And, I'm repeating myself here, but like I said, he would never want me like that."

Renee's face was priceless.

"Honey, he is a red blooded man. Scratch that, he is a red blooded *Texas* man. You blink at him the right way, and I guarantee that he would crawl over cut glass for you."

"Yeah, right, not when he has every woman in five states clamoring after him. It is sickening."

Renee slapped her on the shoulder. "Wake the hell up girl! You are a successful, beautiful, and caring woman. Drake knows this. All you have to do is make him realize that you are up for anything he throws at you."

Nadia rubbed her aching bicep and sent Renee a glare. "Those are nice words, but I know for a fact he doesn't want me like that because it came straight from his mouth."

Now Renee looked really confused. "But I don't see why he wouldn't want you. There is nothing about you that is repulsive. Any guy would be lucky to have you." Renee shook her head. "I just don't get it."

Neither did Nadia. And she had learned it from the horse's mouth, so to speak. She hadn't wanted to believe him, but her young heart had shattered with his words and after that she had never tried to push her feelings or desires onto him. It had taken her months to even think about the conversation without breaking down in tears.

"He picked me up for a dinner date on my seventeenth birthday." Nadia blinked back stupid teenage emotions. "Of course being the naïve and idealistic young girl that I was, I expected something that I never would get. What I got was Drake with a supermodel of his and my night turned crappy from there on. At the end of the dinner date I listened with half an ear to Drake telling Ms. Skinny that her notions of my adolescent crush were unfounded. He managed in mere words to tear down any illusions that I had right then and there."

Blue eyes gave her a long look. "Nadia, that was when you were seventeen. It has nothing to do with now. Surely you realize that."

She just shook her head and remembered the pain from that night. She had primped and planned, strategized to get her look just right, and inside she knew that it was all for nothing. He was an older man and she was a teenager. What would she have done for him? But it hadn't stopped her and by the end of the night she had learned her lesson the hard way. She could still hear his deep voice in her head.

"Chantal, she is just a teenager."

"But Drake I can practically feel her stripping you down in her mind whenever you aren't looking."

"Don't be absurd. She is a child who is lost and looking for someone's help. Besides, if there is anyone that I would be attracted to it would be a certain beautiful blonde, not some skinny, small little woman child. She is like family to me, Chantal. I could never want her like that."

The remembered words tore a fresh wound into Nadia. She could never make Renee understand just how hurt she had been by those offhand words. This was her burden to bear. She would keep those spiteful words and their meaning locked up tight inside her where they would never harm her again. She would move past this, just like she had moved past everything else in life that hurt her.

***

"Tell me that you are joking," Renee said Thursday afternoon as they sat in Nadia's office going over the guest list for the gala event in Dallas that would take place one week from Saturday. The month of June was always busy.

"I'm telling you exactly what I heard from Donavan's secretary." Thank God Natalie was a soft hearted woman; otherwise, Nadia would have found out herself that Donavan planned on going to the gala event even as he knew she would be there. Nadia drew comfort knowing that he couldn't come within 100 feet of her. But still, something inside of her rankled; she didn't trust him one bit.

"That son of a bitch is doing this just to scare you. That's all," Renee said with assurance.

"Well, he is doing a bang up job about it," Nadia muttered, being honest.

"Ah honey, don't worry, you always have security at events like these and this gala has been one of your babies from the get go. Don't you dare let scum like Donavan ruin that, and," Renee's eyebrows rose with implication, "you still have that restraining order."

"I won't, believe me, but I'll just have to put on a brave front and not let his attendance bother me," She said as she moved some paperwork around her desk. "And like you said, there still is the restraining order." Finding what she was looking for, she waved the paper around like the winner of a contest. Then she caught the mischievous look on Renee's face.

"Whatever you are thinking of, stop it right now. I know that look and it is nothing but trouble."

Renee's blue eyes turned positively radiant. "Honey, I have figured out your solution."

"Whatever it is, I'm sure it is bad for me."

Renee's pretty mouth turned down in a pout. "Now, why would you say that?

"Only because your mind is devious and I don't want it to land me in hot water." Nadia spoke truthfully and waited with baited breath to see what her secretary had to say.

"The answer to your problems is right under your nose, literally." Renee pointed down.

Nadia glanced down, looking at the papers on her desk, seeing nothing that stood out. Until her gaze snagged on the card that had come with the flowers Drake had delivered weeks ago. She felt a very feminine, very wicked thrill move through her body.

"No."

"How did I know you were going to say that?" Renee muttered, not to happily.

"Because you know it won't work. Why would I put myself through that just for some form of protection?"

"Because he is like a bull in full rut whenever you are around. He cares about your wellbeing enough to spend the night in your home to make sure you are okay. He rescued your ass from the specific guy that will be in attendance that same night." Renee's blue eyes sparkled deviously and Nadia wanted to smack her. "There are many other reasons. One of them is that you have loved him for forever, he will be within touching distance at all times, you could just reach out…"

"Stop, this is insane. I can't just make Drake tag along to something like this for my protection."

"Why not? He is on the attendance list, isn't he?"

Nadia shut up at that. He was in fact on the list. Matter of fact, he had already RSVP'd her to let her know he was going.

"He already RSVP'd. That means he probably has a date already," She told Renee with a sulky voice. God, was that her speaking like that? Sounding like a two year old whose toy had been taken away?

"Honey, you won't know until you call, will you?"

Damn her for being right. "But I still have the order."

"Girl, you think after what Donavan already had the balls to do to you, that he would stop with some little order? I know we both hope that, but be realistic. The man is nuts. And, if Drake tags along as your date, you know you would be protected from anything that might happen."

Nadia sat there and contemplated what Renee was saying. The bad thing was every word from her friend's mouth made complete sense.

Chapter 10

You are ten times a fool.

Well, of course she was, which was why she was here, walking up Drake's front walk at eight thirty at night, on a Friday night of all things. But his truck was parked in the drive.

She had called repeatedly, both his office and his cell, and he hadn't answered neither. He had told her weeks ago that he had his calls rolled over so that he could pick them up anywhere, but he hadn't answered at any of those locations. And Nadia knew if she didn't get an answer for her specific question tonight, then she just might go crazy.

I can't believe that I'm actually doing this.

Things could always be worse, but for Nadia this ranked pretty low on the list. She never imagined she would be basically reduced to begging Drake for his help. Hell, there were plenty of other guys out there that would bring her, keep her company and such, but Nadia knew Drake could handle Donavan if he got out of line. Right now that was all that mattered-keeping Donavan and his slimy hands off of her.

His front door was unlocked, and Nadia knocked three times before going in. The looming entrance was massive with open beamed ceilings and rustic ambiance.

The quiet of the large house closed in on her and immediately Nadia had a horrible thought.

What if he has a woman here?

Shit. There was no way she was going to barge in on that. Standing there Nadia had a wavering moment. Should she turn around and leave immediately or should she take fate in her hands and look for Drake, ask him what she needed to ask, and get things over with? The option was taken from her when she heard a low, barely audible click-clack on the hardwood floors.

Ah damn, he does have a woman here.

Feeling about as low as she could feel, Nadia turned towards the sound that was coming from a hallway off to the side of the kitchen. What she saw crystallized the breath in her lungs. There was no woman in high heels standing there, shooting daggers at her. Instead there was a very large, very menacing looking, pure black German shepherd. Liquid black eyes categorized every muscle on Nadia's frame. And she made damn sure that she didn't move too fast as she slowly started to inch towards the front door behind her.

"Pretty doggy, you stay right where you are and I'll leave and we can just act like I was never here, okay?"

The massive animal just stared at her with intelligent, all knowing eyes, and Nadia felt stupid for talking to it in such a sing song voice. It was apparent the animal was extremely smart.

"Nadia?"

The questioning voice snapped her out of the trance she was under with the dog and she turned.

Drake stood under an arch that lead to what Nadia assumed were bedrooms. His massive body was nude except for one lone towel, dark blue in color, draped seductively low around those hard hips of his. Nadia's mouth dried to dust. She couldn't even form coherent words. Her eyes were glued to his body. She realized this was as close to heaven as she would ever get. Her fingertips started to tingle.

Large slabs of muscle delineated his chest area where a smattering of dark hair formed a triangle, then moved down in one tiny little line towards the towel, disappearing there. His arms were at his sides but even in rest, Nadia could see tendons roping under hard skin and the beautiful liquid movement of muscle when he propped one arm on his hip. When that arm moved she caught the dark edge of something hiding beneath his towel. Her eyes narrowed and she realized it was the beginning of a tattoo. Her shocked eyes slammed back to his.

He wasn't smiling. Matter of fact, he looked pissed off. Nadia immediately started talking.

"Um...sorry, I wasn't trying to interfere with whatever...um...I need a favor from...no...I need to ask a favor of you. That is if you aren't busy being naked...Oh God, I mean busy making other plans with another woman...Just let me stop talking." Nadia took a deep breath before letting her eyes come back to Drake's face. Now he was smiling. Of course, she had just made an ass of herself. She watched as he sauntered closer and tucked the towel a bit more while he did so, his crooked smile on his face the whole time, the wretch. The massive dog trailed behind him.

One hand gestured towards the huge dog by his side, "This is Lila, sorry if she startled you. She is nothing but a big puppy." Then he looked directly at her again. "Why don't you take a deep breath, start from the beginning, and then try again." His eyes sparkled at her in humor. She didn't find any of this the least bit humorous.

"I need a date for the Dallas Black Tie gala." Her eyes landed on his face only this time, while she licked her lips. "And I need it to be you." There, it was out. Nadia pressed her hand against her abdomen and she could feel her heart fluttering in nervousness. She looked down to where her creased trousers met her peep toe shoes. The bright red shoes were her one concession to shocking footwear. Her wild side rarely came out. Standing in Drake Thompson's house, asking him, basically, on a date, was something she never thought she would do in a million years. Apparently her wild side was calling the shots now.

Rubbing her hands nervously on her hips, Nadia glanced back up and caught the piercing look that Drake was giving her. He walked over to where she was still standing at the entrance to the foyer. Within seconds he was close enough for Nadia to smell the clean, woodsy soap he had used, and she could see water droplets sliding from the ends of his hair onto his shoulders. She balled her fingers into fists as he propped his hip against the back of a tall, decorative table behind his sofa.

"Usually, when a woman asks me out on a date she looks a bit more interested than you do at the moment." His hands came to either side of his hips on the table and Nadia could see the strength in his arms and shoulders undulate beneath his skin.

"It technically wouldn't be a date." How she was able to form those words, she had no idea. Her mouth was as dry as the Sahara at the moment. It seemed every drop of moisture in her body had pooled south.

Oh, don't think about that certain part of your anatomy. The one that is pulsing, clenching, and basically screaming at you to do anything, something, to get your hands on this man.

Nadia blinked, trying to focus on why she was here.

"Darlin,' it would be a date if I accompany you there and stay by your side the whole evening." He wasn't smiling, but Nadia had the feeling that he wanted to. Those eyes of his said enough for him not to.

"The only reason I need you, specifically, is because I have it on good authority that Donavan will be attending. Now I know I have the restraining order but..." She glanced around, trying to look anywhere besides at Drake. She didn't want to come out and say that she felt safe under his watch. Although that was exactly what she *would* have to say if she wanted his help. "I feel...no, I *would* feel safer if you were there with me."

His face was hard and showed no emotion, but she knew he was upset to know that Donavan would be going. Eyes that could be so warm with humor were now as hard as diamonds. "Of course I will go with you, especially now that I know for a fact he will be showing up also."

"What about your date? Won't she be upset?" Jealousy burned in her gut, but she needed to know if he had planned for someone to come with him.

"She'll get over it. Right now you need me more."

You need me more.

Such a smooth talker he was, but she knew from the determined look on his face that he meant every single word.

"Ah…good, thanks, so I need to leave out the day before to make sure things are going according to plan, since my company is heading this gala." Nadia kept her gaze resolutely right over his shoulder. She wasn't too sure if she could handle looking him in the eyes right now. "My flight is scheduled for eight on Friday morning and…"

"Cancel it."

Her gaze flew to his. "Excuse me?"

He shrugged his shoulders. "Cancel it. I have a private plane. We can use that so we can both go at the same time. More convenient that way, don't you think?"

"Um…sure, I guess." Oh God, this was totally getting out of hand. "I can do that. Do you think we can still leave at the scheduled time?"

"I can inform my pilot and he will schedule accordingly." Strong, hard arms wrapped around each other in front of his huge chest.

"Okay," She mumbled. This was all starting to feel a bit surreal and totally out of her control. "I'm staying at my usual, the Coventry Condos Villa. I can call and see if they have another opening for you. Unless you stay somewhere else whenever you head up there?"

"You can cancel that too, if you want. I have my private condo downtown, not too far from the ballroom where the gala will be." Caramel eyes sparkled at some private joke. "Unless you would feel safer across town, far away from me and ten minutes out of the way from police, should you need them."

Lila chose that moment to sniff at Nadia's fingers. Since she was in such a daze from the turnaround that the past ten minutes had given her, she barely noticed the dog's attention. Just how could she turn down that offer when it made so much sense? And he knew it, the wretch. He knew he could get her with that last statement, offering her protection and safety basically on a silver platter, holding it right there, under her nose.

"I'll think about that." Oh and she would, but it would be for totally different reasons.

"I'm not trying to bulldoze you darlin,' but you need to realize that Donavan is not what you thought. I'm not saying he's going to try anything, but wouldn't you feel more secure if you were with someone you knew, and not by yourself across town if he did try something stupid?"

She listened and realized he was telling the truth. She honestly didn't think Donavan would do anything, but how did she know for sure? Look at what he had done when she had thought she'd known him.

"You're right," she fiddled with her purse strap. "Okay…whatever." Damn, she felt so lost. What in the hell was she doing? She was putting herself in a load of trouble.

"Good, everything's gonna be fine, you'll see. At least this way I can watch you without having to worry about you being so far away with no protection."

She really wished he wouldn't say things like that. Nodding absently she studied the fine grain on his wood floors.

"I need to go. But thanks for agreeing with me on this." She told him, finally able to look him in the eyes, before tearing her gaze away and turning back for the door. Her fingers closed around the metal handle when she felt his hand come up to her shoulder.

Please don't touch me. You'll only make things worse, so much worse.

He turned her and immediately pulled her into a hug. Her body was small, so very small against his, and she only came up to his upper chest. All the sexual tension she had been feeling for the past ten minutes faded as he gave her a comforting hug, one that meant to console, not arouse. Nadia blinked back tears as his hands caressed her upper back. So much strength in his hands, and never once did he move to an area that he shouldn't touch. He stayed perfectly proper, and her heart all but melted when he spoke deeply above her head.

"I'm glad that you came to me with this, you hear?" His mouth nuzzled the top of her head and Nadia felt faint. "Don't ever assume that I won't drop everything to help you."

Tears slipped out from beneath her closed eyes and she nodded. Her fingers were clasped around his hard upper arms and his skin was scorching hot, but to Nadia it felt like home, like somewhere that she had been searching for, for a long, long time.

"Things will get better and regardless of Donavan being there or not, you will have a good time next week. I won't allow it to be otherwise." He gave her crown a gentle kiss then pulled away and opened the door wider. "Goodnight, angel…call me when you get home, kay?" His hands moved her hair away from her face, tucking it behind her ears as he gave her a gentle, killing smile.

Nadia nodded, not knowing what to say in return, and walked out the door.

**

Was he trying to kill himself? Did he really have to make things, or parts of his anatomy, any harder than they should be?

Drake shook his head and let Lila out to do her business in the backyard. She belonged to Alana, a fellow Druid. He was only watching her for the weekend while Alana had business to deal with in Houston.

Thinking back to Nadia, he wondered just exactly what good could come from what he had done. He had practically invited her to spend the night with him, *in his condo*, in Dallas. Not to mention he would be around her *all night* long at the gala, because there was no way in hell that Donavan would get within those 100 feet that he shouldn't be in at all, not while Drake had anything to say about it.

At first he hadn't believed his eyes when he saw her standing in his foyer. He had heard her come in, but he hadn't known who it had been. If he had, he might have put some clothes on first. Then he remembered the awed look on her face. Nah, if he had a chance to do it over again, he would do it the exact same way. The look on her face had been priceless.

She had been flustered beyond all reason. Her speech and mannerisms had given her away. Drake couldn't make his body frame smaller than what it was, and he doubted she was actually afraid of him anyway, but he sensed that his largeness had something to do with her anxiety. But the vitals she had shown him in those few minutes were very telling. Blood had pulsed low in her body. He could almost *feel* the clench of feminine muscles, and taste the sexual excitement boiling in her blood. Yeah, there was no doubt in his mind that she was attracted to him, deathly so. God, he didn't need that, not tonight. He would go to sleep tonight with the look of her imprinted on his brain. Prim, tailored pantsuit, crisp red undershirt peeping out from beneath the starched edges of the lapels, bright red high heeled shoes had almost given him a heart attack. Those sexy, red pumps had given him a small glimpse into Nadia's head and he knew she had a sensual, wild side hidden deep inside somewhere. Dear God, he wanted to be the man that made it come out, with a vengeance.

His fangs pricking his lower lip, Drake growled, but knew he had to stop these images from bombarding him. But he couldn't, he couldn't stop from seeing Nadia standing there so primly in his home, long black hair falling past her shoulders, light green eyes huge in her face as if shocked by the way she was responding to him. He couldn't stop from imagining his hands pulling the clothes from her body and showing her how good it could be between them.

No, don't do this to yourself Thompson! She can't be yours. Remember Marie, remember what happened. Don't fall into that tailspin again.

Of course, he knew better. But the lines between Nadia and him were starting to blur a bit, and he wasn't so sure he could stop himself from doing something delicious and utterly forbidden to her if he had the chance.

His phone buzzed with an incoming call, knocking him back to the present.

"Thompson here."

"Drake, just wanted to let you know I made it home," Nadia said, her breath coming fast against the phone. Drake wondered just what she had done, or was doing, that was causing that to happen.

"Good, and what we talked about earlier, if there is anything that you aren't comfortable with, don't hesitate to tell me, okay?"

Don't cancel, don't cancel, I want you with me.

"No, the plans are fine. I was just acting childish. The situation warrants a smart decision and there's no reason why I can't stay with you."

"I will do everything in my power to keep you safe, darlin'."

She sighed. "I know. It's just that I never expected you to become so easily involved in my life."

There was a quiet moment where Drake could almost taste her hesitancy, her wariness in the conversation they were having. He needed to keep her upbeat and keep her on the phone. The last thing she needed to do was to get worried over something that he would control completely.

"Lately we've been having some really good conversations. So it's almost as if we are salvaging our friendship, wouldn't you say?"

She laughed lightly. Drake felt himself beam like a 100 watt bulb.

"If that's the question, cowboy, you owe me an answer for your first crush."

Drake smiled, "I believe her name was Marianne, but that could be the dementia talking."

A full out, low contralto laugh came over the phone. Drake settled himself onto his bed and imagined Nadia here with him instead of over the phone, miles away.

"Touche! Touché! I get it now. No more jokes about you're failing health."

"Damn right, I get touchy on that subject, woman."

She laughed again, and once more Drake felt as if he could move mountains.

"So, this might be catching on, don't you think?"

"What's that?" She asked, after Drake heard her take a breath.

"Our conversations that take place over the phone, late at night…while we're both in bed." Drake smiled, but knew he had caught her off guard a bit. And if there was one thing Nadia hated, it was being off guard.

She cleared her throat, "I don't mind if you don't."

Well, well, well. He hadn't been expecting her to say that. Drake placed his phone in between his shoulder and the pillow, and got more comfortable on his huge bed. "Honey, we could talk about the weather, and I wouldn't mind one bit."

"I could handle the weather, but I would have to draw the line at current events. With you being a business man and all, I wouldn't want to have to debate you on the merits of cutting Medicare, or hear you wax on and on about reforming our health care in this country."

Drake laughed out loud. Leave it to Nadia to give him something to smile about when he was tied up in knots of lust over her.

After finally catching his breath, he said, "So, if you've taken all of that off the agenda, it leaves us with a few things."

"I would say we don't have much left." She countered.

Drake smiled, "Honey, there's always something to talk about, especially between you and me."

Quiet rang over the line, and Drake could have sworn that he heard a whispered, "damn" from her end.

"There is actually one thing I would like to know," She asked, catching him unawares.

"What would that be?"

"What is your tattoo?"

Drake chuckled, amused that she had noticed it, and loving that she was interested. "Damn, you have some sharp little eyes, don't you? It's a cross, but with some tribal artwork surrounding it." He made a disbelieving sound. "I can't believe you were able to see it, I didn't think my towel was that low."

"Oh, did it hurt?"

"Nah, not really." Then being the devilish man that he knew rumors made him out to be, he said, "Remind me, and next time you can see the whole thing, up close and personal."

"I might just hold you to that."

Drake's breath lodged in his throat. "Don't make false promises."

Another shuddering sigh, then quiet came over the line. Drake was just thinking he might have gone too far and then she spoke, her words catching him in the gut.

"God, you do this so easily…"

"What's that?"

Silence echoed back to him. Ah, now she was turning shy. Drake mentally shrugged; he would bring her back to the conversation in whatever way he could. It was past time for her to know just how sexy he found her.

"I believe I know what you are trying to say, angel."

"Really?" Her voice sounded harsh, unused, gruff to his ears.

"Yes, and I burn for you too."

***

Damn, Nadia was sure her ears were on fire, not just her whole body. The heat between her legs was hot enough to power her electricity for the next month. She tightened her thighs, hoping to still the pulse of blood down below, but it didn't help. Actually, it made it worse. A sigh escaped her mouth unwillingly, and Nadia tried to move the phone away before her desires became known. It didn't work.

"Ah honey, I'm sorry. I didn't mean to get you like this. But I love knowing that you are feeling just as excited as I am right now."

Something in his voice told Nadia that he was lying. He wanted her exactly the way she was right now, worked up, with no way of getting around it. Confusion swamped her. He had done a complete turn-around. But she had no idea if he'd had these feelings all along. Was he really attracted to her, or was he just giving into what she wanted so badly?

Are you seriously questioning this, Nadia?

The minutes she had spent in his house, seeing him in that towel, wishing she could lick every inch of his skin swept through her, tightening places on her body that throbbed with awareness. She could just imagine his voice coming over the line, asking her to touch herself, to please herself from his words alone.

That thought spurred her to say, "I have no idea what you are talking about."

God, she sounded so damn prim and uptight, even to herself, even though after this conversation her body was leagues ahead of her mind in the arousal department.

He didn't chuckle this time. His voice was deep, dark and dangerously sexy. "Honey, damn…I could help you through it, if you want me to… I can't believe I'm saying this but…"

"No"

He instantly stopped talking at her statement.

What is wrong with you? Do you have any brains in your head?

Nadia ignored that. What was going on right now was amazing, but she couldn't handle it all at once. It was almost too sexual, too intense, and she didn't want to embarrass herself on the phone with Drake. And, he still hadn't said anything.

"I'm sorry…I have to go…I'll call you soon."

Like the coward she was, she hung up the phone, not giving him a chance to say anything. Silence burned across her bedroom while her body burned, period.

Chapter 11

Nadia peered into the mirror with a discriminating eye.

She had to leave in ten minutes to meet Drake so that they could leave for Dallas. She tsked and pulled on the lightweight khaki jacket. The cut and color were good on her, but she wasn't sure if she wanted to wear it or not.

She wanted to be businesslike and comfortable, since she would be running between the kitchens. A makeshift office had been set up around the ballroom somewhere, while at the same time she would be giving Derek, her Houston director, enough orders to make him dizzy. Comfortable was winning at the moment.

Would anyone really care if you wore jeans? Would the world come to an end?

No, it wouldn't, she conceded as she stared at a *very* comfortable looking pair of jeans.

Ten minutes later she was pulling away from her driveway and trying to calm her ragged nerves. At least she was wearing comfy jeans.

Their phone conversation from the week before was still affecting her now. She wasn't sure if she would be able to go through with this. It wasn't as if he was just some guy that she wanted to have a good time with. This was Drake, the man that had captured her attention and her heart at a young age. He had been the first man to make her feel desire. The nearness of his body caused hers to come alive, as if from his touch alone, her senses went into overload. She would never feel this way for another man. She knew it with a determination that astounded her, which was why every conversation, every glance from those beautiful eyes of his, was a bittersweet pill to swallow.

And now she had something new to worry about.

The conversation had turned deliciously naughty the other night. Some of the things he had said had shocked Nadia speechless. Sure, she had been flirted with before, but when Drake was the one doing the honors, her body flared to life at the mere thought of what he might say, and she wouldn't stand a chance. What really surprised her was that after all this time she had been under the assumption that he didn't find her attractive. Needless to say their conversation had opened her eyes.

Nadia parked the Rover beside a few vehicles and one low slung, very expensive sports car at the private airstrip that Drake had told her to meet him at. Minutes later, holding her two travel bags and her laptop, she was heading towards a metal hangar where a few men were milling around a small plane.

One of the men, a handsome, sandy haired guy stepped away from the group and came up to her. When he got closer he smiled brightly and said, "Let me take those for you, ma'am."

"Thank you so much, Mr.--?" Nadia asked as she handed over her bags.

"Brian Leigh." Blue eyes twinkled. "You can call me Bri, everyone does." He gave her a jaunty wink.

Nadia smiled, instantly at ease with his blatant flirting. This she could handle. He was like an overgrown puppy. "Thanks again, Brian." Nadia stuck out her hand but then she remembered he was full of her bags at the moment. Pulling her hand back she told him, "I'm Nadia."

He flashed another bright smile, "I know."

She wanted to question that but kept her mouth shut as she realized Drake must have told them to expect her this morning. "Apparently my reputation precedes me."

"You have no idea." He told her, then turned back to go towards the plane. "C'mon Nadia, we're about to leave."

Now she really wanted to know just how much this guy knew about her.

***

Monster, magic man, yellow-eyed demon, and warrior of spells…the list went on and on.

Drake had heard every name used to describe what he was. The real truth behind it was an ancient spell that had been cast among a group of Druids practicing their potions and spells before 'witch' was even a word. The ancients were smart, diabolical humans with unique abilities to heal or frighten off other wary ones such as themselves. They kept their secrets very secret and in turn no one could have imagined what would occur. Now, centuries later, their descendants lived among humans, sharing their lives, their families, and their world.

Drake downed the cold soda he was drinking and grinned as Nadia's long legs ate up the distance between her truck and the plane. She followed resolutely behind Brian with a smile on her face. As he looked at her a highly erotic thrill moved through his body. She was the only woman he knew that could make him react like a randy teenage boy, which was something he hadn't been in a very long time.

She made him feel almost human again. He had come to terms with what he was long ago. Now here was a human woman that made him want to hide his gifts from her. He wanted her to want him as if he were normal. Yeah, he was seriously losing his mind.

Long black hair was loose, thank God, flowing down her shoulders where wisps at the end touched her lower back. Her eyes were covered with chic dark sunglasses. She had dressed comfortable today, which surprised him. He was used to seeing her in nothing but suits and dresses. A *very* nice looking pair of jeans clasped her legs and her hips, making Drake's fingers itch to grab and mold to her small frame. Her shirt was frilly, feminine, and buttoned all the way up. Each tiny little button begged Drake from across the tarmac to rip the offending material off and lick every inch of her pale, beautiful skin. His tongue, gums, and teeth heated in response. If he let it, the slide of his fangs would be complete in seconds, so would his other Druid abilities.

Fuck. This was not what he wanted.

Whatever, you keep telling yourself that buddy, while your body knows the whole truth.

Drake blinked, pushing the burn of his amber eyes back to where he could breathe easier knowing they wouldn't pop out in a moment's notice.

Seconds later Brian and Nadia waltzed right up to him beside the plane.

Seeing Nadia from far away was nothing compared to seeing her up close. Her forehead was creased and Drake sensed the nervous energy inside of her, along with the rapid movement of her blood. Pretty light green eyes studied him for mere seconds before she turned and thanked Brian once again, her soft voice a sensuous slide against Drake's ears.

"I've got it now Bri, thanks for getting everything ready. Go ahead and get on in. I'll get Nadia settled." Drake told Brian as he took Nadia's bags and stowed them away.

He turned back to her, smiled his charming smile and held out his hand, "C'mon darlin', otherwise we'll be late."

Her face was a picture of non-expression, but Drake didn't need to read mannerisms to know how she felt. The nervous energy from moments ago had heightened and now a pretty flush rested on her cheeks.

She ignored his hand, from what he sensed was cautiousness, not her wanting to be rude, and walked up the lowered steps to enter the plane. She was skittish and totally closed off from him. He knew it had to do with their talk from last week. Never before had he hinted at any attraction to her and in one phone call, he had blasted her with not only that truth, but the knowledge that he was burning up sexually for her also.

Drake sensed that he would be apologizing for their conversation pretty soon; otherwise, Nadia would never smile at him again.

***

*Talk about things that don't have to do with the way his jeans fit him so well, or the way the sunlight had glinted off of his tiger eyes. Don't concern yourself with thoughts of that phone call last week or the naughty things he **could** have said to you on that phone.*

Nadia glanced around at the more than spacious and luxurious interior that she had stepped into. She had heard him say private plane, but she hadn't been expecting this. This was sumptuous leather, rich wood accents, and generous space. This plane was a beautiful and costly expression of Drake and what kind of life he led. He wasn't only the owner and proprietor of an animal shelter/vet office. He was a ruthless businessman and investment guru. He probably had the ear and favor of more than a few Wall Street icons.

"With the way you're staring at it, I assume you must be pretty thirsty?" Drake's voice knocked her back to the present, and Nadia noticed a young, dark haired woman offering her a drink. She thanked her and took the cold water bottle.

"I'm admiring your plane. I wasn't planning on seeing such an opulent affair." She took a sip of her water and congratulated herself on not spitting out, *'I wish I wouldn't have hung up the phone the other night. I wish I would have let you keep talking. I wonder now what would have happened, what would have been said.'* She shut her mind off.

"Darlin,' this is a G500, a very nice plane, not to mention, mine." His eyes held humor, but a spark shone in those caramel depths. "I'm a very private man, and I don't like sharing my personal space with other people." Those eyes burned along her length and Nadia controlled a tremble. "But right now, I'm not minding the intrusion one bit."

"Your privacy is obviously something that you pay exorbitantly to insure," She told him as she took another sip of water and watched him over the edge of the bottle. Brilliantly beautiful eyes catalogued her every feature while she took in his jeans and the soft, dark colored tee shirt that covered his large frame.

"Money is no object if something is important to me."

Apparently not, Nadia thought as she turned her head and watched the flat low land rush by as the plane taxied down the runway. It obviously wouldn't take them long to get to Dallas, since he had this very nice plane. Thank God she had turned; she could feel his eyes lingering on her and she knew he was going to bring up their phone conversation, knew it like she knew the burn of desire in her gut would never go away.

"Angel, I'm sorry about the other night," his gruff voice begged her to turn back around. Her eyes slid back to his. "I know we have known each other for a long while now, but what I said slipped out. For a minute there, I forgot I was talking to you, my past employee's child, instead you were a beautiful woman…" He stopped talking and Nadia was kept in limbo, wanting to hear what else he had to say…but she couldn't allow him to keep going. She had to stop this now.

"Apology accepted." She let her eyes stay on his. "I guess we both thought of things we shouldn't have." Then she turned back and tried to ignore the warning in her gut that was screaming at her that this wasn't over yet.

He chuckled deeply from the other side of the plane and Nadia bristled. "Thinking is sometimes just as bad as doing."

The condensation on the water bottle pooled into her hand, jarring her back into reality. She knew better than to get herself worked up over a few things he had said on the phone. Just because they had spoken with such erotic intent didn't mean that she should let her shield fall and do whatever she wanted with him.

That was like inviting the Devil over for supper. You knew you shouldn't do it, but boy were you tempted. And no matter how much Nadia wanted, yearned, and ached for Drake, she knew in her heart that she would be deathly hurt if his flirting was something that he was using just to try and get a reaction out of her with. If she ever got a chance with him, her whole heart would be tangled up in whatever they were doing. It would knock her blindsided if his intentions changed and he left her hanging on by a mere thread, trying to pull him back to her with all she had. She would never be that woman-that woman that was left broken and bleeding while the man she loved waltzed away without a care in the world.

The chirp of Drake's cell pierced the silence of the cabin. He answered the call.

His deep drawl was short, precise, and pure business. Long fingers held the cell to his ear while his other hand grabbed a sheaf of papers that was sitting in front of him on a small desktop. Within minutes he and the other person were speaking of contract terms and disputes while Nadia studied him. The no nonsense businessman that she knew was back. There were no hints of a seductively naughty crooked grin, no hooded glances from under long black lashes. This was Drake at his most ruthless. He had always seemed faultless and slick when it came to the world that she had entered only a few years before. Nadia envied his smooth, unruffled approach.

She, on the other hand, had to build up her energy for monthly board meetings and group events. She loved her job, but it had taken determination and drive to succeed in something that she hadn't been prepared for. She liked to think that she had done a decent job of it. With the ratings out every month on magazine sales that showed a steady uphill climb, and retail sales of her boutiques topping what they had made in previous years, she came to the conclusion that whatever she was doing was more than enough. The small town girl that had been born into a working middle class family was now running a top company and keeping it afloat. That was success to her. That was what her life was now.

She looked at Drake and took in his massive frame. Long ago she had come to terms with her feelings for this man. The phone conversation from the other night slipped into her mind, but Nadia ruthlessly pushed it away. It didn't matter if he had only been playing with her or truly flirting, the truth was that she would probably never know. Nadia looked away and out the window. She told herself to be happy that she was allowed this close to him, that he considered her a friend or even someone as close as family.

She told herself this but that small, young and impressionable sixteen year old that had fallen in love with him still lived inside her, and she knew better.

***

After arriving in Dallas, Drake and Nadia made their way to his condo. The morning was hot and stifling, but the air conditioning in his condo was blessedly on and cooling the huge area, as per his instructions.

The large space was comfy and inviting. It should be. He had spent lots of time and money to get the look just right. The spaciousness and decor resembled that of his log house in Beaumont. He was sure that Nadia was comparing the two similar looks as she walked towards the extra room she would stay in.

The slow, sweet way that she walked drew his attention, and the punch of emotions that tried to tell him she was off limits was lost amongst the surge of raw, hot lust that permeated his body. She was a pocket Venus, darkly attractive and sweetly shy. The mix of innocence and a smoldering sensuality that he sensed hadn't been tapped yet burned under his radar. Drake wanted more than anything to give her everything that he sensed she wanted. It didn't matter if it was only one slow dance or something more; as of right now, at this moment, he had committed to being there for her.

"Thank you again for letting me stay."

Her soft, smooth voice snapped him out of his trance. "No problem. I would rather you be here anyway." She visibly shuddered as she placed her bags on the large bed. Donavan still managed to crawl into her mind every now and then. Drake knew she was worried about the other man.

"Now I see the wisdom in being here." She turned to him, her green eyes warm with a friendly light that sometimes she didn't let show. "I think we both know he won't try and mess with you. And even though I have that restraining order, I still feel safer with someone else around." The words 'with you' were there in what she said. Drake heard them loud and clear, even if she hadn't actually voiced them.

His mind brought up images of the night he had found Donavan pushing her against the vehicle. Battling down the rage building inside of him, he cooled his thoughts and focused on getting that man's name out of her vocabulary once and for all.

"From now on, he doesn't exist." Her eyes widened slightly then relaxed as she tried to show him no expression again. "That *man* was part of your life. You trusted him, you confided in him, and you did all of that because of me." Now shock stiffened her body. There was confusion in the green depths of her eyes and he knew he had truly surprised her by stating what he knew as fact.

"I realize now that you were trying to show me that you didn't need anything from me. You wanted to make it without my help, which I still don't understand why, but it doesn't matter anymore because all of that is in the past."

He slowly walked closer to her and stopped when he was near enough to grasp her hand in his. The coldness of her fingers shocked him, but he held on anyway. Not a whisper emerged from her lips.

"I don't know exactly what went on between you and Donavan, and more than likely it isn't my business, but as of right now…" Drake's fingers rubbed over her soft, cool ones and he looked deeply into her wide green eyes. Her emotions were rampant, her blood singing hotly through her veins, telling him that she felt something, he just wasn't exactly sure of what it was. "You are under my roof, and he isn't allowed between us." A slight jolt traveled through her system. "He will never…*ever* hurt you again. I will not allow it."

With a slight rub, he caressed the small, delicate fingers of her hand and leaned down, wrapping her body in a slight hug. She resisted, keeping her hands between their bodies, but her heart was pounding and he could hear the rush of her emotions, like a breeze along his body.

This woman was his and his alone. No man would cause her harm ever again. A wild, fierce protectiveness bloomed deep in his chest as he brushed his hand down the silk of her hair. It scared him, the way she had crawled under his skin so fast without even knowing it. Drake had never been able to turn her away. With the emotions sliding through his system now, he knew that he would do anything for her.

His chin settled right over the crown of her head and with the alignment of their bodies, Drake knew he had never felt anything so *right* before. Strands of her hair tickled his mouth and he knew he should move, right now, before other thoughts turned this moment into something much more than friendly.

"Go ahead and unpack your things. Whenever you need to head out for the ballroom to make sure things are running smooth, let me know."

He unwillingly released her and left the room without looking back. If he did that, he might just turn into something that she couldn't handle yet.

***

The annual Black Tie Gala was an all-star event. Held in Dallas, it catered to the fabulously elite and wealthy, but the rewards were enormous for charity. It was a good thing that the event was held at the Ritz-Carlton because the ballroom there was the largest in Texas, a massive 9,500 square feet.

Since yesterday, Nadia had worked in conjunction with her assistants and Derek, making sure the hotel and her staff were all working in sync with one another. There were only a few moments when things went wrong, but Nadia managed to get it under control. She was determined to make everything run smoothly before she had to return to Drake's condo and get ready for the gala tonight.

The incident yesterday morning had stunned her completely. To know that he knew part of the reason of why she turned to Donavan still sent tremors sliding over her skin. For a moment there in the guestroom she had thought she would lose all sanity. She had expected him to say that she had used Donavan as a wedge between them because of the way she felt for him. When he had told her that he didn't know the true reason for why she had done it, a small bit of relief had slipped inside her body. What really scared her though was that Drake was now determined to keep her within his sights. She would be in close proximity to him from now on, if he had any say so.

Now, standing in Drake's condo, staring into the guest bathroom mirror, Nadia trembled. She ran her fingers down the soft, supple material of the gorgeous dress she had gotten Derek to bring in from her Houston boutique.

A gray silk slip made up the underneath of the dress. There was a deep **V** shape neckline and split that came up to right above her left thigh. The top of the dress was an ivory lace overlay. It clung to the under dress with delicate stitching and gossamer threads. Nothing about the dress screamed sexy, but Nadia knew as she finished her hair, with a low knot on the back of her neck then placed a large cream Camilla among the dark strands, that her Spanish heritage was there for everyone to see.

Her father's father had come from Madrid. He'd settled in Florida and married Nadia's very American grandmother. They only had one child, her father, Matthew Morales, and like his parent's before him, so had he. Nadia had fringes of memory about her grandfather, since he had died when she was nine. A tall, dark, silver haired man with an accent used to hold her when she was a tiny scrap of a girl, and he repeatedly called her, *carino*, "darling" in Spanish. Nadia's family had lived in Florida until her grandmother, Elizabeth, had died from breast cancer. Just six months later Antonio Morales joined his wife in the hereafter. Nadia always liked to believe that he couldn't live without her.

With the soft, cream colored lace overlay against the darker grey of the dress, her skin glowed with a light tan. Her green eyes were large and with her hair pulled back, she appeared younger than what she was. Nadia turned from the mirror and sat at the small vanity. Her silver strap shoes were easy to slide on and then she stood, grabbed her clutch from the bed, and tried to calm her racing heart.

Walking out of this room was going to be tough, simply because she knew that Drake was ready and waiting for her on the other side of the door.

This isn't a date. This isn't a date. It became a mantra inside her head.

But why did it feel like one? *Because you are allowing your mind to make up this little fantasy, that's why.*

Nadia stiffened her shoulders and her resolve. She was determined to get through this night without anything drastic happening.

She grasped the handle of the door and turned the knob. The hallway was lit up by an antique lamp hanging from the opposite wall. She turned and made her way into the large living area, her heels making clicking noises on the hardwood floor.

The lights were on in the massive room and when Nadia walked all the way in she noticed Drake standing against the large, floor to ceiling windows. He was on the cell phone again, his deep voice talking about a merger that should take place next week. Nadia heard every word he was saying, but none of it registered in her scrambled brain.

The sharp, slight smell of cologne hung in the air, along with a heated dampness that told her he had also taken a shower. The right edge of his jaw clenched and rippled with muscle as he spoke and even as far away as she was, the smooth closeness of the shave he had just gotten was visible. The ruffled edges of his hair were still damp. Nadia's fingers curled against her palms.

This was that closeness, the oneness that she would never have with him-to walk into a room and smell his recent shower hanging in the very air around her; to see the damp ends of his hair and want to run her fingers through it because they ached so much from wanting to touch him in some way; to know that he wasn't fully ready yet when she saw the onyx and silver studs of his cufflinks sitting on the counter between them, and be the one to go up to him and wordlessly help him with that small task.

In the back of your mind you knew this. Don't act like you hadn't thought of this already.

Just as she had cleared that thought from her mind, Drake turned. His eyes flashed a beautiful bright golden color, but then he blinked. Nadia chocked it up to the sun dipping down behind him and the lighting in the room.

Nadia stood there, patiently waiting, as he held up one finger to her and then tried to maneuver off of the phone. She took in the sights while he did that.

A beautifully cut, exquisitely made, black tux covered his large body from shoulders to ankles. Black dress boots, shined to deep ebony, were on his feet. A blinding white shirt was under the black jacket, and a black vest and tie completed the clothing. His burnished skin was starkly tan against his white collar, where it sat open, showing Nadia a glimpse of the hollow of his neck and strong edges of his collarbone, studded with dark, swirling hair. Her traitorous fingers throbbed with the need to touch.

The click as he slid the cell phone closed reverberated in the room around her. Nadia jumped slightly as her eyes came back to his face.

"How do you ever get any relaxation? Every time I'm around you, you are working." She knew if she talked about mundane things that would keep the subject on mundane things.

Don't think about how he is walking closer to you, his mouth cocked in that sensual, crooked smile. Don't think about those two buttons, still undone, still flashing you teasing bits of his hard, muscular chest. Don't think about how massive he is compared to your small body, and of how safe that makes you feel. Just don't think and you can make it through this.

"Some things don't have a time frame, and I have no way of ending it unless I get it done right away." He stopped when he got within two feet of her. The slightly spicy, all male smell of his cologne and him wrapped around her nose, teasing her.

"But you need to relax sometimes; everyone does."

"Darlin,' that is the pot calling the kettle black." His eyes twinkled. "You should take your own advice. Besides, this is relaxation for me." His large hand came up beside her and out of instinctual reaction, not from fear, she knew she shouldn't allow him to touch her; she moved slightly. The hurt look in his eyes was there and then flashed away so quickly that Nadia thought she had imagined it. His lips tightened, "I would never hurt you."

Nadia stood immobile as his hand hovered over her shoulder. "I know and I'm sorry…I don't mean to move away, it's just…" Her mouth worked but no reason came out. Instead of touching her shoulder, his finger softly landed on the corner of her mouth. All the blood in her body rushed to her head. She locked her legs to keep standing, while her mouth and skin tingled like the undercurrents rushing through a charge.

"Shh, I understand, I understand everything." He wasn't smiling anymore. The tip of his finger traced the skin around her mouth, not enough to disturb her lipstick, but just enough to scale the rise of her upper lip and then the indention that ran from her nose to her top lip.

Nadia's lips trembled, as his eyes were transfixed on what his finger was doing. There was no way he understood how she felt. The burning, all-encompassing ache to let her know how it was to be touched by this man, burned through her.

He was closer now. When had he moved? So close that if she stood on her tiptoes she could lick the edge of his chin. That maddening finger of his moved from the indention that gave her lips a peaked look, down to the edge of her jaw. She couldn't control another tremble as it moved across her skin and teased the tip of his finger. She sighed, embarrassed at her reaction to him, and jumped to move away. Her eyes started to burn with heat, a forerunner of tears threatening, when she glanced back up and saw something that should frighten her out of her mind. Instead, she stilled, even the blood in her body felt frozen. She dropped her clutch on the floor.

His eyes, the gorgeous eyes that had always been a light delicious caramel, were now glowing hotly. Bright golden striations replaced the light brown honey color. How was this possible? Just as she thought that, he closed his eyes and slid his hand behind her neck, pulling her into his hold.

Nadia didn't struggle, simply because this was Drake; she had known him since she was twelve. She trusted him implicitly with her own life, so of course she didn't fear him.

His voice, so deep, slid into her ear, "Do you trust me?"

Without any hesitation, she conceded. "Yes, of course." Then as if the moment wasn't unreal enough, she let out a hysterical laugh. "Otherwise, I would be across the room by now." His hold on her upper body increased. One of his large hands was still under her hairdo, warm on her nape and the other was on her lower back, keeping her pressed close to him. Her face was against his strong chest. She could hear the pounding of his heart thud against her ears. What was going on?

"There are things I should tell you Nadia, things that would shock you and probably send you running." He exhaled, and to her he sounded disgusted with himself. "I can't do it now. There is so much to talk about, but when we get back, I promise you, we will talk."

"It can't be that bad." She mumbled against the material of his jacket. Her fingers dug into his sides.

He nuzzled his nose into the delicate strands of hair that fell around her temples. The heat of his breath touched her, and she wanted to slide down his body into a puddle of want right then and there. He inhaled, as if he was breathing her in like an animal scenting its prey, and there was a surge of moisture between her legs. All ten of her fingers dug deeply into the material covering his sides. Dear God, he was killing her, slowly, ever so gently. And this was from a man that claimed he didn't want her like that, didn't desire her in anyway. What she felt was not one-sided. It wasn't possible. Her brain screamed that fact loudly.

"Not bad, but different." He moved his hand from her lower back, and used it to tilt her chin up to meet his eyes.

Nadia paused, but allowed him to move her face up to his. She was scared, scared stiff. Not knowing if he was going to try and kiss her, touch her, or do whatever.

She didn't know if she could handle not knowing, but she also didn't know if she could handle whatever he would do to her. She opened her eyes when he stopped, but her body started to tremble uncontrollably.

Instead of seeing him looking at her, he kept his face pressed against the side of hers, his mouth resting so very close to her own. Nadia burned inside. She wanted to move, just a bit, to where she could lick the seam of his lips right across the middle and suck his tempting lower lip into her mouth. The thought crystallized in her mind. She had never thought herself to be a wanton woman. Apparently only Drake made her want to do wicked things. Her tongue throbbed in response.

His voice surprised her. "Promise me that whenever we get back tonight that you will sit and listen to what I say, no matter how shocking or unreal it sounds."

She nodded immediately. Still focused on the placement of his lips and of how when he spoke they had rubbed against her cheek. The singe of fire in her core slid down her legs, making her clench her fingers even tighter against the long muscles that stiffened under his tux.

"Ah…Nadia," he growled the words against her skin.

Nadia shook against him. She had never felt like this before. As if one intimate touch from him would send her over the edge. And she wanted to go over that edge. Her body was one big, swollen erogenous zone. She had never felt this turned on before, this hot, this explosive.

His mouth touched the lobe of her ear, reverently, almost with a hushed silence that was similar to worship. A sigh escaped Nadia's lips. Then his tongue, *God*, his tongue slid delicately along the rim of her ear. Heat burst along her spine, slipped into her bloodstream and uncurled inside her body as if it had been there all along, waiting for Drake to wake it up.

"Oh…please," she didn't care if she sounded like she was begging. She only cared that he continue whatever it was he was doing. Her fingers clenched again. Drake growled into her ear, and then he stopped.

Nadia opened her eyes to find herself being held again. Reality started to invade her mind and she went to move away from his arms, stunned and embarrassed at how easily he could reduce her to insanity and he had only licked her ear.

"It is past the time for us to leave, don't you think?"

His voice sounded husky, deep with nameless emotion. Nadia just nodded. He slowly let her go. Wordlessly she walked to where his cufflinks sat and grabbed them with shaking hands. Avoiding his gaze, she walked back to him, standing deliciously close to his body, while hers still shook with longing.

He raised his hand to take the links away from her. "Let me, please?" She wasn't sure why, but she wanted to do this on her own. He let her place the jeweled links on the starched material of his shirt cuff. Nadia relished the feel of every part of his skin touching hers.

Silently, she grabbed her clutch and they left the condo.

Chapter 12

For most of the night things had gone astonishingly well. Except for his slip earlier with Nadia, Drake felt as if the rest of the night would be fine, and so far it had been. But everything would come to a head tonight, after the gala. The ice forming in his veins told him so.

He hadn't meant to show her the drastic change of his eyes. That had been his first step to destruction. His next was the small, desperate kiss on her ear. Hell, that one simple, innocent touch had been hotter than some of his previous sexual encounters. All because there was no pretense with Nadia. What she felt broadcasted to him so easily, and he knew from the way she had shook in his arms, the way her breathing had hitched with suppressed desire, and the way her body had molded to his that she had wanted that, and whatever else he could give her just as badly as he did. And that he knew without using *any* of his Druid skills. If he had let that part of him go free, he would have had her up against the wall in seconds, pounding himself deeply, and oh so hard, into her body.

The thought of that made his eyes and gums burn. He ruthlessly shoved that down and focused on his dance with the mayor's wife. There was no need to give the older woman more excitement than she could handle.

Wherever he went, his eyes and his senses stayed attuned to Nadia. She was constantly checking things, the caterer's orders, the guest list to make sure no one had been left out. Her actions were telling to Drake. She was nervous and she was attempting to work off that nervous energy. Tonight, if she let him touch her after their conversation, he could give her a relaxing spell, something to help her sleep better and not worry about the desire she felt for him instead.

Just how far was he going to go with this? Should he tell her the whole truth? Should he put all of this on her right now? Or should he tell her part of it and try to stop lust from taking over. Because if she knew everything, Drake had the bad feeling that she wouldn't come near him again. But he could be wrong. Maybe she was different; maybe he was being too hasty with his judgment. He would have to wait and see.

An hour later Drake found Nadia at a table talking to a number of people. He looked at her and felt a jolt of excitement curl through his blood. Her glorious hair was pulled back into a low bun on the back of her head where a large, beautiful Camilla rested amongst the black satin strands. The deep **V** of the front of her dress was echoed in the back, and Drake knew that he had never seen anything as stunning as Nadia in that moment.

The curve hugging dress was entirely lace, the only saving grace was the under dress that was a deep gray color. The cream colored lace combined with the gray color was unique, and the total package was astounding on Nadia's frame. She looked like a picture perfect senorita, one that he couldn't wait to hold in his arms again, even as his head told him not to contemplate that.

No matter how much he knew it *shouldn't* happen, he found himself thinking of ways that it *would* happen. She was so lovely, so innocent and artless that Drake wasn't sure he could *not* touch her again. It would happen. His fingers would glide along her skin, slip into the heat that was under that heavy fall of hair against her neck, rub along those ridiculously long legs, and at some point in the near future, his fingers, his tongue, and his body would be inside of her, bringing her nothing but pleasure-something he was sure she had never felt, at least not the way she should have by now.

His gums throbbed as he walked up behind her. The conversation had stopped as some of the group had left to go dance. Drake let his body come up close, not close enough to touch, but close enough to let Nadia know he was there. He let his breath whisper out along the side part of her neck. Immediately chills popped out along her skin.

"I haven't seen Donavan yet, have you?" She was breathless as she spoke.

His cock throbbed at the way her body reacted to him without conscious thought. And that was just from him standing behind her. Damn.

"He is here, but he is staying clear of you, as he should."

"Where?" Her head turned automatically scoping out the area. The ballroom was massive, but Drake knew if she took her time she would find him.

Drake didn't even look in Donavan's direction. He didn't have to. Thank God the bastard had stayed in the same spot for the hour he had been here. "Up along the right wall, towards the top corner with a group of about ten people. Do you see the tall blonde with the long white dress?" Drake waited for Nadia to glance in that direction. "That is his date for the night. She isn't from Texas, which I guess is why he picked her to come."

He felt Nadia stiffen. Apparently she had spotted him. "Who is she? I feel like I should go over there and warn her about who she is with."

"Annabelle Scrota, daughter of an Italian photographer. I have no idea how he met her, but she seems to be a bright girl. Maybe she will catch on by herself." Drake walked up beside Nadia and then stepped in front of her. "You know damn well you can't go over there. You would be violating your own order."

"I know. I just feel horrible about any woman getting entangled with him."

Drake caught the worried look in Nadia's eyes. He sent out feelers across the ballroom and scoured Donavan's aura, looking for any anger or antagonism directed towards the lovely Annabelle. He didn't pick up anything of the sort. Now there was fury, but that was clearly directed at Drake and Nadia. He turned and sent Donavan a quelling look. The bastard knew better than to fuck with him or the woman at his side again. Drake turned back to Nadia.

"She's going to be fine. She is stronger than she looks."

Nadia's green eyes landed on him. "How do you know? Have you met her before?"

Ah, jealousy, a new emotion from her, to be sure. He tried not to smile. "I have met her before, but it was long ago." The blood in her body began to move a bit more feverishly. Oh yeah, she was not happy about something.

"I'd say she made an impression." Nadia did everything but huff in his face.

The smile he had been holding broke over his face. "She is a lovely woman, smart too." Yes, he was baiting her on purpose.

Green eyes landed on him full of fire. "Maybe you should have asked her to come instead."

Whoa. Someone needed to hand him some ice. Nadia was hot enough to start fires. He wasn't sure he should say what he needed to, but he might as well let the truth out; otherwise, she would find out from someone else and then he would have hell on his hands.

"She was my date." There. He said it. "My original date for tonight. She had called me about two weeks ago and asked me if I had an invitation and then if I had a date or not."

Nadia's green eyes sparked flames at the tall blonde. Drake was amused, but he kept it to himself. He had never imagined that little Nadia would have been jealous over another woman, especially one that had been connected to him. The new things he was learning about her were eye opening, to say the least.

His eyes travelled once more down her small, compact, but very lovely frame. She had no reason to be jealous of another woman. Even if that woman was with him or not, she was beautiful in her own right. Apparently the guys she'd dated before had never informed her of that fact. Drake had never thought of her as having a low outlook when she viewed herself. This was all very surprising. Nadia was turning out to have more layers than he had originally thought.

"She is a very beautiful woman. I'm sure you both would have had a great time tonight."

Then she turned and walked away, leaving a very shocked Drake standing there with his mouth gaping.

***

Tears burned in her eyes and fell over the lower lids, scalding down her cheeks. Nadia sniffed and hastily made her way out into the lush courtyard that surrounded the ballroom. There was no way in hell she could have stood there any longer and stared at the woman that Drake had *intended* to take with him here before her plan came into effect. She was beautiful, tall and golden, so unlike Nadia in every aspect.

A mature climbing rosebush was situated in front of her with a latticework arch where the branches twined around the wood. She stopped there. The hot night air brushed along her skin, but the heat did nothing to stop the tears that ran unchecked down her cheeks. She knew it was stupid to get upset over the fact that he dated beautiful women. She had known it for years. It was no surprise to her at all.

But after what had taken place at his condo…What? What had taken place there? Not a damn thing. Not enough for a well-seasoned man like Drake to take anything into consideration. Not enough for him to go crazy with desire, not enough for him to ache in places like Nadia was right now, not enough for him to get hysterically jealous over any man that had dated her or found her attractive.

You're being idiotic, Nadia.

Clearly she was taking this to extremes, but she couldn't stop herself. It was like a spring had been uncoiled inside her body and only he could set it back to rights again.

The pain of not allowing herself to give into her emotions for over nine years sucked her down. The ache caused her heart to hurt, and her insides to churn. The incident in his condo was some delicious figment of her imagination; it had to have been. But to Nadia, it had woken up every single trembling inch of her body in a way that only Drake could pull off. Added to the emotions she experienced when he was around, she became a mess of a woman.

She grasped the beautiful material of her dress and wanted to rip it off of her body. It didn't matter what clothes she dressed in, what circles she moved in and everything she did to make her life better, nothing could make Drake feel for her what she felt for him. Nothing she did could make her anything like that tall blonde woman in there. Nothing could make her enough for him. And if he hadn't felt anything for her by now, would he ever? Probably not.

The truth caught Nadia deep in her chest and sent pain radiating outward. She hiccupped and then a loud sob tore from her chest. Oh God, it hurt so bad. It always had, but now she knew how he could make her feel with the barest touch from him, and knowing what she could never have hurt even worse.

Her hands tore at her hairdo, loosening the pins and dislodging the beautiful Camilla she had so lovingly placed there. Her shoulders hunched over when the weight of her hair fell down in cascading waves around her arms. Tears poured from her eyes as she tried to calm her breathing. She could never go back in there like this, never.

"Nadia?"

At his voice in the darkness, Nadia immediately halted all sound and movement. She barely even breathed.

No, please make him go away. I will never be able to explain all of this.

Her mind screamed at her to turn in the other direction but she couldn't. The only way out of this hidden arbor was back in his direction. She hastily began to wipe the tears from her cheeks, even as fresh ones started again.

Seconds later she felt those telling tingles erupt over her skin, and knew that he was standing close. She sniffed as delicately and quietly as she could manage, but she knew that he had heard her. Hell, how couldn't he have? It had been as loud as a train blast.

He didn't say anything, but he moved closer. Soon his large body was next to hers and Nadia could smell his scent on the hot breeze. Everything about him was familiar. Then his hand came up to rest on her shoulder, and Nadia knew he was going to turn her around.

When he applied pressure she went with it. There was no use in trying to stop him. His blinding white shirt came into view, and the lovely expanse of his thrilling skin was now hiding beneath buttons. Nadia wanted to rip it from his body.

"Angel…why are you crying?"

His soft, deep voice sparked fresh tears, and even more humiliating than that was her lip started to shake, then her chin, and soon enough she hiccupped again.

When his arms came around her, Nadia knew she should be running in the other direction, but she couldn't. So she turned to the one man that was the reason why she was the way she was. She allowed him to pull her close, to comfort her while she cried, and she allowed him to pity her for what she was doing. At the moment she didn't care. She was past caring. Her tears fell quietly now.

Her face nestled right up against his large chest and her arms stayed at his side. He was hot, so very hot under his tux. His hands held her so close to him that Nadia doubted a ray of light could have moved in between their bodies. She soaked his tux and his shirt, but all he said was 'Its okay' over and over again, while his large hand caressed her back up and down.

Seconds ticked by, then minutes, and soon Nadia was starting to feel childish for her jealous comments earlier. Her face was surely wrecked, her hair was a mess, and she had cried all over Drake. Her night was ruined. And she had ruined his too.

"I'm sorry," she muttered against his tux, trying to make him see that she really was. Her fingers continued to clench against his side, where she could feel muscles vibrate when he moved his arms away from hers, and pulled her face up to his. Embarrassed, she finally lifted her eyes and looked at him. He looked pissed off. Nadia didn't take that as a good sign.

"Why exactly are you sorry?" He gritted those words out so low that they shook through her from where she was pressed to him.

"For making a scene, and for you seeing me like this, and for acting this way. There is no excuse." The words dwindled at the fury that was coming over his face. For a brief second Nadia became scared, even as she knew he would never hurt her.

"I never thought I would say this, but you are turning out to be one infuriating woman."

That took her aback. And set her temper off. "If you don't like it go back inside to *Annabelle*. Maybe if you are quick enough you can steal her away from Donavan and finish your night off with her." Furious and hurt all over again, Nadia pulled her body from his embrace and took off with determined steps back to the ballroom.

She got only as far as a few feet when she felt his hand pull her back around.

"Oh no you don't, Ms. Spitfire. Stop right there. We are going to finish this right here." He pulled her close once again, and she shoved. Now that he had gotten her riled, her blood was boiling at its peak.

"Let go of me!" She shoved again, only managing to make herself get tangled with his arms.

He chuckled, and that really set her off. She hauled back and lifted her hand. He stopped her on the upswing, his fist crushing her small wrist. She looked up into his face, but he was in a half shadow. Still, Nadia could sense his fury, and she knew she had almost overstepped the boundaries between them. But that didn't stop a furious remark from leaving her lips.

"How dare you!" She spit the words at him, but she knew she was the one that was in the wrong.

He pulled her close to his body. "I dare whatever I wish, Nadia. You should know that by now." His deep voice caused the hairs on her arm to lift in warning.

"Brute! All men are the same. They try and bully a woman into th-,"

He pulled her against him so abruptly that she stopped speaking all together. Now she realized the danger. Now that she was close enough she knew that he was going to punish her for the assumption she had just screamed at him. The insult hung in the air. His body was hard and so very large against hers.

His voice growled, while his eyes glowed hotly at her. "You dare much by slinging that insult on me. Maybe you are the one that needs to learn a lesson in curbing what you think."

Without a second to spare his lips captured hers. Nadia ceased to move, breathe and even think.

Her body was at his mercy. He held her in a bruising grip, his hands hard around her arms and his body punishingly close to hers. Then she realized her legs were dangling from the ground. He had actually picked her up. His mouth forced hers open in a vengeful kiss, one that she had never seen coming, and he took over from there.

Hard lips forced hers open, plundering her mouth, stealing the very breath from her lungs. Nadia moaned against his mouth while her hands tried to move against his body, but she couldn't. He held her so closely and so hard against him that any movement was prohibited.

This wasn't what she had expected from him. But she knew she had pushed him to this. Tears bit at her eyes again, and slipped over to slide down her cheeks to where he violated her mouth with his. Almost immediately he slowed, gentled his mouth, as if the tears had touched him, and he realized just how rough he was being with her. His hands let off of their bruising grip. He continued to hold her up, but softly now. His lips brushed against hers tenderly, setting off little sparks of excitement against her lips.

"So sorry," he mumbled against her mouth, his nose bumping up against hers as he adjusted his hold on her body to where she was leaning against him rather than dangling above the ground.

Ever so gently his tongue caressed the seam of her lips, not roughly like before, but with a cautious lick that dared her to open so that he could prove to her that he was sorry. Hesitatingly she moaned against his mouth and opened slowly. One of his hands went under her bottom to keep her anchored high against his body, while the other came up to gently swipe her hair away from their faces. The strength in him amazed her and she trembled again.

"I'm sorry, so very sorry. Don't be scared. Please." The need, the abject honesty in his voice caused fresh tears to well in Nadia's eyes and with a trust born of years of knowing him, she slipped her arms around his shoulders and opened her mouth fully against his, willing to take whatever he would give her.

Even though she had basically given him permission to correct what he had just done, that in no way let Nadia establish a pace with their kisses. Drake was a very dominant male. He liked to set the pace. He liked to call the shots, and he was doing exactly that with her right now, albeit a bit slower and more gentle than what he had started off with.

With his forearm snug against her bottom and his other hand now cupping the delicate line of her jaw, he teased her lips, tilted his head and caressed first the top then the lower rise of her mouth into a dance that she didn't know the steps to, but she was learning. His breath soughed into her mouth, giving her air to breathe, since he wouldn't let her go long enough to catch her own. A large, work roughened thumb moved across the side of her cheek, while his tongue licked at the entry to her mouth. Nadia clenched her fingers in his hair and timidly let the tip of her tongue catch his. His tongue felt like wet, smooth sandpaper, but his taste was hypnotic, drugging, with the faint hint of whiskey.

The growl that reverberated through his chest erupted inside her mouth. His forearm pulled her even tighter against him, while his thumb applied pressure, causing her mouth to open even further. Drake plunged inside.

Pleasure danced along her nerve endings and sang in her veins. Heat flooded her body and where minutes ago she had felt pain and such agonizing torture, she now felt like the most wanted woman in the world. His mouth moved over hers with such skill and passionate intensity that Nadia wondered how women weren't lining up around the block for a go with this man.

Oh yes. Liquid, molten satisfaction bubbled in her blood. She had wanted this, craved this for years, and now he was giving it to her. And boy did he know how to give it. His mouth never stopped moving, teasing, licking, sucking, and caressing her own. Just when Nadia had gotten the hang of things, he switched on her, going from teasing the inside softness of her lips, to plunging his tongue deep, the way Nadia knew his body could do to hers.

Seconds later he pulled away slightly. She still rested on his forearm, and against his body, but now his mouth only whispered against hers, giving her fantastic tingles that trembled along the top of her lips and skin. His eyes were closed and Nadia didn't move away, but stayed to where his lips brushed hers with soft, so very tender nips.

"I have to stop, angel…if I don't, I might do something that I'm sure would shock you."

Nadia smiled slightly, and answered truthfully, "I can't possibly be more shocked than I am now."

With his strong arm he lowered her slightly. Nadia felt his hard body under the material of the tux, so very powerful and sexy. All at once a large, hard, and extremely long part of his body came into contact with her core. Her eyes shot open even wider as she glanced down, trying to see around what she was pressed up against. "Oh."

A crooked, sensual grin tucked up one corner of his mouth. "You got that right."

Nadia had the wild, insane and totally wanton urge to let her legs fall open so that he would press right up to where she was aching. Just the image in her mind of her opening her legs, the slit in her dress allowing for more room, while his massive body pressed so intimately against hers, caused a renewed flash of heat and moisture to gather at the juncture of her thighs.

She wanted to wrap her legs around his taut waist, jerk her hips against his and feel him fully. Her insides trembled at the thought, while her inner muscles clenched with ferocity.

Just when she thought she might actually make a move and shock *him* for a change, his arm shifted, dragging her down that delicious hardness and for a second, Nadia thought she might explode from that torment alone. Then seconds later, he set her down in front of him. With her legs shaking and her heart in her throat, she braced her hands against his chest.

"Damn…we are both screwed, aren't we?"

She thought that pretty much summed up the entire situation.

***

Nadia sipped the tea he had made for her when they had arrived back at the condo. It was full dark and nearing midnight, but Drake wanted to get this out right now. There was no need to put it off any longer.

In his mind he knew that Nadia wasn't some errant society girl that would take the knowledge of what he was going to tell her and spread it around carelessly. She was caring and loyal to a fault, and he knew if he trusted her with his secret that she wouldn't take that trust and stomp it in the ground. Just getting to this point was monumental enough. There had been women in his past, even two that he had married and had loved in his own way, but that physical and emotional connection between his two previous wives had never been as strong as the one he feared was growing between him and Nadia. What he had felt for Loraine and Marie had never been this physically powerful.

With her bright green eyes and lips still swollen from his kisses, Nadia looked like a teenager curled up on his loveseat in her pajama set. His eyes settled on the soft green tank top and green plaid flannel pants that she had on. Drake couldn't remember when he had last seen a woman wear normal sleep clothes to bed. Usually the women he had over for the night wore silk teddies or nothing at all. It was refreshing to see her wearing something else besides what he was used to.

He had also changed. They both needed to get comfortable, as he had told her when they walked in from the gala. Instead of telling him anything smart, she had surprisingly agreed and walked off to the guest room without another word. Her quietness was worrying him. Before their kiss she had kept apologizing for her tears and her jealousy. That was the last thing he had wanted to hear. Why didn't this beautiful, desirable woman see herself that way? What had the men in her life done to her to make her think that she wasn't up to par with other women?

To put it mildly, Drake had seen red. He couldn't believe she had the frame of mind to even think she wasn't good enough for him, which had been exactly what she had been thinking before she had started crying and ran out from the ballroom. The emotions inside of her had been so volatile at that moment.

After the words they had shared, then the kiss, Drake was ready for round two. Hell, he was ready for any round that allowed him access to her and making her feel good. He was so hard for her that it was surprising she hadn't been staring at his crotch for the past ten minutes. So far her eyes had stayed glued to the mug she was holding.

Drake stretched his shoulders in the plain tee shirt he had on, straightened his legs in a pair of black pajama bottoms, and curled his palms against his forearms which rested across his chest. Usually he didn't dress for bed. He only made the concession of clothes because she was here.

"Are you tired?" he asked her.

She jumped a bit. Apparently he caught her off guard. Drake watched her eyes flutter, black eyelashes sweeping across her smooth cheek and once again his cock twitched. He almost groaned. It seemed everything she did was a turn on for him. "No, I'm fine, and besides we need to talk…about earlier."

Heck, she didn't know the half of what they needed to talk about. "First off, let me apologize for that." He cleared his throat and leveled his eyes on hers. "The kiss started out pretty rough, but that was because of what you had said seconds before." Making sure he had her attention, he deepened his voice and held her gaze with his, injecting a slight glamour into his tone. He wanted to make sure she took what he said to heart. "You are a beautiful woman. And no matter what any person says, you always have been and always will be. You will stop downplaying your attributes right now. I don't want to hear another word on the matter."

Huge green eyes took him in warily, but she managed to nod in his direction. He could sense she was reasonably calm, but he knew with the slightest word or touch that could change.

"Now, the other conversation we need to have."

She nodded again.

Drake sat quietly for a second, building up his courage. It wasn't an everyday occurrence that he ensured the safety of him and his brethren to someone else, even though he trusted Nadia implicitly, he would never know how she would react to what he had to tell her. He looked to her again. Her light green eyes watched him, and he sensed that she was waiting to hear something totally different from what he was about to say.

"Earlier, before we left for the gala, something happened. Do you remember what I'm talking about?" He asked her carefully.

She bit her lower lip then slowly let it roll out. Drake could have melted to the sofa cushions. "I remember looking into your face, and your eyes…the color had changed, and they were…they were glowing." She hesitated as if he was going to laugh in her face about what she had said.

He nodded slowly. "Yes, the color was a deep golden color, almost bright amber. Am I correct?"

At her slow nod, he continued.

"Were you scared? Because I remember asking you if you trusted me, and you had said that if you didn't, you would be across the room."

She smiled slightly and her fingers curled around the mug in her hands. Drake felt her heart kick up a notch. "I wasn't scared." Those green eyes of hers landed on his face, searching deeply. "You don't scare me. You never did."

His breath hitched in his throat. *Keep talking man, tell her what you need her to know and don't think about sex right now.* Christ, he was so hot from that kiss earlier that he still hadn't cooled down yet. He had never been one to practice abstinence, but something about Nadia screamed that he should take his time. And he knew down the road something would happen, he had already given in to those emotions that she roused in him so easily, so now it was only a matter of when and where they would eventually get together. And for Drake the added knowledge that she wasn't his usual flavor of woman was making him nuts. He wanted to be patient and caring for her. He wanted her to see a side of him that he had never shown anyone else. He didn't question why.

"My eyes change colors when I'm at the peak of certain emotional levels, such as pain, pleasure, or even anger. The bright amber color symbolizes the unique traits I carry inside of me."

The utter confusion on her face spoke volumes. "What?" She shook her head slightly and placed the mug on the small table beside her. "I don't understand." Her eyes stayed on him while her brow furrowed deeply.

Drake tried again. He had never been good at explaining, especially when people rarely believed what he said. Usually he had to do more of a show-and-tell experiment instead.

"I have other abilities also."

"Abilities?" She stayed on the sofa, still relaxed, but Drake could pick up the tempo of her blood coursing a bit faster through her veins. "Just what kind of sci-fi kick are you on, Drake?"

"Believe me angel, there are no sci-fi kicks going on right now. Everything I'm saying is the God's honest truth. If you remember, I asked you earlier to listen to everything I said with an open mind."

"But when you say things like that, well," she gulped deeply, "It's kinda hard to believe you. I mean you are saying that your eyes glow." She didn't scoff at him but she came damn close to it. "No one's eyes *glow*, Drake. You only hear about that stuff in books or movies."

"But you just admitted that you saw it with your own eyes." He didn't want to point out that obvious fact again, but he did anyway. When he saw the utter confusion on her face, he felt horrible. "If you want to…and God, please listen to what I'm saying here because I sure as hell don't want to scare you, I can show you very easily just what I can do." He let his eyes rest on hers, testing her courage and feeling the excitement that battled with just a touch of fear inside of her. "But if I do please remember that I'm still Drake. I'm still the same man you have always known, okay?"

With a determined, but still confused look on her face, she nodded then said, "Okay, and of course I know who you are. Why would I believe otherwise?"

Drake didn't say anything, but deep in his mind he prayed that she wouldn't bolt when she saw what he could do. With a deep breath, he gave her one last look. "Please just keep trusting me." He told her, his eyes serious on hers, then he closed them and the change begin. With just a slight burning sensation in eyes, Drake was finished. He kept the fangs on a short leash. That was one thing that he sensed would send her over the edge. Taking a deep breath, he opened his eyes.

She gasped, clenching the edge of the sofa with her fingers, her knuckles showing white. Drake instantly began to send out feelers, automatically taking in whether there was any show of real fear, because if there was, he would immediately halt whatever he was doing. He never wanted to scare her.

What he felt was confusion and a deep seated curiosity; there was no fear at all apparent to him. He figured the clenching up of muscles was just because of her nervousness.

"How is it possible?" Her green eyes were glued to his and he could see that she would need answers, but she would also need to *see* whatever he could show her too. He prayed for her acceptance to continue, especially with everything else that he needed to tell her.

"There are things about me that you don't know yet, many other things besides just my eyes that change." Drake took a deep breath. "But as for my eyes, we believe it is simply a way to show that my Druid side is awake and open for full change."

That got her attention. "We, there are others? And what do you mean when you say your Druid side is awake and open for full change?" She sat on the edge of the sofa while her hands continued to curl around the armrest. Drake didn't sense that she wanted to bolt yet. It was only a bad case of inquisitiveness that had her looking so earnest.

"Yes, there are others, and like I said there are many other things about me that change at certain moments, sometimes when I most need those special abilities."

"So when your eyes change, does it cause you to have some special seeing ability?"

"Not only when my eyes change, but at every moment of everyday I have enormous seeing abilities, and I can see in the dark, very clearly."

She pursed her lips, and Drake could see that she was starting to move her fingers together nervously. He tested her emotions, and he could sense the heightened interest moving around inside of her. She not only wanted answers to her questions, but Drake would bet money that she wanted to touch him, to see if he felt any different to her. He fought down the urge to give her a full access free for all.

"Amazing…what else happens?"

"I can send out spells." He threw that out there not really knowing what her reaction would be. "I can also move faster than you can blink, read your emotions, heal pain, and live an extremely long, long time."

Her eyes got bigger, if that was possible. Now she seemed totally in awe. "I want to see something. Show me how it works." She sounded tremendously inquiring, as if she couldn't stop herself from asking.

Before she had closed her mouth, Drake was standing before her. The breeze from his fast movement just then lifted a few strands of her hair where it lay on her shoulders. Now the look in her eyes was priceless. "Oh my God….." she said wonderingly, still too hesitant to touch him. In a half second, he was back on his chair facing her.

"Do you want to know more?" he questioned her and watched the wonder build in her features.

"There's more? My God, how is that possible?"

"Oh, it is quite possible, believe me."

"I do have a question." She asked him before he started up again. "When you said you live a really long time, just what do you mean?"

Drake exhaled. This was a biggie, considering everything else was so easy to take. "I was born on August 28th of 1784, in a very small town right outside of San Antonio."

"1784?? That makes you over 220 years old." Now some wavering showed in her face. "It isn't possible."

"It's very possible. I have a family bible that proves it. I also have my parent's marriage license and two of my own, if you want to inspect those." Drake watched her eyes grow huge again.

"Two marriage licenses? You were married twice?"

"When you have been alive as long as I have, time seems to move extremely slow, Nadia." He answered honestly. That was the only hated concession, in his mind, of being an Amber Druid, the slow time progression.

"But then how do you stay in one place?" And in the next breath, "No wonder I could never guess your age. I was stuck between thirty-five and thirty-eight, because you always had been so hard to pin down."

"I move around every twenty years or so. People are easy to manipulate. If I need to, I can do something we call a mind scrub; it is like eliminating me from your memory."

"You can get in someone's mind?"

Drake grimaced. "No…not really, but there are certain spells that can remove my memory from your mind, or other spells that I can put to use that will make you see me in any way that I want you to, so it's not really 'getting in your mind,' more like making you think what I want you to think."

"Oh," she still sounded like she had a ton of questions.

"Want me to explain something else?"

"What about healing pains, and when you said "strong," just how strong are you?"

"I can heal minor pain and make emotions such as depression, sorrow and sadness, calmer for the person experiencing them. I can't stop blood flow. Kale, another Amber Druid, is the only one I know of that can do that. I'm very strong. If I'm under full change mode there isn't much that I can't lift, and even as I am right now it still isn't a problem for me to lift two times my weight."

"So when you go into full change mode, and when you experience certain things like pain and anger, you change also, automatically?"

Drake nodded. "Even when I'm aroused…things happen." His eyes pinned her to the sofa with an intensity that probably startled her.

"That's why your eyes were glowing…what else happens? I assume that isn't it?" She sounded breathless.

Drake shook his head negatively. "My senses heighten. I can practically taste emotions from people that are around me, not to mention feel what they feel, albeit stronger. There are a few physical changes, but the strongest are my eyes and my teeth." He took a deep breath after he said that, waiting for her fear and for her to storm out of the room and maybe leave him when she found out about his fangs.

"Teeth? Your teeth change too?" Yeah, there was that confusion, the wondering. She didn't understand. Drake remembered the past and the other women that had known about him then. No…Nadia isn't like them. "Can you show me?" Her whispered words slid under his skin. Even without prompting from him, his fangs elongated from the sound of her voice. The Druid inside of him rallied to the fore, breathing fires along his spine, wanting to break out of his bonds and show Nadia the real him.

Running his tongue along one edge of a strong fang, Drake gathered his courage. "Just remember who I am angel, okay?" He knew his words were a bit slurred because of the fangs, but the look on her face egged him on. She really wanted to see. His little Nadia was curious about him, and so far she had taken everything else like a pro.

He let his mouth fall open a bit, just too where the very tips of his fangs showed through the opening. As he did that, he watched her face for the barest hint of fear. She wouldn't make it out of the door if she did try to move because Drake would stop her. But if he knew her, he knew she wouldn't run. She might get scared, she might go quiet, but she wouldn't run.

She inhaled deeply. "Fangs…I didn't think…" Drake watched as she gulped deeply. "Do they hurt?"

Now that she had seen them, Drake made them disappear. "No, they don't hurt and they are practically there for show. We don't drink blood, nor do we bite. That is, unless you want me too." He didn't smile, but he wanted to when he saw the red blush move over her skin. "I was just so terrified that you would be scared to death."

She cocked her head to the side, much like a little animal trying to find all the answers, and Drake felt his insides erupt with heat. She was so beautiful. "I'm not scared of you. How many times do I need to say it?"

"Apparently I need to hear it more. You know I have a thick skull." He smiled at her and she smiled back. Right then Drake felt as if everything were alright in his world.

She yawned, and he realized it was almost two-thirty in the morning. They both needed to get some rest. "Look, there is so much more, but this can all keep for later. I know you are tired."

She nodded, "I have many more questions for you, so get ready."

He smiled, "Whenever and whatever you want answered, let me know, I don't mind telling you anything."

She hesitantly got up from the sofa and turned towards the hallway that led to the bedrooms. He watched her with hunger burning up inside of him. He wouldn't be able to touch her like this. It would turn into the scene from earlier all over again. He would be too rough with her, and that was the last thing he wanted. Whenever he touched her again, he wanted to kill her with seduction. He wanted her to feel what she never felt before.

"Goodnight angel," he murmured to her, knowing she heard him.

She turned a bit and gave him a small smile, "Goodnight." Then she turned and walked away.

Drake groaned as he slumped against the sofa cushions. There was no way he would be able to sleep tonight.

Chapter 13

He was over 220 years old. He had fangs. His eyes changed color. He was oddly strong and really, really fast. He could stop pain, heal hurt, make someone feel better and make them forget all about him. He was still a human being, but so very much more than that. And Nadia had never been more confused in all her life.

Never before had she even given the paranormal world any thought. She had never thought of anything like that being real. Sure, she watched movies, read books and enjoyed fantasy like any other person, but that didn't make it real. Flesh and blood real. That didn't make it 6'6" of gorgeous, mind boggling, sexy man real. That didn't make it Drake, her Drake, with golden glowing eyes, sharp, dangerous looking fangs, real. God, wasn't he deadly enough to her? Oddly enough none of those things scared her. Sure, she was skeptical. Who in their right mind wouldn't be? But, he had given her proof, right there in plain sight. There was no way to deny what was so obvious.

And somehow those things that should scare her, had given her a warm, electric thrill instead.

The sight of sharp fangs peeking from inside the edges of his sensual mouth had almost given her a heart attack, both in a good and bad way. She wanted to touch them, test their sharpness with her fingertip.

Pounding the pillow with her fist she turned over in the bed, determined to make her mind stop thinking, and hopefully slip into a blissful sleep. But images and thoughts of Drake kept interrupting her slumber. She wanted to know about those two women he had married. She wanted to know of things that had happened before she had even been thought of. She wanted to know what he had been like as a younger boy, and then as a young man. She wanted to know if his power ever scared him.

She wanted to know more. She wanted to know it all, right now, this very instant.

With the darkness shrouding her it seemed so simple. He wouldn't turn her away if she wanted more answers now. He would tell her anything. Hadn't he said "whenever"? Yes, yes he had.

But surely he didn't mean at three o clock in the morning!

How would Nadia ever know that if she didn't bite down her nervousness and take a chance? Hadn't he taken a chance on telling her the truth? Hadn't he put his and these other Druids' existence on the line by telling her what he had? Yes, he had. He trusted her.

Warmth bloomed deep in her chest. Hugging the soft coverlet to her body she smiled. For ten years, she had fancied herself in love with him, never thinking a day would come when he might confide in her some deep, dark secret about himself. Well, in one day he had kissed her senseless, opened her body up to what passion really felt like, told her something about him that she never would have guessed at, and just the reminder of all of those things made her eyes tear up.

She rubbed the tears away and stared at the ceiling. She should wait until morning to bother him. He had to be tired.

Ten minutes later she huffed and tossed again.

Another ten minutes passed, and Nadia knew she wouldn't be getting any sleep tonight.

***

Hot, sweltering, humid heat covered Drake.

He soaped up in the shower, and tried for the hundredth time to get Nadia out of his head. But those images wouldn't budge. Her eyes sliding closed as he kissed her for the first time in that garden right outside of the ballroom. Her arms at his sides, while her nails dug into his skin like little needle points.

She had been so hot, so turned on, and Drake had wanted nothing more than to lay her down, or up against something and show her just how sizzling things could get between them.

He remembered her hesitant tongue when he had kissed her, and the way her hands had slowly crept around his neck after he picked her up. She was twenty-five, yet to him she seemed so very pure and untouched compared to women her own age. He had the insane urge to protect her, but at the same time teach her everything she would ever need to know about sex, lust, passion…love.

She had trembled and moaned against him, and Drake had been hard enough to do some serious damage.

He looked down his body, where water was sliding and coursing, and noticed he was still hard.

There was a simple way to ease this temporary ache. He knew it would only take the edge off because the moment he saw her, all of this would happen again. Fuck. He had never had the urge to do this himself, because most of the time he had a woman around to do it for him.

He always had some way to ease off his sexual needs. There was never a shortage of women, and Drake never had a problem getting off before. Until now. Now, he had Nadia on his mind 24/7. Images and thoughts of her were always in abundance. And he knew that no other woman would work. It would either be Nadia or no one at all.

Unless he did the deed himself.

Disgusted, but with the taste, smell, and image of Nadia in every pore of his body, Drake clenched his jaw, and let his hand close around his hard, aching cock.

***

No, this wasn't right. She should be going back to her room.

But as she went down the hallway, and saw the crack in his bedroom door, Nadia stopped herself once again. She wanted answers, and she couldn't wait. And in some corner of her mind she knew he wouldn't turn her away.

With trembling hands, she padded quietly over to his door and noticed the small bit of light coming from the gap at the side and on the bottom. He was still awake. She wouldn't be intruding. Gathering up her courage, she knocked quietly, just in case he had fallen asleep.

"Drake?"

No answer. Standing in the hallway, she peered into the small opening and pushed it a bit wider. "Drake, are you sleeping?"

Still no answer, but Nadia could make out the massive four poster bed that dominated the room, along with very masculine furniture in one corner set up around a large bookshelf. The colors on the bed were deep burgundy, gold, and a startling green so profound, that in the darkness it shimmered like liquid emerald fire. Nadia wanted to run her fingers across the lovely material. She chased that thought away and focused on where he could be.

As she walked fully into the room she saw what could only be the bathroom door cracked open along the side wall. Steam gathered and curled from the edges of the heavy wood and Nadia's stomach seesawed when she realized he was in the shower.

Images of hot, wet, muscular Drake were now singed on her brain. And thanks to her overactive imagination, she was sure she would be stuck with them for a good while.

Even as she told herself she shouldn't, her feet propelled her silently towards that door. The steam continued to escape, and the closer Nadia got the more she realized she was doing something really, really wrong. She was invading his personal space.

When are you going to get another chance to spy on him in the shower?

Um…even she could answer that question. As soon as they left Dallas, Nadia feared their life would resume the same way it had been before they got here, very, very dull indeed. The kisses would be forgotten, the hot looks, the scorching touches, all of that gone to be replaced with work life instead.

Nadia didn't want to forget and besides, when had sheever done anything remotely wild before? Nothing could be as wild as getting a look, only a look, of a very beautiful man, a man she happened to love, while he showered. It would only take a second.

A harsh groan erupted out of nowhere and Nadia almost jumped out of her skin. Just what in the world was that?

The bathroom door was easy to push open, now that Nadia had to make sure that he was okay. Humid air rose around her in tendrils and she could make out the shape and colors of the bathroom dimly through all of that steam. Now that she had the door open slightly some of it was escaping, clearing the area for her just a bit.

It was a large bathroom with a Jacuzzi tub in one corner and a massive, stone shower in one. And oh God, the doors weren't glazed glass, they were clear. Two large hinged doors were closed, but with the evaporating steam she noticed the doors in no way hindered Drake enclosed behind them.

Steamy rivulets of water clung to the surface of both doors, but even with the patchy steam in the way, Nadia could make out Drake's form behind it. He was standing sideways, his left side facing her, while the water fell from a large shower head at the top, and one hit him from the side wall. Glorious naked muscular skin rippled when he moved his left arm and plowed his fingers through his hair.

Another groan slid through the heat drenched room, and that's when Nadia noticed his other hand, and what he was holding.

Her fingers dug into the door and the frame along the wall. She was half in the bathroom and almost left it completely, but a burning curiosity held her in a shocked stupor. Her legs trembled while her heart sped up so fast that it was a wonder she didn't pass out. Heat flared to life between her thighs, burning her, but in a good way.

Thoughts of any questions fled her mind.

Drake's hand was wrapped around his erection. Nadia couldn't have been more shocked than if she had found him with another woman in bed. His large, overwhelming body shuddered, and she shook along with him while sweat popped out along her upper lip. Then his hand started moving. Nadia lost her sanity along with her breath.

With his left hand now propped on the shower wall she had a full side view of him stroking himself, while the hot water rained down over his body. She could have never even imagined such a sexually charged scene, even with *her* imagination. His burnished frame was like a massive sculpture. One that made her fingertips throb in excitement. Moving with rapid speed, his hand grasped that most male part of him and stroked fast while his body undulated with pleasure. Nadia's core flooded with moisture.

The dark ink from his tattoo winked at her from in between puffs of steam and the slightly watery glass. She couldn't see it clearly, but she wanted to touch that almost as badly as she wanted to touch him.

At the moment though, his hand on his hardness was enough to keep her spellbound, more than his tattoo did. She watched the ease and assuredness at how he touched himself. There was no shame, no embarrassment in what he was doing. His grasp was sure and strong and so was his stroke. He switched tactics in front of her eyes, stopping the stroking and sliding his hand under…apparently he hit the right spot because another rumble of a growl leaked out, startling her so badly she almost dropped to the floor.

With his hand out of the way Nadia got her first full look at Drake aroused. She gulped deeply. Damn, but he was as large as the rest of him. And immediately she wanted to touch it, she wanted to be the one grasping his massive erection in her hands. Her, Nadia Morales who had never once initiated anything in her life with the opposite sex, wanted to be the one making this sexual, so very striking and gorgeous man growl with pleasure.

She wanted to replace his hands with her own.

She moaned and immediately stiffened when she heard just how loud it was. With her heart pounding in her ears, her body flushed with a fierce blush as she met Drake's eyes through the glass doors of the shower.

Molten gold had taken the place of his light caramel brown eye color. He looked fierce, deadly, and extremely scary as he stared, but Nadia didn't feel terrified. She watched as his tongue crept out to lick a bit of water on his lips, and that's when she noticed the tip of his right fang. Oh God, he was changing, but that's because he was aroused. Nadia remembered him saying that earlier. And for some reason it made her insides pulse with heat to see those eyes staring her down, a fang winking at her from his mouth, while his hand…her eyes looked down and yes, he was still holding himself. Heat bloomed along her cheekbones. She licked her dry lips and didn't say anything. She wasn't sure of what *to* say.

Drake didn't say anything either. It seemed as if they were both frozen in this odd moment. And then she watched carefully as he moved his hand away from his hard erection. Something inside of her snapped.

"Don't," just one word, but with the way his eyes slid to her face and glowed even brighter, you would swear she must have said something else. He stopped moving his hand though.

He moved one second later, then the water was off and he was opening one of the shower doors, although he wasn't making a move to leave. Nadia got her first glimpse of him head on, naked and aroused, and almost slid to the floor in a puddle of want.

"Don't what?"

The words got her attention, but so did the fact that he was, once again, clasping his erection with his fist. Even with her barging in on him, and watching him *masturbate*, he still wasn't humiliated. The abundance of masculine swagger was so thick in the room that Nadia could have choked on it.

She let her eyes come back up his body, past the thin line of dark, *wet* hair that bisected his muscular stomach, then his chest and past his angular jaw to land on those golden, glowing eyes of his. Then she whispered what she wanted, "Don't stop doing it."

If it was possible for his eyes to burn more, they were doing so now. His gruff voice slid along her nerves, and to Nadia it sounded like a deeper, animalistic growl. "I won't," his tongue swiped at his lips again and Nadia saw both fangs clearly, "but, instead of being a voyeur…why don't you come over here and participate?" His hand stroked one more time down his length and Nadia shivered.

Then she damned herself for all eternity and stepped closer to the shower.

***

He would not push her away when the look on her face told him more than any words at that moment could have. She wanted something. She wanted it badly. Drake wasn't sure if she could handle sex with him right now, and actually, he wasn't quite sure he had enough control over his Druid side to calm down enough for her. With her slight frame and noted different sexual appetites than he or the women he messed around with, Drake would take any notions of what sex between them could be like and turn it into something primal, dark, raw, and utterly different than what she was expecting or used to. He didn't want to shock her, but that would be exactly what would happen if he tried to slide inside her body right now. He wasn't looking for soft words and softer kisses. What he wanted was someone experienced, and just as aggressive as he could handle. He wanted rough, bruising, scream my name, and claw my back sex, and no matter how bad he wanted it with her, he wouldn't subject her to his wilder, carnal appetites.

Although, the look in Nadia's eyes when he had caught her staring had not been ashamed. Instead, she seemed like the cat that had found the secret bowl of cream *and* the prize in the Cracker Jack box all rolled in one. He hadn't missed the self-indulgent smile on her face and he would probably dream about it for days now.

The delicious throb of blood in her body sung inside *his* veins as if he was the tuning fork and she the vein of gold he had been searching for forever. He couldn't stop the glide of his tongue over the tips of his fangs the closer she got. It didn't dawn on him that she might see that and become terrified, nor did it dawn on him that she would do what she did next.

Her slightly built body sidled right up to the glass door that stood hanging open beside him, and without hesitation her hand came up to his face. Delicate fingers reached out, caressing his mouth at first and then without warning, she slid her finger between the opening of his lips and touched the tip of his fang. For Drake, it was like stepping off the edge of a cliff and hitting freezing cold water at fifty miles an hour. He was instantly awake to every thrum of blood in *both* of their bodies, the excitement level for both of them and the wild zing of pure lust that was coming from her in waves. He knew she was past the point of worrying about what they would do when they woke up tomorrow. She was only thinking about right now.

She exhaled deeply and Drake could feel passion, indecision, confusion and a very, very strong emotion rolling off of her and into his feeling range. But for right now, he concentrated on the passion and did his best to make sure she held onto that feeling and let it flow through her. He wanted to give her so much.

With a slight growl, he mumbled, "The thought that you were in here watching me this whole time has me very, very hard." She shuddered from where her fingertips pressed against his speaking mouth. Her green eyes were huge and she still had a major blush riding on her cheeks. Drake let his lips close around one tip of her finger, and he nudged the end of it with his tongue. Her eyes closed halfway and she gasped. He let go, slightly. "Are you going to put me out of my misery or join me there?"

As an answer, she slid her finger away from his mouth, and let both hands slide over his chest. The look she gave his body was so deep and flooded with such want that a warm tickle took place in the vicinity of his heart. She acted as if she had never run her hands down a man's chest in appreciation. She acted as if the sigh of breath leaving her mouth had never been voiced over the experience of feeling her fingers embed themselves deep into hair, muscle, and tough, sun warmed skin.

She was trembling, he realized, and pretty soon the haze of desire that had clouded around him blurred away until Drake was faced with the realization that Nadia had never done this before.

It was all there, the slight hesitation in her touch, the wide eyed look that she still held on his body, the shiver that trembled through her fingers when she encountered the hard ridges of his stomach. She was as green as any other woman out there that hadn't indulged in a bit of wicked sex yet.

Two different emotions pushed in on Drake at once. The first one was shame. How could he go on with this when he knew now just how inexperienced she was? How could he ruin her purity that way? But with that thought came another one. How would he be able to let her walk out of this bathroom tonight without them both reaching fulfillment? Would he rather some other man introduce her into the ways of passion? Fuck no. Protectiveness poured through his veins, hardening his body even more. She was his.

"You're so…big," she whispered on a high indrawn breath. Drake could see the awe in her face as her hands crept inside his chest hair and her fingernails raked a path from his pecs to his waist. He barely stopped himself from throwing his head back and growling like some animal. Bad enough, his growl escaped, which caused her eyes to come back to his face.

Green, half lidded eyes held him enthralled, while her fingers tested the strength of his skin along his waistline. "I knew you were large already, but you really are such a…," her eyes traveled back to watch her fingers and Drake watched too. She had let one hand creep over the tattoo on his left hip, "very impressive man." Her fingers drifted over it softly, fleetingly and

Drake had to stop himself from thrusting his hips towards her.

His hand was still wrapped around his cock and he, absurdly, didn't want to let go. In his mind he would explode the minute her soft, small, hot little hands touched his hard dick. He wasn't sure he would be able to stand if that happened. Trying to put matters back on an even playing field, he leaned down and ever so gently got her attention again by placing his mouth over hers.

She exhaled into his mouth and Drake suppressed a deep groan. He kept his hand on his dick and the other holding onto the door with all of his might. He didn't want to touch her until she was ready for him to do so. Right now her hands were still on his waist, but one of them had moved back up to curl around the back of his neck. She canted her mouth, tilting it just so to give him better access, since he was so much taller than she. Drake nibbled at her half open lips, licking the bottom one, then the top. He created a pace that was slow and sure-lick, nibble, and swipe his tongue along the seam of her lips. Then he would repeat it over and over. He didn't want to plunge into her mouth with his fangs right there and scare her off. If she wanted a deeper kiss, she would have to let him know.

Seconds later, she grew impatient. Her other hand moved to his lower back while she stepped over the bottom railing and into the shower with him, pressing her body up against his where not one single iota of light could shine between them.

His so called slow and sure pace evaporated. He let go of the door to the shower and placed both of his hands under her ass, like he had done earlier. With very little prodding, her legs were wrapped around his waist while one of his massive hands stayed under her ass, keeping her right where he wanted her, sitting astride his cock.

His mouth ate at hers, thrusting deep then retreating and doing so again and again. She answered back as best she could. Her small tongue was swift and deadly accurate, giving him a deep lick on the roof of his mouth that caused him to growl against her. When her tongue laved his fangs, one after the other, he twitched his cock against her molten core. His hardness jumped against her and she moaned deeply, and then she thrust delicately against his hips, her heat riding his cock.

Drake left her mouth and made his way down her jaw line to her neck. She allowed him access, as she thrust her head back and murmured, "Please…" deep in her throat. When he dipped his head and ran his tongue down the sexy line of her neck, he felt a surge of heated moisture against him and his knees almost buckled.

Thank God he had picked her up. If she would have stayed standing and tried to touch his cock with her hands, or heaven forbid her mouth, Drake would have embarrassed himself like some adolescent with his first screw. This he could handle. As long as her hands stayed elsewhere on his body and her mouth above his waist, he was fine. And if he kept it up they would both be able to find some measurement of pleasure this way, besides, this was a whole heck of a lot better than his hand. He had a warm, willing and very wet woman rubbing his cock instead. He shuddered and started a slow roll with his hips.

Long, beautifully slim, and surprisingly strong legs were wrapped tightly around his waist. Her ankles were locked together in a fierce grip, but Drake could feel a fine trembling had started, and he knew as he rocked his hips a bit deeper against her feminine core, feeling the dampness from not only the shower water off of his body but her own wetness through the fabric, that she wasn't very far from reaching her climax.

He tongued her earlobe, wishing they were on a bed to where he could reach every delicious inch of her body, but he would take what he could get at this moment and besides that left an excuse to do all of this over and over again, but to do it right the next time.

God, she was so hot. The heat rolling from her core singed his cock. His hands were now settled right under her ass, holding her tightly against his body while he controlled the movement he was giving her and just how hard, soft, or fast his dick slid over her sensitized, but material-covered flesh. He could feel the thrumming of energy that was growing from inside her body. Her nerve endings were singing in pleasure. Dew had formed on her forehead and Drake leaned away slightly to notice that her eyes were closed. Dark eyebrows were lax, not drawn down in aggravation like they usually were whenever she was with him. Instead, right at this moment she was so lost to sensation that her armor was no longer up.

He wanted to see and watch her come so badly that his own pleasure took a backseat to hers.

***

Nadia felt as if her world had tipped on its axis and would never be right again.

Every hot fantasy she had ever had about Drake, starring Drake, or imagined Drake in was now happening to her. She had never known he was this *unrestrained* with his sexuality; she never could have imagined him doing what he had been doing, much less her walking towards him after a few suggestive words from him.

He was so strong. He had held her up with one arm earlier and had been doing so again, but now both of his hands were placed right where the crease of her bottom met her thighs, and every once in a while, all ten of his fingers clenched against her flesh.

The very hard and very long length of his erection was sliding, *sliding* along her core. Thank God her pajama pants were very soft and now, very wet, but since he was giving her slow, sure strokes she didn't think he was hurting himself in anyway. At the moment she hoped, no, she prayed that he wouldn't stop. It just felt too damn good.

The thought that this was Drake, *her* Drake doing this wicked thing to her filled her with emotions so close to exploding that Nadia wasn't sure if she wanted to kiss him continually for a month, start crying from pure joy of finally getting a chance with him, or combust from pure, unadulterated want. All she did was keep her head back so that he could lick his way along her collarbone like he was doing now. She didn't want anything to be over too fast, but she knew that the fire racing along her nerve endings, the fine tremor that had overtaken her body along with the frantic gusts of air spilling from her mouth, were all signs that she was going to implode in a firestorm of sensation, and it wouldn't be far from now.

Years of agonizing wonder on her part sent her hips into a slight repetitive motion. She started to counter his thrusts with her own. She didn't know the first thing about what she was doing, she just knew that it felt good and he hadn't stopped her yet, so she was going to keep doing it.

His left hand moved from her bottom and slid over the wet material to her lower back. Long fingers dipped between material and skin, and seconds later his massive hand was sliding under the elastic waistband of her pajama pants. She felt as if she were touching a living flame; he was that hot. Her eyes slid open halfway at the same time that he turned them and settled the upper half of her back against the wet stone wall of his shower.

Scorching eyes the color of ultra-bright, molten gold peered at her from hooded eyes. Nadia took in everything from the sweat dotting his forehead, to the gleaming, menacing points of his fangs from where his mouth was opened slightly. Heat pulsed low in her core and she flexed against him as his left hand gripped her bottom and moved the fabric low enough so that his other hand could join in. Now both of his hands were holding her naked bottom, as he kept up a wicked thrust against her.

Nadia just laid there in his arms, held by the wall, his hands and his dick moving under her, and felt so alive and in tune with her body in a way that she had never felt before.

This is what she had been missing for years. This intensity, this passionate, strong, sexy man had done this with so many other women…no…she wouldn't think of that. She pushed the thought away and gripped her fingers in his wet hair, bringing his face down to hers once more. She wanted this moment for him and her only. She wanted to remember this forever, and by God thoughts of the women in his past would not taint it for her.

With his lips barely touching hers, she whispered, "Your hands feel good on my skin."

He shuddered in mid stroke and let his fingers rasp ever so closer to the crease of her bottom. Passionate fire raced through Nadia as one of his fingers dipped down, then even further, until she knew he could feel the slickness of her core.

"Oh…" She stopped moving against him and focused now on that sinful finger which was moving into territory that had never felt the presence of a man before now, before him. Flames licked at her stomach, branching out into her body, burning everything they came into contact with. She felt as if everything hinged on him either touching her intimately or burying himself deep, so deep inside her body.

"Damn angel, you're so hot, so fucking wet…" his breath puffed out against her lips and Nadia felt as if a demon had moved inside, taking over her body when she let her tongue come out to lick his upper lip. That seductive touch along with his frantic cursing made her feel disjointed and unhinged from reality.

His carnally divine finger was slippery now and slid so very effortlessly down through the crease of her bottom to the very sensitive, very swollen flesh of her core. With one bare flick against her responsive folds, she jerked, then moaned deep in her throat, "Ohyesohyesohyes." Between the hardness of his dick under her, still rubbing against her body, his fingers slipping down teasing her wantonly, and his mouth nibbling hers, Nadia was more than mystified. She just knew that she wanted release and she wanted it now.

"Ah…you like that, don't you, honey?" Another lick from his divine tongue and she let hers out to duel with his. That turned into a deep fiery kiss, until he broke away and nuzzled the soft area where her shoulder met her neck. His fingers flicked her receptive core, that small hidden flange of nerve filled flesh, and Nadia shuddered as his dick continued to move.

She started to imagine that when he moved, he was sliding inside of her and the visualization coupled with his fingers and body moving against her helped the arc of pleasure grow to astounding heights deep in her body. A bolt of heat attacked her from nowhere and her inner muscles contracted.

"Ah…yes…please don't stop."

He licked her earlobe and said, "I'm not stopping. I'm never going to stop, even if you come once, twice, or even three times…you are going to have all the fucking satisfaction you can handle from me."

Nadia shuddered against him as he smiled against her neck.

"You are so close angel, so very close. You want to feel it don't you?" Another lick along her neck and her womb tightened with heat, "You want to feel me there, sliding deep into your body. Not my fingers," a deep wracking sob flared up from out of nowhere and escaped her mouth. She was so close, so very close to that elusive bliss that she needed, "but my cock. I'm hard for you angel, only you…"

At those words, Nadia saw nothing.

Her body exploded with want. For a second there she hung, suspended in a world filled with such wanton bliss that she didn't want it to end. She stiffened against him while her mouth opened on a soundless scream. Tremors sidled through her while her core felt imbued with fiery heat and a flood of moisture. Tears burned behind her eyes as she held onto his body with everything she had.

He growled against her chest, sounding like a wild animal, and she felt the tank top she had on loosen a bit around the neck. Then the shudders that had just torn her apart with pleasure, wracked through him. He surged his dick against her now swollen and extremely responsive core, and Nadia felt her shirt give way completely.

Then…silence. Neither one of them moved. Nadia knew she couldn't at the moment anyway. But Drake kept his head down against her chest where she could now feel his hot breath on the heated skin of her upper breast. Her fingers played in his wet hair and she was more than happy to stay right where she was until he deemed it would be time for them to move. Besides, his body still covered her up against the shower wall.

He sighed harshly against her, "I think I ruined your shirt."

Nadia looked down onto the crown of his head, and then he lifted, looking into her eyes while he did so. It took her a few moments to notice that her shirt was ripped and gaping open, but not enough to expose her breasts out to the open. What held her enthrall though was the material of her ripped shirt hanging from his fangs. A deep, dark and very wicked shudder wracked her frame.

She smiled weakly, "I don't care."

He slipped his hands free from her pants and one hand removed the material from his mouth. "Good," that was all he said before he let her slide down his body then turned away to flip the knobs for the shower again.

***

Exquisite, simply exquisite, but Drake fought down the red hot brand of possession that was battling with his mind. Nadia was more than just some woman that he had shared a very sensual moment with; she was fresh faced, purity in a small perfectly wrapped package, wide eyed with what had just happened between them and Drake watched her with a feral quality that he knew he had to nip in the bud.

Tone it down buddy. She still doesn't understand exactly what happened to her body yet. Give her a chance to calm down before you go primal on her.

He put a clamp on his reaction to brand her as his and instead let his recent orgasm satiate his mind as well as his body. He would need a very relaxed state if he wanted to get her bathed and out of this shower.

She was trying to stay in her corner of the shower when Drake moved and let the force of the water hit her. He hadn't turned on the top showerhead only the side one. With his left hand he grasped the edge of her torn shirt and let his hand slide under to rest on her warm, beautiful skin. Her stomach was soft, decidedly female and even though she was such a slight woman, she still had a small curve to her belly that Drake thought was just precious. He had never liked women with more muscles than curves.

"You okay?" he whispered as he rubbed his thumb across her delicate navel. The tip of his thumb fit right into the slight hole there. God, she was so small. His whole hand could grasp the middle of her body.

She nodded, and Drake knew her shyness had kicked in. He tipped up her chin with his other hand and gave her a crooked smile.

"There's no need for you to go all shy on me now. Not after everything we just did in here."

"I know. I just can't help but feel as if I'm dreaming." The redness of a blush tinted her cheeks and she looked everywhere but at Drake.

"Tell you what, let's get washed up then we can really do some dreaming in that big bed out there."

She didn't answer him, but nodded. His hand moved on her skin again and he grasped the edge of her shirt in his fingers.

"Mind if we get you naked so that I can go ahead with that plan?"

The red blush stayed, but she nodded again, apparently at a loss for words.

Before he was allowed to change his mind Drake grasped both edges of her torn shirt and pulled them away from her skin. Without giving her or him a chance to do anything else, he took the waistband of her pants in his grasp. "Do you want to do it, or are you gonna let me?"

She pressed her face into his chest and whispered, "Go ahead." giving him the permission he needed. He knew she was having a tough moment right now and he didn't want to make things any worse by being a rude, overbearing barbarian.

After he had pulled off her damp pajama pants, along with her panties, Drake didn't give himself much of a chance of looking, knowing that she would be waiting for that. Instead he reached for some dry towels that he kept on a ledge over the top of the showerhead and grabbed a washcloth for her and him. Turning, he caught her trying to cover up her body with hands that were too small for such a large job. It was almost funny, but he stopped the grin forming on his face. The last thing she needed was to be laughed at.

The washcloth forgotten in his hand, his hand came under her jaw. Tipping her face up to his, he leaned down and placed a very chaste kiss on the corner of her mouth. Then he leaned back a bit.

"You are lovely, exquisite and simply gorgeous. There is nothing, nothing on your body that I would find remotely ugly, and with what just happened between us, you need to know that if I stay in this shower with you, naked, any longer than I have to…things are going to happen."

He let his eyes take in her huge green ones, travel down her neck to a delicately sloped chest, where breasts so beautiful and so delicately made sat awaiting his perusal with dark, coral tipped nipples thrusting proudly up at him. Burning eyes continued on, taking in her very feminine curves, her insanely small waist to very womanly hips, where closely trimmed dark curls protected her from his view. Her long legs trembled, and when Drake finally looked back up he knew his eyes were glowing again.

"Those things would involve your tight little body welcoming me inch by inch." He swiped his thumb along her shaking lips. He could feel her arousal thrumming around both of them again. "But I can't do that without going a bit crazy, so let me clean up real fast then I will leave you to do your thing, kay?"

At her nod Drake handed her the washcloth then turned, took a deep sigh and washed his body with record speed. Not even two minutes later he grabbed a large towel from the top, placed it on a side rack for her to grab when she was done, and then grabbed himself one to wrap around his hips. He turned, gave her a quick kiss on shocked lips and said, "Take your time. I'll be waiting when you're done." Then he left the shower.

***

Nadia went through the motions of washing as if she had cotton for brains.

The things that they had done and said in this shower couldn't even be surmised in one word. She wanted to weep from the pleasure he had shown her, but on the other hand she wanted to do it all over again. She wanted that rush of emotions, fire and excitement thundering through her veins to happen again and again.

She rinsed off, her mind still in a daze and turned off the water. Grabbing the huge dark green towel, she dried her body and then wrapped it around her. When she stepped out, she stopped in front of the mirror and found out that she didn't look any different; except for puffy lips and a few red marks on her shoulders, she looked like the same old Nadia that had allowed herself to be seduced into getting in the shower with one of the most sinful men she had ever known.

Then she realized she would have to walk in front of him to go back to the guestroom for something else to sleep in. Embarrassment tried to creep in, but she shot it down. She couldn't be mortified every time he did or said something to her.

She gripped the door handle in her hand and turned it, walking out into his bedroom and to where he was now sitting on the edge of the bed. Dark, tousled hair stood up on end and went in every direction while caramel eyes tracked her movement as she walked into the room. His body was bare except for a pair of black boxer briefs and a crooked grin that she was coming to know all too well.

Nadia felt as if her feet had become planted to the floor. She tried to continue walking but she couldn't.

"I pulled out a shirt for you to wear, if you want to wear it, that is." He gestured beside him and Nadia noticed a plain white tee sitting on the bed beside him.

She bit her lip and walked closer to him, glad that he didn't reach out to touch her because she might just come again, simply from one carefully placed touch. Her inside muscles throbbed with renewed ardor.

She reached out and grabbed the shirt with one hand, while the other held a death grip on the towel.

"Thank you," she said, as she pulled the soft shirt closer to her body. But then she wondered how was she supposed to just walk out of the room after what had happened? How could she just tell him goodnight and then leave to go back to her guest bedroom…alone?

"You're welcome," he told her in his deep voice. The little hairs on the back of her neck stood up. He was so very close now. Nadia glanced in his direction and found her eyes captured by his. He was no longer smiling. Skin, glorious, hard, hot burnished skin was inches away.

"I guess I should go to my room now…" Well, she had sounded like a petulant child just then.

"There's no need for that."

"No need?" Nadia parroted back to him, nervously twitching the shirt in her hands.

"No, you can sleep right here…with me."

"With you?" God, she needed to stop this.

A smile tipped the corner of his mouth, one he was unable to hide from her this time. "Nothing will happen, angel. I'm perfectly capable of holding you and falling asleep." He let his hand come up and tangle into her damp hair. "So, why don't you go put that shirt on and then come back and meet me?"

"Okay," Nadia turned and left the room so fast she was surprised there weren't flames behind her.

She didn't contemplate anything on her trek back to the guestroom. Apparently for the past hour she hadn't been thinking too clearly anyway, so why ruin the night with thoughts? She tugged on the shirt, inhaling Drake's particular smell, then pulled on panties, and raced back to his door. She slowed when she reached it, not wanting to seem too eager to spend the night in his bed. In…his…bed. Dear God, she was going to be in a bed with Drake. Her mind reeled.

After chewing her lip to pieces, she finally made her way into his room again to find him already under the covers. Slowly, she walked over to the large bed that she had admired an hour ago and before she could reach the covers to pull them back, he was doing the honors. Nadia glimpsed at his strong, muscular torso before she snuggled down for the night, IN HIS BED.

Within seconds he had wrapped his strong arms around her, whispered good night and pulled her into his body. Nadia took a deep breath and prayed for sleep never to claim her.

Chapter 14

Drake let Nadia's deep breathing that rustled over his chest wake him up by slow degrees. A quick glance at the clock on the wall proclaimed it to be very close to seven in the morning. Too early on a Saturday morning to worry about what time it was.

Another breath across his skin and Drake inhaled deeply, taking in the scent of freshly washed cotton, the mountain fresh soap he had in the shower and one smell that he couldn't catalogue no matter how hard he tried, pure clean warm woman. His feelers were awake all of the time, unless he shut them down with a glamour, and right now since she was asleep he figured there was no reason to know what she was feeling.

Long black strands of hair were coiled around her body, from her crown to her back. Shiny locks wound around one arm and then lay against the dark green of his sheets. Her slight body was curled towards him, but not resting against him. Even in sleep she was too skittish to touch him. A very feminine and long fingered hand rested palm up on the sheet beside her body. Her other hand was under her frame, out of sight from Drake.

She looked so comfortable and so deep in her slumber that he doubted he would be able to bring himself to wake her. Then he remembered the flight wasn't leaving until this afternoon, so there was no need to wake her now.

The bright white of his shirt was startling against the darker colors of his bedding. The neckline was so huge on her that one shoulder had made its way through the neck opening. Beautiful, translucent skin peeked at him through the fall of her long hair. Drake knew she had been embarrassed last night, but even with that embarrassment she had allowed herself to let go and give into her emotions. Now she needed to realize that he wasn't going to do anything to mortify her. She needed to get accustomed to his body and his presence.

He had known that not giving her an option would help, which is why he told her to join him in his bed. Since he hadn't given her a choice, she hadn't brought one up.

With the softness of morning light beginning to make its way into the room, Drake watched her sleep and felt the hard mold around his heart break free. He had felt heavy emotion before. He had allowed his heart entry into both of his marriages, and he dismally remembered how that had turned out, which was why he now only allowed women close enough to have sex with him. Now looking at Nadia curled up so trustingly by his side, he knew he had been remiss in thinking that he could only enjoy her and not let her deep into his heart.

It was too late. She was deeply embedded in his psyche and he doubted he would ever be able to remove her.

***

Stretching, hiding her mouth behind a yawn, and uncurling her body from the position she had been in, Nadia woke, like she always did, by slow degrees, noticing things one at a time. A beautiful four poster, natural pine bed with deep greens, gold, and other colors was what she was lying on. The rumpled bed linens were heavy and comfortable, with soft down filling. Nadia yawned one more time and let out a slight sound with it as she took in the room around her.

A deep burgundy pillowcase was in the way but Nadia shoved it away, focusing on the massive corner bookcase against the far wall. Old leather spines were visible from here, but she couldn't make out the writing, while huge leather-wrapped, masculine furniture sat at angles to the books, inviting relaxation and ease.

Her eyes had just found the heavy wooden dresser where she could see a man's watch, some cufflinks, and a few odds and ends, when the door to the bedroom drifted open.

Drake strolled in looking more than rumpled, wearing nothing more than an old pair of worn, button up blue jeans. Nadia immediately started to run her fingers through her mussed hair and straightened the huge shirt she had on. He stopped beside the bed, sat down right next to her hand and placed a large mug of what smelled like hot tea on the bedside table.

"Mornin' angel," he told her, as his hand came up to a strand of hair which he moved out of her face. Nadia felt her heart thump somewhere around her ankles.

Extremely aware of morning breath, she mumbled, "Morning, thanks for the tea."

"You're welcome."

She took a sip, found it not too hot, but not lukewarm, perfect. She licked her lips and her eyes went right back to his face. Gorgeous eyes warmed like liquid heat as they roamed over her face and then down her chest. She willed her hands not to yank the covers up and over her body.

The things they had done, the things she had seen him doing last night, whirled around in her brain and Nadia took a deep breath, trying to focus on the present.

"So, our flight leaves this afternoon, right?"

"At six," he said with a nod.

What in the world was she going to do with that much time on her hands and a sexy devil of a man around her at every waking moment? A sexy devil that had touched her, in places that no other man had touched, a sexy devil that had made her feel things that she had never felt before. She was going to have to learn to employ some damage control and fast.

"I guess that gives us plenty of time to laze around and do nothing." She looked up into his face, "Unless you have something that you have to do?" She waited for him to say yes, that he did have something to do, something to keep him away from her curious hands.

A crooked grin touched the corner of his mouth. Nadia's breath freeze dried. "No angel, I have nothing to do but sit right here all day, if I want, and watch you lick that delicious mouth of yours."

And just that easily the sexual tension in the room was back.

Nadia felt a blush work up and over her shoulders. Drake, meanwhile, had dropped the smirk and was now watching her as if she were being hunted slowly, methodically and dangerously. She gulped, but whatever was left in her mouth turned to ash. Her body, that he had awakened to desire so easily last night, now flamed into a hot conflagration, the flames worked through her nerves and into her stomach.

"I love when you blush. Your delicate skin flares with heat."

Nadia had never heard it put like that before. "Blushes are never pretty, Drake."

His finger swept a line from her neck to her nose. "Yours are," he said, simply.

She placed the mug back on the table before she dropped it on herself then made a move to get up. His massive hand swallowed hers on the blankets. Nadia could feel the heat inside his body. Her own clenched in renewed hunger.

"I wanted to tell you that I enjoyed last night. I had many, many dreams about you, my hands touching you, and your hands touching me, but I think it is safe to say that what happened eclipsed every single one of them."

He had dreams of her? Nadia shuddered as heat washed over her. The image of Drake, his hand moving on his erection, bringing himself pleasure was like HD in Nadia's brain. She hadn't gotten what she originally had wanted. Instead she had gotten something surprising, even to her, but she wanted that primal, raw moment with him back. She wanted to test her boundaries with him. *She* wanted to put her hands on him and bring him ecstasy.

No, you don't!! Think before you speak. Don't allow yourself to get pulled under. He is only screwing with your desires.

Nadia watched him as he gave her a slow, heated perusal from those hot eyes of his. He might be a man that switched from one woman to another with quick and efficient ease, but why would he do that with her, with the one woman he was always in constant contact with? Wouldn't that be crazy?

But on the same hand that didn't mean he was going to pledge undying love to her and drop down on one knee either. Besides, he had been married twice already. That was still shocking to her. She realized right then that even though she did love him deeply, she didn't want something from him that he did out of pity. If Drake wanted her, then he simply wanted her. She wouldn't be rash and tell him of how long she had loved him and cared for him. That was her secret, her burden for herself.

What she had with Drake last night was a guilty pleasure, one that she wouldn't mind repeating if only she could unglue her tongue from the roof of her mouth. Even if she could, Nadia knew it would take a bit more persuasion for her to ask anything from him, especially sexually.

Licking her lips, she said, "Thank you for your patience with me last night and from earlier at the gala. As you can tell, I'm not as experienced as you and what you showed me…last night…was simply…incredible." Those words came from her heart; they meant something and by the way Drake was looking at her that he realized that.

The look in his eyes was fierce, but tender all at once. His hand traveled from her jaw to her neck and then to her chest. Fire bloomed along the places where he touched, but Nadia kept her cool. His hand, large against her body, stopped right above her left breast, where the beat of her heart was strong, rapid and sure.

"Just when I think you can't surprise me more, you do. You walked in on me doing something that probably would have shocked or disgusted another woman, but instead of running you barged in, all wide and hungry-eyed."

"I wasn't thinking…just feeling." She told him honestly. He blinked and Nadia noticed a gold film creeping over his irises. He was beginning to change again, apparently from arousal.

His hand stayed in place, fingers flexing against her skin. "I know, and when I saw you standing there I wanted you so badly…" his words started to lisp and she noticed the tips of his fangs peeking out from his lips. "You make me burn, angel, burn so hot for such a small, delicate woman."

"Surely you don't think you would hurt me?" She eyed him with a curious look. "I'm sure you realize that women's bodies are made to," Oh God, was she going to say this out loud? "accept different sizes." Her face had to be bright red right now.

An amusing look slid into his golden eyes. "So sweet…" His hand left the thump of her heart and slowly ever so gently, made its way lazily over the curve of her left breast. The long fingers of his hand cradled her gently and Nadia felt as if she had stepped from a cliff into a free fall. Her nipple hardened to a painful peak, but he never touched her there, he just cradled the weight of her in his hand, while his thumb brushed the sensitive skin above her nipple. Nadia felt her vision haze a bit from the pleasure he gave her.

"Yes, I'm a very large man and no, it isn't my size that worries me, it is my Druid nature that scares me. I don't want to get too rough with you, but once I get inside your body it won't be any other way."

Just the thought that he wouldn't go easy on her sent shivers crawling along her skin. His hand left her breast and Nadia couldn't stop the pouting sound that left her mouth as he did so. She opened her eyes and he was closer than she had first thought.

"I don't know why this happened all of a sudden, but I do know this. I will have you, you will be mine, but I won't ever force you to do anything that you don't want to do." His eyes blazed at her while his breath tickled the skin of her neck. "I will teach you anything that you need to know, and think about that because, angel…I've been alive for a very, very long time."

He made sure that thought had settled in her fogged brain before leaving her to think about everything they had just spoken to each other.

***

You sure know how to put yourself in situations that will make things extremely hard on you, don't you?

Drake ignored his mind muttering at him and turned his attention to the scroll of the stock market on the bottom of the flat screen in his office. Usually he didn't watch the market that closely, but right now he needed a distraction from thoughts of Nadia, so the stock market was it.

After making a few calls, checking on the clinic and a few of his business partners, he turned his attention to getting Brian on the phone. He wanted to make sure the plane would be ready to go at the proper time.

An hour later he was knee deep in the background file of a possible business partner when a slight tap echoed through the room. Drake looked up and noticed Nadia standing there. Her long black hair had been pulled into a ponytail. A bright yellow tee covered her chest while Capri pants and some little sandal-looking shoes completed her outfit. She looked so very young and so carefree standing there.

"Hey," he told her as he moved the papers around and placed them in the requisite file.

"Hey back," she replied with a small smile. "I was wondering if you were hungry. It's almost lunchtime." She twisted her fingers nervously and Drake caught the flutters of anxiousness in the air between them. A tense, uneasy woman had never attracted him before, but now that he knew *he* was the reason why she was this way, he overlooked that and tried to think of ways to make her overlook it too. "I was thinking maybe we could go get something to eat."

He didn't waste a second before answering. "Sounds good, what are you up for?"

The sudden acceptance of her question apparently stunned her for a moment, until she snapped out of it. "Uh…how about some awesome steaks?"

He stood up from behind the desk and came around to meet her at the door. "Angel, I'm a red blooded Texas man. I'm always up for steak."

She smiled and Drake *felt* that smile like a punch to the middle of his chest.

"Good, I know just the place."

"Well, lead away darlin.' I'm right behind you."

***

They settled on Mexican instead, since the steakhouse she wanted to go to didn't open until five-o-clock in the afternoon on Saturdays. Now they were sitting in Drake's living area and he was watching her sip the rest of the martini she had from the restaurant. Noise from a golf tournament on T.V. echoed in the background.

"That was delicious, but the juicy, tender, fall apart in my mouth steak that was calling my name at The Capital Grille could have easily topped it." She smiled in his direction over the coffee table. "But the company couldn't be topped." What really surprised him was that she only blushed a little when she said that. She was getting a bit more comfortable in his presence.

He nodded his head in her direction. "You got that right."

She took a sip of her drink and Drake took advantage of the moment to study her profile. Her forehead was smooth, unlined, and free of worry. The tapered end of her nose was cute as hell, and Drake had a hard time holding back the urge to reach over and tweak it. Her lips were naturally pink and plump, and glistened from her tongue that had came out to catch stray drops of her mango martini. She was slowly but surely growing at ease around him, which he took as a good thing, of course.

"You know, out of pure curiosity, I just can't help wondering how you got to be the age you are without the amount of experience that I would have guessed with being twenty-five." He watched her as he said that, and she did blush, but not as fiercely as he'd expected. "Young women these days are much more sexually active than they were when I was that age."

"It wasn't as if I were a recluse or anything." Huge green eyes came up to his face and Drake wanted to reach over and kiss her right there. "I'm sure you remember how painfully shy I was when I was younger. Well, that didn't lend me any attention at all."

"I just can't get over the fact since you are so gorgeous. Back then you were a lovely young woman too, so it just doesn't add up in my mind. The guys nowadays must be blind."

She rolled her eyes and waved him away with her hand. "Drake, you're being silly now."

He leaned over the coffee table and grabbed that hand with his, letting his thumb rest on her pulse as it fluttered in her wrist. "I'm not being silly. You are a gorgeous, tempting young woman and it boggles my mind how you stayed so damn innocent in a world that prides itself on eradicating purity." He could see the shock on her face and feel it emanating from her body. "And don't act as if I don't find you attractive." He let his eyes rest on hers, burning her from the inside out. "You should know better than that, especially after our little tryst in the shower, love."

She licked her lips and Drake imagined that tongue on his body. "T-Thank you for the compliment, but I never really felt as if I had to jump into bed with the next available guy to learn about sex and relationships. Apparently I give off a do-not-touch-vibe."

Drake smiled. "Darlin', you are so untouchable to some of us men, that the arrogant, *important* ones find that immensely exciting." He leaned over as close as he could. "We want to see how far we can seduce you before you allow us a touch, a kiss or even a glance." Smoothing his thumb over her soft skin he continued, "You are a temptress, a woman that unthinkably knows how to seduce a man with those very hesitation tactics."

She arched an eyebrow at that. "So, if I'm listening to you correctly, you are one of those *important* men that want to run me to ground and *teach* me what I have been missing all these years, not only that, but I also unknowingly tempt you beyond reason." She didn't hide her eye roll. "The day I become a temptress for a man like you is the day that hell will freeze over."

He gripped her wrist a bit harder with his fingers. "After last night, how can you doubt the reaction I get around you?"

She looked down at her to go cup and licked her lips again, then whispered, "I'm not stupid, Drake. I know that you were touching yourself with the sole purpose for a quick release. Just because I happened to walk in doesn't mean that I'm the one that made you that way. I just helped you accomplish what you wanted in the first place. Any warm, willing woman could have done that."

Now he was seeing red. "Let me tell you something. Do you remember our argument in your house when Belle died? I can see by your face that you do. Remember when you screamed at me for being away and as you so eloquently put it, "fucking Ms. Vintage Valentino"? Well, I wasn't fucking her, but she did have the experience, the 'know how' and the sexual intelligence that we could have ended up in bed together."

Nadia tightened her fist and tried to move away, but Drake wasn't done yet. "She was even on her knees, her dress pushed down with her breasts out in the open, her hand on my body…her mouth inches away from my cock, and you know what, angel? She still couldn't get me hard." He watched her breathe a harsh curse. "All I thought about while she undid my pants was *you*. All I saw when her hands touched my body was *your* hands doing the touching." He caught her eyes and held her there, trapped with his gaze. "All I wanted was *your* mouth inches from my cock."

Nadia breathed so deeply that she shuddered from the force of it.

"Now you try and tell me how any willing, warm woman can make me come hard enough to bust a couple of ribs. Tell me that so that I can find a way to get you out of my mind."

Furious with her, he dropped her hand and left the room, not trusting his rapidly fraying control one second longer.

***

Nadia sat on the plane beside Drake and listened to him talk on his cell once again. It was amazing that he had even been able to step foot out of his house without people hunting him down. She had known he was a busy man, but sometimes things got out of hand, as it seemed to be now, unless he was relishing every call because that took the strain off of their being alone.

She sighed and looked out the window again. He had been furious, beyond agitated that she would get the idea in her head that she wasn't the reason for his inability to have sex or even get touched by another woman. She, on the other hand, just found it amazing, simply astounding that the beautiful goddess that she had seen in the picture with him weeks ago had placed her hands on him and he hadn't been able to do anything with *her* stimulating him.

Maybe he's telling the truth. Have you ever known him to lie anyway?

No, she had never heard him lie or be dishonest in all the years that she had known him.

So he is being truthful. You are the only woman right now that can get him aroused.

Just the thought that he was right sent shivers down her spine. To have the full attention of Drake Thompson would send her into a tailspin. How would she be able to stop herself from falling ever deeper and more dangerously in love with him? And with his sensory abilities how could he not sense the way she felt? Damn, did he sense it now?

Red burned her cheeks, so hot that her skin throbbed. *It's a little too late to worry about that now, don't you think?*

The two or so hours they had before leaving his condo were spent packing and making sure she had everything she needed. When she'd finished, she placed everything at the entry door to make sure she didn't forget a bag and to do so she had to walk past his bedroom door. Just the images from last night were enough to scorch her brain. What would happen when they got back to Beaumont? Would things go back to normal, or would he become the man she had been waiting for forever, attentive, dedicated to her wishes, sharing his time with her and only her?

She shook her head. Things like this were needless to dream about because they would never happen. Drake would never allow himself to get in over his head. Nadia knew that without having to be told. And his little slip about them having sex, at some point in the near future, Nadia would take that with a grain of salt. Not that she doubted his diligence, she didn't, but it was better to get real than to let dreams haunt you forever. She had enough with loving him for so long that if things ever really changed, she wouldn't know what to do.

Later, when she felt the jostle of the plane touching down, she looked over and noticed that Drake was still on the phone, this time with another business partner. The stewardess came to help her exit and without meaning to, Nadia turned towards where he was sitting one more time. Bright brown eyes held hers for a second then he placed his hand over the phone and told her, "I'll be done soon, don't leave yet. We need to talk."

She nodded and exited the plane. Minutes later she had managed to pull her bags to her Rover with help from Brian. She thanked him, and then stood there like a numbskull waiting for Drake.

Why couldn't he have talked to her in the two hours they had left while they were packing? Why couldn't she have told him that she now understood everything he had said at the restaurant? Why let that crazy scene hold reference over them? Nadia toed a small weed trying to grow from in between the cement slabs of the walkway. Now that she understood what he had been trying to say, she wanted, needed to tell him that she did. She wanted him to look at her again like he had this morning and last night.

Heavy footfalls interrupted her musing and she looked up. Drake was walking towards her and the setting sun tossed a good amount of light into his hair, causing the locks to look like russet colored satin. His body was powerful, with an easy, rock from the hip gait that made her insides clench with the heat that he had awoken in her. That man, that gorgeous, leanly muscled, but massive man had held her body up with his arms and had shown her so much pleasure last night that she had almost cried from it.

She shook that thought off whenever he got close enough to touch her.

"Sorry it to--,"

"I understa--,"

They both started to speak at the same time. He smiled and gestured to Nadia to go ahead.

She licked her lips and realized he was standing close enough for her to feel his breath when he exhaled. It drifted over the top of her head, sending strands of hair flying. "I understand now about what you were saying earlier. I'm sorry for getting you so worked up, although I never realized such a conversation would do that."

His hand tilted up her chin and without any warning he let his lips close over hers. Nadia inhaled sharply as her body came to instant life. He kissed her top and then her bottom lip, licked the crease between and cut it all too short for her liking.

With his mouth still whispering against hers he said, "Everything I told you was true. I think at night of the ways that I can have you touch and kiss me. I dream of the ways that I could turn the tables on you and show you just what I have learned after being around for as long as I have."

Nadia bit her bottom lip at that. His hand clenched on her chin.

"I want to know you as a friend, someone you would call in the middle of the night when you need them." He smiled against her lips, his thumb touching one corner in a sensual dance. "And I want to know you as a lover, one that would know every delicious place on your body…I do realize that this might take time, but darlin,' I can be a patient man." Another swipe of his thumb, "Are you up for that?"

She nodded, half dazed with passion already. Hell, what could he do to her when he *really* turned up the heat?

"Then we should get cozy tonight. How about you come over in a bit, we'll have a bite to eat and maybe watch a movie." He gave her another heart stopping lick across sensitive lips, "maybe I'll even get lucky enough to hit second base. What do you say?"

She grinned at his ego coming through. "I'll be there." And even though it took every ounce of guts she had, she turned from him and went to her vehicle.

***

Drake pushed his workout extra hard when he got home.

Knowing Nadia was coming was incentive to keep his simmering lust under wraps, rather than unleash it on her unassuming body. Well, she now realized that he would get a little out of control, but no amount of telling her would prepare her innocent mind for the realization. He would have to be precautious.

After he finished that, he showered and fixed a light supper consisting of sandwiches and a salad. He was pulling out some movies when she called and said she would be there in a little while.

Drake stood in the center of his living area, grinning like a sixteen year old who had just been asked to the prom.

He had lived for over two hundred years, seen countless things, war, and famine, seen his family grow old and pass on, and still he was astounded to know that there was something in this world that could amaze him. There were still things she needed to know about him and his Druid side, things that he hoped she would take well, as well as she had taken the rest last night.

There was also the fact that he was tampering with a woman, a woman he had known since she was twelve, that would never stoop to just having a sexual relationship with him. And even knowing all of this, knowing that she was fairly innocent, sweetly demure and totally not his normal brand of woman, he kept throwing out invitations and keeping her on a short chain when around him. The last thing he wanted to do was hurt her, but for some reason he couldn't allow her out of his sight.

He hadn't thought of his past and usually tried to keep from doing so, but thinking of deep feelings for women made him think of the women he had been married to. He was an old fashioned guy when it came to marriage. Even though his standards for relationships now weren't that way, his marriages had been carried through, at least on his end, with deep feelings of love for each woman, and a hope to make them understand who and what he was. Neither of those things happened, and each marriage had been shortened because of the fact that those women had turned out not to be the right ones to handle that information.

His sexual preferences were a bit unrestrained and too wild, which had led to his second marriage with Marie, being totally disastrous. Even though numerous years had passed, Drake could still see the unforgettable fear in her eyes when she looked at him. Trying to dispel that fear and calm her hadn't worked; she had stayed far away from him, bundled in the corner of their house, shaking from head to toe in terror. It hadn't taken long for her to leave him. He later learned that she had gone berserk in a town in Arkansas, the town deeming her unfit to live alone and they had placed her in a mental ward. The memory of Marie with her long black hair, beautiful curvaceous body and hauntingly sad dark eyes rose up in his mind. He had loved her, more so than Loraine, because something in Marie had needed him, needed his protection, his love, and he had wanted more than anything in this world to give her that. In the end, he hadn't been able to.

The emotions he had felt for those two women had been the strongest in his life so far. Yet nothing, not even those combined, could touch what he felt for Nadia. He had known back when they danced at Cole's party that something life changing could come from him knowing that she secretly desired him, and he could feel it happening, had felt it for a while. He had tried to restrain himself, tried to badly to keep what he felt for her under wraps, but he knew if he went any further with her those hidden feelings he had they wouldn't be so hidden anymore.

She was the one that could turn him into a raving sexual lunatic or surprisingly enough calm and control the beast, like she had last night. The fact that he hadn't taken her against the wall in the shower was proof enough that his Druid side calmed from her touch. More than likely it realized the purity of her and the strong feelings that Drake had and it held back, trying to save face in front of such an unexpectedly strong woman.

Drake stepped out onto his deck and listened to the night sounds around him.

He would let himself as close to Nadia as he could get. There was no point in denying the inevitable. She would be his. It was only a matter of time. And as far as Drake was concerned, he would do his damnedest to make sure that she never felt threatened, forced, or terrified of him in anyway. If he had to go at her pace, he would. Doing without wouldn't kill him, and besides he had some control; he would just have to learn how to use it.

You won't scare her off Thompson. She is tougher than she looks. Just be gentle.

Ah, now his conscience was *for* this relationship. Amazing how accepting things could also make things much easier. He smiled into the night and waited for Nadia to show up.

Chapter 15

Nadia pulled on the edge of her tee shirt and glanced down to see her bare toes peeking from the edges of her jeans and the flip-flops she had on. She wasn't exactly the epitome of sexual seductress, but Drake had said to get comfortable and she had. Now she was walking up his meandering steps, and she could hear music blaring from inside the house while security lights blazed all around.

Nickelback sang loudly about "something in your mouth," and Nadia couldn't help the smile that broke out on her lips. Drake listened to just about anything, but she had never thought that the large Texan would like that particular band. Apparently the lyrics made it more interesting.

Taking a deep breath she knocked as hard as she could on the front door, hoping he could hear her through the loud music. Seconds later she saw a massive shadow appear behind the hazed glass, and then music lowered and he was pulling the door open.

His eyes were dark in the low light of the foyer and those tingles traveled over her body once again. "Hey angel, come on in."

"You didn't have to turn the music off. I like Nickelback," she told him as she walked in, noticing the music was off now. "But that's okay because on the way over here I remembered some questions I have for you."

One dark eyebrow rose suspiciously. "I like a woman who wants to know more," he leaned down slightly and winked at her, "that means you're in it for the long haul."

Nadia laughed, but quelled the fluttering of her heart in her chest. With his strong abilities he probably could sense everything she felt right at this moment. It would be best to keep her feelings close to her chest, not out in the open for him to feel. Was she even able to hide them like that, or could he still feel them regardless?

He took her purse from her and said, "I know the last two times you were here you weren't exactly able to see the whole house. Do you want to now?"

"Sure…my mind whirls when I imagine just how many rooms you have in here," she told him as she took in the large expanse of his living area. Intensely masculine leather sofas and loveseats were the furniture. He even had a huge lump of driftwood sitting on the hardwood floor that was holding up a large glass coffee table.

"There are four bedrooms, each with their own full baths. I also have a gym, a library, and a game room, not to mention my office."

She heard him, but her eyes were glued to another fabulous driftwood piece that dominated the furniture. "That has to be the most unusual piece I have ever seen."

He chuckled, "I get that a lot."

Nadia let her eyes roam over the beautiful natural colors on the walls and the exposed beams of the ceilings. It really was a man's house, but even though it was intensely virile and sturdy, she felt at home and more than welcome here. An extremely large, but low fireplace was in the middle of the living area and she noticed as she looked closer that she could see another room through the huge opening. "It is double sided?" she asked him with another glance through the opening.

"Yeah, the other side is the den, which is where I spend most of my time besides being on my deck outside." He walked up behind her and placed his hands low on her waist. "C'mon, you know you want to see it."

She laughed and let him push her around the corner of the living room gently. His hands were large on her waist and so very hot. Pushing the thoughts away, she focused on the questions she wanted to ask him and the rest of the house she was desperate to see, trying to keep sexual arousal out of her mind.

"This is my den," he told her with a sweep of his hand.

The room in question was cozy and smaller than Nadia would have first thought. Off to the right, she could see part of an arch that led to the kitchen which apparently connected to the living area via a large hallway. The den was painted a deep beautiful red, which Nadia found surprising, and on the walls were stunning paintings and photography of wild animals. The furniture was overstuffed and looked very inviting and in one corner Nadia could see the large music setup that was still glowing, telling her it was on but muted.

"Well, I like this room too." She turned her gaze towards him and slyly let her eyes take in everything from his jeans to his green tee shirt and bare feet. The tips of his hair were still damp and her fingers itched as she remembered his damp hair from last night and the way it had felt sliding through her fingers.

"I have some sandwiches and a salad if you are hungry." His voice was deep and it was what she needed to snap her out of her perusal of him.

"Sure" She cleared her throat, "I'm starving."

He smiled and then gestured for her to follow him.

The kitchen was through the arch and it was massive too. Large industrial sized equipment gleamed chrome in the light. A gigantic two door refrigerator was one of the staples along with a six range oven. "Dear God, you can't tell me you cook this much?"

"I love to cook, and I do whenever I get the chance." He grabbed the salad from the refrigerator and another platter with sandwiches then turned to the bar that ran along the back of the island. "I would have cooked tonight if we would have had more time, but it's already going on nine 'o clock, so I think this will do."

"Of course, I love simple suppers."

"What would you like to drink? I have beer, soda, water, basically everything under the sun." He told her with a smile.

"Soda is fine." She said and then grabbed her some salad and sandwiches from the platter. Minutes later they were both sitting at the bar and going through the food quietly. Nadia found herself looking at him while he ate his beautiful jaw clenching as he chewed. Why couldn't he smack? Why couldn't he shove food in his mouth like a slob? Did everything about him have to be gorgeous?

"Is something on my face?"

Her eyes flew to his. "Uh…no, I'm sorry." She tucked her head back down and berated herself for being crazy about him.

"It's okay." Things got quiet again until, "You want to ask those questions now or later, because it wouldn't bother me either way."

Wiping her mouth with a napkin she looked at him. It was still amazing too with everything he had told her and shown her the other night, that he was actually some paranormal being. "Okay, I was wondering…you said there were others, right?" At his nod she continued, "Well, I'm assuming that not every single one of you are all the same age and from the same place, so how did you all find out about each other? Like if there is an Amber Druid from France how would you ever find out about him or her? Is there some sort of website you all go to?"

He took a sip of his drink and smiled at her, "I'm pleased to notice that you gave us this much thought."

Nadia couldn't control the smile that came out at his words.

"All right, let me start at the beginning, or what I assume to be the beginning." He smiled then continued, "There was a small group of Druids practicing in Scotland so many centuries ago. Somehow they found a way to attach their abilities and gifts into one single spell. They cast that spell onto themselves so that their ancestors would be graced with extraordinary speed, agility, sensory abilities, and a warning to any enemy that may come around."

"Amazing," she breathed, thoroughly engrossed in the story.

He gave her a wink and kept on. "The Amber Druids I know have all come to the same conclusion about our eyes being the reason for the Amber part of our name. We all have amazing eyesight, fiercely strong abilities, fangs, and the talent for calming, soothing, or wiping a mind of our image. Now with that said, we each have different gifts', mine is the capacity to converse with animals."

"This is the reason why your clinic is so successful."

He nodded at her. "Very plausible deduction Nadia. I am continually amazed at your mind's capacity."

She wrinkled her nose at him. "Smartass."

He ignored her jibe and continued, "Now after having said that, as far as I or any of us know, every Druid we come into contact with has Scottish ancestors, and we all have the same marks on our bodies which have been there since we were born. Our Druid mark denotes us as special, and lets us know on our twenty-fifth birthday that we will go through the change that makes us fully capable with our powers."

Nadia knew her eyes had to be huge again with wonder. "So this mark is like a birthmark?"

He stood in that swift Druid way of his and seconds later was pulling away the left half of his button fly, showing her his tattoo, set permanently into his skin right under his left hipbone. "See the circle in the center? That is the mark. It is a small circle with many different sized red dots inside."

"So the tattoo isn't part of it, it is just the circle that is the actual mark?"

"Yes," he told her and in seconds he was once again buttoned up and sitting. "Now as for the reason we all know each other, and like you said, we aren't all from the same place, whenever another Druid goes through the change, a shockwave of sorts travels to each and every mature Druid out there." He looked deeply at her, "You still with me?"

She nodded, still deeply intrigued.

"Okay, just wanted to make sure. So all the mature ones feel the shockwave and at the same time we all catch this distinctive and very clear picture of who and where this person is. The change to become a mature Druid is very, very draining and at times has been known to kill a lesser human being, one that hasn't the strength of mind or body to stay in control through the transformation."

"Oh my," she said in wonder.

"Did you have another question?"

Nadia tried to think past the astonishment that was crowding through her brain at the moment to remember what she had wanted to ask him. "Oh...is every Druid born a Druid, or is there another way to make someone like you?"

"I can 'gift' you into my world, but as far as I know there have been very few successful attempts. It is accomplished with a simple spell that I mentally chant into action over your body and then I ask you if you are willing to have this special gift; if you agree, I bite you, not to suck your blood, but more or less to inject you with the same powers that I have."

"Like a vampire...this is all so unreal to me," Nadia told him. "It is like a science fiction movie that I'm stuck in." She smiled at him before a horrible notion dawned. Oh God, how come she hadn't thought of this before? Her stomach heaved and she was sickly faint all of a sudden. Tears immediately burned behind her eyes.

"Nadia, what's wrong?" He was by her side in an instant, his strong arm pulling her out of the barstool to stand in front of him.

She swallowed a painful lump in her throat as she realized just how much he must have gone through in the past just to be where he was now. "I just realized that you had to have had a family and that they must be gone, unless you 'gifted' them over. How did you survive knowing that you would live on and on in the years to come, all alone without them?"

His large hand cradled her cheek and surprisingly enough he smiled at her, even though she could plainly see the sadness in his eyes. "Ah my little angel, so worried about me, but honey, I've had years and years to get over the pain. I was the only one in my family that was marked and it was extremely hard because we were so close, but no, they wouldn't accept my gift, and I couldn't force them to take it."

Hot tears scalded her cheeks as she imagined the suffering he had gone through to watch his family leave him one by one. Her heart broke for him. She roughly grabbed his waist and pulled him to her, sniffling into his shirt and trying not to bawl like a baby. "I would have begged you to bite me if the other option was to die without seeing you again." She wanted to bite back the words the second they left her mouth, but all she could do was squeeze his chest even tighter.

He'd stiffened beneath her hands when she said that, but now his large hand was smoothing her hair. "Sweetheart, you don't know what you would have done in that situation. A lifetime is a very long time when you know you can't die normally. It would take decapitation or extreme bodily harm to kill me. As it is, I never get sick, so I won't die from infection either."

She was glad he hadn't put too much emphasis on her words. Instead he had turned the tables back to what he was. She nuzzled his shirt, inhaling his luscious woodsy smell. "I'll bet this isn't the sort of night you had planned, was it? I distinctly remember you saying something about second base."

He laughed, and it rumbled into her ear where it was pressed against his shirt. "Honey, we have all night to worry about second base. Right now you need to make sure you understand everything I am."

Her insides warmed at the fact that he wasn't abandoning her seduction. Even though she knew she was headed for heartbreak, she wanted to feel him touching and kissing her again.

***

Drake looked over at Nadia as she licked ice cream from the spoon. His body stirred to life the instant she had crossed the threshold of his home; now he was merely biding his time before he could touch her.

They were sitting in the den, in the deep, overstuffed and extremely comfortable loveseat. She hadn't drawn in on herself after their question and answer session in the kitchen, or even after her heart stirring emotional words she had uttered into his shirt. Drake could have sworn his body had turned to mush at that moment. To know that she would ask him to do that overwhelmed him. Becoming something like him wasn't a small undertaking, and neither was the change that anyone would have to go through. He wasn't sure he could ever do that to her, knowing she might not come out of it alive. But then he remembered how she had argued with him in her home, standing toe to toe with him and accusing him of sleeping with some other woman. She had spunk, which was definitely good. The stronger the mind and body, the easier the slip into being Druid.

"You're melting on yourself."

Her voice slipped into his head. "What...I'm sorry?"

She nodded towards his hand where his ice cream had overflowed to the top of his small bowl and was now dripping onto his fingers.

"Damn, I need to pay attention."

She smiled at him then took another spoonful of ice cream into her mouth. Drake almost groaned. In two or three bites, he had most of his ice cream finished.

"Thank you for being so patient with me, answering all of my questions."

"I would rather you know all about me than be frightened off by assuming I'm some kind of monster," he admitted, remembering his two failed marriages.

"So, you were married twice?" She asked, placing her now empty bowl on the table beside the sofa and leaning back on the soft cushions, close enough for him to reach over and touch.

"Yes, my first marriage was to Loraine. My second wife was Maria."

"You loved them very much, didn't you?" Her green eyes were curious in her face and Drake didn't have the heart to lie to her, even though he knew that the truth would upset her.

"I did, very much," he told her, taking his hand and placing it behind her shoulders, wanting to reassure her even though he hadn't touched her yet.

She nodded, but didn't say anything until seconds later. "They must have been very beautiful women to attract your attention."

"They were beautiful, but they weren't strong enough to handle me and my Druid side, Nadia." He had to let her know somehow, that those women and she were nothing alike. "Loraine lasted longer than Maria, but Maria was nervous around me for months, before finally gathering the courage to leave me. She just couldn't take it anymore. Living with me, sharing my bed, was too much for her to handle. I was too much for her to handle."

Nadia didn't say anything, and Drake wasn't sure of how to take that. Then he felt her hand come over his thigh to capture his left hand with hers. "I haven't run yet." The words were softly spoken and even through the loudest racket on Earth, Drake would have heard them. He smiled, absurdly pleased with his little angel.

His hand along her shoulder dipped down, tracing her right arm through the material of her shirt. "No...you haven't, which is why you are so special to me, honey. You have no idea how at ease I am when I realize that I have nothing to hide from you. From now on you know everything that there is to know about me. You know me...period."

The need she'd felt last night was back and no matter how hard, she would never be able to hide it from him. He could almost taste it in the space between them. He could feel the emotions rising inside of her, battling at her defenses. There was also the underlying hint of passion tinting her aura. It still amazed him that he had missed that certain aura until just weeks ago. Apparently there were still some things that could stay hidden, even from him.

Turning his body towards hers, he closed the space between them. He left her hand on his thigh and reached out with his left hand touching her jaw, smoothing his fingers over her fine grained skin. "I pulled out some movies if you want to look through them, or is there something else you would rather do?"

Drake's insides burned. He still didn't have a clear view on her exact wants or needs but he could see the delicate fluttering of her pulse in her neck and the deep swallow she took. That alone told him so many things without hearing the words. But she would have to make the moves or tell him what she wanted.

"I would think that after last night you wouldn't need to be shy with me anymore," he told her. She smiled at him and when she turned her face in his direction, Drake felt it like a punch to his gut.

"You have no idea how badly you shocked me," she whispered, her cheeks tinted a delicate pink.

"You have no idea how aroused I had been. I wanted you so badly that I had to take the edge off somehow." He countered back.

Her smile dimmed and she gulped again. Drake let his fingers play in her beautiful hair from where it rested on the back of the sofa. She turned suddenly, facing him. Seconds passed while they looked at each other and Drake knew he had never felt as intimate with a woman than he did right then. Even with something as small as a shared glance, she made it feel like spiritual contact. Her legs were drawn up in front of her body while her head rested in the same place, still able to let his fingers sift through soft strands.

Her bare feet were pressing up against his knee. Drake let his left hand fall onto her calf muscle and then to her foot. He noticed her toenails were painted a bright pink color. "I like that color."

"It's called Shock-me-pink." Her voice was husky and soft. Her eyes watched his fingers move over the tips of her toes.

"Nice name." But Drake was interested in the way she tried to move her foot away whenever he lifted her foot to his lower chest. "Ticklish?"

She nodded, but didn't say anything. He pushed the bottom of her jeans out of the way and rubbed his hand along the top of her foot. Her skin was smooth and so very soft. She had delicate feet, a rising arch that begged to be tickled, and her toes were cute as hell. Drake was not what he considered to be a foot person, but looking at hers was tempting him to change.

He knew his stomach muscles jumped against her sole every time her foot twitched in response, but there was nothing he could do about it. Sliding his hands over her ankle, he then traced her calf muscle, and next, the soft skin behind her knee. She jerked her leg against him when he did that.

"You might want to stop the urge to move, unless you want me to know all of your ticklish spots." His fingers scraped gently there again. Once again her leg moved and she smiled, biting back a laugh.

"Maybe another time I can test out those same spots on you." Well, he hadn't been expecting her to say that.

"I believe you just propositioned me."

A berry bright flush heightened the tops of her cheeks. Drake noted the drowsy look in her eyes and the slight smile on her lips. Oh yeah, she was more than relaxed right now.

"I can't believe that after knowing you this long, watching you with other women, seeing the way they look at you like you're some kind of God, that I'm now sitting in your house while you are seducing my leg."

Drake couldn't help it; he burst out laughing. It took more than a few seconds to stifle the sound. When he looked back at her she was smiling too. "Damn, that is a different perspective."

"I'll say so," she twitched her toes against the material of his tee shirt. "But that doesn't mean you have to stop doing that though."

"What, seducing your leg?" he asked her with a smile and another swipe behind her knee. He tried moving his hand higher, scoundrel that he was, but the jeans were more fitted to her thighs. There was no way he was going any higher. "Why couldn't you have worn shorts?"

"You pig," she said then nudged him in the chest with her foot. He caught her foot up high, her calf across his pecs, her heel sliding over the edge of his shoulder when she tried to kick him again. Then Drake looked at her face. She wasn't smiling anymore. He could easily, so very easily, push her other leg out of the way and lean over her body, pinning her to the loveseat with his body, feeling her feminine curves press against him.

"I am a pig. You guessed right." He told her as he did, indeed, lean forward. He pulled her other leg to slide her under him. Grabbing her upper thigh, he tugged her until her inner thighs were holding his hips. He felt the shock roll through her system as he settled there, letting her feel how hard he was from their teasing moments earlier. His hands left her leg and moved up to her face, framing the softness, letting his thumbs swipe over smooth skin. "God, you have no idea of the things I could do to you, do you?"

"I have a very active imagination," she muttered, and Drake could see her eyes take in everything about him. The words surprised him. She was always saying something he least expected.

Instead of saying anything in return, he pressed his lips to her eyebrows, then her cheeks, feeling the fire of her blush against his lips. "Last night was so good angel, but there was so many things that we didn't get the chance to do." He heard her indrawn breath and her chest moved against his. Placing a kiss to the edge of her mouth, her soft skin trembled beneath his kiss. When was the last time a woman had actually *trembled* for him?

"But there is no need to rush. We'll take things slow and see where they lead. How's that?" he mumbled against her lips, fighting the need to plow inside her mouth and body.

"Okay," her hands rose up to touch his hips and Drake couldn't stop the hip action that ensued. He could feel each of her ten fingers through the denim, like little hot needles.

"What do you want angel? Do you want me to kiss you? Do you want me to touch you?" Drake licked her jaw and then down her neck, feeling her pulse thrum against his tongue. "Tell me, baby, tell me what you want."

***

Delicious, spine tingling heat infused Nadia. Her hand twitched against his denim clad hips as she took stock of the way he felt under her fingers while lying against her. She had never assumed that having a man lie against her would be so stimulating, now she realized her error. Drake was a very, very masculine, virile man. He was hard in the places he was supposed to be, and soft in areas where he should be too, like his lips, which were now nibbling their way down over her collarbone.

Thank God this loveseat was one of those newer models with deep, wide cushions. Nadia felt dwarfed, while she knew that to Drake it was probably a decently sized sofa. He was expanded over her, holding her body down with his much larger one, and she didn't mind one bit. It was exciting to feel the ridges of his muscular body stretched out over hers.

Her mind reminded her that he had asked her a question. *What did she want? What didn't* she want, was more like it. She wanted everything and anything he could give her, but she didn't want to feel the heartache and pain that would surely follow whenever he decided he had had enough with her and dumped her for the next woman. She wanted him to herself, knowing that he would never get tired of her and never want to end this so called relationship they were beginning to have.

That will never happen.

Of course it wouldn't. She wasn't that lucky. But she knew one thing, she would take whatever time she had with him and use up every drop of it, hoping to change his mind along the way.

Her fingers left his hips and slipped under the edge of his shirt to the hot skin beneath. She tugged on the material, and called on her inner wild child, "I want this off." He stopped nibbling at her neck long enough to not even question her statement; instead, he lifted high enough to grasp his shirt behind his head and pull it from his body. Glorious burnished skin appeared right before her eyes. She stopped all movement for a moment, taking him in, and God above there was *a lot* of him to take in.

With the wild beating of her heart surely slipping under his radar, Nadia let her eyes travel slowly over his upper body. Fantasies she had dreamed of when she was sixteen flashed through her mind swiftly. This was that man. This was the man that had caused her dreams and daydreams to be X-rated. This was the man that had unknowingly taught her the way a woman responded to a man she was attracted to. Now he was here, right at her fingertips, resting on his elbows above her body, letting her call the shots.

His neck was corded with tendons and supple skin that led down to prominent trap muscles and a delineated collarbone, just sharp enough to see the dip of his clavicle in between. Broad, wide shoulders were packed with ripped muscle, making his biceps seem massive when actually, he was just built according to his size. Dark hair started at his collarbone and took up most of his upper chest until where his pecs curved down into his stomach. The hair formed one single line that ran down to his navel then into his pants. His stomach was corrugated and flat, tempting Nadia's fingers to reach out and touch. But what really held her attention were the side muscles that ran along his waist and veered down into his jeans. Long swimmer's muscles were smooth and so very masculine, not to mention extremely sexy.

"I have to admit that if I would have known my chest would get this much stare time from you I would have gone shirtless long before now."

She smiled at his words, noticing how deep his voice had gone. Her eyes moved up his body again, stopping on his flat male nipples and realizing they were hard. Her fingertips moved up to investigate. "I wouldn't object to that at all." When she touched him there, he growled, long and deep in his throat. Nadia glanced up to see wild amber eyes and the barest tips of his fangs emerging from between his lips.

Pure fire slid inside her body. To know that he was like this because of her was exhilarating, and she reveled in it. Leaning her head towards his chest she inhaled his scent, wild, pure male. Her nails scored his nipples sending another groan her way as she gave him butterfly kisses along his chest then onto his neck. Seconds later she was at his mouth, hesitating long enough only to feel the very edges of his fangs with her mouth. His large body shuddered, but he seemed to give in a bit, leaning more towards her, sending her into a relaxed pose against the soft cushions of the loveseat. Nadia took that movement as acceptance and slid her mouth over his.

She sighed breathlessly onto his lips, not being able to hold back the pure excitement that streamed in her veins from being near him. The kiss was a study for Nadia. The taste and texture of him was amazing. She couldn't stop her lips from feeling, touching, and sampling every inch of his mouth. He tasted so good, so mind numbingly delicious, that she slipped easily into this bottomless pit where nothing existed but her and him, and what they were doing to each other.

He pulled away and she moaned, not wanting to miss the erotic kisses he was giving her.

"Shh…," his hand swept down her body in one long touch ending at the edge of her shirt. "Tell me that you give me permission to remove this shirt and touch you. Tell me that it is okay." His warm fingers slipped against her waist, singeing her with their heat, and Nadia didn't stop the reaction that had her hips move against his slightly. "I want to see and touch your skin so badly." His mouth nibbled along her jaw line and Nadia wanted to melt to the cushions.

She didn't hesitate. She knew that if at any time she wanted to stop, he would, although she doubted there would be a time in the near future where that would be an option for her. When he touched her, stopping wasn't an option.

"I want that too."

"Angel…" He murmured against the skin of her neck while the fingers resting at the edge of her shirt immediately lifted the fabric and shucked it from her body. Apparently he wasn't wasting the time it would have taken for her to change her mind.

Within seconds, Nadia was bare from the waist up except for her dainty, flesh colored, wispy thin bra. With the cooler air brushing goose bumps along her skin and Drake resting his large body above hers, snuggled up against her hips with his glowing eyes peering at her bared skin, Nadia couldn't remember another time where she had ever felt this exposed. Every nerve ending was alive and fairly pulsing with energy. Her fingertips were throbbing against his chest, where she was still tangled in his chest hair.

With a completely absorbed look on his face, Drake let his fingers trail from her not so firm waist to the soft material of her bra. Nadia never felt as undeserving as she did then. He wasn't used to a woman that wasn't top of the line beautiful and stunning. Still, his eyes catalogued every movement, and she couldn't help but be mesmerized at the simple, honest look that he was giving her as he touched her. It was as if he had never seen the same thing before, on tons of other women. As if he had never trailed his fingers across their skin, watching it react with quivers whenever he moved over it. The slow, methodical touch was absolutely mystifying to Nadia because she, and every other woman in Texas, knew that Drake was no innocent. He had bedded many women, and he had been doing it for some time.

When his fingers touched the soft, delicate flesh rising above the small cups of her bra, Nadia suppressed a shiver and her eyes sought his. With his golden eyes watching her, he slowly maneuvered the straps of her bra down one arm, and then the other. Other than an indrawn breath, Nadia made no move to stop him. And even though she loved him and wanted him as she had no other man, she was still embarrassed at her complacency, and stunned at how much she was willing to let him do to her.

Without removing her bra completely, he left the straps dangling from her shoulders, holding her arms prisoner against her own body. Seconds later he leaned down and trailed soft kisses from her collarbone to the delicate edges of the cups on her bra. Even though the contact was minute, Nadia felt the impact shatter through her and her upper body reacted stiffly, shoving up from the cushions and clearly telling Drake that she was enjoying what he was doing.

"Ahh…"

"Angel…feels good, doesn't it?" His mouth moved over soft skin, his tongue slipping out, wetting flesh and sneaking in under the material of her bra. Eyes closed, mouth slightly open, air disappearing from her lungs rapidly, Nadia slid her hands around to his shoulders then the ends of his hair. She gripped and held on, trusting Drake to show her everything she needed to know.

Chapter 16

The refusal to give into the baser emotions and wants of his Druid side, were giving Drake hell, but he would not push or prod Nadia into a decision that would somehow turn ugly afterwards. If there would be any consummation of their relationship, she would call the shots. She knew that, he knew that; now, he only had to make sure that he didn't blow those plans to shit. She wasn't making it easy on him, not one bit.

Underneath him, with her thighs open enough for him to rest against, her hair was a long black curtain, simultaneously hiding parts of her shoulders, and upper body, and giving him little pulses of heat when strands moved against her pale skin. The sight of her lying there, open to him, bra straps dangling, was more than enough to heighten everything he felt. But it was the docile, trusting light in her eyes and the natural, relaxed aura around her frame that told him the truth. Nadia was at ease right now. Drake felt elation fill him up from the inside.

Her hands were deeply entwined in his hair, while her body shifted and moved with little undulations beneath him. She was turned on, desperately so, if her body was anything to go by. Not only that, but Drake could also *feel* the pulsations of blood beneath her skin and the stunning force of it moving so swiftly told him that with the slightest inclination he could make her come.

He so wanted to make that happen again...and again. She deserved to feel good and he felt ten feet tall because he was the man that was going to make it happen.

With his mouth on her soft skin, his hands under her back raising her up to meet him and his hips settled right over hers, Drake couldn't imagine a better place to be at the moment. His eyes took in the delicate edges of her bra, and he knew that it wouldn't take much to flick the material out of the way. Settling an openmouthed kiss on her sweet skin, he breathed deep, imprinting her taste to memory and savoring it at the same time. His tongue rasped along the edge of the cup, slipping under and catching the pebbled skin of her nipple. Immediately he went after it, like a drowning man needs air. Swiping at the erogenous zone, he heard her breath stop altogether then he moved his hand and used his thumb to move the bra cup away, baring her nipple to his mouth for a full onslaught.

Her fingers all but pulled the hair from his head when he slipped the heat of his mouth fully over her sensitive nipple. That just made Drake more than determined to ensure the complete overstimulation of every one of her senses. He gently sucked her nipple into his mouth, loving the way her breathing hitched, and then escaped on a rough draft of air, as if her very soul were being torn apart. He was gentle enough to keep his fangs out of the picture, but diabolical enough to use the very tips to scrape along the tip of her stimulated skin. He wanted her out of her mind with want.

"Drake…" Her fingers grasped even tighter in his hair. He feared he would have patches missing once he finished.

He let her nipple slip from his mouth then he moved to her other breast and without any fanfare, slipped it from the cup of the bra and out into the open. Instantly her nipple pebbled, hardening right before his eyes. He let his thumb run over the tip again and again, causing her to tremble beneath him.

"What's wrong, baby?" Another rub over her skin then another shiver, "Do you want me to stop?" *No*, his mind screamed. *Please don't say you want me to stop*, but deep inside Drake knew that he was looking at her in the middle of some full blown erotic moment and she didn't want to stop. His heart raced in his chest.

Her lips trembled delicately and fire burned deep inside his body. "No…please don't stop." Her head twisted on the cushions, tangling her gorgeous hair around her head and then she whimpered. His heart twisted. God, she was so beautiful, so innocently sensual that he had to stop himself from ripping the jeans from her body and slamming into her, claiming her in a way that would mark him and her forever together. Then she said something that made him freeze. "I've waited so long…so very long…"

Drake let his head fall in the valley of her breasts. He drug in deep breath after deep breath, the reality of what she was saying slamming into his brain and body.

He knew by the tone of her voice, the sincerity that came out even in passion, that she was speaking honestly and she probably didn't even know it. He could play with her, drag out more words, make her feel as if she was incriminating herself, but he couldn't. He couldn't be harsh with her, not Nadia. He wanted to feel her, teach her everything she didn't know about passion and sex. He wanted to be the man that made her burn. To know that she had waited for a moment like this between them made Drake feel low, extremely base. She had known him forever and in all those years he had never caught on to the way she felt for him.

Apparently he wasn't as strong in his abilities as he thought he had been.

Then something occurred to him. He knew some women thought sex equated to love. He knew that their emotions came into play more than a man's did. And ever since she was old enough to know better, Nadia had seen him with a different woman every week. He had paraded them on his arm as if he was showing off a new toy. And she had seen him do it. The pain she must have felt was probably overwhelming. Because he knew, deep down, that Nadia cared for him, those feelings of lust were deeply intertwined with feelings she had for him.

Drake took a deep breath and she shuddered beneath him. Damn, he had been quiet and still for too long. She knew that he was thinking, sorting out what she had just said. When her fingers left his hair to shove him away, Drake knew he had to do something to keep her there with him, otherwise she would run away, deathly embarrassed by what she had said, and he would never see her again.

He leaned up, and in seconds she was out from under him. Drake got a moment to glance at the beauty of her body, her breasts free of the bra, her hair wild around her shoulders, and her mouth thoroughly swollen from their kisses, before his eyes settled on hers. Tears were welling there and his heart sped up. Just as she was slipping the straps of her bra back on her shoulders, he grabbed her arms pulling her around to face him on the sofa. She tried to get away, but she was fighting a losing battle, and she knew it.

He didn't say anything. He just pulled her fighting mad body closer to him, and let his mouth capture hers. She instantly stopped, giving into the kiss, becoming so malleable in his hands that he could have picked her up and whisked her away to his bed, but he didn't.

Seconds later, just when he was deepening the kiss, she stiffened, then shoved him away. After a slight scuffle he caught her arms again, pulling her close against him.

"Stop this…you're only doing this out of pity." She threw at him, catching him off guard with her words.

"Pity? You think I pity you?" He arched his eyebrows and gave her a cross look, mixed with enough anger to showcase his glowing eyes. She stopped moving, trying to get away from him and stared, her heart all but beating from her chest. He held her close enough that he could feel the soft weight of her breasts, still sitting outside the cups of her bra, pressing against his chest. Not above using his body to get what he wanted, especially from Nadia, Drake used his hands to move her upper body, causing her sensitive breasts to rub against his chest hair. He knew that would stimulate her, and by the way she stiffened against him once again, he knew he was right.

Her nipples turned to hard little brands against him. When she moaned and shook, letting her head drop against his body, he almost passed out, knowing he had stopped her from running out on him, but now he had to keep her there with him.

"I don't pity you." His hands lifted her high against his chest and she gasped sending her arms out to close around his shoulders. "We won't speak of pity again. I don't like how you put yourself down whenever you are around me. That's enough of that." He placed a sweetly chaste kiss against her lips and noticed the tears were disappearing. "I want to give you pleasure, angel. I want you shaking in my arms, screaming my name, pulling my hair, clawing my back, hell pretty much whatever you want to do…except run out that door. You won't be doing that, no matter what you admit to me." He smiled at her. "Are we understood?"

She nodded, her eyes a wide and luminous green as they peered at him. Drake felt that look in his soul.

"Good."

Without another word, he placed her sitting back on the loveseat. She immediately used her hands to cover her breasts, but Drake would have none of that. He tskd his disapproval and gently pulled them away.

"Please don't cover up something so beautiful."

She let him move her hands, but Drake could read the tension in her body. He needed to do something to counter it, to take her mind from it. He opened her legs and knelt between them, settling his body right up against hers. She gasped when his arms came around her waist, pulling her hips into his, and her breasts into his chest once more. Hot little nipples poked him, and he couldn't help the rolling motion of his hips against hers. Her hands went around his waist and she countered his hip motion with one of her own. Drake growled his encouragement.

"Darlin', if at any time you want to do something to me or my body you go right ahead and do it. This is all for you." He had no idea how he got the words out but he did. Nadia murmured something incoherent, but he didn't hear the word stop, so he wasn't going to.

He placed a kiss to the slope of her shoulders while his hand came to the clasp of her bra. He played with the hooks for a moment, trying to feel any hints from her that she might want him to stop, but nothing escaped her mouth other than a few sighs and moans when her hips canted against his. He tugged the clasp open and immediately removed the offending material from her body.

Leaning back a bit, he studied her, the fragile beauty in his arms that shook with passion. Her long hair was a wild mess, her pale skin was splashed with a furious blush, and her breasts, *God*, her breasts were perfection. Beautiful, firm globes tipped with darkened nipples. Drake's pulse raced along with blood rushing to his cock.

He looked into her eyes, caught the hazy, drowsy look that she had and let his head lean down towards her chest. He wanted to worship her body, send her into a tailspin with nothing on between them. His mouth caught the little crest of her nipple and he tugged with his lips. She gasped and grabbed his head, telling him without words that he was doing exactly what she wanted.

He let one hand come up under her breast, plumping it towards his mouth, as he pulled her deeply with a soft suction. He tongued her nipple, being so tortuous to the soft, sweet flesh that her hips jerked against his.

"Yes...oh God yes..." She told him. Drake couldn't stop himself from looking up her chest and watching as she leaned her head back and gave into the furious blaze of emotions that were shaking her at the moment. She wanted this so much that her body pulsated with forerunners of ecstasy. He could feel them arcing onto him, pulling at his subconscious, telling him to let go of his control and plunder, take her.

No. He wanted to give her everything, show her more before she made up her mind about having sex with him. This was, and always would be, her decision.

His hands came to the front of her jeans and he undid the button and soon enough he was pulling the jeans from her body, next were her underwear, and she didn't even blink whenever he leaned her against the back cushions, her body fully exposed to his gaze. Her hands went above her head, tangling in her hair, her chest raised, showcasing those beautiful tipped breasts and small waist. Her hips were uplifted, canted in his direction, making Drake's mouth water.

With his hands on the cushions beside her hips, Drake stared at her, wondering how he had never noticed or responded to this amazing woman before now. A purely primal feeling rose up inside of him. She was his, always his, she would never belong to anyone else, and he would show her that from now on. She was not leaving him. He wouldn't give her the option.

He let his hand trail from her collarbone, down the center of her chest to where her legs came to a V. Short, trimmed hair protected her, but not for long. He settled both of his hands on her hips, letting his thumbs trace the short dark hair there, tempting her beyond all reason.

"Drake…don't stop…" She asked him, her head twisting on the back of the sofa, so earnest in her passion, so wanting. Her legs opened wider, her calves resting against his ass and blood in his body began to boil. He needed to make her come before he attacked her. "I can't believe…this is happening…"

Oh yeah, he needed to shut her up. Apparently being intimate made her talkative. Without another moment to lose, he leaned down gave himself one second to inhale her sweetly sharp woman scent and placed his thumbs on her soft skin, moving her open so that he could settle his mouth on the one place that he couldn't wait to taste.

***

Heaven help her, but he was going to kill her with pleasure.

With a wicked tongue and a sensual, naughty mouth, Drake was sin in its purest form. He was showing her what she had only dreamt about, what she had never thought to experience with a man. And Lord above, but he knew how to make an impression.

At the moment Nadia knew his head was buried between her legs; her legs were locked over his shoulders and his hands were holding her wide open for his and her pleasure, but she didn't see the shame or embarrassment, like she thought would have been there. Instead, she saw the utter giving of his actions. He wanted to do this for her. He wanted her to scream with satisfaction. He wanted her shaking and clawing his back. He had told her that after all. Nadia felt the need he had inside his body for her, but she also felt the emotion that he rarely showed anyone. He wanted this for her. He wanted her to feel good. Most of all she knew he wanted to be the one to give it to her.

His tongue surged deep inside of her body and she jerked, feeling the fire shoot along her veins, seeming to coalesce out of nowhere and slide like wildfire through her body. He nipped at her, hinting of the power he had with his fangs; he tongued her gently, and Nadia could feel the slickness of her body as he proved to her that he could indeed do depraved things to her.

With all coherent thought flying out of her head by the second, Nadia gave over to the sinfully delicious slide of his tongue against her body. She didn't think of the pain he might cause her later. She didn't think of how he might leave her in the dust after whatever they did together was over. All she thought about was the elusive explosion that would rock her body in mere moments. She knew she was close and with his mouth licking and sucking at her, and his tongue moving against her with so much knowledge for what he was doing, she knew it would be big when it hit.

She grabbed his hair in her hands and gripped, keeping him tucked right where he was, not letting him move. Just as she was letting her body start to come to grips with what he was doing, he thrust his finger deep, sending shockwaves throughout her body and making her moan his name.

Oh God, so close, she was so close.

With his free hand he surged up her body and touched her breast, plying the sensitive nipple with quick fingers. A scream began deep in her body. She wanted to release all these emotions out to him, make him realize what he was doing to her, and then he thrust another finger in and she couldn't handle the pressure…she burst.

With that scream, she gave in, and let ecstasy pour over her in throbbing waves, sending sparks out from her nerves, screaming down her spine and shooting deep within her body. For seconds she didn't feel anything besides the clamoring urge to shake and fall apart, bit by bit while Drake continued to ply her body with his mouth, not letting up one second.

She had exploded into millions of pieces and seconds later her body was slowly, meticulously being placed back together, but with a shaky hand. In slow degrees she finally came down from the surge of pleasure that rocked her. She blinked lazily, stunned with the debilitating drowsiness that was pressing down upon her. In seconds she realized he had stopped and was now leaning over her body, his breath hot against her chest, his eyes glowing feral yellow at her from where he pinned her with his gaze. She shivered.

***

God, she was so damn stunning. With her hair now truly messed up, eyes still half lidded from her recent orgasm and body beautifully flushed, she looked like a sinful goddess lying before him. Drake took a deep, steadying breath and tried to calm down his raging erection.

Her skin was dewy from their actions moments before. His finger took up tracing the soft skin that ran from right under her breast to the slight ridge of her hipbone. She shuddered on every down stroke and soon enough Drake had figured out that she was extremely ticklish. He smiled at that discovery, glad that he had learned something so personal about her, something for only him to know.

There was no reason to move. He was in no hurry to get up even if the floor was uncomfortable; he didn't mind. One of the loveliest views he had ever seen was directly in his sights. He wouldn't rush things right now for any price.

She was still nervous, still unsure despite what had happened between them. From her point of view Drake assumed it was because, apparently, she had wanted him for so long and now with him here, giving her what she wanted, it was still a surreal moment for her. She was still soaking it all in.

Her heartfelt admission from minutes before still rang in his ears. When she had uttered those words, his heart had about stopped. He could still sense her desperation at wanting to take the words back, to make it to where he had never known about her secret desire. Looking at her soft hazy expression, with her barely open, vibrant green eyes and luscious black hair, there was a burn deep in his chest that was alot like tenderness. So beautiful and yet so thoroughly naïve about certain things, didn't she know she was supposed to keep her heart closed off from men? Didn't she know she wasn't supposed to show a man how much their time spent together meant to her? No, his little angel was not up to par in the ways of seduction and sex that he was, and he found himself wanting to protect her all the more for that reason.

She was so exquisitely innocent about things that he knew everything about. That made her inherently dangerous to him, which of course could be why he wasn't crawling over her body right now and plunging headlong into what he knew would be something extremely tight and hot.

For some reason every time he had the barest thought in his mind to do exactly that, his Druid side, which was usually so aggressive, calmed. Nadia's hidden sensuality and apparent emotions obviously kick started his protective side. He would no more hurt her than he would rip off his own arm. Now that he realized that it made things a bit easier for him when he was around her.

A sigh caught his attention. Drake looked up from where his fingers were drawing designs on her skin to see that her eyelids were so heavy she could barely keep them open. With a slight smile, he let both of his hands settle on her midsection. He closed his eyes, focusing on a specific spell that would send her into a much needed deep, comfortable sleep. Within seconds he felt a slight burn in his fingertips and then the incantation was over.

He opened his eyes again to see Nadia lost to him and the world. Being as gentle as possible, he unwove his body from above hers and gathered her in his arms. Within seconds he was in his large master bedroom and was settling her on the bed, under the covers. For a few minutes he allowed himself to lie next to her. With a patience that astounded even him, he watched her breathe deeply and evenly, amazed at the small package of dynamite that had so artlessly and slyly snuck her way into his life, even though she had been there all along. He let his large hand cover hers on top of the blanket, her long graceful fingers slide in and out between his own. He marveled at the delicate build of her body while he knew she had a bulldog persona in business.

Her profile was beautifully relaxed and calm and Drake knew he was partly the reason for that. A faint glimmer of hope burst inside of his chest. What would it be like to wake up beside her every morning, to never feel loneliness again, to never have to slake his lust with women that didn't know his secrets, to make love to her instead of other women, like he had in the past? All the things, the possibilities that they could have as a couple flickered to life, images similar to a movie reel playing in his mind.

Without giving himself too much time to dwell on the future he went back to studying her while deep inside, in a hidden part of him, his very being vibrated with a purely male need to mate and adhere to this one woman who was slowly entangling herself into his very life's thread.

***

Rain awoke Nadia.

The sound of the gentle downpour invaded her ears and then roused her completely as a thunderclap vibrated around her. Eyes still heavy from a peaceful and dreamless sleep, she yawned then stretched, finally settling on her side again, her eyes starting to close once more…when a thought hit her-why wasn't she trembling with tension because of the storm? Even though it wasn't as violent as some of the ones that rattled to life in South Texas, it was still strong enough to cause lightning and thunder, which was more than enough to wake her and keep her in a stranglehold of panic. Her fear of storms was something that always embarrassed her, and it was the reason why she was now instantly curious as to why she wasn't biting her lip and praying every prayer she knew for protection.

She was just about to crack one eye open in pure curiosity when a very large, very warm, very male arm pulled her back against an equally very large male body. For a second Nadia was shocked, then the night before rushed back at her so fast that she became dizzy. Surprise held her immobile for a brief moment as she recalled in her mind the things Drake had done to her, what they had done to each other, and then with a small secret smile she closed her eyes once more, settling deeper against the heated circle of his body.

Maybe an hour later she stirred again. The rain continued to fall outside and while she knew from a glance at the large clock on the wall that it was past nine in the morning it was still very dark outside the massive windows. The warmth of Drake's body was like a cushioned furnace that was safe enough for bed use. She might have to keep him around strictly for that reason. She had always been a cold natured person.

Minutes passed as she savored the ultimate indulgence of being in his arms. The hair along her nape prickled and seconds later his slow Texas drawl rumbled to life.

"What is your favorite color?"

The question was so off the wall that she found herself smiling into the pillow. "I love yellow. It's so vibrant and alive, so obviously different from me." She told him honestly, not holding anything back.

A slight shift of his massive body, and then, "It suits you. I remember seeing the color on you before and noticing how it complemented your tone." Then his strong hand wove under the soft cotton of the sheet and Nadia remembered, a little too late, her apparent nudity. She sucked in a breath, but didn't speak as he settled his fingers against her soft stomach. She held back the urge to suck in her stomach.

"What is your favorite food?" His deep voice was so gravelly in the morning. He sounded like a grumpy tiger.

She smiled as she realized just how personal he was getting with his questions. He wanted to know more about her, *her*. Nadia Morales had apparently grabbed the attention of the one man in the world that mattered to her. Her heart sputtered then picked up speed.

His hand clenched on her stomach. "Believe me when I tell you that I am just as excited to have you in my bed as you are right now."

Nadia's cheeks flamed with color and heat. Just the idea that he could read her body signals well enough to know when she was excited was amazing. She ignored that last statement and answered his question. "Fried chicken."

His chuckle was like gravel being poured into satin, but even so it still fired up every part of her body, especially when it rumbled through her back when he spoke.

"What's yours?" She countered, insanely curious to know.

"Baked apple pie," he said it with such reverence in his voice that she smiled again.

"What is your favorite color?"

"Anything that you are wearing." This too was said with such soul bearing honesty that immediately Nadia stilled.

His fingers began to rub her stomach and once again she bit back the urge to suck it in. There was nothing inherently sexual in his touch. It was more like he couldn't stop himself from giving into the urge to run his fingers along her skin. That thought settled her nerves a bit. Even after the erotic things they had done, without giving into sex, she still had a horrible case of anxiousness where he was concerned. More than likely, it was because she had thought him so far out of her range so long ago that she had ultimately given up hope on even being so near to him.

"I love to listen to music. It calms me, soothes my Druid side sometimes when urges tend to overrule common sense." Another stroke of that devilish finger, "Being near you obviously does the same thing. I've found out in the past two days that I haven't felt the urge to beat a couple of holes in the wall over business, like I usually do."

She thought about that and smiled again, liking the fact that she calmed him somewhat. Biting her lip, she grabbed the bull by the horns and said what she wanted to say, damn the consequences. "You should keep me around then. You never know what other effects I might have on you."

Damn, her heart was really pounding now. That was as close as she had ever come to acknowledging how deep her feelings for him ran. Nervousness caused her stomach to heave.

He nuzzled the hair at her nape, Nadia clearly heard him inhale her smell, and then he growled against her body. "I just might have to do that."

Every particle of air in her body evaporated. It wasn't an outpouring of love, and she wasn't really expecting that either, but it was enough to tell her that he wanted her with him at this moment. Wasn't that all that mattered?

They lay there, together, wrapped up beside each other in his huge bed for at least another hour or two. Nadia didn't want to move and neither did Drake. She came to understand that even though he appeared closed off and arrogant sometimes, maybe he was just as misunderstood as she was. Settling deeper into his mattress, listening to him breathe against her, feeling his fingers on her body caused her to drift in and out of consciousness. At one point she thought she heard him whisper words in her ear, but she dismissed that because of the rain pouring outside the windows. Letting her body be lulled by his heat and the protected feeling he gave her, she dozed in the arms of the man she loved.

Chapter 17

A sharp wolf whistle greeted Nadia when she walked into work on Monday morning. With a smile she turned and caught the sly look on Renee's face. She had known that Renee would have something smart to say after knowing, courtesy of a late night call last night, the slightly condensed version of what happened over the weekend.

"Honey, whatever Mr. Thompson does for you, he needs to keep doing it. I have never seen a smile on your face that big or that bright," Renee told her with a hug. Nadia was immensely glad there was no one else in the office with them at the moment.

"I told you enough last night. There is nothing else left to say," Nadia said as she placed her purse in her desk drawer and pulled up her computer for the day.

"There is always something left out and I can guarantee that there is still something you haven't shared." Nadia couldn't help but smile again. Renee caught it immediately. "See, I told you. But that's okay, because whatever else happened should stay between you and him." Renee stepped up in front of the desk and grabbed Nadia's hand, looking at her with huge blue eyes. "This is your moment. You need to savor it."

Nadia nodded, not sure if she had any response to that or not. But she did know Renee was right. It was about damn time she got her chance with the man she loved. Renee moved away, ending the moment and getting back to business, which was just what Nadia needed to get her mind off of Drake and onto work. But that was easier said than done.

Thoughts of Drake kept popping up all day long. When she went to grab a bite to eat, she was reminded of sitting at his island in his kitchen, eating sandwiches and a salad while they spoke of his abilities. When she met with Andy, the head of photography and design for THE TREND, she was reminded of Drake's luscious colored eyes, when she glimpsed a man with similar eyes as they poured over images to use for their new spread. At the store, as she was grabbing stuff to bring home, Nadia overheard some cowboys talking in the aisle next to her and with their deep, smoky drawls she was instantly reminded of Drake's deep tenor when he had spoken to her yesterday morning while they were in bed.

Her mind, body, and soul were flooded with remnants of him. She couldn't get away even if she tried, not that she would want to. The one man she had dreamed of for years was now at her fingertips. What woman wouldn't be thrilled with that idea?

All day long she'd had daydreams about what she *should* have done instead of basically falling asleep in his lap. She *should* have finally scoured over every inch of his body like she had wanted to do for years now. She *should* have touched every delicious part of him, his tattoo that she hadn't known about until recently, his leanly sculpted chest which was roped with muscles and tendons, begging her fingers to reach out and test his strength. The yearning deep inside of her had multiplied to an overwhelming want that screamed at her to do something about it.

She wanted sex. Wild, rough and unadulterated sex, with Drake Thompson.

She wanted him sliding deep inside her body with every molecule of breath she had inside of herself. The complacence he had shown her triggered something inside of her, something that told her he would never turn her down, would never tell her no, so why not go for it, why not take what she wanted so badly? Because even though she would finally have him, she still wasn't sure if he wouldn't leave her afterwards.

So why couldn't she just have sex with him, satisfy herself and him, and then go on about business as usual?

It wouldn't happen because once she tasted him, once he had buried himself deeply inside of her, she would want him to want her forever. She would never be able to be just casual sex to him. It was a hopeless cause and she knew it.

She wanted the romantic ideal. She wanted forever. There was no reason why she shouldn't have it either. Determined wasn't even close, when it came to describing something that she knew was almost within her grasp. She would dodge bullets for him. She would give up her wealth, notoriety, and position in society for him. Nothing else mattered except what she felt for Drake.

Aren't you tired of wanting and never getting? Aren't you sick of watching other women have their chance with him while you stood off on the sidelines biding your time away with a handful of scarce glances and rare crooked smiles?

Hell yes, she was. This past weekend flashed through her mind and she remembered every moment when he had held her close, kissed her, touched her, and made her feel so very important and loved. She wanted this man and she wanted the rest of her life to be spent with him. It was worth it to prove to him that she was willing to fight for their relationship.

Would she be happy with just a scarce fifty or so years with him? But why should she settle for that? He could 'gift' her over, make her one of his kind, couldn't he? From what he'd said the other night, as long as she admitted to him what she wanted and accepted his gift he could change her. Was she willing to do that, to give up a normal life for the man she loved?

Nadia stared into her bathroom mirror when she got home that afternoon. She looked at the very small fine lines expanding out from the corners of her eyes. She would age slowly and live an indeterminate amount of time, but she would have him by her side for that period. She would be able to make up for almost ten years of loving him blindly, and Lord did she have a lot of making up to do.

Determination was too sedate a word for her feelings.

***

The day had been a bitch.

Once he'd finally made it into work, he'd been reminded of an important meeting he'd somehow forgotten about in Louisiana. He had to haul ass across the state line to barely make it in time. Here it was, after seven p.m., and he was just pulling into his own drive.

All day long he had thought about nothing but Nadia. The phone had been in his hand numerous times, but he had opted not to disturb her. Even suspecting she wouldn't consider it a bother, he still hesitated. He would much rather surprise her instead by showing up at her house later on after he got home and had a shower.

The emotions that pulled at his insides when he thought about her were enough to set off flames. He had felt many things for many women, including love for his two wives. However, now that he'd spent time with Nadia…Really come to know her…He felt more certain than ever before, that this was something special.

After changing over in 1809 and going through a period where he thought he was the baddest thing on the face of the planet, Drake had more time to learn his faults and hone his knowledge than any other man. He had charmed, seduced, and bedded plenty of women, but he could say, in all earnestness, that he'd recognized the ache of being unfulfilled. He had no idea it would make this looming consummation of his and Dia's relationship all the sweeter.

He wasn't a fool. He knew she was innocent and more than likely a virgin, although he still didn't understand how it was possible. But he wasn't turning down that specific gift. The knowledge that he had been the one to basically introduce her to certain things, and things that were yet to come, was a heady thought. Still, it was more than just sex. It was being with her, feeling her trust in him, feeling the way she looked at him, so earnestly, so full of passion and promise.

His body responded by standing up and saluting, but he ignored it. Soon he would be close enough to touch her, hold her, kiss her, but right now he headed for the shower, planning to make record time before heading out to remind Nadia that their new relationship was something he wanted to take to the next level.

***

The night air was warm, but the wind had picked up, bringing in a slight breeze.

The breeze kicked up the edges of Nadia's short trench coat. The cooler air ruffled the very small amount of clothes she had on underneath. The bravado that had been pumping her up for an hour and a half now, had suddenly disappeared, leaving behind nothing but nerves and a weak stomach. But she would see this through. Drake had turned out to be more gentlemanly than she knew him to be. If she waited for him to go all the way with her, she just might be waiting forever. She hadn't ever thought she would be reduced to becoming the seducer, especially since she hardly knew how to seduce in the first place.

She had Love to guide her. That was all she needed. She could muster through anything with that at her back.

Grasping her I-phone, she scrolled and searched for Drake's number. Time to put her plan into action.

Seconds later his deep voice slid over the line.

"Hello?"

"Hey you, am I disturbing anything?" She hoped she sounded more put together than she felt.

"Well aren't you the little mind reader?" She could practically see the smile that she knew was on his face. "I have been thinking about you all day long. It's so good to hear your voice, angel."

A warm thrill shot through her as she maneuvered through the darkness and stopped at the edge of the deck. "It's good to hear yours too. I almost called, but I knew your Monday's were always hectic, so I've been a good, patient woman, although it was hard as heck not to pick up the phone."

He chuckled over the line, "Well, you weren't the only one who had trouble with trying to stay off of the phone. I thought about calling you every hour, but stopped myself. I was going to surprise you instead."

A firestorm of sensation erupted inside Nadia as she glanced through the wooden railing on the deck, seeing the tall floor to ceiling windows that allowed her to look into his kitchen. Seconds later she turned her eyes to his bedroom window and the small amount of light allowed her to see him emerging from the bathroom, with nothing on but a towel. Her stomach and nerves heaved as she watched him walk out of his room and into the darkness of his house beyond.

"Just how were you going to surprise me?" Her breathless voice slid over the line. She stopped at the steps to his deck, not taking the chance that he might find out her hiding place before she wanted him to notice her. She couldn't believe she could actually sneak up on him anyway.

There was a faint rustling, and then, "I can't give you all the answers, darlin', just know that you are going to have a good end to a boring Monday because you are going to see me very soon."

"Really," she murmured, sliding her keys in deep in her trench pocket and willing her heart to stop racing, "how do you know that I'm not about to make your night even better?" She asked him as she let herself place one foot on his deck steps.

Silence greeted her question. Never before had she thought she could make Drake speechless.

She went for all the marbles. "Why don't you step out on your deck and see your surprise for the night?" The last part of her question came out wobbly and hesitant, but she congratulated herself for speaking the words at all, especially since her stomach had caved to her toes, her throat was as dry as dust, her heels were pinching her toes and the clingy silk slip she had on was leaving most of her body under the coat, bare to the night air. Thank God there were no mosquitoes tonight.

The click of a lock pierced the night. Her eyes swung to the handles, as they turned and Drake opened the door from the inside. Nadia slid her phone into her coat pocket and braced herself as her fingers went to the knot holding her coat closed.

***

There had been many things in his life that had made his heart beat faster, but Drake knew this experience tonight would top them all.

Nadia was standing on the edge of his deck, where his steps led downward looking for the entire world like an innocent young woman heading to the gallows. Deep within her green eyes was hardness, a certain wild light that Drake had never seen before. Her aura was deep with want, throbbing with lights of sexual awareness, and it called to him in the basest, most deviant way possible. The lines of excitement were so wavy around her that they pulsated with the beat of her heart, which was pounding harshly.

Drake knew this was hard for her, but that stern light in her eyes was driving her to do this, not to mention whatever her body was making her feel. But he also knew she felt something so utterly wordless and unexplainable that he was seeing her do something totally out of character because of her feelings for him.

Her long black hair was down and her body was covered from neck to knees in an oversized trench coat. He was a fool to believe that she was fully clothed underneath. She had the look of a woman out to get what she wanted, and Drake knew that her new role of seducer was all for him.

Her fingers shook as she fiddled with the knot on the coat as Drake stopped about a foot away from her. What spirit she had! Her eyes held his when she finally let the knot fall away. Drake took a deep breath as his eyes slid downward and the coat slipped from her shoulders. His fingers twitched as his eyes took in enormous amounts of her translucent skin. "Ah, angel..."

Sexy, beautiful, stunning, no words could express how she looked to him in that moment. The black scrap of tight material appeared to be a slip of some kind to Drake. Small, thin straps were on her shoulders, while the neckline was indecently low, baring her almost to her nipples where firm flesh was raised. The spandex material was covered in silk, but still cinched in her already tiny waist and showcased full blown, womanly hips then the material stopped about two inches shy of showing Drake what his mouth watered to taste again. His eyes followed her long legs to where black, extremely high heels were on her feet.

Dear God, kill him now.

The thought had barely cleared his mind before Nadia took action. She was pressed up against him with her hands on his chest and speaking before Drake could slap himself awake.

"I hope I meet with your approval," she purred against his skin, her moist breath wafting against his chest, sending his cock straight up inside the towel.

"Darlin,' any more approval from me and you would be flat on your back on this deck right now."

The words delighted her. Drake could tell from the way she inhaled, and her blood pulsed with renewed urgency under her skin. The abrupt change in her body caused the same for him, teeth elongating and eyes burning.

Sound rumbled from her throat, similar to a purr, and Drake had to lock his hands at his sides before he did, indeed, push her on the deck like some animal about to rut.

"Outside would be different, but for our first time I believe I'm spoiled enough to enjoy the bed…what do you think?" Her words rumbled close to his chest, and Drake still shuddered. Damn, he would have never assumed Nadia to be a seductress. It was a very lovely surprise.

"I agree with whatever you want." Drake stopped before he incriminated himself. He would be willing to do anything she wanted, wherever she wanted and at whatever time. It made no difference to him.

"Well, first off, we are going to go inside to your bedroom and then I will get to do all the things I have dreamed of doing to that gorgeous body of yours that I have been putting off." Her fingers trailed over his skin and Drake swore he saw lightning arc from her to him, she was that hot.

One second later they were standing in his room. Nadia looked at him with a smile on her face. "I totally forgot about that talent of yours, but thanks for reminding me." Then with a wink and a smile she grasped the edges of his towel and yanked.

Drake sucked in a deep breath as the cooler, air conditioned air slid over his skin, pricking every erogenous zone on his body. Although with the heat Nadia was putting out it was hard to feel cold when flames were licking at him. The space around them immediately went from intimidating and sexual, to emotions so heavy and thick that it was hard for him to draw breath. He brought his eyes to rest on Nadia's, and in the semi-darkness of the room he could see the widening of her eyes and the barest hint of tears there.

He could read her clearly now. She was astoundingly nervous with the getup she had on and she was also slightly embarrassed at how easily she had been able to bulldog her way into seducing him. Drake ignored those emotions, because he thought she was flat out stunning and he admired gumption in a woman. What really held his attention at the moment was the open yearning deep in her eyes. *That* was causing the tears, that deep feeling of wanting someone so bad, had caused her to come here in that getup she had on. It had also given her the gumption she needed to get here in the first place. The yearning for him had finally broken her walls down. She couldn't hide just how much she wanted him anymore. The truth made Drake feel like an overdone Christmas tree with too many lights. He almost grinned with the force of emotions running through him but stopped it immediately. He didn't want her to think that he was laughing at her.

Her small, shaking hand ran from his collarbone, down over his chest, fingernails pricking the edges of his tattoo, delicate fingertips coming dangerously close to his cock, so close that he could feel the heat pinpricking him there, and that part of his anatomy lifted to her automatically, without his consent. Drake gritted his teeth, feeling the tips of his fangs bite down onto his bottom lip, but welcoming the pain because it made him focus.

A hushed reverent tone escaped her mouth, "You are so very beautiful…I can't even describe how perfect you are."

Drake didn't say or do anything, letting her have this moment to herself, to acquaint herself with his body like he had already done with hers. And he would do this for her even if it killed him.

Her small hands compressed into tiny fists, as if she were trying to stop herself from touching him. The fragile edges of her face, that had been animated and blushing a fiery red when he first saw her on his deck, were now pale and streaked with salty tears, a testament to how long she had waited for this moment to look her fill.

Drake thought of all the years he had known her and never once had he assumed that she had been attracted to him. Sure, she had sent him glances of teenage crush worship, but he had never seen any sly glances, over long touches or secret smiles sent his way. He chocked it up to blind stupidity. Never would he have thought that Matt's daughter had the hots for him. And if he would have known, he probably would have pushed her away out of some absurd reason to try and stop her from making a mistake on a guy that would never do right by her. But now, standing here naked, with those huge green eyes of hers making him feel like a bug on a pin in some museum, Drake knew that it had happened this way for a reason. It had taken him a little while to open up his mind to the possibility of a relationship, sexual or otherwise, with a woman that he had known since she was twelve.

All he knew was at this moment he didn't feel any familial references to her at all. And he knew she realized that too…Thank God.

***

He was standing right in front of her, proudly showing off his body to her without the barest vestiges of cowardice.

Of course, Drake had always been confident; right now just proved it to Nadia.

With her hands shaking like leaves, she re-clenched the fists she had made and stared anew at all of that hot, hard, muscled flesh that was right in front of her, *begging* her to touch, taste, and feel it against her. She had waited so long, so very long to not only see all of him and have the ability to touch until her heart was content, but to do so when she knew they both felt heightened emotions was like a dream come true for Nadia. The tears in her eyes were a reaction to that.

The joy inside of her body was a simple, reverent joy, made all the more explosive because of the calm, sedate way he stood there, offering her his body as if he knew how much it meant to her.

Nadia's eyes slammed into his. Dark, glowing gold amber peered calmly back at her and she could make out the tips of his fangs biting into his bottom lip. He knew. He knew exactly what she felt. With his abilities he had finally figured out the full breath of her emotions. Amazingly enough, she didn't feel fear at him knowing. Instead, a bright, burning light grew in her center, expanding outward with a slow creep, calming her shaking fingers a bit, giving her the renewed bravery to continue her perusal of his body even as he now knew what she felt for him.

And the best part was now she could tell him everything, everything she had ever wanted and ever dreamed of doing with him was etched deep into her brain. She had never been able to forget lying in bed, late at night, daydreaming of constant scenarios that put her within touching distance from him.

Squeezing her fists she cemented her thoughts. She wanted all of that with him, and she wanted to start right now.

Even with her bravery she still felt a few moments of cowardice, so she didn't look into his eyes as she stepped even closer to him, her high heels bringing her head directly under his chin and her mouth right up to his thick, tendon roped neck. His hot breath eased over the top of her head when she settled against him, head to shoulder, breasts to chest, fingertips to hot skin.

He smelled of soap, which was obvious because he had just left the shower. Nadia looked up and caught the damp ends of his hair touching his ear. When the urge to lick the moisture from his neck took over, she gave in, relishing in the fact that she knew it would get her hot and drive him crazy. He tasted divine, salty, *and manly*. Nadia moaned lightly and her left hand went up over his shoulder and grasped his head closer to her. She licked him again, from his clavicle, over his Adam's apple to the soft spot under his ear where she could feel his heart racing. Flames began to burn inside her body.

He never moved, and she silently thanked him for that. But he did growl and exhale against her. She didn't let that stop her. She wanted time to learn his body…and see how much temptation she could take before exploding.

Her hands ran over large pads of muscle from his shoulder and biceps, down his arms until she reached his wrists and hands, such large hands, capable of pain or gentleness. Bringing her hands back to his chest, she twisted her fingers deep into his chest hair where it was thickest at the top, and then she followed the thin line that ran down his stomach and hard abs to where it came up to his distended erection. Still, she never looked into his eyes.

She licked her lips as she eyed his arousal. God, he was huge…massive, really. From between his legs he rose, proud and hard to rest against the hard flesh of his lower stomach. He was darkly flushed and roped with veins. As she watched a small amount of pearly liquid formed at the head, and Nadia felt as if she were in classroom learning all about men's bodies, but with a live model in front of her.

She started talking to cover up the slight nervousness she began to feel when she watched his body react to her.

"I remember when I first noticed you as a sexual, attractive man, rather than my father's boss." The words were quiet but she knew he could hear her, the sound of his breathing slowed and she could practically feel his eyes on her. She resolutely looked at his body instead. "You and some other guys were fixing one of the barns; I was sixteen, getting off the bus at the Haven and waiting for Dad." She licked her lips again and let her hands come to rest on his leanly muscled waist. She felt him tense up. "I went outside to sit beneath one of the trees and read when a noise made me look up. Then I saw you." Not being able to stop herself, her eyes met his.

Molten amber was all she saw, along with an impressive set of fangs. Facial features had melded into something that resembled Drake, but looked nothing like him. His Druid side was exposed to her. His expression was wild, his breathing was rough, uneven and to Nadia he looked seconds away from losing his mind. But still she felt no fear. She kept talking and her fingers ran along his skin.

"You were shirtless, wearing jeans and boots, and I swore that my mind went absolutely blank." One corner of his mouth crooked up and Nadia smiled slightly. "There was sweat all over you; you were practically slick with it and it was running down your back, into your jeans. I didn't understand the urges I was feeling, not until much later, but my body knew. It knew that there was something going on and it liked what it saw."

Nadia took a deep breath as she focused on his chest again then moved her eyes down to where her hands were coming very close to grasping his erection.

"From then on, every time I saw you, I tried to tamp down the urge to touch you. That urge made my fingertips burn, my body ache, and my mind shut down." Nadia traced the crisp edges of his tattoo. The cross was Celtic in nature with the round piece in the middle that showed his Druid mark. Elaborate tribal markings winged outward and away from it in beautiful designs. She tried to focus on everything except the raging erection that twitched with every movement from her. She would get to that soon enough.

"But it didn't work. Years went by and even with the barest glance from you, I would go home so hot, so turned on that falling asleep wouldn't be an option." She leaned close to his shoulder again, giving him butterfly kisses on his lean muscles, ones that would cause him to jerk and groan against her mouth. "With my sexual nature being awakened by you it seemed to me that no other man could touch me except you. Even the faintest thought of that happening caused me to go ice cold inside." The whispers of words against his skin gave her tongue the excuse to touch him. With every glance her insides went hotter and hotter until she could feel her core contracting with pleasure. She held her thighs together in a vise grip, but that only caused the ache to grow.

"The constant want grew until I couldn't even make it through the day without thinking of you in some aspect. When I would finally get another glimpse of you, you were always with another woman. I began to wonder what they had that I didn't, what they could do for you that I couldn't." Nadia drew a deep breath and settled against his chest in a gross exaggeration of a hug. "It became too much for me to handle. I withdrew unto myself, constantly having to push down my feelings for you, to keep telling myself that you would never stoop to my level." He jerked against her with a deep growl, but corralled it, seeming to know that if he interrupted her now she would never finish.

"When Linda passed and I took over, I remember thinking that the new position would put me in your path even more." She breathed a heavy sigh and leaned her forehead against his chest so that she could see down his body to where her hands were resting on his waist. Her body throbbed with need, but she wanted him to understand just how long and how hard it had been for her to keep all of this inside; she needed to say all of this now. "I almost turned it down, but decided I needed it, the busy world of charity and magazines to keep my mind off of you. At my introduction to society you were there, so was Donavan. It took everything I had to accept a dance from him, but I knew as I did that that I would allow him other liberties…as long as it kept me away from you."

Blinking away tears at how stupid and naïve she had been, she watched her fingers trace his skin. He was so warm, so alive, so very much hers for as long as he allowed himself to be.

"I know in your mind you're probably thinking that if I would have told you any of this you would have gone, left, so that I wouldn't have had the temptation, but that's the one thing I didn't want to do, for that reason. I couldn't have you, but I also couldn't stand to see you leave, to never be able to see you again would be heartbreaking for me, so I kept quiet and put up a front with Donavan for you and everyone, even though it killed me inside to do so."

She picked up her head and started to speak, but stopped when she saw his direct gaze as it plowed into her. His eyes were hazy, as if he was tearing up, but Nadia knew that was ridiculous. She wrapped both arms around his shoulders, pulling his face down to hers a bit, and pressed her mouth to his. The instant heat that arced between them surprised her but she opened her mouth, letting his tongue glide inside, plundering her with deep strokes while her body erupted in flames. His arms went around her back in a viselike grip while he stepped into her body with his hips, placing his erection right where she would react to it most. With one last nibble on his lower lip she pulled away with a moan as he shifted against her. She felt a rush of moisture immediately.

She inhaled and said, "I've waited a long time for what happened between us this past weekend. It was everything I've ever wanted, but now," she trailed a fingertip down his chest to his waist and then to the burning heat that surrounded his erection. "Now I want all of you." With those words he jumped against her fingers as she wrapped them around him.

"Ah angel…" The words sounded as if they had been torn from him.

"So now you speak," she told him with a smile, as her fingers learned the length, breadth and shape of him against her palm. He was so hard, but soft at the same time.

"You were doing all the talking earlier…I'm a gentleman…didn't want to interrupt…"

She laughed a little at that and looked down to see what was going on. Her thumb touched the head where that small bit of liquid sat. She got it on her fingers and rubbed it around, spreading it over him and her both. Almost immediately he growled deeply at her, causing her to look back up, just as he sent his fists into the wall behind her. Nadia swore, and jumped about two feet off the ground, but she never let go.

Breathlessly she looked into his face. His bones were all sharp angles and edges, while the only light she saw came from those glowing eyes of his. He looked…demonic …scary, something she wasn't prepared for, but she held her ground, and him.

"I'm sorry. I knew it would be too much for both of us to handle…" he spoke and Nadia could feel it under her feet. He practically vibrated the floorboards; his voice was that deep and harmonious. But even as his voice became monstrous and his face changed, deep in those glowing eyes was the same Drake she had fallen in love with, and she knew she had nothing to be frightened of.

"I'm n-not scared of you. I never have been, and I n-never will be." With those words, she sunk to her knees before him, prepared to show him just how much she wanted to be with him.

Drake thought he had died and gone to heaven.

He opened his eyes and looked down and realized that he was smack dab in the middle of it and yes, it was really happening.

Nadia was on her knees before him. He wanted to reach down and pull her back up, but yet he hesitated, sensing she was doing this because she wanted to, not because he wanted it, and she was showing him how much she trusted him to control himself.

Oh, he was in control alright. When they had kissed, he had maneuvered them up against the bedroom wall, next to the bed. Now, thank God he had done that, his hands were sunk deep into his drywall, keeping him from touching her when he had no idea how far he could take things, and he sure as hell didn't want to hurt her. It hadn't been like this before, this raw, because he hadn't known the full extent of her feelings until now, and how long she had been like this. Now he knew, and damn, he needed something to tie him down, preferably something metal and strong as heck, so that he didn't overdo it and hurt her on accident.

His Druid nature was riding him almost as hard as his arousal. Never before had he felt this wired and uncontrollable, but it wasn't as if the danger hadn't existed.

Emotions, raw feelings, swamped him, and he groaned, even before Nadia allowed her mouth to settle a small kiss on his hipbone. When that occurred, he sunk his fingers so deep into the wall that he touched a stud. He gripped the wood thankfully, and sent every calming emotion he could think of inside his body. Small dust particles drifted around his hands as he squeezed the wood with strong hands.

Nadia's hands twined around the backs of his thighs and Drake swore out loud as his cock surged to even greater lengths. Fuck, he would have to come at least once before he would allow his hands to go anywhere near her.

"I don't know what to do Drake…can you…"

He stopped her immediately, "Honey, anything you do right now is good. But if you want to touch it, then touch it, by all means, please…" He bit off the last of the sentence when she gripped him with both hands.

Drake saw stars. "Ah fuck, that feels good." It came out sounding more like a base animal growl than anything else, but who the fuck cared? All he knew was that she was touching him, and it felt awesome.

Small, delicate hands framed his cock. Her inexperience was apparent, but she could keep doing what she was doing, and Drake would come in minutes. It didn't matter if she was experienced or not.

"Tell me what you like, please Drake?" Her voice sounded pleading, and he realized that she truly didn't know, and she wanted him to explain.

He licked his lips as her hands explored. "Ah…take one hand and wrap it around the base." He felt her do so, took a deep breath and kept going, knowing he was digging his own grave. "Now, with a tight grip, move your hand up and down…fast." Immediately, she started up a rhythm, and Drake groaned as his balls tightened in pleasure. Damn, this wouldn't take long at all. He felt fire spread through his body and run down his spine.

She moved closer to his body, and kept up the stroke, but when she settled closer to him her breast touched his thigh, and that was all it took for Drake to surge against her hand. As he did so, he felt something wet. Looking down he saw her hand furiously pumping him, while her tongue was at the tip, ready to swipe away the bit of pre-cum that was perched there as if waiting for her mouth alone. But she hesitated, and Drake realized that she wasn't sure about it.

Wishing he could pull his hand from his ruined wall, but knowing he didn't trust his strength, Drake said, "Angel, I may rot in hell for this later but if you want to taste me…you are more than welcome to do so. Think of it as payback for what I did to you." He saw understanding dawn in her eyes, and then all thoughts stopped as her mouth enclosed the tip of him in hot, wet warmth.

Nadia allowed her tongue to swipe under the head of him as she settled her mouth over the tip. She could feel him throbbing inside of her. She could feel the excitement singing through his body, and she wanted him to explode. She wanted that for him so badly.

With one hand still moving in a rapid pace, she explored everything with her other one, the tight muscles of his butt, and the sculpted planes of his thighs. She noticed that the wetness from her mouth eased her grip, so she sucked him as deep as he could go and used that as a tool for her hand. The taste of him was amazing. Her heart was racing, her mind had shut down, and she was so turned on that she would probably come with him when he finally gave in. His body was already jerking against her mouth, and she could feel that he was close.

She let her throat muscles go lax, and instinctively realized that he would love this as she all but swallowed him. Particles of drywall rained down around them as he vibrated the floor boards again with one of his shouts. But Nadia held on, using muscles she hadn't realized she had until now to massage every part of him deep in her mouth. Suddenly he seemed to grow even larger, and then a warm jet of liquid hit her in the back of her throat. Nadia swallowed instantly, not even noticing the taste because she was too interested in this raw, primal side of Drake she rarely saw.

He pulled from her, glistening in the moonlight that poured in from the cracks in the curtains. His body was hard, striking, and warrior-like as he stood before her, shaking from his recent orgasm.

Nadia sat back on her heels and felt the wetness of her own body. Images and feelings poured through her and almost in seconds she felt her body erupt in flames. Her breasts became heavy under the slip, so heavy that they hurt and her nipples throbbed in time with her heart. She reached up to rub the ache away, unknowingly, and the movement caused her core to rub against her leg. Sharp little pinpricks of heat traveled down her spine, and she moaned aloud as she moved, trying to catch that twinge of pleasure again before it left her completely.

Drake stood, albeit carefully, still trying to regain his control after that rocking explosion Nadia had given him. One glance down at her though, and his control disappeared. She was sitting on her heels, her hips moving seductively against herself with her eyes closed and her hands roving her upper body. Ah God, she was so turned on she didn't know what to do about it. She was going with what felt good and as long as she was stimulating her clit, Drake knew she would keep doing it until she came. Bad thing was, he wanted her to come while he was inside her, not watching her.

With hands that still shook a bit, and also had dust from the wall all over them, he reached for her, pulling her up to him and carrying her over to the bed.

"Drake…are you going to do that to me too?"

He didn't look at her as he pulled the straps from her body, baring her upper chest to his gaze and the cooler air. Instantly her nipples pebbled. Drake felt a renewed hardness slip over his cock and just that easily he could come again. Thank God the first orgasm had taken the edge off and he could actually touch her right now. Without much thought he pulled the tight as skin slip from her body then groaned again when he saw she wasn't wearing panties, which left her with only those high heels on. His fangs throbbed.

"Angel, we are going to do much more than that."

Chapter 18

All he left on her were those ridiculously high heels.

Nadia squirmed on the bed, naked, and gloried in the sinful, lustful feelings that were crawling through her body right now. Drake's mouth was latched onto a nipple, and his tongue was swirling and swirling, doing everything but sucking, as she moaned and writhed under him.

His body was hard above hers, and so very large where he was pressed against her from hips to knees. The heat that was moving between them was enough to start a fire, but Nadia knew the fire was inside of her.

"You're so ready, aren't you?" He mumbled to her, his voice slipping gloriously close to being so very deep and scary again, and Nadia knew he was beyond turned on.

"Mmm…hmm…" She mumbled, sighing when he finally pulled with his mouth and let one fang scrape over her nipple. She almost came up from the bed.

His large hand settled at her waist. "Shh…just teasing you, angel. Feels good doesn't it?" He let his hand move south and settle on the sensitive mound at the juncture of her legs.

"Drake…"

She was out of her mind now. There was no going back, surely he would put her out of her misery and slip inside of her body like she so wanted him to do. Her hands tangled in his hair as his hand slid into the slippery wet folds that shielded her core. Nadia's hips rose from the bed and she cried out.

"I know honey, I know. Damn, you are so very wet..." Drake mumbled against her upraised knee and then gave the sensitive skin there an open mouthed, wet kiss as he slid a finger deep inside of her body.

Immediately Nadia gripped him deep inside with her muscles, praying that he would give her his body instead of his fingers.

"Please Drake...I want...I want..." Why couldn't she say it? Her head thrashed back and forth on the bedcovers as his finger slipped even deeper inside of her. She felt so full, so very stretched, but there was no pain. Then he slipped another finger in, and Nadia thought her world might evaporate. She wantonly opened her legs wider, accepting him even deeper.

"What do you want honey? What is it?" His deep voice rumbled next to her ear, and she realized he was now hanging over her, teasing her with his voice just like his fingers were filling her with magic. God, she was so full and it felt so good; her hips couldn't keep up with his movements.

"I want you...I want you...inside me, please."

His forehead settled on hers. "Oh damn angel, damn...I don't deserve you...and I swear I won't hurt you."

Nadia immediately agreed, knowing she was about to get what she wanted. "No, you won't hurt me. Give it to me."

His deep chuckle vibrated the bed. "Someone gets bossy when she's turned on." His fingers left her body, and Nadia could have wept at the loss, but knew he was coming right back.

"Don't tease right now…not now. I just need…" Again, she felt so lost, floundering, until his palm settled on the side of her face. Amidst all of the craziness of the moment, Nadia looked into his glowing eyes, felt her soul break open and stepped into her future. Tears filled her eyes and for one split second, time seemed to stop. "I love you."

An instant later his mouth was on hers and there was no more thought. He pushed her legs open to accept his hips and with a sure, straight thrust, he speared into her body, breaking her heart and her virginity open to him.

Huge, monstrous fullness filled her along with a numbing pain. Drake stilled for all of five seconds then moved tenuously, as though feeling if she was okay. When she just laid there in shock, he tentatively moved his hips deeper, and Nadia couldn't stop the sigh of pain/pleasure that rose up from her throat at that.

With her hands lying beside her head, she closed her eyes and kept her legs open for him. She felt confused for a second, hating the feeling because she had gotten thrown back to earth when the pain had hit, but then he shifted, and put his hand on her thigh, pulling her hip towards him, and her leg over his ass.

"Put your other leg up there, hold me with those sexy legs of yours, pull my cock into you, angel..." When he growled those words into her ear, Nadia felt a spark slide down into her core once again, and when she did as he asked, his body slid even deeper, igniting that spark into a flame and catching her breath at the same time.

Ignoring the twinge of pain, Nadia concentrated on the movement of his body, his erection so deep inside of her that she could squeeze him with internal muscles and make him shudder against her. Hot breath blew out against her ear while the hair on his legs rubbed the backs of her thighs, his hipbones pressed into the backs of her thighs whenever he finished a stroke, and his chest teased her nipples. There were so many facets of this that Nadia didn't know where to concentrate on what felt the best.

The sedate thrust he had going on was costing him, Nadia knew this because he was such a raw, animalistic man, and he was holding back for her sake. When she lifted her hips she was planning to take him off guard, planning to make him lose control, instead *she* moaned when her movement caused him to hit the right spot, so she did it again, and again. Soon, his pace sped up, and Nadia was gripping him with her legs and praying with everything she had for the feeling not to end.

"That's it angel, work for it...I know you want it..." His deep growl shook her body as he set his fangs to her throat and teased her with the tips. Her insides flamed, and burst, sending her into pleasure overload. Her body erupted, and slung her into the air, passion shaking her body and mind.

She was slung back to the bed, and immediately Drake's mouth was pinned against hers, kissing her like she had never been kissed before, so deeply, so mind-numbingly. He was slamming into her, bruising her body inside and out with the force of his thrusts, moving the bed against the floor with each slap of his body against hers, that Nadia came again in a rush of pleasure, her body giving everything it had for the man that was making her scream his name again and again.

With a final jerk, then a shudder, a warm sensation filled Nadia. Then Drake collapsed on the side of her, pulling her body into his and kissing her senseless again as if he couldn't get enough of it, or her.

After everything they had just done, she felt extremely worn out and exhausted, emotionally and physically. Apparently he didn't.

Every single one of his ten fingers was speared deep into her hair, tickling her scalp. His lips and tongue were gentle, but excruciatingly tempting as he kissed her thoroughly. Their bodies were still entangled, and even though he had already slipped from inside her, Nadia could feel heat and the slickness from his overheated skin since he was pressed up against every available inch of her.

Images of what they had done seared her brain. From foreplay to the act itself, Nadia had never imagined anything so unrefined and base between them, but overall every touch, kiss, and slide of skin inside and out, had been loaded with feeling and emotion. Even though he hadn't voiced the words, she knew he felt something terribly strong for her. Pulling back, she let her arms cuddle up between their bodies, while her head tucked under his chin where it fit nicely.

Her body felt more than sore; it actually throbbed in certain places. She knew for certain that his teasing nip from earlier against her neck had left a scratch because her neck was extremely tender now. She yearned to leave the bed, and sink into his Jacuzzi tub, but curled her hands into the hair on his chest instead, lifting her head to find his eyes still glowing in the semi darkness.

"I love you," she whispered, watching as his pupils all but disappeared, swallowed by the golden glow of amber in his eyes. The one thing she had waited years to say, now seemed so absurdly easy, so effortlessly spoken. Nadia reveled in her admission. "For years I have wanted to tell you, to see what your response would be to my words." Her fingers never stopped touching his skin, and when Nadia opened her mouth to continue, his fingers stopped her from speaking.

"I will never lie to you, so I'm telling you now that I did love my two wives. They meant very much to me at certain times in my life." Nadia's heart almost expanded the whole width of her chest. She knew what he was going to say, and her eyes filled with tears. "But never in my life, never, have I ever felt for another woman the way I feel for you." Golden eyes singed her with heat. "You are mine to keep, mine to worship, and mine to love…forever. There will never be another for me, and I would never wish harm on any animal, but I'm so very happy that you brought Belle to me that night;

otherwise, you would have never been planted firmly in my sights, and I would never have realized your true feelings." He settled a gentle kiss to her forehead, as tears streamed down her cheeks. "I thank God for you every day."

"Drake…" she whispered, unsure of how to tell him she wanted to be with him forever. "I want to be yours," she said, her voice low but firm.

His hand dug into her hair. "Angel, I hate to break it to you, but I have no intention of letting you go." A crooked, sexy smile emerged, and Nadia could see his fang tips gleaming in the moonlight. An electric thrill sped through her veins.

"Good…because I want to be yours…forever." She saw his smile dim, then vanish completely. "Forever…Drake, I want you to bite me." She stopped speaking, hoping to gauge his emotions, and watched as his eyes grew stern and hard mouth straightened to a thin line.

Seconds felt like minutes and Nadia felt fear creep into her system. She had assumed that if she shared her body, and her emotions with him, he could never turn her down. Laying here beside a man who'd completely shut down, she wasn't so sure. What was she supposed to do if he didn't agree? Tightening her hands on his chest, she hardened her thoughts, and told herself it would not come to that. She locked onto his gaze, opening herself up to him.

"I will not allow you to get rid of me so easily." One dark eyebrow rose at the force in her words, but she continued. "I want this! I want you and I love you. I see no reason why you shouldn't 'gift' me over into your world." Nadia licked her lips and went for the kicker. "How could you turn me and my love away, when I know you feel the same for me?"

The room filled with a deafening silence.

She felt her face burn with heat and humiliation over her embarrassing emotional display. He didn't respond, but the look on his face was something she'd never seen before. It almost looked like fear.

Stupid! You were so stupid to think he would want this!

She flew out of bed, amazed that he even let go of her, and ran to the bathroom, grabbing her discarded clothes along the way.

"Nadia!"

Ignoring his shout, she hastily tugged on her silky dress slip and trench coat, while her body throbbed with every pounding of his fists against the door. Tears flooded her eyes and fell to her cheeks, but she resolutely determined she would not break down in front of him. That would happen in the privacy of her own home. Only there would she let go.

"God, you don't understand just how big of a step this is!" he said, almost painfully from the other side of the wood.

She knew how easily he could overcome the lock, so rather than giving him the satisfaction of unlocking the door with his powers, she would do it herself.

Checking her emotions, swiping at the tears on her face, and gathering nothing but cool indifference around her, she tugged the door open, only to see her beloved, looking as ragged as she felt, standing there.

He was still in change mode, eyes bright, fangs flashing, and purely, deliciously, naked. Nadia struggled, wanting to cuddle into him, but slammed those thoughts away.

"How big of a step?" She questioned, thrusting her anger and the blazing trail of pain she felt into every vibrating inch of her body. He'd pushed her too far, her Spanish blood was churning. "Is it too much of a step for you?" Nadia shot daggers at him, noting the still blazing burn of his eyes, and those fangs hinting at his dangerous side. But that didn't deter her one bit.

She shoved a finger into his chest. "I've waited years...years Drake, for you, to be with you, to love you, but you think this 'turning me' might be too big of a step?" She knew tears were still rolling down her cheeks, but that didn't stop her words or the finger pointing. "How about you man up, and call me when you do. Or, better yet, don't, because I'm sure it will be too late."

She didn't say anything else, just turned towards the front of the house to leave.

An almost inhuman roar was her response, but other than flinch, she didn't stop. She wasn't sure she would be able to leave at all if she caught one last look of him. Minutes later, in her Rover, she finally was able to take a breath, but her emotions were hanging on by a thread. Peeling out of his driveway helped a bit. Seeing the road flying beneath her tires also calmed her.

Don't think about it yet. Get home, then you can dwell.

The thick forest on either side of the road was almost welcome. As dark and dangerous as her mood was, she should have known better than to expect a smooth departure.

A loud pop, then the Rover swerved, Nadia had the frame of mind to pump the brakes, but that didn't stop her from sliding off the road, into the shallow ditch and kissing the edge of a tree. She was thrown forward, but not harmed, thank God. Scared, more than anything, and feeling stupid now that she was sitting out here, wrecked, and emotionally pissed. She took a moment to survey her surroundings…in the dark, feeling a little stupid, a lot scared, and so unbelievably alone…her car a wreck and in a rut…just like her life.

"Good God, how much more miserable can I be?"

She tried laughing at herself, but ended up crying instead.

After a few minutes of feeling sorry for herself, she stopped. She was on the side of a private road, had wrecked and she certainly wasn't going to be able to drive away from this. She needed to find a way out of this mess.

Climbing out of the vehicle was a bit precarious, but she managed, and then she got a good look at the front of her truck, as well as the blown out tire.

"Damn."

Well, there was nothing to this. She was going to have to call Drake. "Shit."

Seemed like her vocabulary was down to the basics now, Nadia thought, as she grabbed her phone from her coat pocket, tapping out her passcode. She didn't notice until she brought the phone up to call Drake, that there was no service.

"C'mon, really?!" She all but yelled at the offending piece of technology.

Birds chirped, and a breeze sang out as a response.

What the hell was she supposed to do now? Nadia shook her head and glanced around. Well, it appeared she would have to start walking, and hope that her signal would come back.

She trudged resolutely along, noting that the sexy heels that had seemed like a good idea earlier, weren't so much now. The wildlife sounds around her were almost comforting, until Nadia realized that a light growling noise was interspersed with the regular cooing and cawing of the birds. She stilled instantly, and almost, *almost*, ran back to her truck to get the bat in the backseat.

Why didn't you take it in the first place?

She glanced back and could only see her back bumper…a LONG ways away. She would never make it. A light sweat broke out on her skin. Her heart raced. She glanced back to the road in front of her, just as the bushes rustled on the right side, and a large, rotund shape walked out, growling softly deep in its throat when it saw her.

Nadia almost passed out

A bear studied her from about forty feet away.

Chapter 19

Something was wrong.

For fifteen minutes, Drake had been trying to calm down, not that it was working, but he had tried, and now some niggling little breach had tapped into his protectiveness streak. The amazing amount of trust that she'd placed in him to ask him to change her, was thrust away, the love she shared with him was also pushed away. He couldn't put a name to it, couldn't describe it, he only knew it had something to do with Nadia.

Within seconds, he was outside, tapping the air with every ounce of his Druid ability.

She wasn't far, and something was deathly wrong.

Every thought he'd had was now put on hold. A darkness, something vile, and evil was close, and Drake had every intention of getting it away from his woman. She might be angry with him, but she was still his, and he would take care of her.

Within seconds, he was on his private drive, running into the woods, desperate for something, anything, to lead him in the right direction.

***

Nadia had never known fear this deep, this true.

The bear was ambling around in her general vicinity, never coming too close. It seemed to be testing her, seeing how easy it would be to make her break.

She'd been tempted to scream for Drake, knowing that he would be able to hear her, but she was frightened that the bear might take that as something aggressive and attack her. So the scream she wanted to send out was cemented in her throat, lodged there with her tears from their argument, and her hope that she would get out of this alive.

A snort broke into her musing, distracting her so that she stumbled and nearly fell. The bear clearly took that as a threat, and let loose a roar, so eerie, and terrifying, that Nadia instantly burst into silent tears. It began to come closer. And as it did so, Nadia stayed planted in the same position, trying not to antagonize it further.

The animal seemed sluggish, almost sick, and the closer it came, Nadia noted the somewhat frothy foam at its mouth. Rabies. The bear was infected with Rabies.

Shaking took over her body, along with the sudden, overwhelming urge to run. But Nadia ignored that, remembering a show once that said running would only incite further aggressiveness from the bear. So she huddled along the side of the road, while a raving, infected bear stalked her ever closer.

Suddenly the bear halted, turning its nose up, scenting the air.

Nadia immediately took note of this. What did it sense? Was another animal coming? Was it a car? But she nixed that last thought. This was Drake's private road. No one would be showing up at this time of night.

The bear roared once more, causing Nadia to jump again. Then it began to run towards her. Without even thinking, she turned and ran, the silly heels forgotten as the need to save her own life cut in on everything else. Within seconds, she was knocked to the ground. Twigs, rocks and mud shifted under her hands, and as she looked up she could clearly see the ravaged, diseased eyes of the bear not five feet from where she lay.

The scream that had lodged in her throat before, came ripping out easily now.

Just as the bear roared again, and raised its large front paws towards her, Nadia caught a blur coming in from the right. The blur was Drake, and seconds later bear and man tussled right before her very eyes.

He would die! There was no way possible for him to defeat that beast. After having to bear the humiliation of him not wanting her to stick around for a lifetime, Nadia refused to witness his death.

"Stop! Please stop!" But the words came out distorted and wobbly thanks to her tears. She rose hastily, scrounging in the dark, feeling rocks and twigs, searching for something to use as a weapon, while the fighting continued behind her, human and beast, the snarling and growling rippling together to form a deathly orchestra of terror.

Another roar, clearly Drake, made Nadia look back to see him standing, the bear on hind legs, doing everything it could to gut him where he stood. The animal was fierce, terrifying, and enormous, the full moon shining down on its rippling furry body and snarling white teeth. One glance also revealed Drake, clearly in full change, fangs flashing, muscles large and impressive, while his eyes glowed hotly animalistic.

It was a meeting of the two most deadly things she'd ever seen.

Then the bear swiped at him, his claws cutting a swath of red across Drake's chest. Nadia screamed, feeling utterly useless with no weapon, and instantly everything became crystal clear.

The man she loved was fighting for her, battling against something terrifying and deadly, so that she could escape.

But she wasn't going to let him battle alone.

Since she couldn't find a stick, she could distract the beast, and give Drake the upper hand.

Standing up, she let loose a long, loud whistle, gathering the attention of the bear and of Drake, who was clearly not happy about her intervention.

"Nadia, no!"

"You're not going to die for me, you stubborn son of a bitch!"

The bear did exactly what she wanted; it turned and started for her

***

There was only one thing to do. He'd tried coaxing the bear with his abilities, when he'd first heard it roar, but since the Rabies was fully spread throughout its body and mind, the animal was relying on its basic survival instincts. Drake couldn't get through to it, couldn't persuade it to stop, and he sure as hell wasn't going to let it hurt Nadia.

He'd allowed himself to go fully through his change.

Now everything was sharper, focused, clear cut, black and white, no gray areas, no haggling, no dissecting. He was the same as the bear-a beast, intent on saving his woman. Nothing would stop him, except, apparently, for Nadia's misguided attempt to save *him*.

The burn on his chest from the swipe the bear gave him, he barely felt, but the terror in Nadia's eyes burned as clear as the love that had given her the strength to stand up to something she was obviously afraid of.

His brave, beautiful woman, he'd have to make an honest woman of her, and soon, but not before the unpleasant task before him.

Within seconds, he was on the bear's back, his hands around the heavily muscled throat, and for a few terrifying moments, Drake wasn't sure he could end the animal's life, despite the rabies. But one glance into Nadia's fearful face told him this had to be done.

Calling on every particle of his power, he roared, and grabbed the bottom and top jaws of the bear, pulling in opposite directions. The heavy beast fought bravely, but when Drake popped his jaw, it fell to the ground, dead, within a matter of seconds.

Feeling horrible for having to take the life of something so majestic, Drake knelt over the beast, praying for its soul, promising to see it resting somewhere permanently safe in its second life.

Tearful hiccups intruded in on his thoughts. Drake glanced up, and saw Nadia sitting on the ground, looking lost and somewhat dazed. He got up and made his way to her, going slowly because he knew the scratches on his chest, the blood and the change he was wearing might also scare her.

"Angel? You okay, honey?"

He barely had a second to brace himself before she came barreling at him and flying into his arms. So, she must not be put off by the blood and his animalistic nature, Drake assumed.

"You crazy, beautiful man." Her words were hazy and indistinct against his throat, but Drake didn't care. He had her right where he wanted her.

"But if I'm your crazy, beautiful man, I must also lay claim to a bit of stupidity to nearly let you get away."

She stiffened slightly against him. So Drake went for it, letting her have what she wanted so badly.

"You are going to be mine forever, Nadia. There is no way I'm giving you up. If I have to change you to have you, then I'll willingly do it."

His air was cut off as she hugged him to her, but he didn't mind the chokehold one bit.

***

Drake made her wait until Friday night to get things started.

Nadia had thought she would expire from anxiousness when he informed her that he needed some assistance from a few other Druids. She thought they could have done the deed the day after that horrible fight, with each other and then the bear; Drake had informed her otherwise. She would need a couple of days to regroup. She might miss work for an untold amount of days because her newly rewired system might throw her off a bit. The actual biting process was not what he was worried about. He was more worried about after, when the changing would set in and her body, soul, and mind would go through the transformation. He reminded her that for some the transformation was horrid, painful and sometimes deadly. Others felt no ill reminders of their time during the change. Some, he told her, passed with no ill effects and days later were right as rain. There was no way to tell how Nadia's change would go until it began, which is why he wanted help to fall back on, incase they would need it.

Nadia wasn't worried one bit. Love that was returned and felt by Drake flowed in her veins. She knew that she looked crazy happy on the outside, but even if that was the case, she didn't want to dim that. She wanted everyone to know how she felt about Drake, even if he was being a bit more honorable than she liked at the moment. He hadn't touched her sexually since Monday night. Instead he had gone over and over again some of the things she might expect from her transformation, during and after. Nadia was more than ready for that to happen, and since she was being honest to herself, she was also more than ready to jump his bones at any given moment.

It wouldn't be now though, she mused as she watched him go to open the door to his house. She had come over with a bag packed, and ready to go, as per his instructions. Back up for Drake would be three other Druids. He had only told Nadia their specialties and their names, but she knew deep inside she was thankful for them being here and helping both her and Drake through this.

After shutting the huge door and murmuring a few words, Nadia watched from the corner of the sofa when Drake finally ushered his guests into the living area where she was waiting. When she caught her first glance of all three men, she swore Druidism carried a gorgeous gene. Every single man was simply breathtaking. How they were all unattached was a miracle to her.

Two tall, dark haired men broke away from another tall, silver haired giant and made their way towards Nadia. She instinctively stood, and calmed her rapidly beating heart. This was all starting to seem very real to her.

With an outstretched arm, the first dark haired man with stunning blue eyes grabbed her hand and gave it a vigorous shake, "Nice to meet you Nadia, I'm Brenan McKinnon." God, he was devilishly handsome, with a dimple in one lean cheek, and a seductive Scottish brogue. Nadia wondered if every woman in New York was blind.

Looking way up, she remembered to smile in the face of such charm, as he picked up her hand and kissed the back of it, not to mention his deep Scottish brogue when he spoke her name had given her the goose bumps. "Nice to meet you too," she murmured as she pulled her hand back in.

The other dark haired man had flashing green eyes, and was a bit taller than Brenan. "Ramsey McMurray, lass, it is so good to meet you." His voice was a deep brogue also. He didn't kiss her hand as boldly as Brenan had done, but when his fingers touched hers she felt immediately calmer. When he let her hand go, he whispered, "My cousin has the charm, but I have the touch." His green eyes twinkled, and Nadia smiled as she remembered what Drake had told her about his special ability being 'touch.'

Drake charged in between the two Scottish devils, and gave them the hardest looks that Nadia could ever remember him giving anyone. "Okay you two, back off." He smiled at Nadia and grasped her hand in his. "This is Kale. He is the other one I was telling you about with the ability to stop blood flow."

The tall man approached her, and Nadia saw what she had thought was silver hair was actually a light blonde. He was tall, with autocratic features, and a commanding air that implied he was just as stubborn and harsh as he appeared to be.

"Hello, Nadia. I hope your transformation will be pain and problem free. We are all here to ensure that." His silver eyes flashed at her as he shook her hand. His voice held no accent, which she thought was odd but interesting.

The next hour was spent getting everything ready. Nadia joked with Drake that he was only making her upcoming trial even harder, but deep down she understood his hesitation. He wanted everything to go smoothly. Now as everyone crowded inside the huge master bedroom, she gulped deeply, knowing what was coming, but not quite sure if she was ready.

After Drake positioned her on the bed, lying comfortably, Nadia licked dry lips and watched as the men conferred at the foot of the bed. She could hear them talking about pain, symptoms from previous changes, and other things she should be listening to, but as of now all she could focus on was Drake. He was big, bigger than the two dark haired men and at the same height with Kale, but what caught her attention the most was the camaraderie he shared with the other men. It was easy to see they were brothers in arms. At that moment Nadia closed her eyes, said a prayer, and let her love for Drake pour through her. This was no mistake. She loved this man, she would be with him forever, and nothing would happen during her transformation to stop her future with him.

Minutes later, Drake came to the side of the bed. Sitting down beside her she noticed his eyes changing right before her.

"We're about to start soon, love. Are you sure this is what you want?" His hand grasped one of hers while his other hand went to the side of her face, pushing away her hair.

She said the only thing that needed to be said, "I love you." She knew that was what he needed to hear when his eyes closed and it seemed to her that he relaxed somewhat. When he opened his eyes she noticed he was serious. Then Kale spoke from the foot of the bed.

"Nadia Mali Morales, you have extended your wishes to be 'gifted' into the world of the Amber Druids. This matter is not to be taken lightly. Your life will change in immediate and drastic ways, and you have been informed of these changes, have you not?

"Yes," she said, at Drake's nod of encouragement. His grip on her hand tightened. His eyes burned into hers as Kale continued.

"Ramsey, Brenan, and I, have come today as witnesses to this induction into our world. We are also here to provide help, if needed, and a shoulder to lean on should things take an unexpected turn."

Drake's eyes closed at that and Nadia sensed the war he had raging inside of him. He wanted her with him forever, and she wanted that also, but the unknown was killing him. She could tell from the way he clutched her hand and kept quiet.

Ramsey and Brenan moved, each taking the same side of the bed that was unoccupied, while Kale stayed at the foot. They stood—silent, ancient beings. Sentinels, guarding her as Drake introduced her into their world.

"Drake, I assume you are ready to do your part?" Kale questioned.

Drake's eyes opened, his gaze spearing her with heat. "I am," he replied. The base tenor of his voice having changed to deep Druid mode, Nadia shivered, but bravely squeezed his hand.

"You may, at any moment, ask her the question and proceed."

Golden eyes held hers. "I love you, angel."

His timely, though unexpected, admission brought the sting of threatening tears. "I love you too, Drake."

She watched as his lips moved, whispering words, mysterious and ancient as time itself, that she could not possibly understand, into the air above her. Nadia felt no change, and within moments, he finished. He had already told her that when a person transformed, they adopted many spells, wards, and other casting abilities from their specific bloodline's genetics. Abilities not learned, but ingrained. Since she was being 'gifted' over and not changing on her own, she would adopt the same abilities and spells that Drake had. It would be as if he were sharing his soul with her on some level.

When she felt his gentle fingers on the neckline of her shirt, Nadia tensed for a second, then relaxed. She knew the bite had to be on the neck, as close to the heart as possible for the powerful venom to be most effective. She also knew that within seconds after the bite, she would most likely pass out from her body's stress due to the transformation.

"Nadia, do you accept this gift I'm about to bestow on you? Do you accept all of its complications and aptitudes? Do you accept your new life?" His voice was deep, but sure, and as Nadia stared into his gorgeous eyes, she let go and gave into her love for him.

"I do."

His fingers pulled the material away a final time. Nadia took a deep breath, and watched as Drake's mouth opened. Fangs gleamed from within as he lowered his mouth to her neck. She gasped as an immediate and searing pain exploded on the side of her neck. Within seconds, her hands burrowed in his hair, pulling him closer as the pain altered to a sensation of floating blissfulness—and then nothingness, as she passed into an abyss of blackness.

***

Two days had passed.

There had been blood from her nose, a small amount that Kale had staved off. Other than a bit of thrashing from a killer fever, her side effects had been relatively mild. Drake sat by Nadia's bedside in the semi-darkness with only one little lamp giving off light. The guys were still there, in the bowels of the monstrous house doing whatever they wanted with Drake's highly faceted electronics. Every now and again he would hear them exclaim over some sport they were watching. But he knew that if he needed anything they would be there in seconds. The loyalty they all felt for each other was as strong as blood. Even though only Ramsey and Brenan were cousins, to every single one of them they felt as close as family.

The bad phase had passed. And even though Kale told him that, and he knew that himself, it was still hard to sit beside Nadia while she lay unmoving and silent. Power that hadn't yet settled was coursing through her blood. The power he had gifted to her was singing through her veins, taking inventory of its new owner. He could feel it pulsing to him on thick waves, battling against his own power. It was like this with every Amber Druid, but after years of ignoring it, Drake and the others had become adept at not worrying with it. It was similar to a calling card of sorts. The Druid's ways of letting each one know that another comparable to them was coming close.

The change so far had been blissfully quiet. Drake didn't know whether that was a good thing or not. She had had the requisite heightened fever color on her body, and she was hot, eerily so. That was all normal. The body would bloom red, as fever raged, and the transformation began. This was usually the time where they would be able to tell if her soul was strong enough to handle the change. So far so good. With her aura pounding around her body like her blood was pounding inside her skin, Drake kept a close eye out for the violently colored red that would converge over her body. The telltale color was the mark that showed pain at its highest. And that was the reason the guys were here. They could all help with the pain, and the better she handled the pain, the easier she came out of this okay.

So Drake sat and watched and prayed like he hadn't prayed before.

With her long black hair a mess around her small body, she resembled a teenager. Drake remembered every moment they'd shared, not only the most recent, but the ones when he had first met her. They played like photo snapshots in his mind. For what seemed like hours he sat and reminisced about her and her family and then thought about the present and the future.

When all this was over and done, it seemed only perfect that he ask her to marry him.

Shuffling feet got his attention from across the hall; seconds later, Ramsey peeked in. "How is she?" he questioned. Drake motioned him into the room. The large Scotsman entered quietly, and then knelt on the opposite side of the bed.

"There has been no change, hardly any movement as of yet either," Drake told him with a deep sigh.

Flashing green eyes took in Nadia's still form. "That can be good. She seems like she is a fighter."

Drake thought of all the years she had quietly loved him. He also thought of everything in her life she had gone through, and she was only twenty-five. "Oh yeah, she's a fighter alright."

"I took it as so." Quiet reigned for a few moments until Ramsey spoke again. "It is clear to see the feelings you two share. It's almost humbling to be in your presence."

Drake let a smile curve his lips. "Don't even think to steal her away from me, Scotsman. You need to find your own woman to hound. Leave mine alone."

A deep chuckle sounded from Ramsey. "I would never be able to take this one." Green eyes found his and Drake felt a brotherly instinct kick-start inside of him for this man and the others in his vicinity. "She is already yours, brother. You deserve to be happy."

Drake inclined his head. "You do too, so take my advice and find you your own woman. That should be easy for the most eligible bachelor in New York." He almost missed the heartbreaking look in Ram's eyes, as it was, the flash only lasted a second.

An instant coil of movement from Ramsey alerted Drake, and within seconds both men were staring at the bold red color that boiled above Nadia's now thrashing form.

"I take it that we are needed now." Kale's voice from the doorway was a shock, but Drake didn't question the man's eerie abilities, he just nodded.

The next few minutes were hectic as the men each found a space around Nadia to concentrate on. With their hands they touched wrists, forehead, stomach, and ankles, and within seconds there were pain relieving spells rising up to the ceiling.

Drake concentrated hard, feeling his fingertips burn, but not acknowledging the pain. Nadia needed him and the others, and for right now any pain would be taken in stride for her.

For what seemed like hours they called forth their own brand of spells until the red started to dissipate and her body seemed to quiet. Drake watched as she seemed to breathe a bit easier and his body relaxed too. He and the others removed their hands and stood silently by her bedside. They all knew this could go on for hours or minutes. No one knew just yet.

Minutes later the room had cleared out once more. Drake sat back in his chair and kept up his silent vigil beside the woman he loved.

Chapter 20

Nadia awoke on Tuesday morning to a blessed darkness.

In the back of her mind, she went through everything that Drake had told her about after the transformation. She would instantly feel amazingly better. Her new power might take her unawares, so it was best that she not become agitated or upset. She would be able to feel the presence of other Druids, and at first it might make her feel as if she should be on her guard, but he told her that was normal and would always happen. Her eyes would stay amber for a good three to five days, and her eyeteeth would be sporting points for the same amount of time. Any spells or wards would have been implanted deeply in her subconscious, ready to be called forth when the time came for it. Her senses would be enormously awake.

For now, with her eyes open in the darkened room, she felt the press of an emotion that was telling her to beware. When she cocked her head to look to her right, she actually felt her hair sliding on the pillow and the separate strands of thread that made up the material. This senses thing was pretty damn strong.

The feeling that she needed to protect herself made sense when she saw Drake sleeping in the chair beside the bed. A rush of love imploded in her body. She sat up carefully, thankful to note when the sheet fell away from her that she still had on a tee shirt and a pair of sleep pants.

Licking her lips, she stopped short as two pointed pricks snagged her tongue. At first she was confused, then she remembered she had fangs. For a few moments, she had to stop and feel them with her tongue, lips, and even her fingers, trying to make herself realize that this was indeed real. After the shock had worn off, Nadia reasoned with herself that she would have to find a mirror as soon as possible.

As her eyes turned back to the sleeping man beside the bed that thought drifted away and the only one left was that now she was his, he was hers, and they would be together for a very long time.

Everything seemed so much brighter now. Her eyes were crisp with every color heightened in perfect pitch and tone. His hair was a luscious shade of every brown she had ever seen. His skin was sumptuous, a deep, rich warmed tone that was supple and pleasing to her new eyes. Long, dark lashes rested lightly atop high cheekbones and Nadia had the urge to run her fingers over every ridge of his face.

She didn't stop herself from giving in.

With her newfound strength and speed she was kneeling in front of him on the bed within one second. She couldn't stop the air from stirring though, and that was what sent those lovely lashes fluttering up. Light brown eyes focused on her instantly and Nadia felt her heart stutter to almost a stop as he visually checked her for outward signals that would tell him if she was okay or not.

"Hello, beautiful. I see that you survived with no ill effects inside or out."

It was in that moment when Nadia remembered that she could sift through his emotions now. He would never be able to hide from her unless he 'glamoured' himself. Right now that wasn't happening. Everything he felt was there, out in the open and stage center for her to see and read around him. Nadia felt her soul expand when she saw the shimmer of pure emotion hazing around his body. Love, wholesome and real, was there and she felt it in the way his eyes traveled over every inch of her body, in the way they warmed as he looked at her, in the way she heard his blood moving furiously inside of his body.

"Y-yes," she had to clear her throat so that she could speak around all of the emotions in the way. "Thanks to the others and you. Speaking of them, do we still have company?" She asked as she slyly crawled from her side of the bed onto his lap, straddling him as she climbed on.

Burning eyes never left hers. "They have left. Kale knew you were clear about five hours ago." His hands burrowed into her hair. "Thank God they're gone." He smiled his crooked smile and Nadia felt it inside her body.

"How are you handling the push of power I'm giving you?"

She thought of that and answered honestly. "Actually, it isn't bothering me much right now but it is there, in the background."

He snuggled up to her, nuzzling her neck. Nadia felt a surge of emotion and love wrapping her up from her feet to her ears as he kissed her and whispered, "Good…and I'm sure you're dying for a bath, aren't you angel?"

"God yes," she all but growled when he nipped her earlobe.

"Well then by all means, let's give the lady what she wants," he told her, and within seconds they were in his bathroom. That was another AHA moment for Nadia when she remembered that she could now do what he could.

"Oh no ma'am," he told her with an eyebrow cocked in her direction.

"What?"

"You can't try any of that so soon. You need to wait until your body catches up with your new senses. Then you can go crazy."

"You're such a party pooper," she whined and gave him a pout.

He smacked her on the ass, and then gathered her in a strong hug. "We'll see what you say about that whenever you are through with your shower." He silenced her with a gentle kiss then he let her go. "I'll see you when you're done, angel." Then he walked out.

About thirty minutes later, Nadia was staring into the mirror with shock deep in her veins.

Drake had never mentioned anything about her looking so much healthier or vibrant. Her skin was practically glowing with health and even though her eyes were a deep amber color and she had fangs, of all things, the absolute newness of everything floored her. The little laugh lines around her eyes were gone, the grooves on the side of her mouth when she smiled were gone, even her nails looked longer and healthier.

Any other discovery was stalled by a knock on the door. "Angel, you okay in there?"

Nadia sensed the hesitancy in his voice, and even through the door she could feel his anxiousness. He was worried that she hated what she was now. Under all those emotions though was the real thing, the ever present, strong undercurrent of absolute trust that he had for her, which spoke of love to her. With tears in her eyes, she tugged on the edge of her tee shirt and turned to open the door.

Drake's massive frame was hovering there with one arm leaning on the jamb. Nadia hadn't noticed before but he looked tired, strung out, and so very worried about what she had noticed about herself so far.

When his hand came out to trace her face, tears threatened immediately at the powerful emotions that snapped to life inside of her, and the ones that he hadn't tried to hide from her.

"You have no idea how worried I was for you, darlin'."

With a tremulous smile she looked deeply into his eyes. "I see it now."

He didn't acknowledge the fact that his shield was down but said, "I know."

A millisecond later his mouth was on hers. Nadia barely had time to catch her breath before strong arms were lifting her to settle on the edge of the counter. His mouth teased hers mercilessly, sucking and nipping at her lips before catching her jaw with his thumbs and opening her mouth for his tongue. Almost too late she remembered her fangs, but her worry was for naught. Drake effortlessly kept away from her new elongated teeth, only giving her a lick or two down the edge, which caused her womb to throb with renewed want and desire. That little lick had made her feel as if he had stroked her from the inside out.

At that rush of heat, Nadia let her hands creep over his waist and slip under his shirt. She kept the momentum up as she grabbed the edge of it, and ripped it from his body.

Shock had her pulling away from his kiss. "Oh God, I'm sorry…" she mumbled helplessly as she showed him two halves of his shirt hanging limply from her hands.

Instead of replying, he just threw the ruined material in the corner of the massive bath and sent his hands to the buttons on his jeans. Flashing amber eyes were burning down at her as he shucked the jeans from his body and said, "Sorry, but I can't wait…"

Burgeoning emotions, love, passion, a deep seated feeling that this was meant to be burst inside of Nadia as she in turn ripped her shirt off too. God, but she loved this man.

Instantly he was on her again, and not once did he let up. His mouth made love to hers, deftly kissing her senseless while his hands molded to her body. The sensations were sharper for Nadia, so sharp that she could *hear* their skin rubbing together, and she could feel *his* desire, love, and want burning so hot inside of him. It made her burn even hotter to realize just how much he wanted her.

When his mouth left hers, and his hands framed her upper waist, Nadia leaned onto the faucet behind her, the heavy metal cutting into her skin, but she didn't feel it; all she felt was his mouth latching onto her nipple, drawing it so deep inside. She shuddered and wrapped her legs around his waist.

A deep, fearsome growl emanated from his body and traveled into hers from where his mouth was touching her. Immediately a flow of moisture gushed between her legs, and Nadia knew she had to have him now.

"Take them off..." she told him, referring to her underwear that was still in the way.

"Not yet"

"Now Drake," she practically yelled, which of course got his attention. With heavy lidded amber eyes he watched her. Dark eyelashes rested almost on his cheekbones, giving him a sleepy look. Nadia knew he wasn't the least bit tired. She leaned her hips, still encased in panties, towards him and allowed her core to touch his hard erection. When he trembled, she looked into his face and said once again, "Now, Drake."

A determined look echoed her words and a millisecond later, both their underwear were gone.

"You better be ready for me, angel," he growled against her ear as he settled his large frame on top of her.

She undulated beneath him, loving the way he felt on top of her, against her, probing the entrance to her body, especially now that all of her senses were heightened. The knowledge that he loved her and wanted her had tripled her foreplay and cut down the time to mere seconds.

Instead of answering him, she let her hips do the talking as they moved against him.

"You're making it hard for me to go easy on you, honey."

She leaned up and nipped his earlobe with her fangs, "Then don't."

He nudged her with his hips and said, "Look down for me, baby."

She did as he asked, and watched in amazement as his large erection slid between the folds of her core. He was huge, but they fit beautifully. Nadia swallowed, and kept watch as he slid deeply inside of her body.

"God…you are beautiful. Look how easily you take me…"

The words were costing him, deeply, she knew but soon he slid home, all the way in, and wrapped his arms around her. Then the real action started.

With long, sure, deep strokes, Drake caused her body to weep tears of desire. From deep in her core, to the muscles that trembled to hold onto him, he slid against her flesh, giving everything he had to make her explode for him.

"You feel so good, honey…so good." Another deep stroke and Nadia's muscles clenched endlessly, trying to hold him against her. "I'm going to make you mine…you're going to be my woman, only mine…"

God, the words he was saying added to the fuel that his body was giving her. "I'm yours already Drake."

A deep dark chuckle invaded her senses. "Come on angel, come for me…"

As if her body answered only to him, she exploded. Shards of pleasure flew outward, encompassing every particle of her body then almost languidly, they returned and slowly pieced themselves back together, leaving her breathing ragged and her arms and legs trying to grip his body as he too fell into that same endless pool of ecstasy.

Minutes later they were still huddled on top of the bathroom counter. Nadia giggled uncontrollably at the unreality of the moment.

"I love you."

The words stopped her laughter all together. Tears immediately welled as she realized that her love for him had finally come full circle. Now there were no more hidden emotions to get in the way. They knew everything they had to know about each other.

Her hand wove deep into his hair. "I love you too…so much."

"I never thought I would tell you that after we had just had sex on top of the bathroom counter, but I couldn't pick the moment. It felt right, so I went with it."

Nadia giggled again, loving him and how easily he made her laugh.

She felt a shimmer of power, then they were in his room on his bed.

"I *so* have to learn how to do that."

Now he was the one laughing at her. She smiled and gave him a soft kiss.

"You will have my help...if you need it, for an eternity...if you want it."

She stopped when she heard the serious note in his voice. Her heart was beating uncontrollably; her breath was soughing in and out while her hands twined against his muscular chest. She thought of all the years she had loved him silently, never thinking she would have the opportunity to get her chance to love him out in the open. Now it was here.

"I need it, and of course I want it. I want you...forever, and yes, I will marry you."

Drake grasped her cheeks with both hands and kissed her within an inch of her life. After a few minutes he pulled back and gazed down at her with love shining all around him.

"Damn, but you are one forceful woman," he rolled his eyes, "But I guess we can get married."

Nadia slapped his bicep, "You guessed right," she told him with a smile, but then softened the blow with another kiss.

Eternity was going to be a long, long time coming.

About the Author

Trish F. Leger lives in South Louisiana and also has a full time job--other than the writing, of course! She is married and from a loving, boisterous family. Since food is so important in the south, it is also important to her, ranking right up there with writing, reading and watching movies.

Writing with a strong sensual bent, intent on capturing the growing relationship between a couple falling in love, Trish adds warmth and emotion to her stories.

She is a fan of everything from Drama to Historical Romance.

Trish is a PRO member of RWA and has been writing for over ten years.

Please visit her on Facebook under Trish F Leger-author, her website @ www.trishfleger.webs.com . Or email her at wackycajun@hotmail.com.